THE RANCH
BOOK 1

THE RANCH: BOOK 1
by SEAN LISCOM
Published by Creative Texts Publishers
PO Box 50
Barto, PA 1950a
www.creativetexts.com

ISBN: 978-0-578-54032-0

THE RANCH

BOOK 1

SEAN LISCOM

TABLE OF CONTENTS

CHAPTER 1

I have been told by many people that I have lived an extraordinary life. While the past few years have been a wild ride, I don't think that I would go that far. I would be more inclined to say that I have been very blessed. The people who I'll introduce you to, they were the extraordinary ones. I was just lucky enough to call them my friends. In order to keep the memories alive of the ones that we lost along the way; I have decided to put pen to paper. It is in their memory that I tell you this story.

My name is Jason Sterling and my incredible journey began on July 9th, 2015. That was the day I learned that my father had passed away. I was 38 years old and had been working at the same warehouse job for 20 years in Reno, Nevada. I had started there the summer I graduated from high school and the place just kind of stuck with me. Over the years I had risen through the ranks, from picker packer to shift lead. Then from shift lead to warehouse supervisor, then to supply chain manager. That was the position I had been in for the last five years.

Retirement wasn't even a thought yet. Hell, I was only 38, who the hell retires at 38? So, every day I went to work. I was there at 5am and left after the second shift came on at 2:30pm. I liked to have contact with all my people. Maybe that's why I was a successful manager. It's not that I really liked the job, I was just good at it and to be honest, I was comfortable. I had bigger plans for when I did decide to retire. Having never been married and having no kids, I had a lot of options open to me. The one option I was looking at was a huge log cabin in northern Montana. I loved the log cabin look and the idea of retiring and telling civilization to piss off was a feeling I felt more and more every day.

I had been a loner pretty much all my life and that was fine with me. I didn't even start dating until after high school. I think my social life back then was best described as non-existent. That is unless you count the guy that ran the local auto wrecker yard. I had regular dates to go there and hunt for parts to keep my old pickup running. I had a lot of "friends" but none that would help me move a body as the old saying goes. I was just the happiest when I was alone. Every year I would take two weeks of vacation in the summer and go climb mountains or hike into the back country. The farther I could get from people the better. Solitude was my comforting friend.

My family was dysfunctional to say the least. My older brother Braden, well, we didn't have anything in common and never saw eye to eye on anything. We couldn't have been more opposite if we had tried. When we were in school, he was the jock and I was the geek. He was popular and I was nobody. He stayed in Kansas where we grew up and started his own family. I hadn't talked to him in several years. My mother was killed in a car accident when I was only three weeks old, so I never knew her. I only had some pictures and the stories my grandparents, her parents, would tell. My father, so I'm told, pretty much lost it and buried himself in his work and left me and my brother to be raised by my grandparents. Maybe all of that was the reason I preferred to be alone. I'm sure that some shrink somewhere would have a field day with me and my family.

My father worked in the oil and gas business. He also spent a lot of time working for the mining industry. I'm told that he would find deposits of ore or oil and gas. Apparently, he was pretty good at it. He traveled the world on his company's dime, which wouldn't be so bad. I hadn't seen him in over a decade. He used to come around once every other year or so and he would always want to get together for lunch or something. I would meet with him and we would chat about mundane crap and then he would be gone again. I always felt like there was something being left unsaid, something more he wanted to tell me. After my grandparents passed away, the visits from my father stopped. There was no explanation, no card or letter in the mail, no phone call, nothing. After a few years, I had begun to assume that he was dead. There was nothing to lead me to believe otherwise. Until now.

The Meeting:

July 9th, 2015 started like every other weekday for me. I was up at 3:00am and in the gym of my apartment complex by 3:15. Nice thing about that time of the morning was that there was nobody there. The complex manager had given me a key to the place so that he wouldn't have to leave it unlocked overnight. All he asked was that I lock it up after I was done. Staying in shape had been a priority for me after I left home. When I was in high school, I was just a tall, scrawny kid and the object of a lot of harassment from the bullies.

THE RANCH

After I left Kansas, I swore that I would never be subject to that again. It was time for a new life and a clean slate in a place where nobody knew me. At 6'-2" tall, I maintained an average weight of 195 with a pretty chiseled physique. I tried to do my hour every morning in the gym. After that, I was in the shower by 4:20 and on my way to work by 4:45. It was only a five-minute drive to work. That was the normal routine and had been every workday for years. I was always the first person at work, so I was a little surprised when I pulled in to find the Plant Manager's car and a black limo in the parking lot. From outside I could see that the office lights were already on, my office light included.

"Hmmm, must be a surprise visit from corporate," I muttered to myself as I grabbed my briefcase and headed for the front door. I had been through these surprise inspections before, so I wasn't about to let it change my routine. In the front door, past the forklift charging stations and into the employee break room. It was a habit of mine to always start the coffee pots. I knew my people liked coming into work with hot coffee waiting for them. That done, I headed to my office. Let's see who we had to impress today.

Daryl, the plant manager, was in his office but the door was closed, so I proceeded to my office which was two doors down. My door was also closed, and I could see light spilling from under it. I stood there for a second or two trying to figure exactly what to do. Do I knock on my own office door? Do I just barge in like I own the place? This was a first.

"What the hell," I whispered to myself. I grabbed the doorknob, gave it a twist and strode in. There was a very well-dressed man sitting in one of the chairs across from my desk. He stood as I entered and extended his hand.

"I'm Bill Butler and I'm pleased to meet you, Mr. Sterling," he said, as he took a step forward to shake my hand. I took his hand and was a little taken aback by his grip. It was surprising to find a corporate suit with a strong handshake.

"Jason, call me Jason," I said, as I set my briefcase on my desk. "How can I help you today, Mr. Butler? I'm not used to having these inspections so early in the day."

"Mr. Sterling, I'm here to see you. This is not a corporate matter, it's a personal matter," he said as he stepped past me to pull the office door closed. "You see, I was a friend of your father and I am the attorney representing his estate," he sat in his chair and motioned for me to do the same. I realized I was standing there with my mouth open and a blank stare on my face. Finally, I sat on the corner of my desk.

"Mr. Sterling, unfortunately I'm here to inform you that your father has passed away. I'm also here to bring you up to speed on his estate."

"Ummm......" was all I could utter. My heart was racing and I'm sure that I was as white as a ghost. There was so much to be said, but I couldn't form a sentence.

"Are you okay?" He asked with concern.

"I.....ummmmm....."

"Shall I continue, or would you like to take a couple of minutes?" Bill asked.

"I'm just in a little bit of shock. You're talking about MY father, Jack Sterling?" I said starting to regain a small portion of my composure.

"Yes, I am speaking of Jack Alden Sterling. Father to you and your older brother, Braden Allen Sterling."

"My father pretty much went wherever the wind blew him. I haven't seen nor heard from him in almost a decade."

"Jason, at this very moment, an associate of mine is in Kansas delivering this very same message to your brother. He is also going to be given the opportunity to share, equally, in your father's estate. Your father may never have been good at expressing himself or being available to either of you, but he wanted to make damn sure, when the time came, you both would be taken care of."

"Mr. Butler, not to be rude, but I don't think you know squat about my father. I'm pretty sure that he was broke......"

"Before you go any farther, I have known your father for nearly 40 years. In that time, he and I had many, many conversations about his shortcomings as a father. We had many conversations about you two boys. I was there when you were born. I was there when your brother was born. I have been your father's eyes and ears for the last 38 years. He had his reasons for behaving the way he did. Many of those reasons you will never understand, and you may never be able to forgive him for. Right now, I need you to decide for me. I need to know if you want to know the rest of the story or if you want me to walk out of this office, never to contact you again. The choice is entirely up to you," Bill said in a flat, steely tone.

I sat there for what felt like a lifetime. My eyes were fixated on a photo on the far wall of my office. It was a picture of me standing on the top of Half Dome taken the year before at Yosemite National Park. My mind was racing but there was nothing coherent forming. Who was this man sitting across from me? Who was my father? What estate? What was my brother thinking right now? I watched Bill reach into his inside jacket pocket and pull out his cell phone and glance at the screen.

"Jason, I'm going to give you a couple of minutes to think about what you want to do. I'm going to step out and take this call. When I come back, I need your answer," he said as he prepared to exit my office. He made eye contact with me and held it for a couple of seconds before he turned and walked out into the hallway. I sat there, totally dumbstruck. What the hell was happening? Part of me really wanted to know what my father had been up to, part of me was terrified to find out. The thoughts just wouldn't jell in my brain. A few moments later the door opened, and Bill stood perfectly straight and in that same steely tone, asked for my decision.

"I'm probably going to regret this, but I want to know the rest of the story," I heard myself say.

"I am very glad to hear that. I need you to come with me then." He started to turn and walk away.

"Whoa, I can't just leave! I've got a job to do!" I exclaimed.

"I've already spoken to your boss. Your duties will be taken care of. Leave the keys to your truck on your desk and I'll have it taken to your apartment complex," he left my office and began walking down the hallway.

"Wait!" I yelled as I threw my keys on the desk and jogged out of the office to catch up. Bill showed no signs of slowing down so I kept jogging until I had reached his side.

"Where are we going?" I asked.

"Right now, I cannot tell you. I just need you to trust me."

"Trust you? Hell, I don't even know you," I replied tersely. Bill stopped and turned to face me.

"Listen to me. Your father trusted me with everything over the last four decades. The least you can do is trust me for the next 72 hours," he held my stare, then spun and headed for the exit. I was beginning to get pissed off but what else could I do? I followed Bill and we walked straight to the big black stretch limo that was waiting right outside the door. The driver, who was standing next to the car wearing a black suit with light gray pinstripes, leaned over to open the rear door for us and I caught sight of a 1911, .45 caliber pistol under his jacket. He looked at me and smiled. Nothing menacing, quite the opposite to be honest. Bill climbed in first, but I hesitated.

"Don't worry about Mark, he is quite a nice fellow actually," Bill said from the far side of the black leather bench seat. I reluctantly slid in and Mark closed the door behind us.

The Ride:

The first few minutes of the car ride was spent in total silence. The sun was coming up, but it was still near pitch black inside the limo due to the blacked-out windows. I was filled with a mixture of fear and curiosity. What the hell kind of high-priced lawyer needed an armed escort and what the hell kind of estate did my father have that needed a high-priced lawyer with an armed escort?

I knew I should have had some emotions about my father passing away, or at the very least, some questions about how he died. Strangely I had none of that. What I was curious about was what this was all about. It seemed like a lot of cloak and dagger crap just to find out what was left to me and my brother. I was startled from my thoughts when Bill's cell phone rang. He quickly answered it.

"Butler," he said.

"Yes.....Yes......Well that is unfortunate......Yes, we are ten minutes from the airport. We will see you shortly," Bill put his phone away and looked at me.

"Braden has refused to meet with us," he said flatly.

"You don't seem surprised."

"You have not been privy to the information that I have been regarding your brother. No, I'm not surprised."

"You said something about that in my office. You said that you had been Jack's eyes and ears. What was that about?" I asked.

"The short story is this, Jack gave me the task of keeping tabs on you and your brother. He wanted to know everything there was to know about you two. I provided him with that information," again, with the ice cold, flat voice.

"How much could you know about us?" I asked sarcastically.

"I know everything about you and Braden," he said sharply. Okay I thought to myself, let's play this game.

"Who was my girlfriend in high school?"

"What grade?" he asked. Inside I was grinning, I had him now.

"Junior year."

"Hmmmm..." he put his hand on his chin and looked thoughtfully at the ceiling. He looked back at me and smiled. "You didn't have a girlfriend your junior year or any year of high school for that matter. You did have a crush on Carrie Wilson though, does that count?" I couldn't answer, he was totally right. "Your first real date didn't happen until you moved to Reno, a young woman by the name of Hannah if I remember correctly. You hung out in one of two places in high school. The auto shop or the library. You spent nearly every weekend working on that truck of yours. You did not go to one school function. Not one. You had a 4.26 GPA when you graduated," I could tell that he was actually enjoying this a little.

"Ten days after graduation you packed up and moved from Kansas to Reno on a wing and a prayer. You lived in your truck for two weeks while you looked for an apartment. Fortunately, you found the warehouse job within two days of arriving. Shall I continue?" he asked with a slight grin on his face. That pretty much shocked me back into my silence. How the hell did this guy know so much about me?

"Don't worry about it too much, Jason. Your brother is just as much of an open book as you are. Remember when you were 14 and your grandfather's cows got out because you left the gate open?"

"Yeah. How can I forget that? I got my ass tanned over that one," I said, looking back at him.

"It was Braden's fault. He and Tommy Walden had been out in the barn drinking some beer they stole from the grocery store. They are the ones who left the gate open."

"How the hell do you know that?" I blurted out before I could even think. Now I was getting pissed off. This guy knew everything about me, and I didn't know anything except his name, and I was about to tell him so. "Listen here you son of a bitch, I don't know who the hell you are, and I don't know what the hell you're trying to pull here but I've had just about enough of it! I want some damn answers and I want them now! Otherwise you can pull this car over and let me out right now!" I said with my voice rising. I felt the car slow slightly and could see Mark looking at me in the rear-view mirror. Bill raised his hand and signaled to Mark to keep driving. I could feel the car begin to accelerate again.

"I will give you some of the answers you want now. The rest will have to wait until we get to your father's ranch. Some of what you want to know is not for me to tell you. I hope you can understand that," I nodded to him and settled back into my seat. "I met your father in January of 1975. He and I were employed by the same company. He had just gotten the job and it was my job to bring him up to speed on all the legal aspects of his new employment. We quickly became friends and stayed that way for the next 40 years. I introduced him to your mother. She was my secretary. Their courtship was very short, and I ended up as your father's best man at their wedding in July of that year. I was at the hospital when Braden was born on April 11, 1976. I was also there when you were born on April 19, 1977.

Your father was out in the field, Saudi Arabia to be exact, when your mother had her car accident. It was a miracle you and Braden both survived uninjured. I was the guy that had to call Jack and tell him what happened. I was the guy that had to go to the morgue and identify your mother's body," he paused and looked out the window. He took a deep breath and began again. "I was the guy that took you and your brother home, and you stayed with me and my wife for a few weeks, until other arrangements could be made. Jack was destroyed. He blamed himself for your mother's death. He was sure that if he had been home it would never have happened.

Anyway, in August of 1977 I drew up the paperwork for your grandparents to take full custody of the two of you. Your father gave them money every month to make sure you had everything you needed. I also set up the money transfers every month right up until they died," he paused again as the car exited the highway and turned toward the airport. "Let's finish this conversation on the plane," he said, as he pulled his phone from his pocket again.

"Dan, we are pulling up to the gate, warm it up," he undid his seat belt as we pulled through the gate that led to the private hangars. The car slowed and pulled into a hanger that had a Gulfstream G6 private jet sitting out front. The car came to a stop and in a flash, Mark had the door open. Bill and I both slid out and I followed him toward the jet. Its engines were running, and the door was open waiting for us. I must have been in shock. Either that or I was having one hell of a dream.

In less than an hour I had gone from a normal Thursday morning to climbing into a G6 corporate jet headed to parts unknown. We quickly boarded with Mark bringing up the rear and closing the door. Mark took his jacket off and I could plainly see a Sig Sauer 1911 in desert tan hanging on his right hip with two spare 10 round magazines on his left hip. I knew my guns and that was one of my favorites. Mark quickly walked past me and took a seat near the rear of the plane. Bill said a couple of words to the pilots and walked back to where I was sitting. The plane began to throttle up and started moving. Bill removed his jacket and I was slightly stunned to see him wearing a Sig Sauer pistol in a shoulder holster. It was the same model as the one I had seen on Mark earlier. Bill took a seat across from me and buckled his seat belt.

"As soon as we are in the air, there is coffee if you want some," he offered. I looked up from his pistol to his face and saw a slight smirk. "Yes Jason, all of us are armed. Even the pilots."

"This day has gone from totally normal to totally surreal in record time," I said, only half joking. "I was standing in the shower this morning wondering what I wanted to take out of the freezer for dinner, now I'm on a G6 flying off into the wild blue yonder."

Bill smiled a genuine smile. "Jason, I understand your outburst in the car, I get it. I showed up in your life less than an hour ago and totally turned everything you knew on its head. It's only going to get stranger for you as the day goes on. Oh, don't worry, I had my man lock your truck and put the pork chops back in the freezer for you," he said with a grin. I just shook my head and looked out the small window. The plane quickly made its way to the runway and within a few seconds we were in the air. By the looks of it we were heading east.

Once our climb leveled out, Mark undid his seat belt and retrieved three cups of hot coffee. He gave me one, gave Bill one and took the third back to his seat.

"Where were we? Oh yeah, your father had just given custody to your grandparents. Anyway, he gave me a couple of stipulations. One, he wanted all four of you to be taken care of financially. Two, he wanted me to keep my eyes on you and your brother. He wanted to know everything you two were up to. As far as why, that I cannot tell you. Yet," he stopped to take a drink of his coffee.

"That had to cost my father a small fortune. How could he afford your services, the support payments, and the surveillance? We're talking a lot of money spent on a couple of kids he didn't want anything to do with," I said as I took a drink of my coffee.

"It was a lot of money, but he could afford it, and don't think he didn't want you boys. I will tell you that he did what was best for you. As much as it hurt him and you, it was the best thing he could do," I wasn't sure what he meant by that, but I decided to let it go and change the subject.

"You said something about a ranch?" I asked.

"Ah yes. We're flying to Elko, Nevada. We will land there, then drive about an hour to the ranch. Unfortunately, once we leave the Elko airport I'll have to blindfold you so that you do not know its exact location. It was one of your father's stipulations that any outsider not know the true whereabouts of the ranch. Sorry."

"Now hold on a minute...." I started but Bill cut me off before I could continue.

"If you like the ranch and decide that you want to continue what your father started, then and only then will you know the location and all of the secrets that come with it. Your father and several of his associates spent 25 years of their lives putting it together and I will not disobey my standing orders regarding its true location. If this is going to be a problem, tell me now and I'll have the pilot's return us to Reno and you can go on with your day and your life," there was that icy voice again.

"No, it's not going to be a problem. Let's go to the ranch," I said flatly.

"Good, now if you don't mind, I have some business to take care of," he said as he pulled a laptop from a pocket on the side of his chair.

The flight to Elko was just under an hour from the time we boarded the plane to the time we touched down. Instead of going to one of the main gates we pulled up to a small hanger near the end of the taxi way. As we were getting off the plane a black four door Jeep roared up and parked next to the stairs. Mark got in the front passenger seat and Bill walked around to the passenger door on the driver's side. I took a seat right behind Mark.

The first thing that struck me from the outside was that this was a damn nice Jeep. Lifted with oversize tires, big winch bumper and brush guard up front, big bumper out back with a rack above the spare tire. Two steel fuel cans were mounted on it along with a hi-lift jack. It also had a rack on the roof with a second spare tire, a shovel and an ax. The windows were all blacked out and I mean pitch black.

The inside of the Jeep was just as impressive. It reminded me of the inside of a cop car. Up front there was a vertical rifle rack with matching AR-15's. The

THE RANCH

factory center console had been removed and replaced with a radio console and a bank of switches that operated who knows what. In the back seat there was also a vertical rifle rack, again with matching ARs. Mounted to the back of each front seat was a magazine holder that would hold six AR-15 magazines and six magazines for the Sig Sauer pistols. All the slots were full.

The driver was wearing black fatigues with a black baseball cap and black framed sunglasses. She turned and introduced herself as Jill. She extended her hand and shook mine. She looked at me over the top of her sunglasses and just stared for a few seconds. She had the most amazing blue eyes I had ever seen. When she was done eyeing me, she gave Bill a look and turned back around in her seat.

"Okay Jason, time for the blindfold," he said as he handed me a black *shemagh*. "You can put it on, or I can put it on for you," I took it from him and tied it securely around my eyes. I then settled into my seat and fastened my seat belt. As Jill stepped on the gas, I was sure that this Jeep had some work done under the hood. The acceleration was crisp, and the exhaust had a deep throaty growl to it. We were in the Jeep for what felt like forever but was truthfully only an hour. I could tell that there was some in-town driving, a lot of highway driving and some dirt road thrown in there. Jill was more than happy to apply the throttle pedal. It was a little un-nerving being blindfolded. Nobody spoke during the whole drive. When we finally came to a stop and the engine shut off, Bill was the first to speak.

"We are here but before the blindfold comes off, we need to have an understanding," he said.

"Okay," I replied.

"This is as far as Mark and I go. Jill will take you to meet with Allan, the ranch manager. I'll meet you back here Sunday at noon to take you back to Reno. Between now and then you will have a lot of information to take in and process. Keep an open mind is all that I ask. For the most part you will have free roam of the ranch and I would not only expect you to explore the grounds, I would implore you to do so. There are places that you will be restricted from accessing. Talk to Allan and he will escort you. What you see and learn here is never to be passed to anyone and I mean anyone. If you choose to return here and pick up where the others left off, you will be rewarded with full access to the site, but I warn you, it will be a lifelong commitment. If you choose to pass on this opportunity, you will never be contacted again, and you will never disseminate ANY of the information you have learned here. Do you understand what I have told you?"

"I do," was my reply. Curiosity had me in its full grasp now.

With that, the *shemagh* was removed from my face. It took my eyes a moment to adjust but when they did, all I could see in front of the Jeep was a massive steel gate with a stone gatehouse on the left side. Looking out both side windows, was a brick wall that was at least ten feet tall, stretching off in each direction. Jill, Mark and Bill opened their doors and stepped out. I did the same. It sure felt good to stretch my legs.

Mark walked around to the driver's side and Jill passed him, headed toward me. Bill came to the passenger's side and stopped right in front of me. He extended his hand and I took it. Again, I was surprised by the strength in his grip. He gave me a nod before he released my hand and climbed into his seat. The Jeep started and slowly backed away from the gate. A glance at my watch told me it was 8:30 in the morning and the air was already getting warm.

I slowly turned a full 360 degrees, taking in the landscape. Off in the distance to the west, probably 15 miles away, I could see what looked like a lake. About the same distance to the north I could see a housing subdivision. As I turned back to the gate I came face-to-face with Jill. There was absolutely no expression on her face.

"Are you ready to have your life changed Mr. Sterling?" she asked.

"Yes ma'am," it seemed like the only appropriate answer. She spun on her heel and walked to the gatehouse. She placed her hand on a flat screen that was positioned just below the blacked-out window. With her left hand she removed her sunglasses and stared directly into the glass. After about five seconds there was an audible click and the gate began to open outward. Jill replaced her sunglasses and began to walk briskly through the gate.

The Ranch:

Once we were past the gate, which swung closed behind us, I could see that the road we were walking on went about another quarter mile before it reached the main house. Well, houses, I guess you could say. The road wasn't straight either, it snaked its way up to a very large circular driveway and parking lot. Set in the middle of the circle was a giant pond. It looked like it took up a full acre on its own. There was a floating wooden boat dock that extended out to the middle. I spotted a small canoe laying on the dock and one in the water next to it. I could also see a couple of folding chairs. My guess was that there were fish in the pond and that would be the perfect place to fish from.

In the middle of the outer circle was a small log cabin. It was a single story and didn't look much bigger than 1,500 or 1,600 square feet or maybe the size of a small three-bedroom house. About 75 feet from it, on either side, were matching two-story cabins. Both were massive in size and completely identical, right down to the covered wrap-around decks. Then on either side of those two buildings, again about 75 feet away, were two slightly smaller two-story cabins. They were exact replicas of the large cabins. The five buildings formed the outer ring of the circle.

All of them were surrounded by well-manicured grass and low-lying shrub and flower gardens. Directly in front of the center building stood a flagpole with the American flag fluttering in the slight breeze and there was a massive parking lot that spanned the area in front of all five buildings. There was a concrete sidewalk that went from building to building. Parked in the parking lot was another Jeep like the one we had just gotten out of. As we followed the driveway, I could catch glimpses of buildings set farther back on the property. All but one of them appeared to be of the same log construction. The other thing that caught my eye was the fact that every building had a solar panel array on the roof. There were also a couple of pens that I could see and at least one had horses. I could also see a white utility truck parked near what I could only assume was the horse barn. There was something on the door, but it was too far away to make out.

Jill's pace was brisk but constant and we were turning up the walkway to the center cabin in no time at all. She walked straight up to the door, swung it open and motioned for me to go inside. I did and she followed right behind me. She pulled the door closed with a heavy "clunk". At first, I thought the lights were off but as my eyes adjusted, I could see that it was lit only by a bank of computer screens and a small desk lamp. Seated behind the desk was an older man who was wearing blue jeans and a white t-shirt. He was standing in an instant and walking around the desk, his hand outstretched.

"Jason Sterling," he said in a booming voice that seemed out of place in the dark room. I shook his hand and he seemed to be looking me over from head to toe over the top of his eyeglasses. "It's a pleasure to finally meet you in person. I'm Allan West," he said, shaking my hand vigorously. "Walk with me while I talk. We have a lot to cover before you leave here on Sunday," he said as he released my hand and started for the door. Jill replaced him behind the desk. I followed him out the front door. You would think that I would be used to it by now, but Allan had a Sig Sauer pistol tucked in the back of his waistband.

"So, Allan, what is it you do around here?" I asked as I caught up to walk beside him. We were walking around the center building and heading toward the utility truck.

"I am the Operations Manager of this property. I make sure the day-to-day life around here moves along smoothly," he said.

"That does not seem to be that bad of a job. What do you have here? Twenty acres?"

"That's just the main compound inside the brick wall, 21 acres to be exact. Outside of the compound there are 3,000 acres, and 500 head of cattle. Inside the compound we have the security office, where we just came from. There are the two main houses and the two guest houses. Out back here we have two barns, which each holds eight horses. There are also two chicken coops that house about 50 chickens each. Two pens for the hogs, eight in each pen. The center building is our warehouse," he said as he motioned with his hand.

"What's the deal with everything being in pairs?" I asked.

"It was something your father thought of. If you look at this place from overhead and split it down the middle, each side is a mirror image of the other. I will explain that when we sit down for lunch. You are more than welcome to explore the grounds on your own. The only building that is locked is the warehouse. Either Jill or I can give you a guided tour of that when you are ready."

"What about now?" I asked.

"Let me introduce you to our veterinarian and then we can go to the warehouse," he said. That was good enough for me. My guess is that we walked about 100 yards to the horse barn. We were met at the door by a man who appeared to be in his early 70s. White hair, white beard.... Santa Clause was the thought that popped into my head. It was tough to suppress that grin as Allan introduced us.

"Dr. Williams, this is Jason Sterling. Jason, I'd like you to meet Doctor Timothy Williams. He has been our vet for the last 25 years," the doctor extended his hand and I took it.

"Mr. Sterling, it's an honor to finally meet you," he also eyed me from head to toe. "You're taller than I expected," he quipped with a grin. He released my hand and turned to Allan. "I'll come back out next week and take care of the horse's hooves. I cleaned them all and did a little file work, but they need to have shoes put on before the big ride. The rocks are tearing up their hooves. Right now, I got to get back to town, patients to look in on."

"Thanks Tim, I look forward to seeing you then. I'm glad you could come out today," they shook hands and Tim headed for the utility truck. We walked into the barn and it was massive inside. There were ten stalls and eight horses. The stalls were all clean and the concrete floor down the center of the barn looked clean enough to eat off of. All the outer doors to the stalls were open into large outdoor paddocks and there was a warm breeze circulating through the building.

We walked all the way through the barn and exited at the end opposite of where we came in. We took a left and headed toward the concrete walled warehouse. We walked up to one of the main doors and I could see the ten-digit keypad on the wall. Allan stepped in front of it, effectively blocking my view. I heard five beeps then a click as the door lock clicked. He turned the handle and opened the door part way. He turned and looked back at me.

"Remember what Bill told you in the Jeep? What you see and hear on this property is to be kept secret," he said, making eye contact and holding it.

"I understand."

He pulled the door open and we walked inside. The warehouse was about 200 feet long and 100 feet wide. While the outside temperature was already pushing the mid-80s, it was very cool and comfortable in here. From where I was standing, I could see pallets of boxes about four feet tall, shrink-wrapped and double-stacked along the wall. There were also four aisles of vertical racking, exactly like the ones we used in my warehouse back in Reno. They were filled with shrink-wrapped pallets just like the ones along the wall. It looked like they went half the length of the building and the 30 feet to the ceiling.

"What's all of this?" I asked.

"Food. It's all freeze dried food."

"Seriously?" the astonishment in my voice must have been evident and I know I said it louder than I had intended.

"Seriously. We have enough food in this warehouse to feed 18 people three meals a day for five years," Allan said proudly.

"Why so much?"

"I'll tell you what, Jason. I'll give you the tour of the warehouse. When we are done here, we will go to the main house and have lunch, I'll answer your questions then. I'm sure you will have a lot of them."

"Okay," shit just got weird. We walked down the closest aisle and I could see the labels on the boxes. Mountain House, Augason Farms, Wise foods, and those were just the ones that I could remember. There were also MREs, (Meals Ready to Eat). These were not the civilian version either. These were government issued. We got to the end of that aisle and it appeared the other half of the warehouse was a garage and workshop.

Along one side there were four military Hummers angled into parking spots. On the opposite wall was a rack with spare parts and dozens of spare tires. On the end wall was a pair of giant roll-up doors. There was also a lathe, a mill and a tire changing machine. There were a couple of welders and presses on the other side of those and I spotted a steel band saw over in the corner. We circled through the garage area and back down the far wall.

This wall was covered with lockers. I stopped and opened one, military uniforms in desert multi-cam. The next locker was full of the same. There was also body armor, boots, helmets, and packs......everything needed to supply a small army. At no point did Allan try to hurry me along. Quite the opposite in fact. After spending about 45 minutes in the warehouse, we found ourselves back at the door we had come in.

"Anything else you want to see?" Allan asked.

"No, I think I have seen enough."

"Lunch then?"

"Lead the way," I said.

We walked from the warehouse to the security building in complete silence. There were so many things running through my head at that moment. I don't know if it was the summer heat that was making me sweat or the fact that I felt like I had stepped into the Twilight Zone. I was a rookie survivalist and I had a few supplies, but these guys were the big leagues. I felt like I was in way over my head.

Allan leaned into the security office and told Jill that we would be in the main house having lunch. From there we went to the large cabin to the right of the security building. We went in the front door and made our way straight to the dining room. The table could seat 20 people but was set for two. There was a platter of sub sandwiches and a pitcher of water already on the table. I took a seat on one side and Allan sat opposite of me.

"Let me see how many of your questions I can answer before you ask them," he stated as he grabbed a sandwich from the platter. "Twenty-five years ago, your father pulled together a crew of ten people, including himself. I was the foreman for that crew. We all came from different backgrounds in the construction and military fields. About half of us were tradesmen of one sort or another, metal workers, wood workers. Those guys were true craftsmen."

"Of the ten of us, only three remain. Myself, Doc Williams, and Bill Butler. Your father wanted to build a compound that could sustain all of us and our families if there was ever a catastrophic event. He bought the land from the Bureau of Land Management for five bucks an acre in the fall of 1989. The summer of 1990 brought all of us out here and we ran fencing around the entire 3000 acres. It took us eight weeks and I cannot tell you how many blisters," he paused long enough to take a bite of his sandwich.

"The next summer, 1991, we came out and brought some heavy equipment with us. Again, we spent eight weeks out here, this time putting in all the infrastructure. There are four water wells on the property, two down here inside the compound, and two more outside to keep the waterholes full for the cattle. The original plan was to put five mobile homes out here but the summer of '92 brought a change. Your father had found a company that built log cabins and shipped them to where they were to be assembled. That company was floundering, and Jack struck a deal to buy them out. We spent that summer loading all their inventory and equipment into cargo containers and moving it from Caldwell, Idaho, to this location. That entire winter he had truckload after truckload of timber brought here."

"The summer of '93 came around and he hired the crew from Idaho to teach us to run the equipment and help us build the first cabin, this one. The summers of '94 and '95 were spent building the other three cabins and the security building. I stayed on for the winter months of '95 into '96 and built the pond and did all the groundwork for the walkways and pads for the barns and warehouse. The summer of '96 we did all the concrete and asphalt work. We hired a crew to come in and build the wall which is all concrete and re-bar reinforced. It would have taken too long for us to do it."

"The summer of '97 we put up the barns and erected the warehouse. That finished all the major construction projects," again he paused long enough to chew a bite of sandwich. "In the fall of '97 we lost one of our own. Jerry Taylor was our electrician. He had no family, so we had his body brought here and we buried him up in the meadow."

"Starting in the spring of '98 we did pretty much all the finish work. We put in all the landscaping and the crops out behind the barns. Your father spent most of his time working so it was rare that he could make it out here," he paused for another bite.

"What exactly did my father do for work? I mean this, all of this had to cost a fortune," I said.

"Well your father did work for the oil and gas industry as an independent contractor. He would sniff out the deposits and he was very good at it. That was his cover story anyway," he put his sandwich down and gave that a moment to sink in. "He made good money doing that and he had made some really, really good investments but the bulk of his money came from the U.S. government. With his credentials, your father not only had access to just about every country on the globe, but he also had access to their governments and their officials."

"Are you saying my father was a spy?"

"In a word, yes. Bill was his handler. Everything Bill told you on the way here was true, he just didn't tell you all the details. That is my job."

"What details?" I asked.

"Well, while Bill was your father's boss, he ended up being his best friend, too. Bill showed him the ropes and taught him everything he knew. Your father was on assignment in Saudi Arabia when your mom was killed. What Bill didn't tell you was that it was a botched attempt on your father's life. There was a man in the car that night, a fellow agent, who was assigned to your mom's protection detail. The bad guys thought it was your father. They pulled up next to the car as it was traveling down the highway. They shot the agent in the head as they passed by their car. It went off the road and rolled down the embankment. The bad guys kept going and never looked back. Your mother was killed instantly in the crash, she never had a chance."

"Your father flew home immediately and from what Bill told me, he was a total wreck. After the funeral, he went off the grid for nearly six months. Bill had no idea where he was, and he used every single contact he had to try and find him.

He got only one message from Jack and that was to make you and your brother disappear. He knew that was the only way you would be safe. When he reappeared, he told Bill that he found the guys responsible and that they would never hurt anyone again."

"He killed them?"

"Yes, he did and from what he told me; they did not die easily. He kept you in hiding because he was afraid that someday, someone might get the idea to try something like that again. He went so far as to change his name and re-write his history," he picked up his sandwich and took a couple more bites. I sat back in my chair, my thoughts racing all over the place. "Anyway, with your father's connections around the world and inside our own government he managed to pull together a lot of deals under the table. Bill, being of like mind, knew what he was up to and helped him import some stuff into the country. No questions asked."

"It was the fall of '99 when things started showing up here. Usually in cargo containers and usually with orders not to open them until he was present. It was '02 when two flatbed trucks showed up with the Hummers. Two weeks later, two more trucks showed up, one with a M932A1 five-ton six-by-six and one with crates and crates of spare parts and tires. Shortly after that, four of the containers were dropped off and they were full of gear. Boots, body armor, uniforms.....you name it. Then one day in '05 a 48-foot box trailer showed up that was loaded from one end to the other with MREs. I never once questioned where the stuff was coming from. Plausible deniability," he said with a grin.

"In the summer of '06 your dad showed up here and behind him was a long line of cattle trucks. All of them were unloaded and when it was all said and done, we had 250 head of cattle. A year later he showed up again leading three semi-trucks up the road. We backed 'em up to the warehouse and unloaded all of the freeze-dried food. It was also the summer of '07 when we started getting the crew together and we would do the cattle round-ups. We would bring them down here and the good Dr. Williams would make sure they were in good health.

Your father was adamant that this place be as self-sufficient as possible. Doc Williams also pulls duty as our Chief Medical Officer. He didn't become a vet until after his tours in Vietnam. In those days he was a combat medic," he paused long enough to take a long drink of water. "After Bill left the service of our country, he became a pretty high-powered corporate attorney. That was good for us because he made sure everything we did here was legit."

"How do Jill and Mark fit into all of this? They are quite a bit younger than the three of you," I asked.

"They are Bill's kids. There is another brother, Dale. Jill stays here full-time and oversees all of our security operations. She trained side-by-side for three years with Walter Jenkins. He was a Green Beret in Vietnam. He then became a cop for LAPD, retired as a Lieutenant and moved out here full-time. He passed on everything he knew to Jill. What he didn't know, he found a school for her to go to. Honestly, I have never seen anyone run an AR-15 like that girl can. Don't piss her off either, she could beat your ass and not even break a sweat," he chuckled and finished his sandwich.

"Listen Allan, I appreciate the history lesson, but I'm still not really sure exactly what this place is. I mean it sounds to me that you guys have put together a prepper compound here, am I right?"

"You're exactly right. I know you are familiar with prepping. You have done some research on it, been to some specialized weapons training, put some food and water away. You keep an emergency pack in your truck, which by the way, is a beautiful ride. You went and got your concealed carry permit. Why go to all the trouble?" he asked. I shrugged, not sure how to answer. "That's exactly what we have done here, just on a much larger scale. Your father is the one that spearheaded this entire project. He had traveled the world. He had been to some glamorous places and some real third world shitholes. He read the writing on the wall long before many of us put it all together. He knew that someday the defecation was going to meet the oscillation. And it will. Not if, but when."

"Sooooo, he put a crack team together to do what? Hide out here to live out your days?"

"No, not at all. We are very involved in the well-being of this county. We have donated millions of dollars to our schools and different charities. Donated tons of food to food banks. We bought the sheriff's department new cruisers and sent their guys to some high-end schools. We bought the county road department two new snowplows when the state didn't have the money. The local volunteer fire department needed some heavy rescue equipment and we got it for them. We did all of that and never asked for anything in return, nor will we. As a matter of fact, all of the donations were made in total anonymity, thanks to Bill and his law firm."

"So, what does this place gain from anonymous donations?" I asked.

"We get a stronger and healthier community. A community that could recover faster from a catastrophic event."

"I keep hearing about this event. What is it that you think is going to happen?"

"Does it matter? Financial collapse, EMP (Electro Magnetic Pulse), pandemic..... Does it really matter? The result is the same across the board. Most people have no clue what can happen in a disaster and it has been right in front of their faces this whole time. We have Hurricane Katrina, the earthquake in Haiti, the tsunami in Japan. The list is endless, and everyone thinks the same thing. It can't happen to me; it can't happen here. Sadly, when it does happen, many will perish because they were too preoccupied with the football season or the stigma of being one of those crazy prepper guys," Allan said.

"Yeah but those were all localized events. Help was there within a couple of days. What makes you think something so bad is going to happen?"

"It has happened before. Fortunately, our highest level of technology was a telegraph back then. I know you have investigated it but look hard at the Carrington event that happened in September of 1859. If something like that happened today....." his voice trailed off. He poured himself another glass of water and picked up another sandwich. I realized that I was hungry, so I took one and began to eat. "Listen to me," he began again. "Things have happened before. The Carrington event, The Spanish Flu, the dustbowl and that's just to name a couple. If any of those things happened today, the results would be devastating. Those are just natural events."

"Let's not forget the kind of shit man can create. Nuclear war, weaponized Ebola, super EMP weapons, terrorism and on and on. The world is a very dangerous place, Jason," I sat in silence as he again went to work on his second sandwich. Yeah, I had investigated those things but considered all of them to be remote possibilities at best. I kept the supplies that I did because I lived in an area where earthquakes did happen. We ate in silence for a few minutes before Allan spoke again.

"We are not a bunch of weirdos, Jason. This is not some sort of cult. Your father shared a lot of information with us over the years, things that he should have taken to his grave. All the information was backed up and verified by Bill. This place is the real deal."

"Why did he choose you and the other guys to help build this place? How have you managed to keep it secret for all these years?"

"From what your father told me, he spent almost two years looking us over from a distance. He knew everything there was to know about us before he ever contacted anybody. He met with each one of us in person before he got us all together. He met with me as a job applicant. He took a dog in for a checkup with Doc Williams. Walter Jenkins taught a concealed weapons class that he had enrolled in. He did that with everyone. We all came together one weekend in Denver, Colorado. Yep, he lured each of us there under false pretenses. All of us thought we were going to some seminar that pertained to our field of expertise. I thought I had been given a free trip to Denver to sit in on a contractor's conference," he chuckled a little as he took the last bite of his sandwich.

"We were all pretty pissed off, but he convinced us to stick around and hear him out. By the time he was done with his hour-long monologue, we were hooked. He told us that he needed specialists to help him build his new ranch. The first stint would last eight weeks, and the work would be brutal. He didn't lie. I know a couple of us wanted to haul ass after about the third day of stringing barbed wire and pounding fence posts. I think the only thing that kept us from doing so was the money. Your father paid very, very well. It was the last night of our stay here that first summer when he told us what he was really up to."

"We were all sitting around the fire pit, bellies full of steak and potatoes and a little bit of old whiskey. I'm pretty sure that he already knew that we would all agree to be back the next summer and it wasn't just the money that would bring us back. By the time that night was over, we knew that we had all made lifelong friends. As far as keeping it a secret, it's not really a secret at all. If you ask anybody that has been by here or knows we are here, they think it is a retreat for high-powered corporate executives. That's what the sign at the turn-off from the main road says anyway. We had a sheriff once that snooped around hard. When he looked around the warehouse, he thought he had us nailed to the wall."

"Of course, we produced the paperwork for everything in there and he bought the excuse we gave him for the military gear," he grinned. "We told him that we ran military-style 'team building' exercises with airsoft gear. We even showed him all the airsoft guns and videos. He left but he wasn't happy. Swore up and down we were up to no good but had absolutely no proof." The grin just got bigger. We talked for about another hour and between the two of us, polished off the sandwiches and water. I glanced at my watch and it was just about 1pm. Allan stood and picked up the plates. He headed for the kitchen and I followed behind him with the pitcher and glasses. He quickly washed them by hand and left them in the strainer to air dry.

"Jason, I have some things to take care of and I am going to be busy for the rest of the day. You are more than welcome to wander the grounds. All the cabins are unlocked, and you are welcome to check them out. If you need any assistance, Jill will be in the security office until 5:00. Dinner will be at the other main house at 6:00," he said as he extended his hand, which I took. "I am glad you are here, and I hope you choose to stay with us. It would be nice to have a Sterling in charge again," he smiled and released my hand.

When Allan had left the room and I heard the front door close, I leaned on the counter, put my face in my hands and closed my eyes. I had always wondered what kind of man my father was, and as of now, I was no closer to discovering that. He was even more of an enigma now.

I had almost five hours to kill before dinner. Allan and Bill had both told me to explore the place, might as well start right here I thought to myself. I pulled the tie from around my neck and stuffed it in my pocket, rolled up my sleeves and began my tour.

The kitchen was large and had a very big center island that was home to a six-burner stove. The sink was a large stainless-steel industrial unit. The fridge looked like it should also belong in a restaurant, not a home. It struck me as a little odd that there was no dishwasher. I found that the pantry was a massive walk-in affair. It had fully loaded shelves all the way around the outside wall. It was about ten feet deep and eight feet across. I spotted a handle recessed in the floor and gave it a firm pull. The trap door opened and there was a narrow set of stairs leading down. The light had come on when I opened the hatch. I went down and realized that it was a root cellar. It too was well-stocked with everything from potatoes and onions to carrots. I closed everything up and went to explore the rest of the first floor.

I walked into the living room with its massive stone fireplace. There was a huge sectional couch that wrapped around a handmade pine table. Two overstuffed recliners sat on either side of a smaller table. The mantel over the fireplace had pictures of my father and nine other people. My assumption was that this was the group that founded this place. I found what I assumed was the study. It had a beautiful, hand-crafted oak desk in the center of the room and an overstuffed leather chair behind it. Bookshelves lined three of the four walls. The fourth wall was covered in maps. Local maps, regional maps, world maps. I also found what appeared to be a bedroom with a private bathroom on the ground floor. There was also a second, full bathroom in the hallway. The dining room had a massive wooden table that was surrounded by 20 chairs. Nine of the handcrafted chairs ran down either side with one at each end.

When I found the staircase, I was faced with a choice, up or down. I went up. The second floor had two master bedrooms, one at each end of the floor and between the two of them, they took up the entire floor. They were very modest in their furnishings. Each had a handmade pine-framed bed and headboard. Both bedside tables, the dressers and the chests at the foot of each bed all appeared to be handmade. Lots of closet space and a very large bathroom. Both rooms were mirror images of each other. It was at this point that it donned on me that I had not seen one TV or computer in the house, and while all the rooms had electricity, there were old-fashioned oil lamps and candles placed as "decorations" around the rooms. Both master suites also had wood-burning fireplaces. The floors throughout the entire house were hardwood. I don't know who did the housekeeping, but I found no dust anywhere.

I went back downstairs and kept going until I got to the basement. There was a big change down here. The stairwell went from wood to concrete and the walls went from log to cinder block. The stairs ended and a long hallway began. I could see three doors on either side. I opened the first door on the right. "Storeroom" is what it said on the nameplate and that is exactly what it looked like. Medical supplies to be exact. I.V. supplies, sutures, bandages large and small, gowns, masks, gloves, surgical tools....... Enough to supply a small hospital. In the back of the room there was a small fridge with a padlock on it. I could only assume that it was a drug locker.

I left the room and went to the one across the hall. There was no nameplate on the door. It looked to be another storage room. This one held blankets, sheets, towels and other linens. The next three rooms were all identical. Two sets of bunk beds, four wall lockers and four-foot lockers. The sixth room was a modest bathroom. At the end of the hallway was a large locker. The nameplate on it said, "Cleaning Supplies". Other than that, there was not much to see down there. I went back to the main floor and glanced at the wall clock. I couldn't believe I had spent nearly an hour looking around the main house.

THE RANCH

From there, I went out the front door and was immediately assaulted by the early summer heat. It donned on me that while it was about 70 degrees inside the house, I had seen no air conditioning unit or even a thermostat for that matter. I went to the slightly smaller version of the house next door. The exterior may have been the same, but the interior was very different. I stepped in the door and was standing in a smaller version of the kitchen. This one was furnished pretty much the same but set up more like a restaurant kitchen. The dining room had a long table with 20 chairs, ten on either side. There were three bedrooms on the ground floor, all with their own private bathrooms.

The upstairs reminded me of the old military-style dorms. Again, there were two massive suites but each one was filled with ten bunk beds, ten wall lockers, ten-foot lockers, and a bathroom that had four toilet stalls and four shower stalls. There were four matching sinks with a full wall mirror across from the showers. Very industrial in feel. All stainless steel and tile. The one similarity was the oil lamps, candles and wood-burning fireplaces. This cabin also had a basement, but it was also set up very different. There was a large conference room or at least that is what I called it. It had a huge oak table and was surrounded by a dozen chairs. Like the study in the main house, this room also had maps plastering one wall. Opposite of that was a huge whiteboard. Outside of the office was a large, well-furnished weight room. The only other thing down here was a cleaning supply cabinet just like the main house.

I made a quick pass through the other main house and guest house. Both were exact mirror images of the other two. The only difference was that the two master suites in the main house were being lived in. I assumed one belonged to Jill and the other to Allan. With nothing left to see in the living quarters, I decided to check out the barns. Both barns had eight horses and ten stalls. The outer doors that led into the outdoor paddocks were made of thick timbers probably four inches thick and framed entirely in steel "C" channels.

There was a loft in each barn, and both were full of hay. The concrete floor that ran the center of the barns was in fact a coated concrete. The gray rubberized coating looked like concrete but was much easier on the horse's hooves. The main doors at each end of the barns were built just like the paddock doors except that these doors covered the ten-foot-wide spans and rolled to the sides instead of swinging outward. All the horses were friendly and obviously well taken care of.

All the stalls were clean and so were the outdoor paddocks. While it was warmer inside the barns, the cross breeze felt good as it flowed through the structures.

The chicken coops were also very large affairs. Each structure was about 40 feet long and 20 feet wide. Each was a lean-to type of structure with the coop itself being the enclosed ten foot by twenty-foot hen house. The rest of the covered area had a plywood base that went from the concrete foundation to four feet high. The next four feet up was a very tightly woven chicken wire. There were two entrances to each one. One was a gate into the yard, the second was a door into the henhouse.

The pig pens, the chicken coops, and the horse barns were all the highest quality. The materials used, for the most part, appeared to be hand-hewn. What had to be purchased looked to be high quality and everything was well taken care of. The buildings that were farther back appeared to be two pole barns and two greenhouses, all of which were very large. As I got closer, I could see that there was heavy equipment and other equipment parked in both barns along with hundreds of bales of hay. There was a Case 780D 4x4 backhoe, a Case TR310 front end loader, a SV185 skid steer and a whole host of sawmill equipment. The latter I assumed was the equipment that came from Idaho. The Case equipment all looked to be new. Each pole barn had matching heavy equipment minus the sawmill equipment. That was the only thing I had seen up to this point that had not been doubled up on.

After I wandered through the greenhouses I headed back toward the main house where Allan and I had met earlier. A quick glance at my watch told me that I only had eight minutes before dinner was to start. I picked up the pace and hurried back to the house. I didn't want to leave a bad impression and be late to the first dinner. I made it with a couple minutes to spare. After washing up in the bathroom I went to the dining room.

There were three places set at the end of the table. One at the end and one to either side. There was a platter with lettuce, sliced tomatoes, sliced onions and pickles. Jill came from the kitchen with another platter of hot hamburger patties. I almost didn't recognize her. Gone were the black fatigues and combat boots. They had been replaced by a pair of black spandex shorts, a tight-fitting black tank top and running shoes. Her sandy blond hair was pulled back into a ponytail. Her athletic figure was one of the best I had seen in a very long time. Her clothes fit tight enough that you could see the chiseled muscles beneath. She stood about 5'8" and probably went 130 pounds, all of it muscle. She wore no make-up and she didn't need to. Her natural beauty was stunning. I could never recall seeing a woman with such perfect features and proportions.

"Are you going to stand there and stare or are you going to sit and eat?" she asked flatly. I almost had to force my eyes to look away and I could feel myself turning red. I stepped to the side to get out of her way and did my best not to make eye contact. "Well-done are on this side of the plate and medium are on that side," she said as she set the platter on the table. "Allan is going to be a couple minutes late," she spun on her heel and went back into the kitchen. I caught myself watching her walk away. She returned a moment later with the condiments for the burgers. She took a seat in the chair to the left of the one at the head. I started to sit in the chair to the right side, but she quickly waved her hand. "That's where Allan sits. Your place is at the head of the table."

"Jill, I'm just a guest here, I don't think...."

"Your last name is Sterling, right?" she demanded.

"Yeah but...."

"Then sit your ass in the seat. That seat is always filled by a Sterling and guess what, that's you," she snapped but softened it with a half grin. "Jason, if you decide to stay here, it won't be as a guest. You will be the new head of this organization. We all have roles to fill around here and your role will be at the head of the table. Try the chair out and see how it feels," I sat but I was uncomfortable as all hell. She passed me the buns just as Allan walked in the front door.

"My apologies," he said as he sat in the chair to the right side of me. He never even gave me a second glance. "I am having trouble getting the ranchers set up for the big ride next weekend."

"That's twice I've heard about this ride, what is it?" I asked.

Jill took the question since Allan was taking a long drink of water. "Normally we get together on the Fourth of July weekend and round up all the cattle. We had to push it back this year because we have been busy with the passing of your father. Allan has had to start working with some of the local ranchers to get their help pulling it off. We have been running a little shorthanded the last few years."

"Yes, she is quite right and unfortunately, the ranchers' prices go up year after year," Allan said as he refilled his glass from the pitcher on the table. "We used to be able to do it ourselves but just cannot muster the manpower anymore and we have quite a few more cattle than the previous years."

"How many people do you need to round up the cattle?" I asked.

"We always managed to do a decent job with eight riders," Allan replied as he passed me the platter with the hamburgers on it.

"How many riders could you get right now from the ranch personnel?"

"Let's see." He looked thoughtfully at the ceiling for a moment. "Seven. If we pressed every adult into service, we could get seven riders."

"So, earlier you said that there were ten people including my father that started this place. Was the invitation not extended to their families? Why are there so few adults?" I asked, slightly confused.

"This is where we were a little short-sighted in our planning. Of the ten of us, only three ever married and produced children. Bill, Tim and a fellow by the name of Chad Thompson. Chad, his wife and all four kids moved to Costa Rica about ten years ago. Rumor is that he wanted to put together something like what we have here, just smaller in scale. We were all Type "A" personalities and tended to live hard and die fast. Attrition has been a cruel adversary to us."

"What you're telling me is that the people who know this place inside and out are getting fewer and fewer and that you are losing the specialties that my father was looking for when this all started. Correct?"

"Yes, and I fear we may be past the tipping point of recovering that talent. We had Special Operations guys from the military, law enforcement, medics, craftsmen and so on. Everyone was cross-trained, and everyone was very good at their jobs. Jill here is the closest thing have to someone who can wear all those hats. Bill and I can do some of it, but we are getting too damn old. Mark is a good security guy but lacks the training on the medical side. Dale would make a good farmer but can't hit the side of a barn with the target nailed to it. Tim, that guy has put more stitches in my body than any ER doc. He is damn good at it too, but he has the same problem Bill and I have, too damned old. His kid, Samantha, is going to medical school in San Francisco and we haven't seen her in well over five years," he said, exasperation creeping into his voice.

"The ranch came together better than anyone expected," Jill started. "The problem we have is that we are running out of people and don't know what to do about it," I made eye contact with her but just couldn't hold her gaze after getting caught staring at her athletic body. She seemed totally unfazed by the incident.

"When I'm at my job, I manage 28 people and I do a pretty good job of it, or so I've been told. I'm also in charge of hiring the people to fill those positions. Let me think about this, there has to be a way around it," I said.

THE RANCH

"Our biggest problem is that we just can't run an ad in the local paper for help wanted," Allan mused.

"You need specialized talent, I get that. Why don't you poach the talent from other organizations? I mean, like the military, there are lots of men and women who are leaving the service and I'm sure there are skill sets there that would fit right in around here."

"Then that brings us right back to the original problem, outsiders," Jill said.

"I'm an outsider, yet here I sit," I said quietly.

"I didn't mean it like that, Jason. You're a Sterling, you have a right to be here," she said apologetically.

"Jill, it's okay. Up until twelve hours ago, I had no clue about any of this. I may share the same last name as the guy that put all of this together, but the similarity ends there. Regardless, I'm still an outsider," I said. She shared a look with Allan, and it looked almost like he was scolding her without saying any words. We finished our dinner and after we cleared the table and washed the dishes, Allan and I moved into the massive living room. Jill appeared right behind us and set a bottle of Yamazaki single malt scotch on the table between the two recliners. She also placed two glasses next to it.

"I'll see you two tomorrow. Go easy on that stuff, it will sneak up and bite you in the ass!" She laughed and pointed at the bottle of Scotch. With that she turned and headed out the front door.

"Where is she off too?" I asked.

"She is usually in bed by eight. That kid gets up well before dawn," Allan said as he poured both glasses half-full and settled into his recliner.

"Kid? How old is she?" I asked as I sat in the other recliner. I picked up the glass and took a small sip.

"Twenty-six," was the answer.

"I see. Listen Allan, I wasn't trying to be an ass earlier and I certainly didn't mean to get Jill into any trouble. The thing is, you guys are going to have to change your ways or eventually there will be no one left to run the ranch."

"I hate to admit it, but you may very well be right, Jason," he said with a heavy sigh. He and I talked of things large and small for the next two hours and polished off half of the bottle before we too turned in for the night. After Allan left, I wobbled my way upstairs and collapsed into the very large bed. Jill was right, I got bit in the ass.

CHAPTER 2

Friday July 10, 2015.

The next morning, I awoke at eight, unusual since I hardly ever slept past five, even on my days off. The hangover was not nearly what I feared it would be. I rolled gently out of bed and went into the bathroom to relieve myself. On the counter were fresh clothes. Black BDU pants, T-shirt, cap and a set of black military boots in my size. There were also underwear, socks, deodorant, toothpaste and toothbrush, everything I would need to freshen up. I took a quick shower, dressed and headed downstairs. I was more than happy to trade my slacks, dress shoes and button-up shirt for the utility clothes.

There was a bowl of fruit on the island in the kitchen, so I grabbed an apple and went out the front door. I stood on the deck for a few minutes and surveyed the area. Everything was so clean out here. That was odd to think because we were in the middle of the high desert. The colors were crisp, the air was clear, and the quiet of the wide-open spaces was deafening. For the first time in a long time, I could hear myself think. Once I had finished my apple, I returned to the kitchen to throw the core away. There was a fresh pot of coffee in the coffee maker, so I searched the cupboards until I found a mug. Steaming mug in hand, I walked back out the front door. This time Jill was standing on the stairs.

"Well good morning, Jason. How is the headache this morning?" she asked cheerfully.

"Honestly, not as bad as I figured it would be. How are you this morning?" I returned with a smile. "Can I assume that you picked the wardrobe for the day?" she looked down at her black BDUs then back at me, a sly smile played at the corners of her mouth.

"I am afraid that the answer is yes. The good Lord knows that if I were to wear what I was wearing last night, you would be pretty much useless today," she said. I damn near blew coffee out of my nose and I could feel myself turning darker and darker shades of red. Now she was grinning from ear to ear. "Look at the bright side though."

"What bright side?" I said wiping coffee from my face.

"We now know that you do indeed have a good choice in women," she said with a wink. "Are you ready to get going today?"

"Yes," I mumbled. "What's on the agenda?"

"I thought I would take you up to Hightower, let you get a good vantage point to see everything from."

"Sounds good, what is Hightower?" I asked. She stepped off of the deck and motioned me to follow. We stood on the walkway between the security office and the main house. She pointed to a mountain peak in the distance to the east.

"That is what we refer to as Hightower. You can drive all the way to the peak. On top is an old fire watch tower that stands almost 50 feet taller than the peak. You interested in checking it out?"

"Sure, I don't have anywhere else to be," I said. She chuckled a little and we turned and headed for the front door of the security office. After I closed the door behind me, I could see Allan sitting at the desk. He was writing on a clipboard.

"Jason and I are going to Hightower then maybe on our way back, I'll take him downtown," Jill announced as she motioned for me to follow her past the desk into one of the back rooms. There were lockers lining one side of the room and a gun safe on the other wall. She went to the third locker and opened it. She reached in and pulled out a gun belt. She handed it to me and then took one for herself. On the left side of the heavy belt were four magazine pouches and a pouch for a water bottle. On the right side was a drop-leg unit with a full retention holster mounted to it. I fumbled with mine for a minute, trying to get everything adjusted correctly.

Jill had put hers on already and I could see that it came out of the locker with everything but the gun. She walked across the room and punched in a five-digit code on the safe. From the safe she pulled out a Sig. She eased the slide back a fraction of an inch to see that there was a round in the chamber. Then she dropped the magazine and made sure it was full. After replacing the mag, she reset the safety and slid it into her holster. Reaching back into the safe she pulled out four ten-round magazines and handed them to me. I checked to make sure they were full and slid them into the pouches. A moment later she pulled another Sig and repeated what she had done with the first one then she handed it to me, butt first. I re-checked it and slid it into my holster.

"There are bears and mountain lions that like to hang out up there, that's why the guns," Allan said from behind me. "There was a hiker mauled up there about a month ago," the last thing Jill gave me was a full canteen to put in its pouch. She looked at Allan.

"You all good here?" she asked.

"I will be just fine, you two kids go have fun," he said sarcastically.

"Yes, dad," she fired back with a wink and a smile.

We walked out of the security office and climbed into the Jeep that was parked out front. Jill fired it up and slipped the automatic transmission into gear. We followed the circular drive around and picked up the main driveway. Just before we got to the main gate, I could see that there were two dirt roads, one going either direction inside the brick wall. We followed the one that went to the northeast. As we approached the gate at the northeast corner of the brick wall, Jill picked up a hand mic and spoke, "Rover Two, approaching gate two." A moment later the gate began to swing open. As we passed through, she again spoke, "Rover Two, we are clear, see you for dinner."

"Copy that Rover Two. Be safe," Allan answered.

The drive to Hightower took about 45 minutes. The view from the top of the fire tower was something to behold. You could see to the horizon in every direction. It was a nice clear day, so the viewing was exceptional. Jill leaned against the railing and took a deep breath, and when she let it out she began to speak.

"I really hope you decide to stay here Jason; we need you."

"Jill, I just don't know. You guys have hit me with some heavy shit in the last 24 hours. I'm comfortable with my life in Reno, this is all way out of my league," I said as I waved my hand at the countryside below us.

"We could teach you what you need to know. You could be comfortable here, too. Life here is slower and the rewards are pretty nice."

"Don't get me wrong, Jill, this place is awesome. It's every dream of mine come true. I just don't feel like I belong here though, I feel like this is someone else's dream and I'm invading," I said.

"I understand that and you're not too far off. This place was your father's dream, but you and Braden were a part of his plans from the beginning."

"I'm not so sure about that. It seems to me that he put a lot of thought into this place, but we were just an afterthought."

"I knew your father, Jason. You and your brother were hardly afterthoughts. From day one, he had plans in place to get you and Braden here if things went sideways," she said. I turned to face her with my elbow still resting on the railing.

"When Walter was the security chief, Jack had him draw up extraction plans for both of you. When I turned 21, I was assigned to your team with Mark. I was going to the University of Nevada, Reno, taking classes to become a lawyer like my dad. Mark worked as a limo driver and security guard for his law firm. We were there to get you out if we had to. We were to do whatever we had to do to extract you. Up to and including knocking your ass out if it came to that."

"My brother, Dale, and a young man named Alex were assigned to your brother. Our orders were very clear. Get you two here by any means necessary," she reached into her thigh pocket and pulled out a small notebook. She looked at it for a second then handed it over to me.

"What's this?" I asked.

"It is one of many journals your father kept. He gave me that one to give to you should we ever have to extract you. I have carried it for five years in my "Go-Bag" but never once opened it to read it. Dale also has one to give to Braden." I stared at the faded black cover of the small composition notebook. It was well-worn and a little frayed around the edges.

"Why give it to me now?"

"I hope it helps you understand your father and what he wanted to do here. I hope it helps you understand what you meant to him and I hope it helps you make up your mind about staying here."

"You said "many" journals?"

"Yeah, I think your dad wrote down everything. They are all kept in the library of building two, the house I stay in."

"Mind if I swing by and check it out this evening?" I asked.

"You bet. Fair warning though, I think some of it is coded."

"What makes you say that?"

"Well, all of the pages are handwritten of course, but in the margins of some of the pages, there are number strings and a symbol. I don't know what they mean but they look like some sort of code. I have played with different ciphers, but nothing seems to work. It's just a hunch," she said as she glanced at her watch. "Ready to go downtown?"

"Yeah, can we stop at a corner store? I'd love a tall cold beer with dinner tonight," before I had even finished speaking, she was giggling. "What's so funny now?" I asked

"Downtown is what we call the gun range," she said, smiling a genuine smile. "I thought you might like to get some trigger therapy while you had the chance."

"Seriously? I'd love to get on the line with one of these Sigs!"

"Well, quit yapping and get your ass in the Jeep!" she laughed.

We drove back down the mountain and headed in the general direction of the compound. About halfway there we turned up another dirt road and followed it for about ten minutes. It snaked its way around the base of the foothills. When we came to a stock gate and cattle guard across the road, Jill asked me to get out and open the gate. I did and we drove on down the road after I closed it behind us. When we pulled up to the range, I was a little shocked, again. There were several different lanes for high-powered rifles. Jill told me that they went to 1,200 yards, past those were bays for carbine and pistol use. At the far end was a building that had "Funhouse" in big bold letters above the door. That's where we parked.

Jill opened her door and climbed out. She walked to the rear of the Jeep and opened the rear cargo hatch after she swung the spare tire out of the way. She pulled out a black armored plate carrier and put it on like she had done it a million times. I was standing slightly behind her when she stepped to the side and told me to grab one. I pulled one out and donned it. It already had six loaded AR-15 magazines in the front pouch. She stepped back in and pulled two helmets out. One had no nametape on it so she handed me that one. The other was obviously hers. She closed the back hatch and walked back to the driver's door. She leaned in and pulled one of the AR's free. After checking it, she attached it to the sling points on her plate carrier. She reached back in and pulled the other one free and passed it to me.

"Ready to go throw a little lead?" she asked with a big smile.

"Hell yes!" was my reply.

We went through the front door and up one flight of stairs onto an overhead scaffold system. It was like being on the second floor, but the floor was see-through. Below us was a maze that looked like the layout of any typical home with an office building thrown in. At the far end two vehicles sat at odd angles. Both had been shot to hell.

"Here is the deal," Jill began. "This is our shoot house. There are between eight and 18 hostiles positioned around the building. There are several more non-hostiles. The standard drill is to double tap all the hostiles. You do not know for sure how many will be in there so make sure you are very aggressive but thorough in your search," she pointed to the starting point.

"Going to make me do it first?" I asked.

"Yep, as your instructor, I need to know where you are weak. By having you run it cold, I will find out in a hurry what you need to work on," she said, all business now.

"Okay, let's do this then," I said as I stepped to the starting line. There was a timer hanging on the wall above the start point. As soon as it buzzed and started counting, I was moving. It took me three minutes to kill nine bad guys and make it all the way to the end buzzer. Not bad I thought.

"Three minutes 11 seconds," Jill said as she walked down the stairs. "Shooting from your left shoulder can use a lot of work. You burned four mags to kill nine hostiles. That's not very good. You have a good understanding of what needs to be done. The execution needs work though and that's easy enough to work on. Good news is that you are physically in good shape. It always helps to have that," she finished her critique.

"Yeah, it's been months since I've been to the range," I took a long swig of water from my canteen. "You going to run it?" I asked.

"Absolutely. I'll go out the back door and walk around to the front. You walk back through and reset the range. Fresh targets are in the locker over there and you can move the target stands to wherever you like inside. That will keep it completely random. Sound good?" she asked.

I nodded and went to grab some new targets. She walked out the back door and I started resetting the range. She had told me that there could be up to 18 bad guys in here. I was going to make it hard and see if I could trip her up with more targets. I thought I was clever for doing so. Ten minutes later I met her back at the starting clock.

"Want me to tell you how many hostiles and whatnot?" I asked.

"Nope, just get upstairs and I'll go tear the hell out of this place," was her answer. I trotted up the stairs and gave her the go signal. Forty-two seconds later she tripped the finish buzzer. I was totally speechless.

"Twenty-three bad guys, six friendlies, right?" The smile on her face was from ear to ear.

"Um, yeah..."

"Let's walk back through and make sure I hit all of them. There should be 69 holes, three per target," we both proceeded to walk back through the range and every bad guy in the place had three holes in him. Two to the chest and one to the head. Her speed and accuracy were astounding. Allan was right when he said that he had never seen anyone run a rifle like her. We spent the next six hours running various drills, everything from transitions to hand-to-hand combat. When I ran the course at the end of the day, I had shaved my time to 1:22. After we were done, we spent half an hour collecting all the spent brass and throwing it into a five-gallon bucket. All the guns were broken down and cleaned before we left the range.

After putting all our gear back in the Jeep, we returned to the compound. Jill parked in front of the security building and we headed inside. There was nobody there.

"Where is Allan?" I asked.

"I don't know but he has his radio and his PDA. Could be up feeding animals," Jill said as she headed into the back room. She opened the safe and placed her handgun inside. I gave her mine and she placed it in the next open slot. Both of us removed our gun belts and she replaced them in the locker.

"What did you think? Did you enjoy that?" she asked, as I turned to leave the small room.

"Are you kidding? I haven't had that much fun in a very long time!"

"You have a really good skills foundation. With enough practice, you might be able to give me a run for my money," she said with a smile.

"HA! I seriously doubt that! I watched you run that course over and over and every time you did you looked like a machine. There was no wasted movement, none," I told her. We walked out the front door of the security building and headed toward the main house where she and Allan stayed. She glanced at her watch. "Its 4:30, we got an hour and a half to kill before dinner, want to join me in the hot tub?"

"I didn't know there was a hot tub."

"Yup, basement of the barracks buildings, back corner behind all the weight equipment. You up for some of that?" she asked again.

"Does the offer include a cold beer?"

"You know where the fridge is, help yourself," she said as we walked through the front door of her house. "Gimme a minute and I'll get you some shorts," she rounded the corner of the staircase and headed upstairs. I headed to the kitchen. Spaten Oktoberfest was apparently the beer of choice. I grabbed two of them and the bottle opener off the side of the fridge. Jill returned a moment later and I handed her one of the beers, she handed me some swimming trunks. She took a long hard drink of her beer.

"Good stuff! You can change in the bathroom down the hall. Grab a couple more of those before we leave," she said pointing to my beer. Then she spun around and headed back upstairs. I went to the bathroom and changed out of my fatigues. The shorts were a little baggy but would do the trick just fine. Five minutes later I was standing in the kitchen again holding four more beers in one hand and finishing the open one with the other hand.

I heard Jill coming back down the stairs and I turned in her direction. She had a towel wrapped around her waist and a dark blue bikini top on. Her hair was down, and it came to just below her shoulders. She took two of the beers from me and handed me one of the two towels that she was carrying. We left the main house and went to the barracks building. Sure enough, there was an eight-person hot tub down there. I must have missed it in my earlier investigation.

Jill turned the jets on and slipped the towel off and placed it on a hook on the back wall. She placed her second towel on the floor next to the hot tub. If I thought the spandex shorts from the night before were nice to look at, seeing most of her body now was off the charts. On her right upper thigh there were traces of a scar that looked to be about eight inches long. I would have to ask her about it someday I thought. She turned and started to get into the water but stopped and grinned at me. "I'm ogling again aren't I?" I asked sheepishly.

"Yep," she answered. She slipped the rest of the way into the water and I joined her. The water was hotter than hell, but it felt good on my tired muscles.

"Listen Jill, I feel like I need to apologize to you for a couple of things," I said seriously.

"What? You haven't done anything wrong."

"Well, last night at dinner, I feel like I might have gotten you in a little trouble with Allan over my outsider comments."

"You don't owe me an apology over that. Allan can just get a little cranky occasionally, it was no big deal," she said.

"I saw the look on his face, and I could tell that he was a little mad about it."

"Don't worry about it, Jason. I'm supposed to be doing everything I can to sell you on the idea of staying here. Allan was mad because I said what was on my mind instead of trying to be a salesperson," she took another long drink of her beer and let out a sigh. "Don't get me wrong, life here is great. I love living here and I love everything that the ranch has to offer and everything it stands for. All of us hope you decide to take over, but I don't want you coming here under false pretenses. I want you to stay because you want to stay not because we begged you to stay. Does that make sense?"

"Yeah, it does," I answered.

"I just want you to know that all of us are being honest with you. When you ask a question, you will get an honest answer. Allan will come off as the wise old uncle and in many ways, that's exactly what he is. I'm more of the bratty type. I tend to say what is on my mind and not sugar coat anything and I can also be very direct. You said last night that you were an outsider and honestly, you are. Then again, at one point or another, all of us were outsiders," she said as she finished her beer and popped the top on the next one.

"I'll be honest too, Jill. I'm in way, way over my head with all of this. I am just a rookie at this sort of thing and you guys are asking me to not only join the team but lead a team of big-league players. I'm out of my element and not real sure I can fill those shoes."

"Like I told you when we were up on the mountain, we can teach you what you need to know. All of us are here to help you in the process of picking up where Jack left off."

"I appreciate that Jill, I really do. I'm just going to need a little time to think this over. I need to let all of this soak in for a day or two," I said as I finished my beer. She tossed the bottle opener over and I opened another one. She was silent for a few minutes and I could feel those eyes looking at me.

"You said that there were a couple of things you wanted to apologize for, what's the other thing?" she finally asked. I was already regretting opening my mouth.

"It's just that......well..... I want to apologize for staring at you. That's not something I normally do," I said meekly. She got a good chuckle from my embarrassment.

"It's quite all right, Jason, it does not bother me one little bit. I have worked very hard to get this body and it's kind of flattering to have someone stop and admire it," she said with a genuine smile.

"Can I be honest, Jill?"

"Of course," she said. I took a long pull from my beer in the hopes the liquid courage would help.

"I have seen a lot of beautiful women in my lifetime, Jill, and I have to say that you take the cake. I have never seen a woman with such natural beauty and ability. You truly are a stunner. Hugh Hefner would be proud to have you grace the pages of one of his magazines or, you could fit right on the cover of Guns and Ammo. You have the girl next door good looks, the body of a super model and this sweet, sincere personality. From what I can tell, God broke the mold with you. And here I am, rambling on like a schoolboy," I took another drink of my beer and I could feel my face flush a little.

"I'll take all of that as a compliment, Jason. Like I said, it doesn't bother me that you like to look. It's nothing to be ashamed of. Thank you for noticing my..... Ummmm ..... Assets," she said with that smile. I decided it was time to change the subject. I had taken about as much embarrassment as I could.

"So, how did you get so good with a gun?" I asked trying to make small talk. She picked up on my discomfort and went with the new conversation.

"I grew up with them. I've been to several very reputable training centers and spent way more hours on the range than I could even begin to count. I have also been told that I just have a natural ability," she said as she popped the top on her third beer. "That and there is not a whole lot of other shit to do around here. I am up at 3:30 in the morning, I spend two hours down here in the gym, and I go on shift at seven and get off at five. Just about every day I go to the range for an hour or so. It helps to kill the time. Dinner is at 6:00 and I'm in bed by 8:00. That's my day," she took another long drink of her beer.

"Today must have been a nice distraction," I said.

"Today was a great day, and I got to spend it in good company," there were a few minutes of awkward silence as both of us drank our beers and closed our eyes to relax a little. We finished up in the hot tub and made our way back to the main house. Allan was in the kitchen when we walked in. Something smelled good and it made my mouth water. Allan eyed both of us.

"You two better get cleaned up and dressed, the roast will be on the table in 15. Hope you are hungry 'cuz there's plenty," he said as he removed a pot of vegetables from the stove. Fifteen minutes later, both of us had changed back into our fatigues and were sitting at the table.

"You were right, Allan. Jill can run a gun like nothing I've ever seen."

"Let me guess, she ran the course in under 50 seconds?"

"Forty-two to be exact," I replied. Allan just looked at Jill and shook his head.

"It takes me 42 seconds to find and shoot the first target!" he laughed.

"Allan, can I ask you serious question?"

"Fire away."

"If the shit hit the fan right now, how many people would make it here? Best guess?" Allan looked across the table at Jill, then at me.

"Best guess in a worst-case scenario? Three to five of us."

"I see," I nodded and took another bite of my roast. "That would be you, Jill, Bill, Tim and Mark?"

"Yes, that is correct."

"What if Bill, Mark and Tim didn't make it? What if it was just you and Jill here in the apocalypse?"

"In that case, Jill and I would cut all of the animals loose, open all of the gates, cut power and water to everything above ground and then we would......" his voice trailed off.

"You would what, Allan? There is still something that I'm missing here, and I think you are just waiting for the right question," I said around another bite of roast. He shared a quick look with Jill and then looked back at me like a deer caught in the headlights of a speeding car. "You haven't explained why everything around here is in pairs. What's the deal with that if I may ask, again?"

"Your father wanted to make sure that we had redundant systems. As far as the houses go, it would confuse the bad guys. Generally, they would want to attack the "big" house because that's where all the loot is. This way, theoretically, they would have to divide their forces to attack simultaneously. In the case of the barns and pens, if one group of animals fell ill, odds were that the other group would be okay. It's the adage about never putting all of your eggs in one basket and one being none and two being one," he explained.

"And three is a backup, Allan. What is it you are not telling me, what is it that you are leaving out?" I said, playing a hunch. Allan stopped chewing and set his fork down. Jill looked up at him and he looked at her.

"Shit, don't look at me, Allan. I didn't tell him," Jill said slightly defensively. Allan looked at me and swallowed hard.

"I always knew you were pretty smart. Yes. There is a third part of this compound. If you would like, we can tour it first thing in the morning," he said.

"I would like that very much. My compliments to the chef, this roast is excellent," I said. Allan resumed eating but you could tell that I had broadsided him. I felt kind of bad. After all, it was just a hunch that there was more here. If he had said that I had seen it all, I would have believed him. We finished dinner and took care of the dishes. Allan excused himself. Jill and I went to the living room and sat on the large couch. She sat a little closer than I expected but I didn't say anything. I produced the journal that she had given me earlier in the day. I hadn't taken it from my pocket since she had given it to me. Just before I opened it, I looked up and caught Jill looking intently at me. There was a smile playing at the corners of her mouth.

"What?" I asked innocently.

"I have known Allan my entire adult life and I don't believe I have ever seen anyone so completely and utterly blindside him. You didn't send one across the bow, you blew him out of the water," she chuckled.

"I know and after I pulled the trigger on him, I felt kind of bad. He is only doing his job after all."

"He underestimated you is what happened," she said as she picked her crossword book up off the table. She leaned back and opened the book. "He underestimated you and you reminded him of your lineage. That was something your father would have done. You laid the perfect trap and let him walk right into it."

"Do you think I should apologize?"

"Hell no! Let him lick his wounds tonight, he will be back to his cheery self tomorrow. He needed to be reminded who he is dealing with. He got the message loud and clear," she giggled again.

"I just don't want him pissed off at me," I said sincerely.

"He's not mad, trust me, if he was you two would still be having it out in the dining room."

"If you say so," I replied. She set her book on her lap and looked at me again.

"He is a little rusty at his verbal sparring skills. You let him walk right into the trap to get the information that you wanted. Don't feel bad about that. If anything, you earned a lot of respect from him tonight. Leave it at that and move on."

"Alright, I'll let it go," I said as I opened the journal. Seemingly content with my answer, she picked her book up again. Inside the cover of the journal was a note written to me.

"Jason, if you are reading this, the worst has happened," it began. "Listen to the people that gave you this journal, they speak for me. I would trust any one of them with my life and you should too," there were several more lines, but I closed the journal again. I felt like I was reading something that was never meant for me. I looked over at Jill and she was intently working on a puzzle. I'd known her for a day and a half, but I did feel that I could trust her. I felt the same about Allan. It was almost as if they were waiting a very long time for the prodigal son to return home.

They had accomplished a lot of work here over the past 25 years, but there was more to do. The generation that started all of this was slipping away and with them went their knowledge. Jill was an amazing woman. She was smart, witty and incredibly beautiful. She blew everyone away when it came to weapons and self-defense. She was amazing, but there was no one for her to pass her knowledge on to. I spent six hours with her today on the range and I learned more than I had in the past six years.

I was sure that Allan was a treasure trove of construction knowledge, after all, he was the guy that turned my father's dreams into reality. Doc Williams was another one, even though he had a daughter in medical school, what were the odds that she would return here? I opened the journal again and began to read. I'm not sure what time I fell asleep, but I awoke at about one in the morning with Jill curled up next to me. I didn't bother to wake her, instead I pulled the blanket off the back of the couch and covered both of us and went back to sleep.

Saturday, July 11, 2015

I woke up again at about a quarter after six and Jill was gone. I began to think that maybe it was just a dream. I laid there for a few more minutes before I decided to get up and go to the kitchen to get a cup of coffee. I took my cup and walked out on the deck. I leaned against the rail and took about half an hour to drink the

THE RANCH

steaming brew. After returning my cup to the kitchen, I headed over to the other main house. I went upstairs to the room I had stayed in before. Again, there were clean clothes neatly folded on the top of the bathroom counter. I took a long hot shower. It felt good on my sore muscles. After dressing I left the house and went to the security office. Allan and Jill were both there.

"Sleep well?" Jill asked.

"Sure did, that couch is very comfortable," I said. I could see a slight smile at the corners of her mouth.

"Are you ready for your tour?" Allan asked.

"Whenever you are," I replied.

"Follow me," he said as he stood from behind the desk. He turned and walked into the small back room. He stopped in front of the row of lockers and opened the one in the middle. It appeared to have body armor hanging in it. He reached all the way into the back of the locker and pushed on something. When he did that there was an audible click. He grabbed ahold of the front lip of the locker and pulled hard. The entire wall locker unit slid toward him about three feet. I stepped back and could see a stairwell leading down. It was very dimly lit.

Allan led the way and Jill and I followed behind. When we got to the bottom, Jill turned and pulled a heavy rope that pulled the locker back in place. We were in a hallway that was about ten feet long and three feet wide. The walls, ceiling and floor were all concrete. At the end of the hallway there was a "T" intersection. Allan stopped there and turned back to me.

"Remember when I told you about all of the cargo containers showing up here?"

"Yes," I nodded.

"We didn't let them go to waste," he started walking again, down the corridor to the left. Here the concrete was gone, and I could tell that I was standing inside of a 40-foot-long container. "We buried all of containers that we used to bring everything down from Idaho. All of that was done before we put the living quarters up. They were sprayed with a rubberized undercoat and are encased in a foot of re-bar reinforced concrete on the sides and 18 inches on top," when we reached the end of this container, we made a right and came to a very well-built door.

When Allan opened it, I could see that it was nearly six inches thick, but he swung it open with one hand. "We put living quarters down here, another security office and enough supplies to last a dozen people five years," we kept walking and in the dim light I could see pallets of freeze-dried food lining one side of the corridor. They went all the way to the ceiling. When we reached the end of that cargo container, there was another door. Once we passed through it we were in the living quarters. It looked as if three containers had been set side-by-side in this case. There was a large set of French doors in the middle that separated three bunk rooms. We went through those doors and walked into a space that housed the kitchen, dining room and common area. In the bunk area there were smaller rooms that were separated by curtains. It looked like there were two bunk beds in each of the nine "bedrooms".

The common area looked like it was also made up of three containers. In here I found the large kitchen and pantry at one end. In the center was a large couch with a recliner at each end. This is also where I found the only TV on the ranch property. There was also a dining table with chairs for 20. At the far end were the showers and bathrooms. Four stalls for each. There were more French doors on the far wall. He opened them and I could see that I was looking down another 48-foot container that appeared to be empty.

We walked to the center of it when Allan reached down and pulled on a small steel loop that was recessed into the floor. A hatchway opened that was four feet square. We went down the narrow ladder and stepped into what appeared to be the armory. One wall was lined with AR-15's and AK-47's. Best guess was 50 of each. The end wall was covered in older 1911 pistols. The other side wall had shelves that were full of steel ammo cans. I brushed my hand across the labels as I walked the length of the unit. 5.56, 7.62x39, .45acp filled the shelves from floor to ceiling. When I reached the end, I removed one of the 1911s. It was clearly stamped "U.S. Army". I cycled the action and it moved flawlessly. After putting the hammer back down, I replaced it on its hook. I next removed one of the AR-15's. I was stunned to see that this was the military version, the M4. It had select fire. Semi Auto and Burst. I quickly replaced it and removed one of the AK-47's, they didn't have the burst selection, instead, they were capable of fully automatic fire. I could not believe what I was seeing. I turned to look at Jill and Allan and both were grinning from ear-to-ear.

"I told you your father had a lot of connections," Allan said with a smile.

"We keep the really cool stuff down here, away from prying eyes," was Jill's response.

THE RANCH

"Come on," Allan said, motioning me back up the ladder. Once we were all up and the hatch was secured, Allan pointed to the far end of the container and told me that there were living quarters and a galley just like the ones I had already seen. Again, with the mirror image thing. Allan pulled on another ring that was inset into the wall and a door popped open.

I looked to the opposite wall and could see another ring placed there. Allan saw me looking at the recessed hatch and told me that the clinic and the security office were behind it. I followed him through the hatch that he had pulled open. This hallway was again made of concrete construction and stretched as far as I could see in the dim light. We followed it for about 50 feet when we came to a four-way intersection. Allan stopped and pointed to both the left and right.

"Those passages lead to the main houses and the barracks buildings. We will go out that way when we come back," he started down the main corridor again. We came to another small room, probably eight feet across by ten feet long. Inset into the far wall were two more heavy doors. Allan opened one of them and we continued walking. We finally came to another door. Allan opened it and this one was almost twice as thick as the others. Again, it swung open with ease.

We walked into a concrete room that was about 30 feet square. There was a steel ladder in the middle of the room that led to what appeared to be a hatch in the ceiling. The far wall was end-to-end with a stout wooden bench that was home to reloading equipment. There was a locker to the right that I opened and found was full of various gun powders. The locker on the wall opposite of this one was full of bullets. All the calibers that the ranch used. Both sets of lockers stretched the entire length of the wall it was sitting against. Next to the bench on the floor that was covered in anti-static matting, I saw the bucket of spent brass from our day at the range.

"You are standing under the horse barn. That ladder leads up to the empty stall. The hatch is obscured by the hay and dirt on the floor. There is a matching reloading room down the other corridor. It is also under the other horse barn. We have enough bullets to reload about 250,000 rounds in each location. We also have the ability to cast our own bullets and enough lead stored away to make about another 250,000 rounds should the need arise. Between the two powder lockers, we could conceivably reload almost a million rounds. All the floor is covered in anti-static matting. The shelves are also lined with it. The lockers are also grounded to a copper rod under the floor. If any temperature of more than 120 degrees is detected in here, the halon system will automatically engage and flood the room. A fire in here would be really bad," Allan said.

I stood in awe. I knew a couple of guys who reloaded their own, but this was on an industrial scale. We left that room and walked back to the four-way intersection. Allan turned to the left and we wound our way around a couple of corners and past another intersection. We ended up at yet another steel door. Allan pushed it open and we were standing in the basement of the barracks building. When Jill shut the door behind us I could see that it was concealed behind the locker that contained the cleaning supplies.

"You can access the underground bunker from any of the main buildings up here and the horse barns," Allan stated as we made our way to the stairs. "The complex is split in two just like above-ground. The only difference is that security is run entirely from a laptop or PDA. Should the worst ever happen, and we must go underground, rest assured, you will be safe there. The doors would take quite a bit of C-4 to blow and the bad guys would be dead before they ever made it that far. We can flood any of the corridors or the reloading rooms and the armory with halon gas. The entire facility has nuclear, biological and chemical air filtration."

"It has its own redundant power supply and enough fuel to run nonstop at full power for five years. Long enough to survive whatever befalls the outside world," we had left the barracks building and gone back to the main house where we were standing in the kitchen. Allan removed two more coffee cups from the cabinet, set them next to mine from earlier and filled all three. He handed one to me and one to Jill and motioned for the kitchen table. We sat and I stared at my cup for a few minutes before speaking.

"I'll be honest Allan; I was bluffing when I assumed that there was more to this place. Before now, this place was beyond anything I could have imagined. This place......... It's incredible what you have put together."

"Thank you, we like it," he smiled.

"I'm a little concerned though," I said, starting to find my footing.

"About?" Jill asked.

"The weapons down there.... Those were all military grade. For a guy like me to own one would cost thousands of dollars and the paperwork is horrible...."

"I understand your concern Jason but believe me when I say that they were all purchased legally. Bill made sure that we jumped through all the hoops. We also have suppressors for every one of them. Those were also purchased legally.

Everything and I mean EVERYTHING here is legit. There are just some things that we do not like to share with the outside world," Allan said.

"Like the sheriff that was nosing around?" I asked.

"Exactly! We have done nothing wrong, but we don't need him meddling in our affairs. It was better to give him the five-cent tour and send him on his way."

"But you have equipment here that was at one time military equipment and cannot easily be obtained by a civilian. The Hummers, those are all destroyed after they are decommissioned, and by the looks of them, they came straight off the factory floor. If I did my math right, they ended up here right after we started tearing it up in Afghanistan.... How is that possible?"

"Bill handled all the particulars but the basic story is that we do business as a military contractor. We were able to purchase them under that contract. Like I said, Bill knows the details and is the one who set it all up," I sat in silence for a few more minutes and drank my coffee. The look of concern on my face must have been evident because Jill was the next to speak.

"Jason, look, everything here is good to go. My father is one bad ass lawyer and he made damn sure that there was and is nothing illegal about anything we have here. We have 80,000 gallons of liquid propane buried out there. Legit. Five thousand gallons of diesel fuel and 5,000 gallons of gasoline. Legit. Automatic, suppressed weapons. Legit. All the building permits were filed and are legit. There is nothing for the Feds or cops or military to find here that is not legit. If you want the details, my dad will be more than happy to walk you through all of the contracts and purchases that we have made."

"I believe you Jill, it's just that I'm having a hard time putting together how all of this happened."

"You father had a vision, Jason. He had a vision, money to burn and contacts around the world. Once he shared it with us, it became our vision. Even if nothing bad ever happens, look at what we have here. We are self-employed with one hell of a retirement and life insurance plan," Allan said smiling. "We are not demanding that you take control here. It is simply a request. If you choose to go back to your life, your job and your little apartment, so be it. That is entirely up to you. If you choose to stay here, maybe, just maybe you can help us make this place viable in case of disaster....."

"What does that mean? Viable in case of disaster?" I cut Allen off.

"It means that if the shit hit the fan right now, this place would fall. I think that is what you were hinting around at last night. We do not have the manpower to make it work. The fresh vegetables are from the green house. We will not be planting crops this year, again, no manpower. We cannot afford to hire the workforce needed to do that. As it is, we had to work out a trade agreement with the local ranchers so we could get the roundup done this year. Don't get me wrong, we are not in danger of losing what we have, not yet anyway. We just cannot maintain what we have," he said looking into the bottom of his coffee cup.

"You were right when you said that this place cost a fortune. All ten of the original members poured everything into it under the assumption that future generations would do the same. So far, Bill and his family are the only ones who have been able to do so. He pays all our legal fees out of his own pocket and works for us for free. The jet you flew out here on belongs to the law firm he works for, not us. It just so happened that he had business to take care of in Elko. Almost all the capital that built this place is gone and there is no replacement income coming in. We used to sell a lot of the crops we produced and what we didn't sell, we would donate. Same with the cattle. We try to maintain 500 head; the excess is sold for their meat after each roundup. With all that said, we can't afford any further expansion."

"Jason, neither of us," Jill stated as she pointed to herself and Allan "draw a salary, we are paid by living here. We are not in it for money. We do it because it's the right thing to do," there was more silence. Jill stood up and got the coffee pot and refilled all the cups. I felt like I should say something profound, but I needed some time to think. It was then that Allan's cell phone rang. He looked at it and stood up.

"Got to take this, it's Sheriff Case," he said as he walked into the living room. Jill sat back down and looked at me. She put her hand on top of mine and spoke quietly.

"Jason, I hope you choose to stay with us. I was truthful when I told you that we need you here. Yes, you are just one man, but you are smart enough to help us get through this. We need fresh thoughts and ideas. The plan your father put into place only carried us so far. It's time for the second act of this play," she said with those ice blue eyes staring directly into mine. Just then Allan walked back into the room, the phone still at his ear.

"You bet Louie, have your deputies and Search and Rescue people here in 30 minutes," he said. "We will have the Jeep and the horses ready to go......Not a problem, see you soon," he put his phone back in his pocket. "Jill, get ten horses saddled up and ready to ride. The sheriff has two missing backpackers up around Hightower," Jill started to stand.

"Who is leading the SAR party?" she asked.

"He is sending Marvin up..." she quickly cut him off.

"I swear if he starts his shit, I'm going to knock him out!" she blurted.

"Louie warned him to be on his best behavior," Allan said as he headed for the door. "You two get the horses saddled up and I'll get the Jeep topped off," then he was out the gone.

"Come on Jason, time to earn our keep," she said as she started for the door. I followed her and we walked quickly toward the horse barn.

"Who is Marvin and what kind of shit does he start?" I asked.

"He is one of Sheriff Case's deputies and the guy is an asshole. Thinks women should be barefoot and pregnant, not doing "mans" work," she said heatedly. "Son of a bitch thinks he is God's gift to cops and women. Little prick!" she muttered. "I did a hand-to-hand combat class with the sheriff's department last year and he made a big deal out of me being there! Said I should be making them all sandwiches instead of trying to be one of the boys! Can you believe that?" she asked to no one in particular. "During lunch on the second day, I had a little one-on-one time with the instructor. I told him that I wanted a go at Marvin when it came time for the final practice session. I'd had enough of his remarks."

"Did he give you the chance?" I asked.

"Sure did! It was great! I toyed with him for a few minutes, I was trying to get him to lose his cool and boy did he! Called me a whore and launched a haymaker at me!"

"Oh shit!" I said.

"He paid for that outburst with a broken nose!" she laughed. "The instructor signaled us to stand down, but Marvin was having none of it. He kept lunging and throwing punches. None of them made any serious contact. The instructor tried to step in, but I waved him off, I wasn't done yet. We ended up going to ground with the fight. I nailed him in the ribs and heard a couple of them break. It ended when I choked him out. The paramedics were called and took him to the hospital. He physically recovered but I know that one of these days he will try it again. He just can't let it go," her story ended when we got to the barn. She showed me where the saddles and bridles were. It had been years since I had saddled a horse, but it quickly came back to me. Jill had brought two more horses from the other barn and we had them all saddled when the first sheriff's car pulled up.

"That's him," Jill said with a nod as she started toward the cruiser.

"Deputy," was her one word greeting.

"Butler," was his. Allan pulled up in the Jeep and was leading two big Ford Excursions. Four deputies and four firefighter paramedics piled out of them. They all got backpacks out of the cargo are and everyone congregated around the hood of Marvin's car where he had a map laid out.

"Okay people," Marvin began. "We have two backpackers missing some-where around Hightower. They were supposed to meet their ride up there at 4pm yesterday," he went on to give their descriptions and the basic route they were supposed to have taken. In his briefing he mentioned that they both had FRS radios but, nobody had been able to contact them. He also said that both had cell phones, but they couldn't get a ping off either of them.

"Excuse me deputy," Jill said as she stepped up to view the map.

"What?" Marvin asked, annoyance evident in his voice.

"If they have radios and phones but can't be reached, there are only four places they could be....." Marvin cut her off.

"Miss Butler, this is my operation. If we need your assistance, I'll let you know," he shot back. She seemed unfazed.

"They will be in one of these four canyons," she pointed out four different locations on the map. "Those are the only four areas on that mountain where cell and radio signals won't reach," she finished.

"Then why don't you make yourself busy and hike on up there. Leave this to the professionals," he hissed. Jill glared at him for a full 15 seconds before she backed away from the car. Marvin went back to his briefing. Jill walked around to where Allan was standing. I followed her.

"Allan, I'm going to take two horses and Jason. We are going to go to the canyons and check it out. This jackass couldn't find his own ass with two hands and a 20-minute head start," she whispered.

"All right, be careful. If you find anything, pop smoke and I'll get the SAR helicopter to your location," he said. Jill nodded and motioned for me to follow her. Once we were out of earshot, she began her rant again.

"That son of a….. I should have handed him his ass right there!" she blurted. "If those hikers are in trouble, it will take him days to find them the way he is going!" I didn't say a word, just followed a step behind her. She was pissed off and nothing I could say was going to calm her down. She kept talking until we reached the barn. We jumped up on the horses and headed for the security office. Once there, we tied the horses to the flagpole and went inside. Jill once again issued the pistols and leg holsters. She reached into one of the large lockers and pulled out two red packs with big white crosses on them. Obviously medical equipment. Next she pulled out two jackets and handed me one. "It gets cold up there after dark," she said. Once she closed the lockers we headed back out and got on our horses. We took off at a moderate trot headed for the gate we had gone out the day before. It was almost an hour before Jill spoke again.

"See, I told you he was an ass," she said.

I chuckled, "Ass doesn't even come close. As a matter of fact, I think that's an insult to asses everywhere." I said, Jill chuckled a little.

"We will be going into the first canyon, just around the bend up here. The trail is narrow so just let your horse have its head, she won't get you into trouble. Keep an eye for any disturbances on the ground on either side of the trail. It's steep so it's real easy to slide down. If you see something, let me know. Do not try to get off the horse otherwise you could slide down too," she instructed.

"You got it," was my answer. We followed the trail for an hour when we finally came out of the top. Neither one of us had seen anything to indicate the hikers had been here. We followed the ridge line for a little bit before we started down the next canyon. Jill had explained that we were going to go up the first canyon, down the second one, up the third and so on. We were three quarters of the way up the third canyon when Jill brought her horse to a stop. She pulled a small pair of binoculars out of her medical pack and looked at the far side of the canyon. I looked in that direction and could barely make out what appeared to be a red jacket.

"Crap," she said. "I see one of them, not moving. It looks like the other one kept sliding," it was then that I could see the fresh slide marks going downhill past the red jacket. "Let's get to the top of the canyon and work our way down," she said as she put her binoculars away and started up the trail again. Once we got to the top, we got off the horses and took their bridles off. "Don't worry, they won't go far," she said. "If we tie them up, they wouldn't be able to defend themselves."

"Ahhhhh, okay, I get it."

We grabbed our packs and jackets and started down the trail where Jill had seen the hiker. It only took us about half an hour to get to where they had slid off the trail. She yelled for them but there was no response.

"Let's go about 50 feet that way," she pointed down the trail. "That way if we kick anything loose it won't fall on them. Once we had moved 50 feet down the trail, Jill pulled her pack off and dug around in the side pocket. A moment later she produced a canister that looked a lot like a grenade. She pulled the pin and tossed it another ten feet down the trail. A bright red smoke began to pour from the smoke grenade. She donned her pack and looked at me.

"If either one of us slips and starts to fall, we cannot try and catch each other. My guess is that is what happened here. One fell and the other got dragged down with them. Understand?" she asked. I nodded and with that she started over the side. She was basically climbing down backwards, digging the toe of her combat boots in with each step. I let her get about halfway to the first hiker before I started over the edge. Using the footholds that Jill had dug into the side of the hill, I was able to catch up to her as she reached the first hiker. He was very pale, and his left arm was twisted at a grotesque angle at the elbow. Jill reached down and felt his neck.

"He is still alive," she said as she pulled her pack off. "Get down to that one and tell me what you got." I worked my way past her. The 50 feet to the next hiker was slow going. I didn't think the hillside could get any steeper, but it did. It was damn near vertical when I got to the second hiker. He was wedged under some brush and tree roots. I reached down and felt for a pulse. I was just about to give up when I finally felt it. It was very weak. I didn't want to remove him from the tree roots as they looked like the only thing keeping him from plummeting another 200 feet to the rocky canyon floor. I started assessing his injuries and didn't find anything serious until I felt his abdomen. It was hard and when I lifted his shirt, I could see that it was one giant bruise.

"Jill!" I yelled. "This one is alive too but I'm guessing he has got some pretty bad internal injuries!"

"Okay, give me a minute and I'll come down there," she yelled back. I kept up with my assessment but could not find any other obvious injuries. I looked up and could see Jill working her way to my position. It took her a good ten minutes to make it to me.

"Ever started an I.V.?" she asked.

"Nope."

"All right, there is an I.V. kit in your pack, get it out for me," she instructed. A moment later I handed the kit to her. She started the I.V. in his arm and hung the bag from the tree we were under. "Cover him with your jacket and just hang out with him. The chopper should be here before too long. I'll have them take this guy first," she said as she started back to her patient. I had my legs wrapped around the largest tree root and had managed to stabilize myself pretty good and it's a damn good thing that I had done that.

As Jill started past me, the rock she was stepping on broke loose and she started to fall. She was grabbing at brush and tree root but was sliding away fast. I flipped on my side and managed to grab her left wrist. I knew I wasn't going to fall; my foot was still wedged under the root. I made eye contact with Jill and could see the terror in her eyes. There was absolutely nothing for her to grab onto. I was the only thing standing between her and certain death. I had an iron grip on her wrist, I just didn't have any leverage to pull her back up.

"Jill, I can't pull you up. Use my arm and climb back up," I told her. "I'm not going to let you fall but I need you to help me with this," my eyes never left hers and I could see a subtle shift in them from terror to determination.

"Okay, okay. Please don't let go!" she pleaded.

"I got you Jill, now start pulling yourself up!" She took a deep breath and swung her right hand up and grabbed my wrist. I was pulling with everything I had but again, just didn't have the leverage to help her.

"You sure you got me?" she asked. "I'm going to have to swing my legs up."

"Do what you got to do, Jill. I got you."

"Okay, on the count of three I'm going to swing to my left and see if I can get a foot on that root over there." She took another deep breath. "One...two....three!" she kicked off of the dirt hard and swung toward the root. She managed to get her heel on it and pulled herself toward it until she could get her knee hooked around it. When she swung, I felt something in my shoulder pop and the pain was excruciating. I had to dig deep to keep my grip firm.

Once she had her knee hooked, she pulled herself back up over me. She pretty much collapsed on top of me. She was breathing as hard as I was and both of us were sweating profusely. I could feel her whole body trembling. She looked into my eyes. "Thank you," she said as she just laid there a moment to collect herself.

She rolled off me and got back to her feet. I pulled myself back into a sitting position. My left shoulder felt like it was on fire and my arm didn't quite work right. Very carefully and slowly this time, Jill made her way back to her patient.

It was about 20 minutes later when we heard the chopper. They knew the general location and within minutes had us pinpointed. Jill was talking into her radio when they got over the top of us and pointing in my direction. The chopper was hovering directly over me and I could see a basket and medic hanging out the door. Within moments they were winched down and on the ground next to me and my patient. The medic unhooked the winch cable and I could see that another medic was waiting in the doorway. Within minutes, he too was on the ground.

The two of them loaded the hiker in the basket and one of the medics and the basket were winched back up. The remaining medic worked his way up to Jill's position. I collected my pack and jacket and followed him up. It was slow going and I didn't get there until the basket and second medic had returned. When they loaded Jill's patient into the basket, I could see that he was now conscious. The first medic went up with the basket and the cable was lowered back down. Jill said something to the remaining medic, and he gave her the thumbs up. With that he was winched back up. The chopper turned and headed back down the canyon. Jill and I worked our way back up to the trail and Jill could see that I was favoring my left shoulder heavily.

"Are you okay?" she asked.

"No, I think I tore something in my shoulder," I said.

"Crap, here, sit down and let me look at it," she said as she pulled her pack off. I slid mine off and sat on the uphill side of the trail. "Take your shirt off, too," Jill ordered. I did so and could immediately see the swelling. She examined my shoulder and the surrounding tissues. She pulled an instant ice pack from her pack along with two triangular bandages followed by a role of sports wrap. She secured the ice pack with the wrap and then secured my arm in a sling and swath. She dug into her pack again and handed me eight ibuprofens.

"Sorry, that's the strongest thing I've got." She handed me her canteen and I washed the pills down with a long hard drink.

"It will do for now," I smiled and stood up. There was no way to put my shirt on, so I wadded it up and put it in one of my cargo pockets. I threw my backpack on my good shoulder and picked up my jacket. We slowly made our way back to the horses and sure enough, they hadn't gone far. Jill put both bridles back on and helped me into the saddle. We made our way back down the mountain in near silence. Once we were able to use the radio again, Jill called Allan and told him what had happened. She also told him that I would need to see the doctor and would probably need x-rays. Allan told her that he would have the Jeep waiting when we got there. It was nearly 4:00 in the afternoon by the time we got back to the security office and Allan met us by the flagpole. We got off our horses and Allan handed Jill the keys to the Jeep. "Doc is expecting you," was all he said to her as he collected the horses' reigns and started toward the barn.

CHAPTER 3

The drive into Elko was only about 30 minutes and that had me a little confused. "You guys gave me the runaround when you took me to the ranch from the airport," I stated breaking the silence.

"We did," Jill said slightly smiling. When she looked at me, her eyes went to my shoulder and the smile faded. She looked away and continued driving. We didn't go to the hospital; we went to Doc Williams' office. She took me to the vet! As we pulled into the driveway I started laughing. Jill shut the Jeep off and looked at me, confusion evident on her face.

"I've been told that I'm as big as an ox and I've been called a dog, so I guess it's fitting that you take me to the vet," I started laughing harder. "If I have to wear the cone of shame I'm going to be pissed!" Jill just stared at me then slowly started to giggle and then she burst into laughter. Doc Williams opened the front door and stood there staring at us. He probably thought we had lost our minds. It was probably three or four minutes before we settled down and got out of the Jeep. Doc was still staring at us.

He took us inside and took x-rays of my shoulder. After reviewing them he announced that there was no major damage and it was only sprained. I think Jill was more relieved than I was. The Doc told me to take ibuprofen and keep ice on it. Jill helped me get my shirt back on and Doc put my arm back in the sling. He showed us out of his office, and we drove back to the ranch. It was just after dark when we got back. Jill parked in front of the security office and shut the Jeep off but made no move to get out. I heard her take a deep breath before she spoke.

"Thank you for what you did today, Jason. I owe you my life," she said quietly.

"You owe me nothing Jill. Had the roles been reversed, you would have done the same thing."

"I don't trust very many people Jason. Today you earned my trust in a big way. You literally held my life in your hand. Risking your own life, I might add. When I looked into your eyes, I knew... I knew that you weren't going to let me fall and if I were going to fall, I wouldn't be falling alone." She paused and wiped at her eyes. "I have never had anybody put their life on the line for me and you did that today, no questions asked, you just did it."

"Jill, I was in the right place at the right time today, but you need to look at the bigger picture. You saved two lives today. You knew where they would be. They would have died up there today if you had let that Barney Fife idiot have his way. "

"I know, Jason. I just can't get over what could have happened today. I can't believe I was so clumsy...."

"Stop it, Jill. The rock you were standing on broke. I used that same rock for a foothold, twice. It was an accident that had a tremendous ending. Yes, you could have plummeted to your death, but you didn't. Mark this one in the "Win" column and be happy. We risk death every time we get out of bed, any day that you make it back home is a win in my book. Now, I'm hungry and I could really use a little liquid pain killer, maybe even another trip through the hot tub. Are we done out here?" I asked, she wiped her eyes again and sat up straight.

"Yes, we're done here," she replied as she opened her door and got out. I got out of the Jeep and walked around to her side. I stopped and stood in front of her.

"You going to be okay?" I asked. She surprised me by throwing her arms around me and pulling me in for a hug. I had to bend over a little bit, and she buried her face in my neck. The embrace only lasted about 20 seconds, then she pulled her face back and looked me in the eyes.

"Thank you for the pep talk and thanks again for saving my ass today," she said quietly. She gave me a kiss on the cheek and released her embrace. With that we went in the house. Allan was sitting at the dining room table with a steaming cup of coffee and a notebook. He looked over his glasses at us as we came into the room. He smiled and closed his notebook.

"How's the shoulder?" he asked.

"Doc says it's a pretty good sprain but no permanent damage," I said as I sat in a chair.

"That's very good news!" he stood and headed over to the stove. "My guess is that you two are looking for some grub."

"That and a little something to warm the soul," Jill said as she went past me to the pantry. She returned with a bottle of Jack Daniels. Stopping by one of the cabinets, she grabbed three shot glasses. Allan said nothing but you could tell he was a little surprised. Jill filled all three glasses. After passing them out, she raised her glass for a toast.

"Here is to the "win" column!"

"Hear, hear!" Allan said and I chimed in and then all three of us downed the amber liquid. Allan went to make sandwiches for Jill and me from the leftover pot roast from the night before. Jill poured herself another shot, I slid my glass across the table, and she filled it again. She gave me my full glass and I raised it to her.

"Here is to being in the right place at the right time," I said quietly.

"Amen, Jason," she said and shot me a wink. Allan brought our sandwiches to the table and sat down.

"I talked to the sheriff just before you got back. He said that the one hiker had a badly broken arm and that both were severely dehydrated. The other one had some severe internal injuries and had to be rushed into surgery. It looks like both will live to tell the tale."

"That's great news," I said.

"Sheriff Case also wanted me to thank the both of you for taking the initiative to get the job done. He also apologized profusely for sending Marvin out. Apparently, all of the SAR people filed a complaint when they got back to town and from what I understand, Marvin is in some pretty hot water over his handling of the mission today," he said with a slight grin.

"Good, Louie needs to fire that jerk before he gets someone killed!" Jill blurted out.

"It may be headed that way. The medics and deputies were all hot under the collar after you two hauled ass. At one point I thought it was going to come to blows. The teams on horses didn't leave here for almost another 90 minutes after you left and he sent them in the opposite direction. The look on his face was price-less when you popped smoke."

"If it's all right with you, I'm going to call Louie tomorrow and see about filing my own complaint," Jill said looking at Allan.

"Please do. Marvin is a danger to the department, and I think Louie is gather-ing all of his momentum to finally force the guy out. Getting a civilian complaint will certainly help," Allan stood up and picked up his notebook. "If you will ex-cuse me, I believe I will be turning in for the night. Don't forget, Jason, Bill will be here at noon tomorrow to give you a lift back to Reno."

"I know," I said with a sigh. Allan looked from me to Jill. I could see her shrug her shoulders slightly out of the corner of my eye. After he left the room and it was quiet for a moment.

"Did you get enough to eat?" Jill asked as she took my plate.

"I did but I think I could use another dose of painkiller," Jill put the dishes in the sink and returned to the table. She refilled both glasses and sat back down. I stared at my glass for a moment.

"Let me ask you something, Jill."

"Anything," she replied.

"If that had been me and any other member of this team, if I had been the one to slip, would the outcome have been the same?" there was no hesitation when she answered.

"Yes. Any one of us would have done everything possible to save you or die trying."

"I see," I raised my glass and knocked back the shot. Jill did the same. This time I refilled the glasses.

"You gave me very explicit instructions and told me to not do exactly what I did, right?"

"Yeah, yeah I did," she said, staring into her shot glass.

"Would the others have disobeyed that order?"

"Probably. I know these guys and they would have had the same gut reaction that you did. Orders be damned," we sat in silence for a couple of minutes before I started again.

"What happens to this place if I leave here tomorrow and never come back?" concern and panic flashed across her face.

"Well, eventually all the livestock will be sold off. Then we start selling the fuel we have on hand. Once that is gone, we start selling off equipment. Then guns and ammo. Then we sell off the food stores. It would take quite a few years but eventually this place will fall into disrepair."

"Tell me about your dad. I've spent three hours with the guy, but I don't really know much about him."

"My father? He's a tough one. He has always been the sort of guy that has an all business demeanor. He was tough on us kids growing up although I think I had it better than my brothers. I was his baby girl after all," she said with a smile. "He is one of those guys who works 16-hour days and probably will until the day he dies. He brokers multi-million-dollar deals between corporations. Land deals, tax deals, take-overs, those sorts of things are what he lives for. It got even worse after mom died," she paused for a few seconds. "He's a great guy and as honest as they come, he's just got a real tough shell that he rarely comes out of."

"I didn't know about your mom, I'm sorry."

"It's okay, there is no way you could have known."

"What about your brothers? What are they like?"

"Well, Mark has always kind of been the screw-up of the family. He dropped out of college, worked about a million jobs and had about twice that many relationships. He is a great guy, would give you the shirt off his back but, as dad says, he can be kind of flaky. Mark is as happy as he can be, but it drives dad nuts that he just won't settle down. He is the oldest and dad thinks he should get his shit together. As for Dale, he is the opposite of Mark. He is married, has twin boys who are just about to turn 15, works a small farm just up the road from your brother and he does pretty good at it. That guy has a pair of green thumbs!" she chuckled.

"What's Allan's story?" I asked.

"He ran his own construction company in the 80's. It was back east, New Jersey, if I remember right. He was a self-made man and was doing quite well. He never married and never had any kids. He had the fast cars and the nice houses, but he walked away from all of that to move out here full-time. He will tell you that he wanted out of that lifestyle and that he wasn't happy, but sometimes you can tell that he kind of misses the luxuries that he had back then. He really is a sweetheart, but I think he's been just as frustrated as I have been."

"Why have you been frustrated?" I asked. She sat back in her chair and let out a long sigh.

"This ranch has so much more to offer but we are not exploiting that. Life around here has come to a standstill."

"What do you mean by that?"

"Well, the shooting range for instance, we could open it to the public and charge admission. Five bucks per person and you get the use of the outdoor range for the entire day. We still have all the old airsoft equipment so why not open the shoot house and charge each person 20 bucks to play airsoft. It would be a great source of income for the ranch. Mark has talked about opening up his own wilderness survival school but keeps getting shot down by dad and Allan."

"If we could start getting money rolling back in, that would be a start. If we could find some new people to add to the staff around here, that would be great too. Even if you do decide to come live here, that only puts three of us here full-time. If we look at the scenario you put out last night, we still couldn't hold the ranch together if the world ended. It makes me mad to think that we are squandering your father's vision and it makes me mad to think that we could conceivably lose this place. The whole damn mess just irritates the piss out of me!"

"You are one hell of a firearms instructor. Have you ever thought about opening your own school? Maybe teach concealed carry classes."

"I have, trust me, same thing happens to me that happens to Mark. I go down in flames every time."

"Let me ask you this then, what happens if I stay? What sort of miracle do you expect me to perform?"

"Our hope is that you can bring new ideas to the ranch, that you can bring the vitality back." She paused and looked away. "Our hope.... my hope.....Jason, this place is my life. I don't want to lose it. I hope you can figure out a way to help me keep this. Your dad left this for all of us and I can't stand the thought of losing it on my watch," I could tell that she was on the verge of tears again. She turned away and wiped the corners of her eyes.

"Do you want me to stay?"

"The ranch needs you."

"That's not what I asked," she turned back to face me, her eyes locked with mine.

"I want you to stay," she said barely above a whisper. Holding her gaze I leaned back in my chair and I let the silence linger for a few moments. Truth be told, I had already made up my mind. I leaned forward again and raised my shot glass. Unsure of what was coming next, Jill slowly raised hers.

"Here is to lasting friendships, the ranch and the future. May we always be in the right place at the right time," I said quietly. The fear in her eyes was instantly replaced with joy. Both of us threw back the shots. "All I ask is that you keep this under your hat. I still need to talk to Allan and your father. They may not be as happy as you are about it because I am going to make some pretty drastic changes."

"Time for a changing of the guard?" she asked.

"So to speak, but you're going to play a crucial role. I am going to need you and your skills," she looked puzzled. "Jill, you are the Chief of Security for the ranch and you are an awesome instructor. You have skills that I plan on using to our advantage. I'll talk to Bill and Allan tomorrow to give them a better idea of what I want done in the next two weeks. I must go back to Reno tomorrow and tie everything up nice and neat. I'll be back in two weeks and that's when things are going to get fast and furious. After I talk to Bill and Allan, we are going to have a meeting with everyone. We will get your brother, Dale, on the phone for a conference call. This is going to affect everyone in a big way," she simply nodded. "One more thing, you and I will probably be taking a road trip to Kansas to see my brother."

"Okay."

"I have to see him one more time and give him one more chance. I may tell him more than anyone wants me to, but he is my brother and I owe him that much," she totally understood.

We talked for another hour before Jill excused herself to go to bed. She gave me another big hug accompanied by a peck on the cheek. She thanked me again and took her leave. I settled into the overstuffed couch and again started reading my father's journal. I could see why Jill thought some of it might be in code. There were sets of numbers in the margins, all in sets of three. The numbers seemed to go from one to 100, nothing higher. It was perplexing but I continued to read. I finally went to sleep sometime around midnight.

Sunday, July 12, 2015

When I awoke the next morning, a quick glance of the wall clock told me it was 5:00. It wasn't a whole lot of sleep, but I did feel refreshed. The coffee pot was already on. I filled what had become my cup and went back to the other main house to see if there were any clean clothes. There were. After my shower, I dressed in the black fatigues and t-shirt. I didn't put the sling back on. My shoulder was sore as all hell, but the sling was just pissing me off. I looked in the medicine cabinet and found a bottle of ibuprofen. Eight of those ought to do it I thought as I washed them down with lukewarm coffee. I went back to Jill and Allan's house to refill my cup. Allan was sitting at the table enjoying his first cup.

"Morning," I said

"You're up early today."

"I had a lot on my mind last night. There is a lot I want to see today so I thought I'd get an early start."

"I see."

"When Bill gets here, I need to talk to both of you, together."

"That can be arranged. I take it you have come to a decision?" he asked.

"Yup," was the only thing I said. I took my now full cup and walked out of the kitchen and out of the house. I walked the grounds again, taking mental notes all along the way. I spent a lot of time in the greenhouses and going over the equipment in the pole barns. One of the greenhouses was devoid of plants. It was ready to be used but nothing had been planted. The second one was only about half full. There was lettuce, tomatoes, potatoes, peppers, green beans and corn. All in all, a pretty basic crop to supplement meals for two to three people. My assumption was that the greenhouse was used year-round to continuously grow food.

The sawmill equipment was older but was very well maintained. All the bare surfaces had a light coating of oil to keep the rust away. The blades were all sharpened with care and the belts had all been removed to prevent them from stretching and dry rotting. I then turned my attention to the heavy equipment. All of it was very nearly new and showed little wear.

I continued my walk until I found where the crops were normally planted. This was an area outside of the brick wall. It looked to be about 20 acres but had not been worked in quite some time. The entire plot was surrounded by barbed wire, to keep the cows out was my assumption.

My next stop was back inside the fence. I walked to the pond in the center of the circular driveway. I walked all the way around it, then I walked toward the gated entrance. I went inside the guard shack. There wasn't much to see. A notebook on a simple desk and a chair. I realized the glass was bullet-proof. There was a closed-circuit TV camera positioned on a tripod on the desk. I realized that was what Jill had looked into that first day. The pad on the outside of the window that I thought was a scanner of some sort was nothing more than a piece of black, 1" thick Lexan plastic. It was odd to see it in black. Normally, it was clear and used to make unbreakable windows. The fancy entrance was all for show. Allan could see Jill in the camera and unlocked the gate from the security shack. "Well played," I muttered.

I went back outside and inspected the gate. It was no joke. Whoever built it knew what they were doing. I glanced at my watch, 11:00. Another hour. I worked my way back up the winding drive and it was then that it dawned on me. The drive was not straight because if it were, attackers would have a straight shot to the houses. While the fence on either side of the drive was no real obstacle, it would slow them down.

When I got back to the security office, I stopped and turned a full 360 degrees. It was a slow turn as I wanted to take everything in one more time. I was now positive of what I wanted to do with this place. I was not sure how well it would be received by Bill and Allan, but I had to give it a shot. It was time for the second act as Jill had said.

I could see the black Jeep approach the gate. A moment later it opened, and the Jeep came up the driveway. It came to a stop right next to the one that was already parked in front of the security office. Bill and Mark both climbed out and we traded pleasantries. Jill came out of the security office and hugged her brother and father. Allan was right behind her and he shook hands with both men. After a few minutes of small talk, we made our way into the main house where we had shared meals for the last couple days. Bill and Allan took their places at the table. Jill and Mark had stayed outside.

"I believe Jason has something he wants to tell us," Allan told Bill.

"I do." I remained standing. "You brought me here in the hopes that I would pick up where my father left off. You have asked me to give up the life that I have made for myself and build a new life here. If that is to happen, we will need to make some drastic changes in a very short time," Bill and Allan looked at each other. I had them off balance and it was written all over their faces. "This place needs a crew to run it. It cannot be done with only three people here on a full-time basis. You are planning on people showing up here after some sort of disaster and that's fine for those who actually survive the apocalypse."

"Will there be enough people to defend what has been built here? I think not. From what I have learned in the past couple of days, this place may not last long enough to fall in a post-apocalyptic world. Financially, we are hanging on by our fingernails and not much else," I paused for effect and Bill started to say something. When I raised my hand, he fell silent. "We need to change the way we think around here. We need to run this place like a business if we want it to succeed. We need to take a step back from the high-tech and revert to low-tech, real low-tech."

"Here's what I propose; number one, sell all but 100 head of cattle. Number two, sell half of the earth moving equipment. Three, open the shooting range and shoot house and turn it into a shooting school. You have one of the best instructors I've ever met, put her to work. Four, open a wilderness survival school. Five, draw in some new talent from those schools. If it's done right, the survivalist community will come to the classes that are offered. Poach the talent from there. If someone stands out, watch them. If they look like a good fit, research them. If they clear all of that, make them an offer. Six, poach talent from the men and women who are leaving the armed services. And last, bring Dale and his family back here. He is a farmer by trade, and we could really use his knowledge to get the crops in next season," I put my hands on the back of the chair and leaned forward slightly. Both men just stared at me for ten seconds or so. Bill was the first to speak.

"If we bring in outsiders, they will know what we are about and that could end very badly!" he protested.

"Outsiders come here all the time. There was a dozen or so cops and firefighters here yesterday. You brought me here, I'm an outsider. Do you think they are a danger to us? Do you think I am a danger?" I asked.

"The others could be, but I didn't think you would be a danger!" Bill said defensively.

"Then turn it around, make those types of people the solution, not the damn problem. Get them to be allies even if they don't know it. For them to work with us, they do not need to know everything about the ranch."

"What about the cattle and the equipment? We cannot sell it off and maintain the redundancy that we need!"

"We can and we will. The cattle replenish themselves and while I like steaks, I can't eat them faster than they can be replenished. As far as the equipment goes, we do not need two giant backhoes with air conditioning. What we do need is equipment that will not be left useless by an EMP type of event. We need to lose the dead weight around here and do it fast."

We argued, sometimes heatedly, and talked for well over an hour and a half before we came to an agreement. I pretty much got what I wanted in the end. Jill and Mark were invited in and we got Dale on speakerphone. Dale seemed genuinely happy about moving his family back to the ranch. Jill was astonished when she was given her assignment; put together a tactical shooting school. Everything from long-range to hand-to-hand combat. By the end of the meeting, Mark had decided that he too would be moving back to the ranch to run the wilderness survival school. It was a passion of his and he looked forward to it. When it was all settled, it was nearly 5:00.

We all said our good-byes and Mark and Bill were already in the Jeep. I shook Allan's hand and he turned and walked away. Jill walked up to me and I extended my hand. "Screw that!" she said as she wrapped me up in a big hug. It lasted a little longer than the last hug and again ended with the kiss on the cheek. "Hurry back," she whispered into my ear before she pulled away. She turned and headed for the security office. I turned around and climbed in the Jeep. Bill and Mark first looked at each other then looked at me.

"What?"

"Jason, the last guy that tried to hug my daughter got a knee to the groin," Bill laughed.

"SHE hugged me!" I said awkwardly.

"She must like you. She doesn't hug anyone other than family," Mark said as he started the Jeep.

CHAPTER 4

The five-hour drive back to Reno was uneventful. Bill and I spoke at length about the changes that were coming to the ranch. He told me that he would make the arrangements to sell the cattle and equipment. Mark already had plans for setting up his survival school and was genuinely excited about it. He said that he had already done a lot of research on the subject and getting people to come to his school should not be that hard. There were a lot of people who were hungry for knowledge and many would pay just about anything for good training.

I asked Bill to get with Dale and find out what equipment we would need to keep the ranch running after an event like an EMP. He said he would get him on the phone first thing in the morning and get his thoughts on it. They dropped me off at my apartment at 10:45pm. I went inside and went straight to bed. I was tired but sleep didn't come quickly. I stared at the ceiling and listened to all the noises creeping into my room. It wasn't until now that I realized how quiet life at the ranch was.

Monday, July 13, 2015.

The alarm clock went off at 3:30 Monday morning and it felt like I had just closed my eyes. I laid there for ten minutes or so before I finally put my feet on the floor. My shoulder still hurt like hell so there was no way that I was going to the gym. Instead I took a very long, very hot shower. I dressed in my usual work attire. The slacks, button-up shirt and dress shoes didn't feel like they fit anymore. The tie felt like it was choking the life out of me. They felt foreign to me.

The only thing that did feel right was my old truck. She was my pride and joy. A 1977 Dodge Crew Cab four-by-four. I'd poured a lot of money and even more time into it. One of the first things to go was the tired old 318 engine. It now had a 6BT Cummins turbo diesel engine under the hood and a five-speed manual transmission behind it. The half-ton axles had been replaced with the one-ton axles from the same truck the engine and transmission had come from. The interior was all modern except the gauges. I had kept all of them the old-style manual gauges.

As a matter of fact, there were no modern electronics on the truck at all except the stereo system. As always, she fired right up and took me to work.

I arrived right at 5:00am. As always, I was the first one there. I went inside and started the coffee like I had done for the past five years. When I got to my office my briefcase was still sitting on my desk, right where I had left it. I sat in my chair and just stared at the pictures on the wall. Everything here felt like it was from another lifetime. I was still sitting there when I heard Daryl, the plant manager, coming down the hallway. I heard the keys jingle as he unlocked his door. A few moments later he was standing in my doorway.

"What are you doing back so soon?" he asked.

"Huh?" was all I could say.

"Bereavement, you can have up to five days. I figured you would take all of it."

"Oh, um, no, I won't be needing it but we need to talk," I said as I motioned for him to sit down. "You're not going to like this, Daryl so I'll get straight to the point. I'm giving you my two weeks' notice. I'm leaving the company," I said. He looked like he had just been sucker punched. "You should promote Ann to my job. She works her ass off, and she already knows most of what I do. Hell, she has covered for me when I've been on vacation. I can show her the rest of the ropes in the next two weeks."

"Why? You have 20 in this place.... What happened this weekend?"

"Daryl, you know me. I have always been a straight and narrow kind of guy. At 5:00am last Thursday, my life took a very hard right turn. Everything I thought I knew was shaken to the very core. For the first time in my entire life, I was in the right place at the right time...." The reference to Jill made me smile a little. "I came back here this morning out of habit but everything about it feels wrong. It's time for me to move on."

"Okay," he said. "As soon as John from HR gets in, we can go make it official. Do you want to tell Ann, or do you want me to?" the resignation in his voice was loud and clear.

"I want to tell her," I said.

After I spoke to HR and gave Ann her promotion, the rest of the day was rather mundane. Of course, people came and went with their condolences about my father and about how much I would be missed. I hung out until second shift came in and I met them all in the break room and held a short meeting. Once that was taken care of, I left for the day. The whole day was surreal. By the time the two weeks was over I was surprised at how much I wanted to get back to the ranch.

I stood in the middle of my apartment that Friday afternoon and looked at all my possessions. I took my Auto Ordinance 1911 and my Daniel Defense AR-15 and put them in my truck. I also grabbed the four full ammo cans and loaded them up. I had already packed one suitcase of my favorite t-shirts, several pairs of blue jeans, socks and underwear, and already had it in the truck. There was nothing else that mattered except a half dozen photo books and they too were in the truck. I walked out and pulled the door shut. I climbed in my truck and went to the complex manager's office and dropped off the keys to the place. I told him to do whatever he wanted with the stuff that was left behind. I did not need it anymore.

As I drove down I-80 with Reno and Sparks fading in my rear-view mirror, I finally started to feel at ease. I started to feel like I was really going home.

Friday, July 24, 2015

It was almost 11:00pm when I finally got to the ranch. I had called ahead and told Allan when I would be getting in. I stopped at the gate and sat for a moment before it opened. I slipped the truck back into gear and eased my way up the drive. I pulled up and parked next to the Jeep and shut the truck down. Allan was waiting for me. I slid out of the front seat and closed the door. Allan let out a soft whistle.

"That is one gorgeous truck!" he said.

"Thanks," I said as I looked around him. "Where is Jill?" was my next question. About that time, she burst out of the front door of her house. She was wearing sweat shorts and a tank top. Her bare feet padded across the concrete as she ran up and gave me a big hug. I squeezed her tight and lifted her off the ground.

"I'm glad you're here," she whispered in my ear.

"I'm glad to be here," I whispered back. I set her back on the ground, but she did not let me go. I was in no hurry to let her go either. Allan made himself busy looking at my truck. Finally, she let go and took a small step back. Her smile was ear-to-ear.

"How is the shoulder?" she asked.

"It's healing great. Almost back to 100 percent," I told her.

"That makes me happy," she said. "Listen, I have to get up in four hours, I just wanted to welcome you back. I missed you."

"Okay, better get your butt back to bed. Will you be in the security shack when I get up in the morning?"

"I will be. See you then?" she asked.

"I'll bring you coffee."

"Looking forward to it," she said with a smile. She turned and walked back to the house. Before she went through the door, she looked back at me and smiled again. I was so engrossed in watching Jill walk away that I did not realize Allan had walked up next to me.

"That girl has fallen for you in a big way," he said. I looked at him, but he just stared straight at the house. "I don't think I've ever seen anything like it," this time he looked at me. "What? Don't tell me that you can't see it," he paused. "Come on, let's go in the shack," he said and pointed toward the door. I really didn't know what to say so I just followed him. Once inside he sat back behind the desk and I leaned against the wall.

"You should know some things about Jill," he stated. "There is a lot of history there that I think you should be made aware of. I think it's only fair that you know what you are getting into," he said looking over the top of his glasses. "She came back to the ranch a little over five years ago. She had just finished her third year in college. She had been dating this guy, Joshua, and they were getting serious. So much so that he had proposed to her and of course she accepted. He was a good guy. I liked him; her whole family liked him. He'd even been out here a time or two."

"Then one night, Jill, her mother, Kathleen, and Joshua went out to dinner to discuss wedding plans. About halfway through dinner, two gunmen burst in to rob the place. There was a scuffle and, in the end,, Joshua, Kathleen and one other person were dead. Jill took a round through her thigh and she nearly bled to death before the paramedics made it inside. The bullet had nicked her femoral artery."

"Both gunmen escaped and were never caught. Physically she healed just fine, faster than anyone expected in fact. Her mental wounds were far worse than her physical wounds. To be honest, she was one screwed up kid for almost a year afterward. After 11 months of both physical and mental therapy, Bill and Mark brought her out here in the hopes that it would help with her recovery. She had been here a little over a month when our then security chief, Walter Jenkins, decided it was time for some tough love."

"Walter was the Green Beret, right?" I interrupted.

"He was. Anyway, he wasn't having any of it. It had been over a year since the incident and she was buried under a ton of guilt. She wouldn't eat, slept for 15 hours a day, wouldn't talk.....she just existed inside of her little shell. One day he had had enough. He stomped up the stairs and kicked her bedroom door clean off its hinges and halfway across the room. I'm pretty sure he scared the shit out of her. He got right in her face and gave her what-for and was showing no signs of letting up. He was trying to provoke a reaction."

"It took him about 20 minutes of reading her the riot act in his drill instructor's voice before he got what he wanted. She slapped him across the face so hard that I heard it downstairs. It was dead silent for about ten seconds before he started in again. He was cursing like a drunken sailor on leave and telling her to get pissed. Get angry. Get mad and break shit. It didn't take long before I heard the crack of her palm across his face again, and again he launched another verbal assault. I was getting a little worried so I went to the top of the stairs where I could see what was going on."

"By now she was standing, and her face was nose to nose with his. She was so mad that the little vein in her forehead was popping out. Finally, she threw a punch. It connected but it didn't bother him at all. I think that was what set her off. She started punching and kicking and slapping and screaming this primal, rage-filled scream that I hope to God I never hear again. She threw everything she had at him for the next 15 minutes and he took every hit. She finally ended up in a pile on the floor, totally and utterly exhausted. His lip was split, his nose was broken and one of his eyes was swollen almost completely closed."

"What he did next blew my mind. He scooped her up off the floor and carried her down to the kitchen and set her on the counter. He pulled out some frozen vegetables and put the bags on her bruised knuckles. The entire time she sat there like some impetuous child. She was staring at him with a venom in her eyes that scared me. He again put his nose to hers and very quietly told her something. He said it so quietly that I couldn't hear it and neither of them ever told me what was said."

"Whatever it was worked. That all started at 10:30 at night and by the time they went to bed it was almost 4:00 in the morning. She was back up at 8:00 that morning and the two of them walked the grounds for what had to be six hours. She joined us for dinner every night after that and they walked every day for a week.

After that he started teaching her about weapons and fighting. He taught her everything he knew and when he had run out of things to teach her, he sent her to schools. She excelled beyond what anyone could imagine. She has standing invitations at several of those schools to come back as a guest instructor. After that first week she started hitting the gym and pushing herself harder and farther than anyone thought possible. To say that she is driven is an understatement if I ever heard one."

"What happened to Walter?"

"Cancer got him. It took him fast, too."

"How'd Jill take that?" I asked.

"Well, the day after we buried him, she went to the shoot house and spent the day there. She wrecked two AR's because she was running them so hard. She burned up 15,000 rounds doing it, too. But that wasn't the end of it. She started in on the punching bag and by the time she was done she had torn it from its mount in the ceiling. She had broken three fingers and two toes, sprained a knee and a wrist. The next day she showed up and took over Walter's job and has had it ever since."

"Unreal....." was all I could mutter.

"When she took that fall on the mountain, it rattled her. It made her realize that she is still a human being," he paused and drank from a bottle of water he had on the desk. "She had forgotten what it was like to need someone. If you hadn't been that someone, she would have been dead. She has buried her emotional side under that hardcore exterior, but it's still there and it is still vulnerable. For whatever reason, she has decided that it's okay for you to see that side of her."

"Are you saying that's the reason for the.... flirting and affection?" I asked.

"Not entirely. She is a grown woman and she has needs just like anyone else. I saw the limited flirting before the fall. What I am saying is that you and circumstances in general made her realize that life is way too short to waste the flirting and affection on just anyone."

"Oh, hell Allan, I was here for 72 hours. You cannot tell me that she has fallen madly in love with me in that amount of time, that's stupid."

"You are forgetting one detail, Jason."

"And that is what?"

"She was assigned to extract you in case of an emergency. She has studied you intently since she first joined the security team. She probably knows your habits better than even you do."

"Horseshit!" I fired back.

"Didn't we have hamburgers the first night you were here?"

"Yeah, so?"

"There were two that were well-done, she and I eat them medium-rare. Your clothes were folded and left on the corner of your bathroom counter. Pants and shirt stacked, socks and shorts stacked right next to them. The toothpaste was the same brand you used at home. The deodorant was the same brand you normally use. Any of this ringing any bells?" I was shocked but he was right about everything. "Don't let it bother you too much. It was her job to know you inside and out and she was very good at her job."

"Why so much detail? Wouldn't where I lived and worked be enough?"

"No and let me tell you why," he paused long enough for another drink. "She had to know your habits. If things went sideways on a Friday night at 9:00, she had to know your likely whereabouts. If it were Sunday at noon..... See what I'm getting at?"

"I get it, it just kind of weirds me out a little."

"All I am asking, Jason, is that if you decide to do more than just flirt, don't break her heart."

"I give you my word that I will not do that," I said.

"Your word is all I need," he said.

We chatted for a few more minutes, then I took my leave. I stood in front of the office for a few minutes enjoying the warm, starry night. There was a slight breeze blowing in from the west and it felt good. I decided I would unload the truck in the morning. I left the keys in the ignition and made my way to Allan and Jill's house. I had thought about it on the way out here and figured I would take the downstairs bedroom in their house. It only made sense. Dale and his family would need more space than the rest of us so I thought they could take over the other main house. It would give them the room they needed and some privacy.

The smaller bedroom was not really that small. There was plenty of room for a king-sized bed and a massive oak dresser that had nine large drawers. There were oak night stands on either side of the bed. There was also a very large closet. It had been a long day that started at 3am and I was tired after the drive. The clock above the dresser told me that it was 12:30am. I pulled the covers back, stripped down and climbed into bed. As much as I wanted it, sleep did not come quickly.

I was thinking about everything that needed to be done around here. The cattle were already gone, and the equipment was set to be auctioned in two weeks. Dale was due in about a month and the good news was that he was going to be bringing his four big draft horses and all the pull-behind equipment that he had, which I guess was a lot. He was also going to be bringing his old Massey Ferguson tractor. Mark was also going to be out here in the next month. Luckily he had already decided to stay in one of the barracks. When his school started up he wanted to stay with his students.

Then there was Jill. Once she found her way into my thoughts there was no getting her out. I know that it really should have bothered me how much she knew about me. I think that the fact that it was her job is what made it easy for me to accept. I was glad Allan had told me what had happened to her. It went a long way toward explaining the way she acted when my shoulder got sprained. She really did have a hardcore exterior. I'd go so far as to say that she was kind of a bad ass. She still did have a vulnerable side though, and that was the side I would have to be careful with. By the time I had fallen asleep, I had decided to just let things with her go wherever she took them. Going slow was a top priority. Besides, we were both going to be busy in the coming weeks and months.

Saturday, July 25, 2015

I was up by 5:00am in the morning and I was standing in the door of the security office at 6am sharp. Coffee in hand. Once I was inside and I had given Jill her coffee, I sat on the corner of her desk and sipped at mine.

"Sorry I had to bail on you and Allan last night. Three AM comes mighty early," she said with a smile.

"Don't worry about it," I told her. "I was just happy to see you again."

"I'll tell you this, Jason, even after you said you would be back, I was worried that you would change your mind. You had a decent life back in Reno and all we have to offer is hard work and long days."

"I did have mixed feelings about this place but the day on the mountain sealed the deal for me. Even if nothing bad ever happens, we have the opportunity to help people here and I think I can deal with that."

The smile slipped from her face at the mention of the mountain. "I cannot even tell you how sorry I am about almost getting all of us killed up there. What's worse is that my stupidity got you hurt...."

"Jill, I've told you already, let it go. We walked out winners and I am happy with that."

"I know but...."

"No but, we won, take it and never look back."

"Okay," she said, looking down at the keyboard on her desk. I decided it was time for a shift in conversation.

"Jill...." she looked up at me. "Teach me your job."

"What?"

"Teach me your job. If I am staying here, I need to be able to pull a shift and I am going to need to know what to do and when to do it," I said. "Think of me as a new employee and this is my first day on the job. You are the boss, now show me the ropes."

"Okay rookie, take my seat," she said as she stood up. I sat in her chair and she stood behind me leaning over my shoulder. "This screen on the left is all of the video cameras on the property. Put your cursor right there," she pointed to an icon at the top of the screen. "Click on that and you can toggle through all of the cameras manually. If you leave it alone it will cycle from camera to camera every 15 seconds. If you want to stay on a camera, simply click on it. Once you do that a menu will pop up and you can zoom in or out or pan and tilt. Once you leave that camera, it will return to its normal settings."

"All told, there are 32 cameras inside the wall. All of them have night vision capability," I switched from camera to camera and used the controls to manipulate it. The interface was easy to use. "On the center monitor we have the alarm center," on the screen I could see what amounted to a map of everything inside the wall. Every building and the underground facility were represented. "This will show you whether a door or window is open or closed. It will also register a fire or CO^2 alarm and show you what room or building is involved. This monitor on the right keeps tabs on all our fuel stores and you can remotely turn the water on for the livestock from here. Down in the corner of the screen, see that camera icon? Yeah, click on it. There, see that?" she asked. I nodded yes. "That is the watering hole up in the meadow, if you see it getting low just click on the "ON" tab and you can fill it from here."

"That doesn't seem so bad," I said.

"Oh, don't worry, this is just the tip of the iceberg," she laughed. "In the top drawer you will find the logbook. If you see anything that is odd, put it in the log with the date, time and a description of what you saw."

"What do you mean by odd?"

"Odd, as in not supposed to be there. Six months ago, we had a crack head sneaking around outside the wall at two in the morning. He was looking for a way in so he could steal stuff."

"Really? All the way out here?" I asked.

"Yup. A couple of nights later I watched him carry a ladder all the way from the main road. He put it against the wall and jumped over. It was the exact moment when he hit the grass that he realized that he screwed up," the grin on her face was huge. "The Idiot had two problems. First, he had no way to get back over the wall and his second problem was me. I was waiting for him. It was near pitch black that night because I turned off all the perimeter and interior lights. I was wearing my black uniform and I was using night vision goggles. Poor bastard never knew what hit him," she chuckled a little.

"Best part is when he woke up. He was handcuffed to the front gate. Just as he started stirring, I got on the intercom that runs to the gate and whispered, "God is watching you." He was tweaking hard so my screwing with him didn't help matters!" by now she was giggling. "I messed with his head until the deputy showed up and hauled him off," now she was laughing and so was I.

"I bet he'll think twice before he comes back here!"

"I bet you're right," she said. "Okay, let's get back to it. Over there on the counter you will find the radios, grab one and let's take a walk," I did as I was told, and we headed out the front door. "It's up to you how you decide to patrol the property, just try to be random when you do it. Change your routes and times whenever possible, got it?"

"Yes, ma'am."

"Check the living quarters, the barracks buildings and the underground. Again, whatever order you want is fine," over the course of the next hour and 35 minutes we walked through all of the main cabins. When we were upstairs passing by Jill's door, I couldn't help but notice the distinct boot print on it. She had never cleaned it off. We ended our tour of the buildings in the basement of one of the barracks buildings.

She opened the hidden door and we passed into the underground. After 30 minutes of walking all the corridors and living spaces we came up through the floor of the horse barn. Once the hatch was closed, you could not even tell where we had come from. In the next hour we walked all the buildings on the back of the compound, even going inside the chicken coups. No place was left unsearched. The whole time we were walking Jill was showing me the locations of the cameras. "Just for reference, the distance from the security office to the barns is exactly 100 yards. From the front of the office to the gate is 440 yards. The four lights that illuminate the driveway are one 110 yards apart."

"Okay?" I said more as a question.

"Known distances when you need to shoot at something farther away."

"That's clever. I would never have thought of it."

"That was Walter's doing. He had me spend a lot of time putting together the ranges for everything inside the wall. You ready to stop and grab another cup of coffee?" she asked.

"Sure," I replied as we turned and headed for the security shack. We grabbed our cups and headed into the house to fill them up. Allan was sitting at the table with his laptop in front of him.

"Good morning you two," he said cheerfully. "Jill giving you the rundown this morning?"

"She is. If I'm going to pull my weight around here, I figured now was a good time to start learning how it's done."

"That's good! Jill, Dale says that they may be coming a little earlier than they expected. They had an offer on the farm this morning!"

"That's great news!" she squealed. "I can't wait to see my nephews!"

"I also got an email from Mark this morning. He said it is going to take a little longer than he thought, but that he should be out here at the end of August," Allan said.

"I'll just be happy to have both my big brothers back here! Now if I could just get dad to move back, that would be awesome," she said wistfully.

"I know, it would be nice to have everyone back here. I miss those days."

"Me too, Allan," Jill said as she handed me a full cup of coffee. She pointed toward the door and we headed out again. "Let's take the Jeep, we need to run out to the range."

"Okay," I said as I headed toward the passenger side.

"You drive," she said. "It's about time you chauffeur me around."

"Sweet! I've been dying to give one of these a test drive!" I jumped into the driver's seat and used the controls to adjust it. The first thing that I saw was that the instrument panel was not the factory package. The cluster of instruments was all custom and there was none of the fancy digital crap. I turned the key and the starter made a very distinctive sound, one I had heard a million times in my own truck, before I put the diesel engine in. The engine just purred like a kitten. "Jill, you have to tell me what the deal is with these Jeeps. That is not a stock engine under the hood," I said as I slipped the console shifter into drive. I looked closer at the shifter and knew something else was up with the transmission. It was a three-speed automatic with no overdrive. That wasn't a factory option either!

"Your father bought six of these, all identical, for use at the ranch. He got them from a corporate asset auction, and I want to say he only paid like five grand for each one. The problem was that they all had a load of miles on them. I think the baby of the bunch had 240,000 on it. All of them are 2013s, so they were new, just worn the hell out," she paused long enough to hand me radio mic. "You are Rogue Two, I'm Rover Two, and Allan is Shepherd One. This is gate two that we are approaching. Let Allan know that we want out," she instructed.

"Shepherd One.....Rover Two and Rogue Two are at gate two, would you let us out please?"

"Copy Rogue Two, be safe," Allan replied and the gate started to open. Once we were on the other side of it, I radioed back, told him we were clear, and I watched the gate close in my mirror. Jill picked up the story of the Jeeps again.

"Anyway, your dad had a friend that worked for a four-by-four shop in Reno and in his spare time he liked to build off-road monsters in his own garage. Jack hired him and brought him here. When all was said and done, we ended up with six of these bad boys," she patted the dash. "Under the hood there is a small block Dodge 318 that's been worked over. The transmission is the venerable Chrysler 727, also worked over. He told me what the transfer case was, but I can't remember. The rear axle is a cut-down Ford nine inch, it's got a locker in it and the front axle has an air locker, that switch right there turns it on and off," she pointed to a switch on the console.

"The tires are the same ones that are on the Hummers, including the run flat inserts. The suspension was fabricated by a guy that used to race off road. It's fully tuned to the weight of the vehicle. They added quarter inch thick AR500 armor plate inside all four doors and the tailgate. That will stop pretty much any small arms fire," she finished with a grin.

"I see," I said as I made the turn to head for the range. "You're telling me this thing has a full-race suspension?"

"Pretty close to it."

"Got your seat belt on?"

"Yeah I....." I pulled the shifter into second gear and floored the throttle. The response was immediate. The 318 roared to life and the rear tires kicked dirt and rocks into the air. When we hit 60 I slammed it into third gear, and we were still gaining speed. We were drifting around the corners and catching air every so often. The ride was great, and the power was awesome. I looked at Jill and her eyes were huge! I thought she was going to leave finger imprints on the armrest of her door. As we approached the gate, I brought us to a fast, hard stop.

"Holy shit!" she exclaimed. "That was so much fun!"

"Don't tell me you have never taken one of these out and ran it like that," I asked, she just shook her head as she got out and opened the gate. Once she was back in, we continued to the range at a much more relaxed pace.

"I have always wondered what all the hype was about the Jeeps, I guess now I know," she laughed.

"You've never done that before?" I asked.

"Not even close!"

"These things were built for speed! Whoever built them knew what the hell they were doing," I said as we approached the parking area. "I'll have to teach you what I know about performance driving."

"I would love to learn how to drive like that!" she said as we got out of the Jeep. We talked more about driving skills as we walked the interior and exterior of the shoot house and the range. She explained that there were no cameras out here, but she showed me what to look for in case someone had been here.

"Look for fresh footprints," she pointed to the tracks we were leaving. "See, the dirt out here is pretty soft, and we are leaving tracks that Stevie Wonder could follow."

"Okay," I nodded. As we walked the grounds, she pointed out fresh deer tracks. She stopped cold when she found cat tracks. "Bobcat," she pointed. "I've been wondering when he'd be back."

"Had any problems with him?" I asked.

"Nah, just hadn't seen his tracks in a while. I have spotted him a couple of times, but he always keeps his distance. He's probably watching us right now," that statement kind of spooked me a little. I quickly scanned the area around us. Jill started giggling. "Jeez Jason, settle down! He won't bother us unless we get out there and start screwing with him," that calmed me down a little. We spent about an hour checking the place out. There were no signs that anyone had been here besides us. When we had returned to the Jeep, Jill glanced at her watch.

"We have time to throw some lead if you want."

"I'd love to!" I said and we headed back into the shoot house. We spent the next hour practicing with our pistols. Instead of just shooting, we worked on our weak hand drills and weapon manipulation. After that we drove back to the compound and the security shack. We spent the rest of the shift in and around the security office. Jill was filling me in on the details of security operations. I learned that, under normal conditions, condition three, they could go to town but never unarmed. Everyone carried outside the wall. Inside the wall was up to the individual. When I asked her why she didn't carry inside the wall she simply smiled. She lifted her uniform shirt to reveal a Glock 21 tucked in an appendix carry holster. The Glock was the same caliber as the Sig Sauer's.

"There is always a gun within my reach," she stated.

"You didn't have one the night we went to the hot tub."

"Are you sure?" she asked.

"You didn't have anywhere to conceal it," I smiled at the memory.

"It was in the folded towel that I was carrying."

"No kidding? What about at dinner that first night?"

"There is a pistol in a holster mounted to the bottom of the table. There is one mounted behind the towel rack outside my shower. There is one under the table in the living room. There is one in a #10 can that says peas on it in the pantry. I will never be without a gun," the look on her face was not quite right and her eyes were focused somewhere else.

"You okay?" I asked. She quickly re-focused and answered.

"Yeah, memories from a different life," was all she said.

Over the course of the next month we had settled into a routine around the ranch. I stepped up and took the graveyard shift for security. Jill was on in the mornings and Allan took the afternoon shift. I was teaching Jill about high-speed driving; she was teaching me about armed and un-armed combat and boy did I have some bruises to prove it! It was August 23rd when Dale and his tribe pulled in. I met his twin boys who were 15 years old, Mike and Ben, and his wife, Susan. All of them were thrilled to hear that they would get the other big house to themselves. Dale was quickly brought up to speed about the state of the greenhouses and the fields. He was not happy but said he would get to work on it right away. I was caught off guard when I learned that Susan was an RN in an emergency room before moving here. I had never thought to ask what she did for a living.

Mark pulled in on September 9th. I almost didn't recognize him. He had stopped shaving and was growing a beard. He was dressed in blue jeans and a t-shirt. He moved into the barracks and filled us in on the future of his school. He too settled in very quickly. By the end of September there were eight of us living at the ranch full-time. The dinner table was filling up and there was fresh life around it in the evenings.

CHAPTER 5

By the beginning of October, life had become normal for me again. Almost like I had lived here my whole life. It all felt right, finally. Jill had just put on a shoot class for the Elko Police Department and it had received rave reviews. She already had a class scheduled for the Sheriff's Department the very next weekend. Her nemesis at the department, Marvin, had been fired after the hiker incident. That was considered good news by everyone.

Dale had plowed the field and even expanded it by about ten acres before the weather cooled off. He wanted to give the soil a work-over well before he planted the next spring. Both greenhouses were now in full operation and he had already worked out a deal to get the food to market as soon as it was ready. Susan was homeschooling the boys, but she made time to teach everyone what she could about emergency medical care. All of us learned how to suture on the skin of a chicken breast. Then we got to practice removing them, and a lesson in how to make fried or baked chicken.

Mark's first class was set to begin November 1st and would be a two-week affair. I was right when I said people would pay good money for a good class. The full two-week course cost each student $1,000 and he sold out all 15 positions in three days. People were coming from as far away as Australia for his class. His plans were for one class a month. December was booked solid, so were January through August of 2016. Even he was a little shocked by the response he was getting but he was very enthusiastic about it.

Allan had sold the extra equipment at auction for a very nice sum. We decided that we did not need anything else with the arrival of Dale's old equipment. He had said that he was more comfortable with his old tools and draft horses. We socked that money away. He had also worked out a deal with the local ranchers to purchase fuel from us. While they were getting it cheaper from us, we were still getting it at below wholesale prices, so we made a profit there, too. It was also good because it allowed us to keep the fuel fresh. I was worried about it going bad and this way we always had good fuel on hand. We had not started selling the produce yet and we had money coming in. Things were looking up.

Bill had come out to spend the weekend back in September. He wanted to see all his kids and grandkids. Before he left, he and I had a long private conversation. There were a couple of things I wanted, and I wasn't sure how to go about it. One of those things had to do with my 401k account. It had nearly half a million dollars in it and I wanted it out, but I didn't want to lose half of it to penalties. He said he would get back to me on that and the other things we talked about.

I had been hitting the gym hard at Jill's insistence. At 6'2" and 195 pounds when I arrived here, I was a pretty big guy. Before I came here, I was in the gym five days a week. I did mainly weight training and cardio. After almost three months at the ranch I was pushing 220 pounds of pure muscle. I had never been a runner but would always use the treadmill at my apartment gym. Once I got here, I would run the wall every day after my shift.

Jill and I had become closer, but we had not become intimate yet. Neither of us were in a hurry to get there either. I think both of us were just enjoying the flirting. We spent our free time hanging out and watching old movies. She loved Katharine Hepburn and John Wayne movies. We would hide away in the common area of the underground and use the TV that was down there. We also spent time horseback riding and hiking the local mountains. We were getting to know each other.

I still had not gone to see Braden. I think maybe I was putting it off because I didn't want to fight with him. We may have been related by blood but that was all that tied us together. Part of me wanted to have nothing to do with him. He had made his choice, right? The other part of me felt that I owed it to him, that he really needed to see this place. I was working my shift one night when I was thinking about him a lot.

I had already made my rounds and was sitting in the shack as we had taken to calling it. I started reading my father's journal for what had to be the 20th time when I had a thought pop into my head. My brother's journal. Jill had told me that Dale had a journal to give to Braden. It was just after four in the morning and I knew Dale would be up, he was always up early. I put the journal back in my pocket and left the shack. Sure enough, I could see that Dale's kitchen light was on. I knocked softly at his door and a minute later he opened it.

"Jason, is everything okay?" he asked.

"Yeah, I was just wondering if I could talk to you for minute," I said quietly. I didn't know if anybody else was awake yet.

"Sure, come on in," he ushered me past him and pulled the door shut. He pointed me to the kitchen. "Hungry? Want some coffee?" he asked as he pointed to a pan of eggs he was cooking.

"No, thank you though. I just need to ask you about the journal that you were supposed to give to Braden. Do you still have it?"

"Of course, I still have it, it's still in my pack. Why?"

"I need to see it, please," I said.

"Sure," he said as he got up and went to the coat closet by the front door. He returned and set his pack on the table. He opened it and produced a journal that was exactly like the one in my pocket. He started to pass it to me but stopped. "This is for your brother; you know that right?"

"I am aware of who it is for. I'm not interested in what my father wrote to him. I'm interested in the numbers in the margins of the pages," I said, making no move to reach for the journal. Instead I reached in my pocket and pulled my journal out. I opened it and showed him what I was looking for. "I think it is a code and at least a part of it is in that journal you are holding. There was more my father wanted to tell me and Braden, but I think it is locked away in that code."

"Write down what you need and return it to me?"

"I can do that," I told him. He hesitantly passed me the journal. Before I took it from him, I said, "You will have this back by dinner. You have my word that I will not read the parts for Braden, I just want the code." It was then that I took it from him. He looked like he had just given one of his kids away.

"Okay, sure you don't want coffee or breakfast?" he asked again. Again, I thanked him but declined. He walked me to the door and showed me out. I quickly got back to the shack and opened both journals side by side. I was right! The numbers that were missing in my journal were present in Braden's journal. My numbers were on the even pages, his were on the odd pages. I pulled the notebook from the drawer and began to put it all together on one sheet of paper. I was so intent on transcribing everything that it startled me when Jill opened the door. It was already 6:55 and her shift was about to begin. As usual, she had two cups of coffee.

"What is that?" she asked as she set my cup down on the desk.

"You were right when you said that my father coded parts of his journals. Look here," I said excitedly. She leaned over my shoulder and took a long look.

"Wow......"

"So, these two journals are probably the key to unlock the other journals. He wanted Braden and me to figure this out once we were together again. Now we just have to find the cipher to unlock this message......"

"What's that?" she reached over my shoulder and pointed to a symbol on the corner of the page.

"It's the Sterling Family Crest, it is on every page that has the code on it."

"Why is that so familiar to me?" she asked more to herself than me.

"You have seen this before? In of the other journals maybe?"

"I know that I've seen it, but I'll be damned if I can remember where." You could hear the frustration in her voice. I decided it was time to take a break. As interesting as the puzzle in the journals was, I was interested in the lady standing behind me, too. I closed them and stacked them on top of the note pad. Spinning around in the office chair, I was now facing Jill. She was still leaning over and put her hands on the arms of the chair. Our faces were inches apart. Our eyes were locked and neither of us dared to look away. It was a little game we played, almost like a game of chicken. Her eyes were such an intense blue, they almost didn't seem real. We stayed like that for almost a minute before she spoke, barely above a whisper.

"It's Friday and neither of us has to work tomorrow. It's your turn to choose, movie or hot tub?"

"Actually, I've made other plans for the evening. I was thinking maybe I should ask you on a date. Maybe take you to town and we could sit down for a nice dinner," her eyes betrayed her surprise. Her demeanor stayed perfectly cool. "There is one condition though," I told her.

"Really now? What sort of condition might that be?" she asked.

"You cannot wear your uniform or spandex shorts or combat boots. You have to wear honest-to-God girl clothes."

"You really think you can handle it if I wear girl clothes? You could barely handle the spandex," a smile played at the corners of her mouth.

"I'll be downstairs waiting for you at 7pm this evening, don't be late," I said. She slowly stood up and took a step back. I stood up in front of her. "Do you prefer Mexican or Italian food?"

"I like Italian," she said.

"Good, because I made reservations," I started to walk past her. She grabbed my arm and pulled me into a hug. She held it and then gave me the kiss on the cheek that I had become accustomed to. She let me go and I slipped out of the shack into the cool morning air.

Seven o'clock rolled around that evening and Jill was at the bottom of the stairs. I was wearing the only suit and dress shoes that I had brought with me from Reno. She was wearing a dark red, knee-length skirt with off-white open-toed heels and a low-cut blouse. Her hair was down, and it was obvious that she had spent some time getting it just right. I'm pretty sure this was the first time I had ever seen her with make-up on. She looked, stunning.

"Wow!" was the only word that I could get past my lips. She looked me over from head to toe.

"Not so bad yourself," she nodded in approval. With that we were out the door and into my truck. We drove into Elko and straight to a little mom and pop restaurant that I had scoped out a couple of weeks before. It was supposed to be the best kept secret in town. It was 7:45 when we arrived. I parked the truck in front of the entrance and shut it off. Jill took off her seat belt but made no move to open the door. She just sat and stared at the double doors. I could see her eyes glistening in the ambient light. She looked as if she would burst into tears at any moment.

"You okay?" I asked as I reached over and took her hand. It was trembling. Her whole body was trembling. She kept her gaze on the front door.

"I haven't been on a date in a very long time, Jason. I have spent all day telling myself that I could do this, that I needed to do this," she said in a cracking voice. "The last time I went on a date, three people died....." her voice trailed off.

"If you would rather, we could go do something else," I offered as I squeezed her hand.

"No!" she said sharply. "I have to do this, this is a part of moving forward with my life," she wiped at the corners of her eyes and finally looked over at me. "Nothing bad is going to happen and we will have a great time, right?"

"Yes, we are going to have a great time, I promise," I told her. She sniffled a little and wiped her eyes again. She let go of my hand and opened the door of the truck and climbed out. I was next to her in a flash.

We were seated at a table for two that was lit by a couple of candles. The room was fairly dark, most of the lights were turned down and there was music playing softly in the background. We were the only patrons; all the other tables and chairs had been removed. Once the wine had been poured and the food ordered, we began to talk quietly.

"How did you know I like Italian food?"

"Your father told me."

"When did he tell you this?" she asked.

"When he came out to visit you and the grand-kids. He and I had a long talk before he left."

"Not about me I hope."

"Not all about you, there were other things he and I needed to talk about."

"Now you have me worried," she said.

"It was nothing really. I just wanted to know some things about you but didn't want you to know what I was up to."

"What exactly are you up to?" worry creeping into her voice.

"I wanted to show you a nice time and I needed some details. He helped me out. I thought that after all the hard work that we have put in over the last couple of months a nice night on the town was called for. We haven't been on an honest-to-God date and I wanted to get it right," I said. She blew out the breath that she had been holding.

"Well, so far so good!" she said with a wink.

"What did you think was going on?"

"I thought you were going to pop the question or something stupid like that!"

"Lord no!" I laughed. "I just wanted to give you a nice night but didn't know what kind of food you really liked," by now she was laughing too, as relief flooded across her face. While we never really discussed anything that serious as far as relationships went, it was pretty much understood that neither of us were ready to get married. We did enjoy hanging out with each other and had made out in the hot tub or on the couch more times than either of us could count, we just weren't ready to go the marriage route.

After dinner, she and I enjoyed some slow dancing in the empty restaurant. That was exactly why I had asked the owner to remove all the furniture and that was why I had asked him to play slow music for our visit. Jill didn't know it, but I had also contacted the owner a couple of weeks before our date and made him a deal. I doubled what his normal take would have been on a Friday night so that he would close the place. Jill and I were his only customers for the night.

I had also contacted the local movie theater and made a deal with them. I had rented one of their theaters and had arranged to have a midnight showing of African Queen. Jill and I were the only people in the theater for a private showing. It

THE RANCH

was perfect. The movie let out at 1:45 in the morning and we drove back home. I parked in the circle in front of our house and we both went inside. The entire drive back, Jill kept telling me how much she enjoyed herself and thanked me profusely for the evening. When we left the theater, she had slid from her passenger seat to the middle of the bench seat and sat really close to me. Two months ago, it would have been awkward, now it seemed totally normal.

Mark was sitting on the couch reading a book. He had the graveyard shift on my nights off. The security PDA and radio were on the couch next to him. He looked up at us and glanced at his watch. "You kids have any idea what time it is?" he asked with a mock scowl on his face.

"As a matter of fact, big brother, we do!" Jill proudly announced and tussled his hair as we walked by. He laughed and went back to his book. We walked down the hallway toward the stairs and my bedroom door. Jill was leading the way and she stopped at my door. She turned around and looked at me. I wasn't sure what to do or where this was going but my heart was racing. Jill took a step toward me and used her body to push me back against the wall. She planted a passionate kiss right on my lips and we stayed that way for what felt like a very long time.

Her arms were around my neck and I was firmly pinned between her and the wall. When her lips left mine, she buried her face in my neck. I could feel her ragged breathing as she nibbled on my ear. I felt one of her hands leave my neck and reach for the doorknob that was right next to us. Then I heard the door open and I was sure she could hear my heart beating. I know I could. She put her lips to my ear and whispered.

"The only thing you get on a first date is a kiss," she nibbled my ear for a second longer and then backed away. She turned sharply and went upstairs, never once looking back. I sagged against the wall trying to calm my heart rate and catch my breath. I heard the door upstairs close and then there was a roar of laughter from the living room. Mark had watched the whole thing.

"Damn man, that was hard to watch! It was like a train wreck in slow motion!" he chuckled some more. "Want me to get you an ice pack for that bruised ego?" he burst into laughter. I shook my head and shot him the bird. All that did was make him laugh harder. It was infectious because I was laughing too, by the time I got inside my room and closed the door. I was quickly asleep after climbing into bed. It had been a long day.

After the sultry kiss in the hallway, things were back to normal the very next morning, like it never happened. Neither of us had to say anything about that first date but I'm sure that Jill felt the subtle shift in our relationship. I know that I did. Sadly, we would not be able to go another date until after Thanksgiving. She had classes scheduled, I had to pull extra shifts because of Mark's classes. To top it all off, Bill was coming to spend a week with us. We still made time and excuses just so we could hang out together. We just didn't have time to go to town for the evening and be home at a decent hour.

CHAPTER 6

Mark's December class went off without a hitch. He had just gotten back the morning of December 15th when I told him that he was going to have to pull extra shifts for a few days. Jill and I were going to see my brother and we would be leaving on the morning of the 17th. We had decided to take one of the Jeeps, it would be more comfortable for a long road trip. Neither of us wanted to be in the airports during the holiday rush. Besides, both of us had carry-on that would never be allowed on an airplane, even with our concealed-carry permits.

The weather had been cold but so far, the winter had proved to be another dry one, so I was not too worried about that for this trip. I was worried about the reception I would receive when we got to Hutchinson, Kansas. That was far more likely to be worse than any snowstorm.

I packed my bags and threw in the manila envelope that Bill had given me when he was up for Thanksgiving. I zipped it shut and took it out to the Jeep the night before. One less thing to worry about in the morning. I was heading back to the house when Mark waved me into the security shack. It was just past 8pm and all I really wanted to do was go to bed but I decided to see what he wanted. As I got closer, I could see that he urgently wanted me inside.

"Jason, you got to see this..." he ran back around to look at the computer monitor that had the cameras. "There is someone stand..... Wait, where the hell did he go?" he started switching from camera to camera, obviously looking for something.

"Settle down Mark, what did you see?" I asked.

"There was a guy at the front gate! I swear he was standing right there," he pointed at the screen.

"What did he look like?"

"Ummm, about my height, looked like a black jacket and pants. Hard to tell in the green of the night vision though. He had on a stocking cap, too. I couldn't see a whole lot of his face, it's too grainy in night mode," Mark explained.

"Lucky you spotted him at all, these things are a bitch at night," I said.

"He was smoking, the cherry on his cigarette looked like an atom bomb in the night lens. That's what caught my attention. He was right at the edge of the camera view."

"Okay, stay here, I'm going to get backup and then we will go look around," I said as I sprinted out the door and back to my house. I went upstairs and beat on both Jill and Allan's doors. Both answered their doors at almost the same time.

"Come on you two, we got someone sneaking around by gate one. I need backup to check it out!" I was already turning and heading back downstairs, Jill hot on my heels. Allan had to go back in his room to put shoes on. We burst into the shack and scared the hell out of Mark. He had been intently looking for the person he had seen, and I think he was a little spooked by it.

Jill bolted past me and started grabbing her gear, body armor included. She and I had all our gear on and were headed out the door in such a hurry we nearly plowed straight into Allan. Jill jumped into the passenger seat of the Jeep and I got behind the wheel. I fired it up and punched the gas. The big tires grabbed traction and we roared down the driveway. The 35" tires howled through each turn. We slid to a stop at the gate and both of us bailed out. She took up a position to the right of the gate and I took my position to the left. It was a drill we had practiced a million times. I called to the shack on my radio and was told that they had not seen anything moving and we could see nothing moving in the headlights of the Jeep. I told Mark to open the gate enough for us to get outside the wall.

The gate swung open about two feet and stopped. I went first with Jill covering me. Once I was clear of the gate Jill joined me on the outside. I gave her the hand signal to search the right side and I took the left. We went out about 100 feet but found no one. I was beginning to wonder if Mark was seeing things when my flashlight beam swept across a cigarette butt on the edge of the asphalt. Somebody had been here. A little more searching and I found three more butts crushed out in the dirt about 50 feet from the first one and ten feet from the road. I also found a set of boot prints. It was a full moon night and whoever it was could have been hiding just about anywhere in the shadows of the sagebrush. All I could do was hope we had scared them off. Jill and I worked our way back inside the gate and Mark closed it behind us. We got back in the Jeep and returned to the shack. When we went inside I could see that Dale had joined Mark and Allan.

"Report," was Allan's one word greeting.

"There was somebody out there," I stated. "We found a cigarette butt right where Mark said he saw the person standing. I found three more well out of camera range and found a set of fresh boot prints. They looked to be a military style sole," I paused long enough to pull my plate carrier off. "They wanted to be seen, Allan."

"What makes you say that?" he asked.

"He had a position outside of the camera that gave him a decent view of the houses. If he had binoculars, he would have had a great view. If I am right, he waited until Mark was done with his rounds and he knew he was sitting in here watching the cameras. When he realized that he did not have our attention, he lit that smoke, knowing that would do the trick."

"Who and why?" Mark asked.

"I don't have a clue, but they wanted to make a statement and boy did they." I stepped past everyone and went into the back room to put my gear away. When that was done, I returned to the front room and leaned against the wall. I was totally silent as Mark, Allan and Dale discussed what we should do. Jill was sitting on the corner of the desk watching me. I was lost in thought when I heard Jill's voice.

"Jason....JASON!" she said with her voice rising. "You okay over there?" She asked as I caught her gaze. It was then that I realized everyone was staring at me.

"Yeah, sorry about that. I was thinking..... Allan, when did you have these cameras installed?"

"That would have been 1997, why?"

"Shit..... How the hell did I miss that one? All right, here is the plan. Allan, bright and early tomorrow I want you on the horn and I want new cameras here and installed as soon as humanly possible. Good cameras, no cheap ass crap. I want night vision and thermal at all the gates and I want motion sensor lights at all the gates. The next thing I want you to do is upgrade this shack, get rid of these tiny monitors and plaster these walls with giant, high-definition monitors. Bring this place into the new millennia for hell's sake."

"Mark, I want you to find me some high-power spotlights that can be put on the walls and run by remote from in here. It's dark out there and I want to be able to make daylight. Dale, first thing when the sun comes up, I want you out there with the loader and I want all the brush cleared all the way around the compound, 100 feet minimum. Spend whatever you have to spend, make it happen," everyone was busy writing things down and nobody said anything for a few seconds. When nobody had any questions, I started for the door. Mark called after me before I could get out the door.

"Do you think they will be back tonight?" he asked

"I doubt it. They made their statement and left," I said and left the room. Jill was right behind me.

"Are we still leaving in the morning?" she asked.

"We sure are," I replied as we went into the house. I stopped in the living room and Jill nearly ran into me. I lifted my hand and it was shaking like crazy.

"Adrenaline dump," Jill said, staring at my hand. She held hers up and I could see it trembling, too. She looked up at me and smiled. "Nice job by the way. You nailed it just like we did in our training."

"Why thank you, ma'am," I said. She gave me a quick hug and headed up to her room. I went into the kitchen and got the bottle of Jack Daniels and a small glass. I poured about two fingers worth and returned the bottle to the cabinet. I went to the living room and sat on the couch. I tried to take a sip, but my hands were shaking so bad I almost spilled it. It was about ten minutes later when I heard Allan come through the front door.

"Don't you have to get up at the crack of dawn tomorrow?" he asked from behind me.

"Waiting for the adrenaline to settle down," I said.

"I bet, that had to be scary as hell. You and Jill did a fantastic job. You're a hell of a team, the two of you."

"We need better gear, Allan. We were going out there nearly blind and we shouldn't have to do that, not with our resources," I said, after finally getting a sip of whiskey down.

"Like what?" he asked.

"We need better radios and more of them. We lost a lot of time because I had to run over here and roust everyone out. We need earpieces and mics that are capable of voice operation. Military grade, helmet-mounted night vision would have been great out there. The night vision we have is antiquated and its stored downstairs, not where we need it."

"Well, I'm going shopping tomorrow so I'll see what I can do," he patted my shoulder and headed upstairs. I took my whiskey back to the kitchen and poured it down the sink, then I went to bed.

THE RANCH

The next morning, Jill and I were in the Jeep and on the road before dawn. It was just a shade over 1,200 miles to my brother's house. We had planned to be on the road for two days, spend a day talking to my brother, then two days back. We were planning on being back late on the 21st. We made it all the way to Ft. Collins, Colorado, the first day. The second day we pulled into Hutchinson late and got a room at one of the local motels. Our plan was to be at his little farm at 9am. It was a Saturday morning, so we fully expected to catch him at home. When Dale was staying here, he had a partner, a young man named Alex Perez. We met Alex for breakfast Saturday morning before our trip to my brother's farm.

Dale told me he was young and come to find out he had just turned 19. When Dale left here, he left one of our Jeeps in the young man's care. I was told that it was stored in his father's barn. We finished our breakfast and I told Alex to meet us back here for dinner at 5:00 and to bring his parents. We left the motel at 8:30 and made the short drive to my brother's place.

It had been 11 years since I had last been here. That trip ended in a shouting match between me and Braden that nearly came to blows. Hopefully both of us had matured a little since then. There was no gate on the driveway, so I just eased my way up the drive. As I came to a stop in front of the house, the front door opened, and my sister-in-law cautiously stepped out onto the covered porch. Jill and I opened the doors and got out of the Jeep.

"Oh my gosh! Jason!" Megan said as she bounded down the stairs. She nearly knocked me down when she gave me a hug. She was happy to see me and that was a start. "What are you doing here? Come in the house!!!!" it was all rapid fire in her excitement. She grabbed both Jill and me by the hand and led us into the house. She took our coats and motioned us to sit at the dining room table. Before I knew it, both of us had a cup of coffee in front of us.

"I know this big goon, but I don't believe we have ever met," she said to Jill. "I'm Megan."

"It's nice to meet you Megan, I'm Jill." Jill extended her hand but was quickly pulled out of her chair for a hug. After Jill had returned to her seat, I had to quickly redirect the conversation because I knew Megan would start digging to find out what our relationship was.

"I'm wondering Megan, is Braden around? I really need to talk to him, it's important and our time is short," I said.

"He took your nieces to a friend's house, he should be back any minute," she replied.

"How has he been?" I asked.

"He is doing okay. He has been working here and at the gas station, so he is tired but is in good spirits."

"And you, my lovely sister-in-law, how have you been?"

"I am doing really well. I got a teaching job at the high school. Been doing that for almost two years now," she beamed.

"Allison and Kalin? What are they now? Fourteen and 16?"

"Yes, they are and both of them are doing great......." she stopped when she heard a car door close out front. I heard the boot steps on the deck and the front door creak open. My heart pretty much stopped, and my blood iced over as my brother walked into the house.

"Megan! Whose Jeep is that?" he bellowed from the front room. I stood and stepped to where he could see me when he turned around.

"It's mine, brother," I said. Jill and Megan were silently looking back and forth to see what was going to happen next. He stood erect and still for a few seconds before he finished taking his coat off. He dropped it onto the back of a chair and slowly turned around.

"I thought I told you to never set foot on my property again," he said flatly as he walked into the kitchen.

"You know me, I don't listen for shit."

"No, you don't. I'll tell you right now if this has anything to do with dad, you can beat feet right on out of here. I told the ass that showed up here a few months ago the same thing," he said. I could see Jill tense up when he referred to her brother as an ass. To her credit she kept her cool.

"Actually, you and I have something to discuss. Give me 30 minutes, that's all I ask," I said. He stared at me, then at Jill. Then seeing the pleading in Megan's eyes, he finally looked back to me.

"Thirty minutes, start talking."

"Jill, could you run out to the Jeep and get the large envelope off the front seat for me please?" I asked. She nodded and quickly left to get it. "Braden, as you know, dad is gone. As you are also aware, he left his estate to our care....."

"I don't want anything that son of a bitch left me, I don't want his damned charity," he growled.

"Braden, it's a little more complicated than that. It's something that you need to see in person."

"And I'm telling you that I don't need to see shit. I have one farm that I'm trying to take care of. I don't need some damned ranch 1,200 miles away to worry about, too."

"Hear me out, Braden….." it was about then that Jill returned with the envelope. She returned to her seat. "I'm not here to try and tell you what to do. I am here to try and make some peace with you. I'm here to give you the chance to see what was given to us. If you want to be a part of it or if you want to tell me to pound sand, that's your call. I can't make it for you, but I can give you all of the information you need to make a good decision," he leaned back in his chair but didn't say anything.

I reached into the envelope and pulled both journals from it. I slid his across the table. He made no move to take it. "Jack wrote two journals. One for you and one for me. I have read mine from cover to cover at least two dozen times. I have not read yours. I'm going to leave both here with you," I slid my journal across the table, too. He eyed them suspiciously.

"I told you that I don't...." he started but I cut him off.

"Shut up and listen, you gave me 30 minutes and I don't want you wasting any of it!" he kept quiet but glared at me. I knew that there was no one who talked to him like that in his own house. "I am willing to pay for the four of you to fly out and spend three days with us and I am willing to fly you back home. All expenses paid. All you have to do is tell me when you want to come out. If after three days you still want to tell me to leave you alone, I will," I paused and took a sip of the coffee Megan had poured for us. Jill was surprisingly quiet and still. Braden's gaze had softened, if only slightly. I took a deep breath and began again.

"We don't owe each other a damn thing, Braden. The only thing you and I have in common is the blood in our veins. In the last few months, I have been very blessed. I also know that in the last few months you have had some hardships. Just as Jack wanted us to share in his legacy, I believe that I need to share my blessings with you and your family," I paused and slid the envelope across the table. "My phone number is on a note inside there. The other stuff in there is a gift to the four of you. There are no strings attached to any of this. I just want you to be able to make an informed decision. I hope I hear from you soon," I reached across the table. "But if I don't, I understand," he stared at my outstretched hand but did not take it.

I withdrew my hand and motioned Jill toward the door. I gave Megan a hug goodbye and asked her to wish my nieces well. We made our way to the Jeep and as I opened the driver's door, Braden burst from the house and ran toward us. Jill went into defense mode and so did I. I thought I was about to get my ass beat, again. He came up just short of me and stared me right in the eye. The papers from the envelope in his hand.

"Is this for real?" he demanded.

"It is and you will see that it is all in your name. Nobody has any claim except you," I told him. Megan was now standing behind him.

"What is it?" she asked. Braden was staring at me.

"No strings attached?" he asked.

"None. It's all yours."

"What is it?" Megan asked again. Braden passed the papers to her.

"It's the deed to the house and property," he said with a bit of quivering at the edge of his voice.

"Braden, it's a win for you and your family, take it. Please read both journals before you tell me to piss off. After you have read them, I'll accept whatever decision you come to," I said as I climbed into the Jeep. Jill quickly climbed in on her side. I could see that I had made my point. For the first time in a long time, he was speechless. Megan was standing there reading the paperwork and shaking like an aspen leaf. I started the Jeep and began to back out of the driveway. I heard Braden call my name and I stopped. As he approached, I rolled the window down. He extended his hand and I took it.

"Thank you," he simply said.

"Have a Merry Christmas," I told him. He released my hand and walked back to his wife. I backed out of the driveway and headed to town. The ride back was silent. With all the turmoil in my own mind, I could see that there was something on Jill's mind too. She just wasn't ready to spill it yet. I knew her well enough not to ask, she would tell me when she was ready. The meeting had not gone as well as I had hoped, but it also didn't go as bad as it could have. It could have ended in a fistfight in the driveway. I had to accept the fact that that might have been the last time I would ever see my brother.

Before I knew it we were back at the motel. It was only 10:30 in the morning, and I felt exhausted from all the tension leading up to today. If it weren't for the fact that we were supposed to meet with Alex, we could have just left and started for home. Once we were inside, I kicked off my boots and laid on the bed. Jill laid next to me with her hands clasped behind her head.

"You going to be okay?" she asked me.

"Eventually."

"You tried. You did more than most people would have. The ball is back in his court now."

"I know, I just hope it was enough. Hopefully he can let go of the past," I said.

"How long have they been married?"

"Nineteen years next month," I answered.

"Why haven't you ever gotten married?"

"Never found the right person I guess."

"Did you know that I almost got married?" she asked.

"Allan told me what happened."

"Can I tell you what happened?"

"Only if you want to, Jill."

"I want to...." she said. She spent the next hour telling me every detail of the night her life changed. She was on the verge of tears a couple of times but managed to hold it together. It was almost a clinical account of what happened. When she was done telling her story, she rolled over and put her head on my shoulder and her arm across my chest.

"Everyone said that I was pretty screwed up when I got to the ranch, and I was in bad shape. What no one seems to realize is that I'm still screwed up as far as my relationships go. That night made me who I am today. I lost the man who was the love of my life and the woman who loved me unconditionally. Love is like a foreign language to me now," she paused for a minute and I was beginning to think she had fallen asleep. "Until now I was beginning to think that it was a lost language, but you have me shown otherwise. You have taught me that it's okay to love again. That it's okay to have unconditional love and it's okay to be loved again," again she was quiet for a little while. "Jason?"

"Yes?"

"Do you think you could love the same person for the rest of your life?"

"Yes, I could," I answered.

"I think I could, too," she answered quietly. Then there was silence. About 20 minutes later I could feel her fall asleep in my arms. It felt as if another piece of my life had just fallen into place and I was okay with that.

We met with Alex again at 5:00. He brought his mom and dad as I had requested. It was my understanding that he had a younger sister, but she was at a high school football game. Once greetings were finished and we were all seated around the table, I started the serious part of the conversation.

"I'd like to thank you all for coming tonight. I felt it was important for you, as Alex's parents, to hear firsthand what I have to say. First, the Jeep that is in your barn, I would like Alex to have for all that he has done for my organization for the last two years," his mom and dad looked very confused. "You see, a colleague of mine recruited Alex to help him with some surveillance of a couple of people in this county. Nothing dangerous to be sure. The problem is that we have never compensated Alex properly and I hope the gift of the Jeep will take care of that," I reached in my back pocket and pulled out the folded title. I signed it right then and handed it to Alex. "The next thing I would like to do is to offer your son employment at my ranch in eastern Nevada. I have heard nothing but good about this young man's work ethic and I would be happy to offer him gainful employment," Alex Sr. held up his hand and motioned me to stop.

"He hasn't been doing anything illegal on your behalf, has he?" he asked.

"Absolutely not. Everything was quite legal and, as I said, there was nothing dangerous about it," I reassured him.

"What kind of job are you talking about at this ranch of yours?"

"He would be hired as a greenhorn ranch hand which pays approximately $15,000 a year. He would have full medical and dental insurance and a nice place to live. He would have access to phone, internet, and would be allowed visitors at any time. The job would consist of working with our animals and various construction projects on the property. We have a 100 head of cattle, horses, pigs, chickens and a huge farm plot that we will be planting in the spring. Believe me sir, I know the starting pay is not great, but we have an unbeatable benefits package, and your son will be charged nothing to stay at the ranch."

"I don't know...." the senior Alex stated.

"Sir, if I may, I would love to have you and your family come visit us at the ranch. I offer to pay all of your travel expenses if you will just come take a look around," I was doing everything I could to make this happen. I really needed younger hands at the ranch and Alex was the perfect candidate.

"Can we have a little time to think about this?" he asked.

"You bet, take as much time as you need. For now, enjoy your dinner," once dinner was over, I picked up the bill and wished Alex and his family well. I gave his father a business card with my phone number on it, then Jill and I went back to the motel room.

Jill curled up with me in my bed and for the very first time, we spent the entire night in the same bed. Nothing sexual happened but it still felt as right as anything ever had. Both of us slept well. Neither of us mentioned it in the morning and were on the road at 5am sharp. When we stopped for the night, we again slept in the same bed and again nothing happened, but both of us were completely at ease with it.

For the most part we rode in silence on the way back. Both of us enjoyed the scenery, the nice weather and the music on the stereo. We did talk, but it was never about anything important, it was just conversation. We were about halfway between Salt Lake City and Wendover when Jill reached over and turned the music down.

"Can I ask you a question, Jason?"

"Absolutely."

"Well, it's kinda personal. Are you sure?" she asked timidly.

"Jill, you can ask me anything," I reassured her.

"The other night, when we were in Hutchinson, I asked you why you had never married, and you said that you hadn't found the right person. Isn't that what you said?"

"That's right."

"Can I ask what the right person would be like?"

"Well, uh...."

"You don't have to answer if you don't want to, I'm just curious is all," she said. I had to admit; the question did catch me off-guard.

"You want an honest answer?" I asked.

"Yes, I do, I want to know what you find attractive in a perspective mate. I know that you dated a lot up until a couple of years ago, but you never stuck with the same girl for more than a month or two, why?"

"Oh boy," I said with a chuckle. "I forgot all about you knowing just about everything about me!" now I was laughing. "The honest answer is that I didn't really know what I wanted, but the girls I dated definitely didn't fit the bill."

"What do you mean?"

"I like strong, intelligent, independent, sexy, beautiful women Jill, but I never did find a woman with all of those traits when I lived in Reno. If I was lucky, I could get three or four out of the five but never all of them in the same person," I said, feeling a little awkward. She didn't say anything for a few miles, she just looked out the window.

"Is that why you gave up on dating? Couldn't find what you wanted?" she finally asked.

"That's a big part of it, I just got sick and tired of all the games and drama," I answered. "I just couldn't see the point in wasting everyone's time anymore."

"I see...."

"Jill, I dated a lot of women. A LOT of women. I remained friends with most of them because they were good people, they just weren't what I was looking for. I really hope that you don't think less of me for that."

"I don't think less of you, not at all. You were aggressive when it came to finding what you wanted and you weren't willing to settle, I can respect that. But......." her voice trailed off.

"But what?" I asked.

"It's just that the two of us have spent a lot of time together. We have slept in the same bed, we have made out like a couple of teenagers more times than I can count, but we have never gone past that and I'm beginning to wonder if you're not attracted to me......"

"Let me be clear, Jill," I interrupted. "I am very, very attracted to you. You are everything that I have ever wanted and more. Out of respect for you, I have chosen to go slow, to let you take the lead. The last thing I want is to go too far too fast. I never, ever want to hurt you," I said. She was silent for a few more miles.

"The night that you took me out on that wonderful date, remember what happened in the hallway after we got home?"

"How could I forget?" I said with a smile.

"Jason, I really wanted to take it to the next level that night, but I got scared at the last minute, absolutely terrified," she admitted.

THE RANCH

"Don't feel bad about the way that it went; I was terrified too. Even with the way the date ended, I was as happy as any person could be. I had a great night."

"That's just it, I had a wonderful time with a fantastic person. I really wanted to shove you into your room and have my way with you!" she said with a coy smile. "It's just that I didn't want to….." her voice trailed off again. She was silent for a couple of minutes while she stared out the window again. "I didn't want to dishonor Josh's memory," she finally said quietly.

"Can I ask what you mean by that?" I asked.

"You said that Allan told you about what happened between me and Walter the night he kicked in my door and we had it out, right?"

"Yeah."

"Did he tell you what Walter told me after we came downstairs?"

"He said that he didn't hear what he told you."

"I have always wondered if he did or not, I guess now I know. Walter told me that it was time to get up. When life kicks your ass and beats you to the ground, the only thing left to do is get back up. He told me to never be a victim again, he told me to take the tragedy and turn it into something that honored those that lost their lives that night. He told me to bottle up all the rage, guilt, fear and terror and to learn to control it and call on it when I needed it. He taught me how to do that. He also told me that the grief would never go away, it would be with me forever and instead of letting it eat me up, I needed to let it fuel me. Everyone else told me to let it go, to be free of it. That never worked. They never gave me the tools that I needed to cope. He did. He also told me that if I were ever in that type of situation again, to pop the cork on that bottle and fight. Use the rage and fight. That's why I train the way I do, that's why I always have a gun, that's why I don't let many people see my soft side."

"I don't want to get attached to anybody. I'm afraid that I'll lose that person and that rage will come out with a vengeance," she paused and took a deep breath. When she let it out, she began to speak again. "Jason, I'm falling for you and I'm afraid that something will happen, and I'll lose you. You have brought back feelings that I have not felt for anyone in a very, very long time. That scares the hell out of me! The thought of losing you terrifies me and has been the cause for some bad dreams and sleepless nights."

"I gotta be honest with you Jill, I'm not falling for you. I've done fallen already. I told you that I couldn't find what I was looking for in a woman in Reno.

The truth is that I had to move to a ranch in Elko to find everything in one beautiful package. I find you very attractive and if you had pushed me into my room and had your way with me, I wouldn't have stopped you. Like I said, you are the one setting the pace here," I glanced over at her and those eyes were fixated on me.

"I also gotta tell you that none of us get to choose when our number is up. A meteor could fall out of the sky right now, come through this windshield and kill me dead or I could live to the ripe old age of 120. We don't get to choose. What we do get to choose is how we use the time we have been given. You have chosen to bury yourself in your work and training because that's what you're comfortable with, that's something you can control. You're scared because of something that might happen, and sooner or later, it will happen. Don't cheat yourself out of the joy, the fun and the happiness because you fear the inevitable. You also need to honor those lost in the past by living life, by creating yourself a future. Isn't that what the ranch is all about? Isn't it about creating a future and enjoying the present? The ranch is there for us to enjoy and nurture because of the sacrifices made in the past. The ranch is all about second chances. It's been a second chance for me. Take advantage of the second chance that it has given you, Jill," I finished. I feared that I might have made her mad or embarrassed her because she was quiet for so long.

"Are you really interested in me?" she finally asked.

"Jill, I am very interested in you."

"Even if I have a lot of emotional baggage? Seriously Jason, most guys would think I'm damaged goods."

"Jill, you have scars. Scars mean that you have lived to tell about something. I like your scars because they have made you who you are. They have turned you into the woman that I have fallen head over heels for," I said. Again, she was quiet for several miles before she spoke.

"Thank you, Jason," was finally her response. She reached over and turned the radio back up. Her mood seemed better and I know mine was. I had finally gotten my feelings for her off my chest and I now understood why she had been so skittish every time we came close to crossing the line to intimacy. It all made perfect sense now. It still changed nothing in the way I felt about her taking the lead in the romance department. If anything, that was even more important now.

We didn't get back to the ranch until almost midnight that night. As I pulled up to the gate, a bright spotlight came on and illuminated the whole area. I could see that Dale had cleared a large swath of sagebrush down to bare dirt. We sat for a moment and the gate opened. We proceeded up the drive and parked in front of our house. Mark greeted us. He was sporting a new radio on his belt and I could see his earpiece. It made me feel good that they had jumped on board with the new security protocols. Things were coming along nicely.

Jill led the way into the house and when we got to my door she stopped and turned to face me. She gave me a long, passionate kiss on the lips, her embrace tighter than I could ever remember. Once she released me she stared into my eyes. There was a playfulness there that I had not seen before. Without saying a word, she took me by the hand and led me slowly up the stairs to her room. The lights were left off and once she closed the door, I heard the click of the lock. We shared another long and a sultry kiss. I could hear the quickening of her soft, warm breath on my neck. She pushed the jacket from my shoulders and pulled my shirt up over my head. We moved slowly, savoring every moment when another piece of clothing fell to the floor. There was no hurry as we took time to explore each other's bodies and we were both fearless that night.

CHAPTER 7

After that night, Jill and I moved into the same room upstairs. We had become very, very close and had officially become the new couple at the ranch. Both of us were very happy with the new arrangements and even her family was accepting. That was one of her concerns and it proved to be a non-issue. She continued to run her classes through the winter for police departments across the country. The reviews were outstanding, and her school was highly recommended.

The new security measures were all in place by the end of December and we had not had any more issues with people lurking outside the wall. Allan was drawing up plans for a new security shack because we were outgrowing the one we had. Come spring we were going to start having lumber shipped in and we were going to pull the sawmill equipment out to build it. The school that Mark was running was so booked up that the poor guy was barely ever home. He had a student that proved to be a fantastic prodigy and by February the ranch had a new resident. Thirty-one-year-old Mike Taylor joined the crew and became Mark's right-hand man.

By the end of March, I still had not heard from Braden. Alex and his parents had come out and liked what they saw, he was allowed to stay on at the ranch. On April 19th I turned 39 years old and we had a big birthday bash. The ten of us that lived at the ranch were there, Bill came up from Reno, and Doc Williams was also there. Everyone was a little shocked when the other Doctor Williams showed up all the way from San Francisco. It had been nearly six years since Samantha Williams had been to the ranch. Her father, Tim, couldn't have been happier to see her. Even Sheriff Case showed up. There was a huge bonfire and we had a little bit of dancing in the grass and a lot of alcohol was flowing. Mark and Dale were probably the only ones who were completely sober because they had guard duty. It was about 9pm when Mark found me slow dancing with Jill.

"Sorry to interrupt, you got a phone call in the guard shack."

"Who is it?" I asked

"Didn't get his name, sorry," he said sheepishly. I excused myself and walked to the guard shack with him. We went inside and I picked up the phone.

"Jason," I answered.

"Happy birthday baby brother," Braden said from 1,200 miles away. I was totally speechless, my heart felt like it was in my throat.

"Braden..." I said, just above a whisper.

"I got the birthday card you sent me, thank you. I have been thinking about what you said, and I have gone through both journals that you left me. We need to talk," he said.

"Whenever you are ready, I can fly all of you out here."

"Can you fly us out there on the 29th of this month? I know its short notice, but we really need to talk in person," he said.

"We'll make it happen!" I said. "I'll have all the flight information for you tomorrow."

"Okay, just let me know and we will come see this spread you got out there," he paused for a second. "Jason, thank you for giving me this chance."

"I would do it again if I had to," I told him.

"I know you would. I got to get off here, let me know about the flight tomorrow?"

"I'll talk to you later," I said and hung up. That was about the fastest I've ever sobered up.

"Everything okay?" Mark asked from behind the desk.

"It's great!" I said and trotted out the door. The next morning, Allan made all the arrangements to fly Braden and his family out at the end of the month. I called him a little after lunch and gave him all the details. We talked for a few minutes but kept it short. There was something on his mind, serious enough to make him come all the way here.

I worked it out with Dale so that they could stay at his house for their visit. It was starting to get crowded around here I mused to myself. I would have to bring it up to Allan and see about constructing more residential buildings. Not everyone wanted to stay in the barracks like Mark, Alex and Mike. It had become known as the bachelor pad by most of us.

I was riding on cloud nine. My brother was finally going to come to the ranch, Jill and I were getting along better than ever, the changes at the ranch were well underway, and the dire financial straits we were in six months ago had passed without incident. Things were looking up. It was the day before Braden's arrival, and I was keeping myself busy with small tasks. I was helping Dale in the greenhouses and learning how to use a horse team to plow the fields. It was almost four in the afternoon when Jill drove up in one of the Jeeps. She climbed out and judging by her pace, something was wrong.

"Hey, I need you to come take a look at something," she said quietly.

"What's wrong?" I asked.

"I just need you to come with me, now, please," she insisted. I put my work gloves down and yelled to Dale that I would be back in a little bit. I climbed into the Jeep and Jill made a beeline for the front gate. She stopped short and got out. I followed her and she led me outside the wall. At the very edge of the cleared area she stopped and pointed at the ground. I kneeled and inspected the boot prints in the soft dirt.

"These look like the same boots from December," I said, out loud.

"Yeah, I tracked them all the way back to the main road. I also found several cigarette butts along the way."

"All right, we are going to have to change it up for a little while. Let's go back to the shack and reset the cameras. Whoever this is does not want to be seen, they just want to rattle our cage," I said as I stood up.

"Jason, that's not everything," Jill said coldly.

"There's more?" I asked.

"Let's go," she said and turned back to the gate and Jeep. Once we were in the Jeep she headed for the shoot house. "They left a message this time. A very clear message," within minutes we arrived at the range and on the side of the building someone had spray painted huge letters, "BITCH!" My blood ran cold. Jill stopped the Jeep and started to get out.

"Stay in the car," I said, as I opened my door and got out. She started to protest but I shot her a look that told her there was no conversation to be had about the subject. She pulled her door closed and sat behind the wheel with the engine running. I approached the wall and could see the same boot prints from the front gate. I checked the doors and they were all locked. I couldn't find any prints near the doors. They were concentrated around the graffiti. I got back in the Jeep and told Jill to take me back to the shack. I asked her who was on day shift today and she confirmed that Alex was. She also told me that Alex confirmed that the building was clean when he made his round at 10:00 that morning. Whoever had done this had done it in broad daylight.

"How is your acting?" I asked her. She glanced over at me like I had lost my mind.

"Why?"

"Make it look like we are fighting when we get back to the shack, flail your arms, throw your hat on the ground and stomp off toward the house kind of thing. Can you do that?"

"Car fight kind of argument?" she asked. I chuckled.

"Sure, why not?" I'd barely had the words out of my mouth when she slammed the Jeep into second and floored it.

"Everybody drives crazy in a car fight!" she grinned. "What are we fighting about?"

"Does it matter? I just need it to be believable."

"Of course, it matters!"

"I forgot to put the toilet seat back down! I don't care just, make it look good," I said, as we approached the circle way too fast. She quickly scuffed off the speed and slid to a stop.

"Show time!" she said as she threw her door open and jumped out. It had to be a comical sight for anyone within earshot. Both of us acting out an argument over a toilet seat being left up. It ended when she threw the keys at me, followed in quick succession by her baseball cap. She shot me the finger and stomped off to the house. I shot the finger back and went into the guard shack.

I threw the door open and stomped inside, quickly pulling the door shut behind me. Mark was sitting at the desk with his eyes wide. It dawned on me that he had seen the whole thing on the CCTV system.

"Don't worry man, it was all an act," I told him.

"Huh," was all he could get out.

"Your sister and I are fine; we were putting on an act. Listen to me, I need you to spread the word, quietly, that we are having an emergency meeting at 8pm tonight in the conference room of barracks one. Tell everyone to use the underground passages to get there and back. I don't want whoever is watching us to know what we are up to."

"Okay boss, I'll get it done. Everything's okay though?" he asked.

"Jill and me? Everything is fine, relax," I laughed a little. I grabbed ahold of the doorknob. Put a scowl on my face and stomped back outside. I picked Jill's hat up and threw it in the Jeep, then I slammed the door that she had left open. I stomped my way to the house and went inside. Jill was waiting for me by the couch.

"We just about gave your brother a heart attack," I laughed as I took my hat off and sat on the couch. Jill sat next to me.

"What the hell is going on out there, Jason, this has me more than a little worried," she said.

"I don't know babe, but we will get to the bottom of it. I have called an emergency meeting tonight. I told Mark to get everyone to the conference room in barracks one at eight tonight. We need to take some precautions."

"Okay. I just don't know who I might have pissed off bad enough to pull this kind of shit..." her voice trailed off.

"Run upstairs and get a shower, get out of that uniform and relax a little. Inside these walls you are safe, and I'll make sure you are safe outside the walls, too," I said as I took her face in my hands and kissed her forehead.

"Since it's you telling me, I'll believe it," she said as she stood up. She turned and headed upstairs. I went to the kitchen and got dinner started for the house and I made Jill a cup of her favorite tea, Chamomile. When I took it up to her, she was already out of the shower and drying her hair in the bathroom. I set it on the counter and noticed that her Glock was also on the counter.

"Dinner is in the oven, it will be ready in about an hour," I said as I left the room and went back downstairs. I found Allan sitting at the dining room table.

"Do you want to fill me in on everything that happened today?" he asked. "Mark knew a little bit but I figured I should probably get it from you," I spent the next ten minutes telling him about what we had seen outside the wall and at the range.

"Obviously we need to get some security on Jill. She may be the primary target, but we cannot rule out the possibility of a ruse. Everyone here could be a target. Sheriff Case gets in at 7am, right?" I asked.

"Yeah."

"I want you standing in his doorway when he gets there. File a report and let him know who my prime suspect is. Ask him if he could beef up patrols out this way after dark, too," I said.

"Who is your suspect?"

"Marvin."

"Oh shit, that's right! I had forgotten about that asshole," Allan said. "You know, Jason, we could move Jill into the underground until this blows over."

"She would go ape-shit if we even tried to put her down there and you know it."

"Just remember that it may come to that if we can't get this nailed down soon."

"It's not going to come to that. I am positive that we will have a plan tonight, we will catch whoever is doing this. Whoever it is has patience, we must have more," an hour later the three of us had dinner. When the dishes were done, Jill and I went upstairs to talk. I could tell she needed to vent. I sat on the edge of the bed and she started pacing the floor.

"This shit is really pissing me off!" she started. "I feel like I should be out there, I should be tracking down this asshole and putting my size eight combat boot right up his ass! I'm the Chief of Security! Why the hell am I hiding in here with my damn panties in a knot?" at this point I knew that it was best to let her run with it. "I got some prick running around out there who thinks he can bully me, SCREW THAT! He set foot on MY property, MY PROPERTY! He is playing on my turf and I ain't putting up with that shit!" her pacing was reaching a frenzy, and she was flailing her arms. From the outside it might have been comical to watch. "I'm putting my foot down tonight! I don't give a damn how many extra shifts people have to work; we are going to catch this bastard at his own game. I've had enough pussy footing around!" she stopped and looked at me. "What the hell are you smiling about?" I didn't even realize that I was.

"You're going to wear a hole in the floor if you keep up that pace," I grinned even more.

"I think better on my feet so piss off," she said with a smile. "Come on, I need to get the conference room. I need the white board" she grabbed my hand and led me to the basement and to the conference room. We were the first ones there. She went straight to the board and started drawing a rough map of the compound. I sat at the head of the table.

"When we're in here, that's my chair," she said without even looking in my direction. I got up and moved to the other end of the table. She was still scribbling on the board when everyone else started filing in. Everyone had been seated in silence for nearly five minutes before she put the pen down and turned around.

"Here's our plan. From here on out, no one and I mean no one goes outside the wall by themselves. Minimum of a pair, preferably three or more. No one goes outside the wall without body armor, soft armor under clothes is fine, but I would prefer hard plates. If you must go to town, you do it in pairs and you do it armed. That goes for everyone, no exceptions. Does everyone understand?" her question was met with nods. "Next, starting tonight I want all of the wall cameras in search mode, not stationary. Tomorrow I want someone here to order me about 20 game cameras with the ability to take pictures in the dark with no flashbulbs. I also want three remote-controlled drones with cameras on-board. I need the best money can buy because I need something with some range. We're getting an Air Force!"

"Mark, put together a new roster that puts two people on duty at all times. If we have people that need to be trained, train them. For right now, security just became the number one priority around here. If you have other duties, you will take care of them after your shift or you will train someone else to help you. Every house will have a radio in it and if you are on the property, you will always have a radio on you. Am I clear on all my instructions? If there are any questions, ask them now because you will not have the time to do it later."

There were no questions except technical questions about the drones and the new duty roster. Everyone was told to be at the security office at eight in the morning so they could get their soft body armor and their sidearm if they needed one. She dismissed the meeting, but you could tell she was still fired up. She and I were still in the conference room and she was going over the map she had drawn. She picked up the pen again and drew in the roads outside the wall, then she drew in the shooting range. Next, she put stars where the wall cameras were located and drew a cone to show their field of view.

"SHIT!" she blurted out.

"What is it?"

"Right there!" she pointed to a spot on the map between the range and gate two. "There is a culvert that runs under the road, that's how he avoided the camera! Look here, too," she pointed to a place near the front gate. "There is a culvert here, too. We put them in three years ago because every time it rained the road would wash out. He used them and the wash to avoid the cameras. If he crouched down, he could traverse the entire front of the compound and never be seen by the camera. Clever bastard!"

"So, what do we do about it?" I asked.

"We sneak out there under the cover of darkness and install some game cameras after they get here."

"When do you want to do it?"

"We wait until there is no moon and we put the new NVGs (Night Vision Goggles) to use. I don't think this guy has night vision capability. Every time he has struck has been during a full moon and now in the daylight."

"You're the boss when it comes to this stuff," I said. She put the pen down again and smiled at me.

"Why were we fighting earlier?" she asked.

"I wanted to see if word got around. If it does, we will know that we are being watched and we might be able to find out who told who what. People in town know us and if there is gossip to be had, they love to spread it."

"Smart," she took my hand in hers and smiled seductively at me. "Do we get to have make-up sex then?" I felt my face instantly turn red. She could still catch me off-guard.

Friday, April 29, 2016

Jill and I were both up at 4am and in the gym by 4:30. After a 90-minute sparring session we hit the showers and started getting ready to leave to pick up Braden and his family. Per Jill's orders from the night before, both of us had soft armor on under light jackets. Instead of wearing the standard black fatigues, both of us opted for blue jeans and t-shirts. The big Sig Sauer pistol was hard to conceal so I opted for a small-of-the-back carry. If I didn't bend over or kneel, it would remain covered. Both of us were on high alert as we pulled through the gate and headed for town in my truck.

We arrived at the airport at 8:45 and waited in the parking lot until we could see the flight land. We went inside but stayed well away from the TSA goons. Within five minutes I spotted Braden and waved to him. Megan and the girls, Kalin and Allison, were right behind him. As he approached, I extended my hand and he took it and pulled me into a hug. He patted my back and I knew he felt the armor. He didn't say anything about it when he pulled away. Megan hugged both Jill and me, but if she felt it, she didn't say anything either.

None of them had any bags, just backpacks they used as carry-on, so we were back to the truck less than ten minutes after we had left it. Jill sat between Braden and me on the front seat and the three girls filled up the rear bench seat. They all seemed very happy to be here. We made small talk during the drive but when we turned off the main road, everyone fell silent. The front wall of the ranch loomed ahead of us. We pulled through the gate and wound our way up to the houses. Once we parked and everyone piled out of the truck, Braden was the first to speak.

"Damn little brother, I had no idea it was this big. What do you have here? Twenty acres?" I chuckled a little on the inside because it reminded me of the first conversation I had with Allan.

"There are 21 acres inside the wall, 3,000 outside of it." I said, Braden let out soft whistle. "Why don't we get you guys settled in and then we can relax a little, sound good?" I asked. Everyone agreed so I took them over to Dale's house. Jill had peeled off and slipped inside the security shack. Braden immediately recognized Dale as the guy who had tried to get him to come here almost a year earlier. He apologized profusely to Dale for the way he had treated him. I'm pretty sure he genuinely felt bad about it.

Dale showed everyone where they would be staying and before long his two boys were showing my nieces around the place. Jill had rejoined us as we were leaving Dale's. We went to our house and milled around in the kitchen. Both Braden and Megan were in awe of the main cabins. Their house in Kansas would nearly fit in the living room of this house. Jill and Megan excused themselves and went outside. That left Braden and me alone for the first time in a very long time.

"I had no idea this place was this big," he said again.

"Don't feel bad, I didn't either. I had no idea any of this existed. I figured Jack was destitute somewhere and they wanted money for his burial or something. All of this blew my mind."

"No one ever told me, how did he die?" Braden asked.

"The small plane he was flying went down in bad weather off the coast of Honduras. Parts of the plane were found but they never recovered his body."

"I see," was Braden's reply.

"You have something on your mind Braden, I hear it in your voice now and I heard it in your voice when you called me on my birthday. What's up?" I asked.

"You gave me both journals for a reason, didn't you?" this time a smile cracked his face.

"Yes, I did."

"Then you know about the code on the margins of the pages, right?"

"Again, yes. I swear to you that I did not read your journal, I only copied the code off the pages."

"It's all good," he chuckled a little.

"Were you able to decode any of it?" I asked.

"As of now, a little, but I have a theory about the rest of it," he said as he pulled a folded piece of paper from his pocket. It was almost identical to the notes I had taken a couple of months earlier. "This was my first attempt at getting it all on paper. It is just a string of numbers. I tried the alphabet to number conversion but quickly got nowhere. I was pissed so I put it down and didn't pick it up again for a couple of weeks. Then I rewrote it. I used the three sets of numbers and added commas to separate the groups of numbers. Each page only had a set of three numbers, right?" he asked, I nodded. "I still wasn't getting anywhere so naturally I put it down again. I got on the internet and started reading about different codes and how they used different ciphers to encode and decode them. One type of code stuck in my head, so I decided to try it out."

"The way the code works is that each end user has the exact same copy of a book. I send you a code that looks like this," he wrote down the numbers 39,12,3. "When you receive the message, you go to the agreed upon book, turn to page 39, go to line 12 and finally word 3. You can go even further and instead of word 3 you can add another number to the sequence, say 4. That would then make it word 3, letter 4. See where I'm going with this?"

"Yeah, I do."

"The problem I have is that I believe that my half of the code is in your journal. I know your half is in mine. I was able to decode the words from your code, but it is still gibberish without my half of the code," he slipped both journals out of his back pocket and slid mine across the table to me. "Shall we do this little brother?"

For the next hour we sat at the table and decoded the message, one word at a time. Finally, both of us leaned back from the table. Braden was right in his assumption that his numbers were coded from my journal and mine from his. It was rather ingenious for a one-time cipher. However, it also meant that there was a cipher to discover to decode the rest of the journals.

"Do you want to read the whole thing out loud or do you want me to do it?" he asked.

"You figured it out, you read it," I told him as I pushed the paper toward him. He picked it up and cleared his throat and began to read.

"I always knew you boys were pretty smart. Together you solved this puzzle. If you two work together there is nothing you cannot accomplish. I am sorry that

I could not be there to share in this moment with you. Trust those around you, they are very honorable people and would go to the ends of the earth for you. This ranch is yours to run now. It has many secrets and you may never discover all of them. Some of those secrets are known only to me, not even my most trusted advisers know about them."

"You have been given a great opportunity. Don't blow it. Seek the Family Crest. I love you boys more than you will ever know and I am sorry for everything that has happened. Please, forgive me. If you are reading this, it means that I am probably dead. I pray that you two can work out your differences and come together for the first time in a very long time. If you can do that, this ranch can be a comfortable home for the generations to come. The way it was meant to be. Do not blame each other for the past, instead look to the future together," he finished. We both sat in silence for a couple of minutes before Braden spoke.

"What secrets is he talking about?"

"If I show you what I know, I need you to promise me you will never tell anyone else."

"You have my word on it," he said cautiously. I picked my radio up off the table, holding eye contact with my brother.

"Jill, you got a copy?" I said into the microphone. She answered within seconds. "I need you to meet me at the security office, bring Megan with you please," she acknowledged, and I stood from the table and motioned Braden to follow me. We got to the security shack and had to wait about five minutes before Jill and Megan got there.

"Everything okay?" Dale asked from behind the desk.

"Yeah, everything is fine. I just need you to show these two the third part of the ranch," I said. I could see the concern on Dale's face. "Braden and Megan need to know everything that I know. I want them to make an informed decision just as I did. Show them everything."

"All right, you're the boss," he said. "If you would follow me please," the three of them went in the back room, leaving Jill and me in the front office. Once they had descended the stairs and the locker pulled back into place, Jill began to speak.

"You sure about this?"

"As sure as I can be. Come to the house with me, I have something to show you," I took her hand and together we went to the house. I showed her the code that we had deciphered. She read it repeatedly.

"Okay, I get that your father may have hidden some things from my dad and Allan, but what and where the hell would he hide it?" she asked, still staring at the paper. "And what is with the family crest? I have seen it before, years ago, but I'll be damned if I can remember where."

"Frustrating, right?" I asked her.

"I'm positive there is nothing hidden inside the wall and I'm pretty sure, 95 percent anyway, that there is nothing hidden outside of it either. I have hiked, hunted and ridden horses all over out there and never found anything."

"It would help if we knew what we were looking for. Is it the size of a matchbook or a battleship? I guess we will know it when we stumble across it," I said.

"I hope it's not a battleship, that would be a little hard to explain," she laughed. "I have to know..... How is your brother?"

"I'm still not sure all this is real. We have never gotten along, but something big has changed. Is it because we have gotten older and more mature? Is it because my father is gone? Because I paid off his house..... I just don't know. I'll tell you this though, I'm going to enjoy it while they are here. The last time I saw my nieces they were three and five. Now they are both teenagers. That's kind of hard to make peace with if you know what I mean."

"Take as much time as you can with them. Your sister-in-law is a pretty cool chick. At first I thought she was a flower power pansy, but boy was I wrong! She is just about as hardcore as I am!" she laughed. "Seriously, babe, spend as much time as you can with them. I know you have a partial shift tonight; I'll take it for you. Hang out and finish that bottle of scotch that you and Allan put a dent in. Tomorrow we can take the horses up to the meadow and have a picnic with them."

"You going to be up for that after being up most of the night?"

"Sure, I'll skip the gym and catch a good nap."

"Thank you, Jill, this means a lot to me," I said. We chatted for another half hour and then we started making sandwiches for lunch. Braden and Megan would be finishing their tour soon. We were just putting everything on the table when Dale escorted them back into the house. Both had the famous deer in the headlight look. I imagine that I looked very much the same on my first day here. I motioned for them to sit at the table after they had washed up. I sat in my spot and everyone assumed their chairs. I could see the annoyance on Jill's face but couldn't get the words out fast enough.

"Excuse me, Braden, your seat is at the other end of the table. Opposite but equal to Jason. Sterling's always sit at the ends," she said. I was trying to suppress a smile because I knew what was coming next.

"I'm just a guest......."

"You are a Sterling, sit your ass in that chair," it was at that point that I could no longer take it and burst out laughing. All eyes were on me now.

"Just sit, Braden, arguing with her will get you nowhere in a hurry. Megan, your seat is to his right. From what I have been told, there is a lot of tradition as to who sits where," he shrugged and sat at the opposite end of the table. Over the course of the next several hours, we had a conversation very much like the one I had with Allan on my first day. I was very pleased that both Braden and Megan were very inquisitive about all aspects of the ranch. When Megan asked about the body armor we were wearing at the airport, we told them the truth. There was nothing to be gained by trying to bullshit our way through it. We told them everything including all of the countermeasures we were implementing.

"Be honest Jason, what made you want to give everything up in Reno and move to the sticks of Elko?" Megan asked.

"Well, there were a couple of different things that brought me back here. In Reno I was comfortable with my life, but it struck me that I was content to live the rest of my life in a rut. I had no social life; I found the people un-interesting for the most part. I didn't like my job; I was just comfortable. The only thing I really liked was my truck and my annual vacations. I decided that was no way to live. That was no life. Out here I still have to work, but I enjoy the work and the people I work with. That's the long, politically correct answer," I told her.

"What's the short answer?" she asked.

"The short answer is that I have a case of the "hots" for Jill and it sounded like a lot of fun and a really cool place to live," I said.

"I did ask you to be honest," Megan chuckled. It was finally my turn to make Jill blush a little.

"What catastrophic events are you preparing for?" this was Braden. Jill took the question.

"It doesn't matter what boogie-man you prepare for, just be ready for whatever comes. Some people prepare for specific events. Financial collapse, pandemics, World War III, zombies, asteroid strike, whatever.... The result is always the same. You need food, water, and shelter. We have taken it to another level here, but the basics are covered. Now we are working on the ability to defend what we have from those who would wish to take it or harm us."

"Zombies? People really prepare for zombies?" Megan asked.

"It seems far-fetched on the surface, but what would happen if rabies went airborne and as easy to catch as the common cold. Poof, now you have a zombie starter kit. If you shoot them enough, they will go down, not like in the movies. You've seen what rabies does to an animal, what if that crazy squirrel were a human instead?" she said.

"That's nuts! What are the odds something like that could happen?"

"Very, very slim chance of it happening on its own, but you know how humans love to screw with stuff," it was that conversation that took us all the way to dinner. Jill had excused herself and thrown some burgers on the grill. Megan left just before six to go get Kalin and Allison. We were going to have a meal as a family for the first time in a very, very long time.

After dinner, everyone retired to the living room and we just kind of caught up on everything we had missed over the last decade. When Jill mentioned a picnic and horseback ride for the next day, the girls got excited about that. They thought that would be great. We agreed to meet at the security shack at nine the next morning. It was about a three-hour ride to the meadow. Instead of staying up and finishing off the scotch, everyone decided to retire for the night. I helped Jill clean up the kitchen, after which she kissed me goodnight and headed for the security shack. She would be sharing the duty with Mike Taylor. I went ahead and went to bed but left my radio on the nightstand with the volume all the way up.

Saturday, April 30, 2016

The following day we met at 9am as we had agreed the night before. I had the horses ready to go when everyone got there. Jill and Megan had prepared the lunch for the day and put it all in a backpack with plenty of bottled water. Jill took both Megan and Braden into the security shack and when they returned, they had gun belts on that matched ours. Jill also had a first aid pack strapped on.

"We have big cats that frequent the meadow and the highlands, better safe than sorry," I said, as I patted the gun on my hip. Once everyone was on the back of their horse, we headed out. The path was winding, and it did offer a nice view of a lot of the ranch property. At about the halfway point we stopped so everyone could stretch their legs. We arrived at the meadow at noon, just as we had planned. The entrance was on the south end and it opened to a short grass-filled meadow that was about 100 feet across and the length of a football field. There was a small creek that trickled through it in the spring and early summer months.

On the east side of the meadow was the cemetery. Walter and Jerry had plots there. My father also had a plot even though he was not buried there. There was a fourth plot and I had asked Jill about it the first time she had brought me here. She said that the legend was that it belonged to a miner that had died up here in 1911. After lunch, we explored the grounds around the meadow. It gave Megan and the girls a chance for some adventure and it gave Braden and me time to talk. Jill had to warn Kalin and Allison away from the caves that were on the west side of the meadow as that was where the mountain lions and bears hid during the day. Braden and I were sitting in the shade of a pine tree and taking it all in.

"Can I ask you something, Jason?" he asked.

"You can ask me anything."

"Why did you leave Hutchinson after you graduated?"

"Honestly? I left because of you. I hated living in your shadow."

"What?"

"Braden, you were the homecoming king, you were the all-star quarterback, and you dated all the hot chicks. There was no way I could compete with that. People always compared the two of us and I was always the geeky looser," I said as I watched my nieces picking wildflowers.

"Was it really that bad?"

"It was horrible. I just needed to get out of there and start a new life where no one knew who I was."

"I'm sorry, Jason, I had no idea it was that bad for you."

"I don't think anyone knew and if they did, they didn't care," I told him. He was quiet for a few minutes.

"What made you decide on Reno?" he asked. I chuckled a little.

"When I got to interstate 80 after leaving Hutchinson, I flipped a coin. Heads, I went west and tails, I went east."

"Are you serious?"

"Yep. I left the farm with $933. I put $100 aside for when I got to wherever I was going, and the rest went into gas and food for the trip. If I didn't have to replace that tire in Colorado, I probably would've made it to San Francisco."

"You seriously left home on a wing and a prayer? That's amazing. That took some balls!"

"Like I said, I had to get out of there and it didn't much matter where I went. I just had to go."

"Well, look at you now," he said with a smile. "You have done really well for yourself, even before you came out here. I'm proud of you brother," when he said that I damn near lost it. That was the first time he had ever said anything like that to me.

It was nearly four in the afternoon before we headed back to the compound. That was going to put us in just before dark and well after dinner. Jill had radioed ahead and told Allan that we would be late. After dinner, all the adults settled in the living room just like the night before. The kids had gone to Dale's house and gone to bed. All the fresh air had worn them out.

Megan and Braden were still asking detailed questions about the ranch which was good. My thought was that with the more they knew, the odds became better of them choosing to stay. That was the hope anyway. Neither Jill nor I had to stand a post tonight, so she pulled out the scotch and we let it flow freely. None of us were drunk but the booze helped loosen everyone up a bit. We spent the rest of the evening laughing and joking and getting to know each other on an informal level.

I learned that my gift to them back in December had been exactly what they needed at exactly the right time. Their little farm was on the verge of being taken by the bank. They had a couple of bad harvests and the bank was breathing down their necks. I discovered that they had assumed the payoff of their mortgage came from dad's estate. I didn't tell them that it came from my 401k. It really didn't make a difference to me, so long as they were out of hot water with the bank.

The bottle ran dry and all of us had decided to go to bed at about 12:30am. The next day was to be their last full day at the ranch. I was hoping that being open about everything would help them decide to come and live here. I would respect whatever decision they made. It would suck if they decided not to stay, but I would respect it. Before Jill and I drifted off to sleep, she suggested that we take them to the range in the morning and then to Hightower after lunch. I told her that sounded good. I also told her that I wanted to have a large dinner with everyone present, a big outdoor barbecue. She liked that idea.

THE RANCH

Sunday, May 1, 2016

The next morning after breakfast, all of us headed to the range for a couple of hours. Megan and Braden both proved to have an aptitude for weapons. They both had a lot of fun running both the indoor and outdoor ranges. After lunch we collected the girls and drove up to Hightower. I think they were as impressed with the view as I was the first time I went up there. I had noticed that Jill and Megan had become almost inseparable. I could tell that they had been talking about life here at the ranch. It was also apparent that Megan and Braden had been talking about it.

For the most part, the whole day was very relaxing and mellow. Allan tracked me down after we got back to the ranch and told me that he had heard back from Sheriff Case. Apparently, Marvin had an alibi for the time period around the last incident. He was in Reno and had the credit card receipts to prove it. Braden broke away from the rest of us and did the same thing I did on my last day here. He walked the entire grounds from the gate to the back wall. He joined us for dinner but was unusually quiet. It wasn't until after dinner when we were sitting in the lawn chairs on the front deck, that he started talking.

"Jason, I have a couple more questions for you," he said quietly.

"What's up?

"What happens to my farm if we decide to move here?"

"Keep it. Sell it. Rent it. It's entirely up to you," I told him.

"When do you have to have a decision?"

"There is no pressure, Braden. I brought you and your family here to see what was available to you. Nothing says I must have an answer right now or next year. I just want you to know it is here anytime you want it."

"What happens if we stay?" he asked.

"Well, we can find Megan a job with the school district if she wants it. The girls can go to school in Elko or they can be home schooled here. We put you to work with Dale on the farming end of things, again, if you want it. Everyone gets trained on the security of this place. Hopefully nothing bad ever happens and we live our lives out here quietly."

"If we don't stay?"

"Then life goes on. I hope you decide to return here. I need your Yin to my Yang, your black to my white. You and I have always been opposites and I need that balance. Just know that if you leave here in the morning and decide not to return, you will always have an open invitation to come back whenever you want. I will not close the door on you. Ever."

"I appreciate that." he said quietly.

"Braden, we lost a lot of time that we will never be able to make up. Whatever your decision, stay or go, I plan on doing everything I can to make that up. Of course, I hope you return but I'll understand if you decide not to. I want you to do what is right by you and your family. That's all that I can ask," I told him. He nodded but didn't say anything. We sat and enjoyed the evening for another hour. He never gave me any indication as to his decision.

CHAPTER 8

It was ten days after Braden left the ranch before I heard from him again. He told me that he was very interested in moving his family to the ranch, but he needed to wait until the end of the school year. The last day of school was June 17th. He had some things that he needed to tie up, much as I had to do, and they were planning on moving in by the middle of August. That news put me in a fantastic mood.

During the first week of May, things were going great. Loads of lodge pole pine started arriving and would be twice a day for the next two months. Not only were we going to construct a new, larger security shack, we were going to be building two new houses. They would not be as large as the main houses, but they would be large enough for a family of four to live in comfortably. All the things we would need to do the finish work were already ordered and due to be delivered at the end of May. All the plywood, steel roofing, T&G (tongue and groove) flooring, cabinets and appliances cost us a small fortune but I used the remainder of my 401k money for them.

Allan had pulled the mill equipment out and had been training Mark, Alex, Dale and Mike how to run it. He was also teaching them how to operate the earth moving equipment. They would form the basis of the new construction crew for the ranch. The solar system we had on-site was big enough to support the new construction and the water wells were also more than capable.

Pretty much every adult at the ranch was pulling double duty to cover the security shifts. Mark and Mike were trading off on the survival school, and there was at least one day a week that either Jill or I would pull a 36-hour day to make it work. Everyone was tired but we were making it work.

It was the first week in June when Bill Butler pulled in from Reno. With him came two new recruits. They had lived in Reno for about a year where they had moved from San Diego. Jake was a former Marine and Jessica had worked for Bill as a secretary. They didn't have any kids, so we put them in the downstairs bedroom of the house that Allan, Jill and I lived in. Both were well received, and they proved to be very hard workers.

It was our first dinner together in the house when Jake voiced his concern that he wouldn't be able to do as much as everyone else because his leg had been amputated below the knee. He had a good prosthetic, but he said that it did slow him down. Everyone reassured him that he would be fine and that it was not a problem for any of us.

Jill and Jessica quickly became best of friends and it didn't take Jill long to have her in the gym and on the range. By the end of their first week, Jill had her competent enough to stand a shift, and by mid-June, both had fully integrated into the day-to-day operations. Jake had become full-time security and being a former 0311 in the Corps, he adopted to it fast. Jessica was learning everything Dale knew about farming and when she wasn't doing that, she was with Susan training to be a medic.

By the first of July, the new security shack was up and running and the ground floors were constructed on the new homes. The construction crews had been working from sun-up 'till sun-down. The rest of us did everything we could do to support them. We made lunches and dinners. We took them ice water and made sure they had everything they needed to keep working.

The cattle drive was going to pull everyone from their projects and leave a skeleton crew to run the place but that was acceptable. We were going to have a big barbecue on Monday the 4th of July and set out to round up the cattle before dawn on the 5th. The only people that were not going to make the barbecue were Bill Butler and Doc Williams. Bill had work obligations and Doc Williams didn't want to come until Thursday when the cattle were due to arrive.

Monday, July 4, 2016

It was 9pm on July 4th, 2016 when our lives changed forever. I was sitting at a table with Jill, Jake and Jessica, when my radio roared to life. Alex was in the shack tonight and he was yelling at me to get there as fast as I could. I bolted from the table with Jill hot on my heels. I spotted Mike and Allan coming from the other side of the fire pit. I was nearly to the shack when the whole night sky lit up. I slid to a stop and looked up and slightly toward the east. There was a huge explosion in space. Jill couldn't stop fast enough and hit me at a dead run. Both of us crashed to the ground and laid there, stunned for a moment.

"What the hell was that?" Jill exclaimed. She was looking at the same place in the sky that I was. Neither of us had noticed that everything around us had gone dark. I was too stunned to answer; all I could do was stare at the fading explosion. Alex burst out of the shack yelling something, but I was in a state of shock and didn't hear his words. Jill and I were untangling ourselves when he reached down to help me up. I stared at him blankly for a few seconds when his words started to get through to me. It was like someone was slowly turning the volume up.

"WE ARE UNDER ATTACK!" were the first words I heard. My thoughts were finally starting to form about the time Allan arrived.

"Alex!" he shouted. "Sit-Rep right now!" Alex directed his attention to Allan. His eyes were wide, and his voice was shaky, but he began to deliver his situation report.

"I was watching the East Coast news and there was a live shot of Washington DC, there was a huge explosion. A second later the feed cut out. It looked like a nuke went off! I flipped to another channel and they said that a massive bomb went off in New York, that's when I called Jason on the radio!" he said breathlessly. His words were running together. By this time Jill was on her feet and helping me to mine. Allan put his radio to his mouth and pressed the transmit button.

"All security personnel to the security shack immed...." he stopped and looked at his radio when he realized the red "transmit" LED was not on. "Jill, give me your radio," he demanded. She picked it up off the ground and handed it to him. He keyed it up and the light failed to come on. "Shit," he muttered to himself. "Mark, go find all the security personnel and get them back here as fast as you can." Mark was gone into the dark in an instant.

"What's going on?" this was Jill asking.

"Too early to tell but I think we just got hit by an EMP," Allan said in a stone-cold voice. The shaking of his hands betrayed his calm demeanor. He pulled his cell phone from his pocket and pressed the buttons on the side of it and got no response. "Alex, I need you to settle down," he said as he returned the phone to his pocket. "I need you to go into the underground and check all of the comms equipment down there. Do not bring it up here, just check it to see if it works and report back to me."

"Yes, sir," he said and then he too was gone. Allan started for the shack, Jill and I quickly followed him. When we went through the front door, he pulled a flashlight from the charger on the wall. It came on when he clicked the button. He handed it to me and reached for another one.

"Jason, go to the storage lockers and pull out one of the propane lanterns and bring it back in here, we need to conserve battery power for now," I did as instructed and returned a moment later with the lantern hissing away and lighting up the whole room. Allan took it from me and set it on the desk. Neither Jill nor I had much to say at this point. We were still in shock. Allan had made himself busy with a thick binder that he had pulled from the desk drawer. It felt like forever, but the other security personnel started showing up. Once all nine of us were present, Allan closed the binder and cleared his throat to quiet everyone down.

"I need everyone to settle the hell down and get your head in the game. We have trained for this and we have the ability to overcome it!" he started. "From what I can tell we have been hit with an EMP weapon and quite possibly a couple of nuclear weapons on the East Coast. We have no other intelligence to go off right now, so we are going to go with a worst-case scenario. We will assume that our government has been disabled and no help is coming our way. We will assume that the attack will be continuing. If this were an act of terrorism or the act of a rogue nation, it doesn't matter at this point. From here on out we are on our own."

"Starting right now there will be three guards per eight-hour shift. All projects will be put on hold for now. The animals still need to be tended and the crops are going to be more important now than ever before so when you are not pulling duty or sleeping, you will be working the crops or greenhouses. At sun-up we will do a damage assessment of the electrical systems and see where we need to concentrate our repairs. The vehicles should be fine, but we will also need a damage control team to go through them and make sure they are good to go."

"I'm going to need the Hummers brought out of storage too. Jason and Jill, first thing in the morning the two of you need to go get Doc Williams and bring him here," he paused for a moment and made eye contact with each of us before he continued. "Every cabin has flashlights, candles and lanterns. It's okay to use them but make damn sure you use the blackout curtains and keep outdoor light usage to a minimum."

"Allan," Jill said quietly.

"Yes Jill?"

"Are we going to send a team to get my dad?" she asked.

THE RANCH

"Your dad has a Jeep parked in his garage, he has supplies and he knows where we are. As of now it's up to him to get here," he paused and looked at me. "It's the same for your brother and his family, Jason. I know he doesn't have a Jeep, but he is a clever guy. They will make it; they will all make it. Have a little faith in them," he said. He looked from Jill and me to everyone else in the room.

"This is what this place was built for. This is why you were handpicked to be here. We never had a choice of what the game was going to be, the game chose us. Now it's time to step up and bring everything you got to the table." Again, he paused and looked around the room. "Draw weapons, ammo and body armor. At this time, we are at condition one and will remain there until further notice. Get to it!" he finished.

Once everyone on the security detail had drawn their sidearm, AR-15, body armor and spare mags, Mike and Jessica were given sets of night vision goggles from the underground storeroom. The sensitive electronics down there were unfazed by the EMP blast. The only concern was that there would be another EMP hit. After weighing the odds, it was decided to pull two pair of goggles into service for the roving guards. They would only power them up if they were needed. Alex was to stay at the shack and monitor the radios which had also been replaced from the underground stores. Jake and Mark were going from room to room in every building and pulling the blackout blinds over every window. That would prevent any light from inside escaping.

Allan and Dale went to talk to Dale's family to let them know what had happened and what was expected of them. Dale's boys, Mike and Ben, were going to take care of all the animals in the mornings and evenings, which would take some of the load off the adults. Susan was going to start manning the infirmary full-time. We had turned the old security shack into a makeshift infirmary after the new shack came online. It had a waiting room in the front and the back rooms had been transformed into the emergency room. It was well-stocked. One other thing Susan had insisted on was making sure she had everyone's blood type, just in case.

Jake, Jill and I decided that we should not wait until morning to check on the vehicles. My truck fired right up. The only thing that didn't work was the stereo, no big loss there. Of the four Jeeps at the ranch, only one would not start. A quick change of the ignition parts and it too was running. The fifth Jeep was at the airport, which Jill and I would pick up when we went to get Doc Williams in the morning. The sixth one was in Reno with Bill. All four Hummers fired up with no issues and so did the five-ton truck. The new Case equipment was as dead as a door nail. The old Massey that Dale brought with him from Kansas purred like a kitten.

Tuesday, July 5, 2016

It was a little after three in the morning when the patrol noticed the orange glow emanating from the direction of Elko. Our best guess was that there was a massive fire and with no water pressure and no working fire equipment, the fire was probably running un-checked. Around 4am Allan met up with the three of us and suggested that we should see the sheriff in the morning. He wanted us to extend the offer of assistance if he needed it. Sheriff Case had been friendly to the ranch and we really needed to keep that friendship alive. Jake was a little concerned about showing up at the sheriff's office in head to toe black fatigues, body armor adorned in spare mags, and AR-15's. Allan smiled a little and went on to explain that nothing in the way we were dressed would even warrant a raised eyebrow from the good sheriff.

The plan was for us to head to town at 6am, shortly after the sun was due up. I was a little leery of going to town so soon after the EMP, but Allan insisted. His reasoning was that we needed to get in and get out while everyone was standing around scratching their asses trying to figure out what happened. He was very worried that the medical supplies and drugs at Doc's office would be looted if we waited. I could see his point. At 5am, Jill and I went to our house and grabbed some coffee and a quick bite of breakfast. She also packed some sandwiches and half a dozen bottles of water. Both of us grabbed our "Go-Bags" out of the hall closet and headed to my truck.

Jake was already there with his pack and a sack lunch. We secured the packs in the bed of the truck and climbed into the cab. Jake took the backseat and rolled both windows down. He sat in the middle with his AR laid across his lap. Jill was sitting on the passenger side of the front bench seat. Her AR was pointed down between her feet. My AR was laying on the seat next to me. As we rolled to the gate, I could see the patrol unit heading the same way. They were going to open the gate for us. It would also give Jake a chance to tell his wife goodbye.

The drive to Elko went a little slower than I expected. There were several stalled cars on the two-lane road, so we slowed and worked our way around them.

THE RANCH

As we passed the small sub-division about halfway between the ranch and town, we came across the first car crash. A pickup and an SUV had collided head on and blocked both lanes. There were no emergency services on scene so we made a quick decision to see if we could render aid. Jake stayed with the truck while Jill and I cautiously approached the carnage. Once we checked the vehicles it was obvious there was nothing we could do. Both drivers had died on impact or very soon thereafter.

We got past the wreck using the shoulder of the road and continued the drive into Elko. With the sun fully up, it was easy to see that the fire in town had not slowed any. There was a huge column of thick black smoke rising into the air. We were about three miles from the Elko city limits when we came across a sheriff's deputy walking along the side of the road. I was already slowing down when he heard us and started waving for us to stop. As we rolled to a stop next to him, Jill moved her AR to lay across her lap pointing at her door. Her hand deftly slipped the safety off and her finger was resting just outside the trigger guard.

"You don't know how happy I am to see you guys....." he started to say through Jill's open window but quickly stopped when he saw the body armor and rifles.

"Need a ride deputy?" Jill asked sweetly. "We were headed to the sheriff's office anyway." His hand started ever so slowly toward the Glock on his right hip. "We are the good guys. Please do not reach for your weapon," Jill said. His hand stopped but the confusion in his eyes accelerated. "If you want a ride and a bottle of water, please get in. Otherwise we will have to leave you behind. We have things to do today."

"You're from the ranch, right?" he asked.

"Yes sir, we are. If you need a ride, we would be more than happy to give you one."

"Okay, I guess I'll take you up on it," he moved to the back door and climbed in. Jake had slid over to give him some room. Jill slipped her safety back on and put the rifle back between her legs. I passed him a bottle of water and started down the road again. When Jill asked him if he knew what was going on, we found that we knew more than he did. He had gone to bed last night and overslept when his alarm clock didn't go off. He knew some bad stuff had happened but didn't have a clue as to the extent. Like everyone else he knew there was a fire, but nothing more. He was just trying to get to work to see if he could help.

Fifteen minutes later we were parked in front of the sheriff's office. Deputy Owens climbed out of the truck and headed inside. I told Jake to stay with the truck while Jill and I went inside. We took our AR-15's with us but had them slung across our backs, barrels down. It was nearly empty inside the building. We didn't see anyone until we made our way to Sheriff Case's office. We were a little surprised to see Case and the Mayor. Both looked exhausted and it looked like the Mayor was just getting ready to leave. They shook hands and the Mayor pushed his way past us with an "Excuse me deputies." Once he was gone from the hallway, Louie greeted us.

"Somehow I knew you guys would have your shit together," he said as he shook our hands. "I've got my hands full today, what can I do for you?" Jill stepped a little closer to his desk and spoke.

"Actually sir, we had to come to town to pick up one of our own but wanted to stop and see if there was anything we could do to help," she offered.

"Have you got a working fire truck?" he said jokingly as he sat behind his desk. "Or maybe a working police car?"

"Sorry Sir, we don't have either. Do you know what happened last night?"

"Intelligence is pretty slim, Jill. We think nukes went off in DC and New York. There is also rumor that one went off in San Antonio, Texas. There was another rumor that a cargo vessel in the Gulf of Mexico fired the EMP weapon that hit us. I guess the ship exploded and sank before anyone could intercept it. Mostly just rumors to work with right now, sorry," he said as he leaned back in his chair and rubbed his face.

"If we hear anything over the HAM radio, we will make sure to let you know," Jill told him.

"I appreciate that. We have a guy with a working HAM set up here, we will try to keep you posted, too."

"Okay, if there is anything we can do to help, please let us know and we will do what we can. We have to pick our guy up and we have some stuff we have to get from a hangar at the airport....." he cut Jill off at the mention of the airport.

"Don't waste your time going over there. A big cargo plane went in last night, wiped out all the hangars at the end of the runway and last I heard the main terminal was completely engulfed in fire."

"Oh, thanks for the heads up," she said as she reached across his desk and shook his hand. It was with that, we showed ourselves out of his office. Once we were back at the truck, we filled Jake in on the conversation we had with the sheriff. After a short discussion, we decided it would be prudent to make sure we had indeed lost the Jeep. It was on our way to Doc Williams' house, so there really was nothing to lose. As we weaved our way through the city streets, it became very clear that nearly everyone we saw had no clue what happened. All eyes were on us as we crawled along. It quickly made all three of us uncomfortable.

As we neared the end of the airport where our hanger was, it was obvious that there was nothing to be gained by going any closer. The hanger that the Jeep had been in was just gone, leveled and burned to the ground. We changed course and went to Doc's house. When we pulled into his driveway 20 minutes later, we were surprised to find that there was nobody home. Jill checked the door and found it unlocked, but there was no one inside.

"Maybe he went to his office?" she suggested.

"Only one way to find out," I replied as we were walking back to the truck. It was less than a mile to his office and this road was clear, so it was a quick ride. We checked both the front and back door, locked up tight.

"Anywhere else he might be?" I asked Jill. She thought for a minute before answering.

"I guess he could be at the hospital or the fire department. He volunteered at both," she finally said.

"Where is the closest firehouse? We will try there first," I motioned her back to the truck. She gave me directions and within ten minutes we were pulling up to the station. All three bay doors were open, and I could see that all three rigs inside had the hoods up or the cabs tilted forward. The station captain came out to meet us as we got out of the truck. He introduced himself as Jim Hamilton. The three of us also introduced ourselves.

"I'm glad we finally have some deputies on the streets, people are starting to get pretty spooked." he said as we started walking toward the bay doors. Jake hung back by the truck. That was twice now that we had been mistakenly identified as sheriff's deputies. Neither of us bothered to correct him.

"Yeah, vehicles are at a prime right now," I said. "We're actually here looking for somebody and we were wondering if you might have seen him. A fellow by the name of Tim Williams," I went on to describe him a little.

"You're talking about Doc Williams? Yeah he came by here late last night to check on us after the power went out. He didn't stick around. Jumped back on his bicycle and headed into town. Might try the hospital," he suggested. We thanked him for his time and left for the hospital. It was getting close to noon when we finally got there. The place was chaos, plain and simple. There were a couple of older cars pulled up to the emergency room doors, and it looked like they were using an old army Jeep for an ambulance. The thing looked like it had crossed time and space from the beaches of Normandy.

I pulled around to the employee parking and the three of us got out. I left it running and I told Jake to leave if anyone tried to confiscate our ride. He got into the driver's seat and closed the door. Jill and I grabbed our rifles, slung them and went in the employee entrance. The door was normally locked but the EMP destroyed the electronic lock. I stopped the first nurse that we passed and asked her about Doc Williams. She told us to try the ER, as she had no clue who we were talking about.

When we turned down the hallway that led to the ER, Jill and I both came to a dead stop. The walls were lined with gurneys and patients. Some were covered in blood-soaked sheets. Some had expired and were just left uncovered. There were a lot of horrific burns, from the jet crash I assumed. Others were still alive but judging by their injuries, they wouldn't be for long. I grabbed Jill by the arm and started to pull her down the hallway of horrors.

"Let's find the Doc and get the hell out of here!" I said through clenched teeth. I could see that Jill was as white as a ghost. The smell of vomit, fecal matter, blood, urine and burned flesh mixed with jet fuel was enough to make anyone wretch. She just nodded and we double-timed it out of there. When we got into the actual emergency room, we were greeted by a whole new set of horrors. The screams and wails of the living mixed with everything we had already seen was too much for Jill. She lost her breakfast in a waste basket by the nurse's station. I pulled a bandanna from my pocket and handed it to her to wipe her face with.

A doctor was trotting by us, I grabbed him by the arm and spun him around. He was pissed but at this point I did not care. I gave him the basic description of Doc and told him I needed to find him. To my surprise he remembered seeing him earlier in the morning. He told us to check with the nurses on the second floor and pointed to the nearest stairwell. I sent him on his way. I spun around and again grabbed Jill by the arm and directed her to the stairwell. It wasn't actually stairs but instead a ramp that made access to the second floor easy for the gurneys and wheelchairs.

Jill and I bounded up the ramp and burst out onto the second floor. The smell up here was only slightly better. The nurse's station was directly across from the door but there were no nurses present. I started down the hallway, but Jill yelled at me to wait. I stopped and turned to face her. She was looking at a whiteboard behind the counter. She pointed at it and I followed her finger. Next to room #203, under "patient's name" was Tim Williams. Jill took off at a full sprint toward the end of the hallway. It was everything I could do to catch up to her. She slid to a stop when she got to room #203 and darted in. When I got in the room, Doc Williams was on a gurney with a bloody dressing on the left side of his chest. His face was black and blue, and his right arm was in a sling. He was unconscious and the IV that was stuck in his left arm was attached to an empty bag.

"He's alive but if he stays here, he won't be for long," she said as she pulled the IV bag and laid it on his chest. She started unlocking the wheels of the gurney and I followed her and the gurney out the door. I got ahead of her and started steering it down the hallway. She ground to a halt at the nurse's station, vaulted the counter and kicked open the locked door that led to the room where they kept IV supplies and medications. She returned a moment later with a cart in tow and pockets stuffed with supplies. She grabbed a pillowcase off the linen cart and started stuffing IV bags and other supplies into it. She threw the makeshift bag to me and vaulted the counter again.

"Go!" she said and pointed toward the door. We got to the door at the bottom of the ramp and burst out into the ER. Normally everyone would have been looking at us but today there was just too much chaos, so we went unnoticed. We went back through the hall of horrors and went out the employee door we had come in. Jake was still there. He jumped out of the driver's seat and ran to the back of the truck and put the tailgate down. Jill put the head of the gurney up to the tailgate and jumped into the bed of the truck. She grabbed the corners of the mattress and started pulling. Jake and I each grabbed a side and helped her slide Doc into the back, mattress and all. Jake slammed the tailgate and jumped in the bed to assist Jill.

"Jason, let me get his IV going again before we take off," she said.

"Okay," I replied.

"I'm going to need you to get us to the ranch as fast as possible," the look in her eyes told me everything I needed to know. A minute later she slapped the back window and yelled go.

"Hang on!" I yelled back as I put my foot down hard on the throttle. I darted in and out of stalled and parked cars until I made it back to the main road. There were enough people on the sidewalks now that they took notice. At several points I was driving on the wrong side of the street and completely blowing through intersections. Within a few minutes, we were back on the two-lane road that led back to the ranch. I opened the big diesel up and was pushing red line in fifth gear a couple of times.

When I made the turn off to the ranch, I was on the radio telling them to get the gate open and Susan to the infirmary immediately. I had to brake hard when I blew past the gate at 70 miles per hour. The tires were howling in protest at every turn of the snaking driveway, but she held traction. I locked up the brakes and slid to a stop on the asphalt in front of the medical building. Susan, Allan and Jessica were waiting with a gurney. Within moments Doc was being transferred from my truck to the infirmary. Jill went inside with Susan and Jessica, and she was giving them the information that she had.

"What the hell happened down there?" Allan asked.

"Shit is falling apart fast, Allan. We spent a lot of time looking for Doc. We finally found him at the hospital. That place has turned into a house of horror. It was the worst thing I have ever seen in my life," I paused and took a drink of water. "The place is more morgue than anything else. There was no way in hell we were leaving Doc behind. I don't know what happened to him, but I do know what *would* have happened had we left him there," I paused for another drink and Jake picked up the story.

"The fire was caused by a jet crashing at the airport. We lost the Jeep. Sheriff Case is in the dark about what happened too. The one new thing we learned was that there might have been a detonation in San Antonio, Texas, too. It's just rumors as far as he knows."

"It's not rumor. Our contacts on the HAM frequencies are telling us that New York, Washington DC, San Antonio and Los Angeles were all hit by nukes. From what they are telling us, it was the dirty bomb type not the missile type," Allan interrupted.

Both Jake and I fell silent with that news. I know that I was having trouble wrapping my brain around everything that had happened in the last 16 hours. It was one in the afternoon and I felt like I had aged ten years overnight. Allan excused himself and went into the infirmary. Jake and I made ourselves busy cleaning our gear out of the bed of the truck. Once that was done, Jake took the truck to fill the fuel tank. I was waiting for Jill, but Allan appeared first.

"I'm glad you didn't leave Doc behind. Susan says he has a stab wound to his chest, a collapsed lung, broken arm, broken nose and was very dehydrated. He was awake long enough to tell us that a bunch of thugs jumped him for his bicycle. They've gotten him all cleaned up and are replenishing his fluids. He is heavily sedated now but told me to tell you thank you," he stopped and put his hand on my shoulder. "I want to thank you too. He would have been dead if you hadn't found him when you did."

"No problem Allan, it's what we do. We take care of our own," I said.

"Yes, we do, and I hate to say it, but we are going to be busy for a while," he paused for a few seconds. "I'm going to need you to take Jill and Jake back to town tonight and retrieve Doc's stuff."

"What stuff are we talking about?"

"He has some weapons at his house, and you will need to go to his office and get all of his medical equipment. Drugs, tools and so on. Clean the place out. I'd send somebody else but you three already know what's going on down there."

"We can do it, should be an in and out trip," I told him. It was about that time Jill came out of the infirmary.

"What can we do?" she asked. She looked exhausted.

"Make another run to town tonight and get the Doc's stuff," I told her.

"Yeah, we can do that. I just need to brush this taste out of my mouth," she said as she headed to our house. Allan smiled a little and waved me to follow her. I caught up to her as she got to the front door. We went inside and straight upstairs. She dropped her body armor on the dresser and peeled her BDU shirt off as she went into the bathroom. She brushed her teeth, washed her face and hands. She looked only slightly better when she came back into the room.

"Kick your boots off and lay down for a while, you're exhausted," I told her. To my surprise, she didn't argue. Instead, she did as I suggested. She was asleep before I could get my boots off. Both of us were asleep within mere moments.

It was 6pm when I awoke to a soft knock at the door. There was a second knock, slightly louder, before I had enough cobwebs cleared to call out.

"Yes," I answered. Jill stirred next to me.

"Sir, its Alex. Allan asked me to wake you for your mission tonight," the young voice said. Poor kid sounded scared as hell.

"Thank you, Alex. Please let Allan know that we will be down in a few minutes."

"Yes sir," he said, and I heard his boots on the stairs.

"I wish I had that kind of energy," Jill said from next to me. She still made no move to get up. I chuckled a little and swung my feet to the floor.

"Come on babe, places to go and things to do," I said as I grabbed my boots and started to pull them on. She sat up and did the same. She grabbed a new BDU shirt from the closet and threw it on over her black tank top. Both of us grabbed our body armor on the way out the door. When we got to the kitchen, Allan was waiting for us. I could see that somebody had brought our packs and rifles to the house and left them in the corner of the dining room.

"Did you two get some rest?" Allan asked as he passed each of us a cup of coffee.

"Yeah," Jill grumbled as she sat at the table. I took my cup and joined her. Allan remained standing.

"I tweaked the plan a little for tonight," he began. "You are going to be joined by Jake and Mike. They will follow you in the five-ton. That will give you a little more manpower and a lot more storage space. It will also give you a back-up vehicle in case anything happens to one of them. Mike has already pulled helmets and NVGs. He also pulled the throat mics and ear buds for your radios, all of which are fully charged now. The plan calls for you to leave here at eight tonight and be back by dawn. The rules of engagement are that you will not engage unless you have been engaged. If any shooting starts, be very careful. There are a lot of non-combatants and friendlies in the area. Are we clear?"

"Crystal," Jill said before I could get the answer out. The coffee was starting to work its magic for her. I just nodded.

"For now, enjoy the coffee, get a shower, whatever. Jake and Mike will be here in an hour and we will have dinner before you head out."

"How's Doc doing?" Jill asked.

"He is much better. Susan is keeping him sedated but his prognosis is very good," he answered. That improved Jill's mood even more than the coffee.

It was seven sharp when Jake and Mike came through the door. Allan had showed up about a half hour earlier and started dinner. Jill was back to her normal self after her shower before dinner. When we were done eating and the dishes were cleared from the table, Allan pulled two maps from his back pocket and laid them side by side on the table. On both maps we traced our primary and secondary routes to both objectives. We added rally points should we become separated.

Once we had arrived at each objective, each team had different roles. We set up a communication's plan and checked comms to make sure everyone was on the same page. We rolled out of the gate at 8pm on the dot. It was still light enough that we didn't need the NVG's yet. We were planning on hitting the outskirts of town at full dark. We would go in with all the lights blacked out and go as quietly as the big diesels would allow us to. The going was slow, but we arrived at our first objective, Doc's house, at 10:05pm.

Jill and Mike made entry and quickly located the weapons and ammo. Those were thrown in the backseat of my truck. They made a second sweep of the house and brought back a suitcase of Doc's clothes and some of his personal effects. His work truck was in the garage and they stripped it of all its medical equipment. They did try to start it, but the rig was totally dead. At 10:29 we pulled away from his house and made our way to the vet clinic.

When we got to the clinic, we backed both vehicles up to the door for faster access. Jill and Mike were going to make entry again while Jake and I pulled security. When we were here earlier in the day all the windows and doors were intact, now the glass front door had been smashed. Jill stopped short of entering and listened intently. She signaled Mike that there were at least two intruders. She and Mike moved like wraiths in the darkness. They silently crept through the broken front door and began to clear the building.

They had been inside for about two minutes when I heard Jill and Mike yell at someone to freeze. There were muffled sounds of a scuffle and then Jill announced in my ear bud that they were all clear, coming out with three subjects. A moment later Jill was pushing two guys out the door at the end of her AR-15. Mike was behind her with the third one. All three had been flexi-cuffed already and they were shoved to the ground. Jill told them that if they so much as breathed hard they would get their asses shot off. They must have believed her because they laid perfectly still.

Jill and Mike went back inside and started bringing plastic tubs out and loading the trucks. They were on their third trip when we heard gunshots. They were not very far away but at this point they were not shooting at us. Yet. Jill and Mike were going as quickly as they could, but it still seemed to be taking too long. The bed of my truck was already full, and the five-ton was nearly full when we could hear more gunshots. These were close. Jake and I could see flashlight beams dancing up and down the street in front of us. There was shouting that couldn't have been more than half a block away. The trucks were blocked from their view by a six-foot block wall that separated Doc's clinic from the property next door. That wasn't going to last much longer.

"Jill, Mike. We are going to have company in about 30 seconds," I said quietly into my throat mic. I looked over at Jake and could see that he had his rifle laid across the front bumper of the five-ton and he was using it as cover. I laid my rifle across the hood of my truck and waited for the crowd to appear. Jill and Mike slipped out of the clinic and moved silently along the glass front to the brick wall. They worked their way up to within two feet of the end of the wall and waited. They were pretty much hidden from sight by some tree branches and shrubs.

There were four of them stumbling down the middle of the street. One was armed with a pistol that he was waving in the air with one hand and he had a big bottle of booze in the other hand. All four were in the bag drunk. Two of them had flashlights that they were shining around. I was praying to myself that they would just keep going up the street, but I knew there would be no such luck. One of the flashlight beams played across the front of the clinic and stopped when it got to me. I centered the lighted reticle of my sights on the guy with the gun and flipped on my high-power flashlight.

"Keep moving and nobody gets hurt!" I said loudly. They stopped dead in their tracks and the second flashlight beam landed on Jake. He lit them up with his light, too. The thugs were obviously taking a moment to decide what to do next. They had no Idea that Jill and Mike had them covered from a third angle. "If you so much as point that gun in this direction, I'll shoot your stupid ass. Now get moving!" I shouted.

They were so distracted by me and Jake that Jill and Mike had slipped from the wall and taken cover on either side of the street behind them. They hit them with their flashlights at the same time and startled the hell out of them.

"Drop the gun!" Mike shouted from behind them. Apparently, this was enough to break their will. The guy with the gun dropped it on the asphalt. "Good choice asshole. If you have any other weapons, they better be on the ground in the next three seconds!" he demanded. There was an assortment of knives and a hatchet that all clattered to the ground very quickly. When Mike yelled at them to haul ass, they did, and they did it in a hurry. Mike and Jill collected their weapons and threw them on the floorboard in the back of my truck. Jill went to the three guys that she and Mike had captured earlier and knelt next to the one that appeared to be the leader. She whispered something in his ear and then pulled her fighting knife from its sheath on her lower leg. They all laid perfectly still while she cut their restraints. They remained face down and unmoving until we had pulled out of the parking lot.

We left the clinic at 12:30 in the morning and were pulling through the gate of the ranch at 1:30. The drive back was totally uneventful and that was fine by me. My adrenaline was just starting to settle down from the confrontation with the thugs. The trucks were unloaded and refueled by 3:00. Jill swung in to check on Doc and returned a few minutes later with a smile on her face. He was doing very well. Dale had the night watch, so Jill and I met with him and gave him a briefing on how the mission went. Overall, he was very pleased.

Jill and I finally went to bed just before five in the morning. The nice thing about the blackout blinds was that it seemed like nighttime when we slept during the day.

CHAPTER 9

Wednesday, July 6, 2016

"What?" I answered. It was just after 7am when there was a knock at the door.

"Jason, its Jessica. Allan needs you at the security shack pronto. Sheriff Case is here, and he needs to speak to you. Sorry."

"All right, tell him I'll be there shortly." I sighed and rolled out of bed. I dressed as quickly as I could and headed to the security shack. Jill was so tired that she didn't even stir this time. When I got to the shack, I was still trying to rub the sleep from my eyes. Allan and Louie were the only ones in the office when I walked in.

"Morning sheriff, Allan."

"Jason, Louie has some questions for you about last night, mind giving him the briefing you gave Dale a little while ago?" Allan asked. Over the course of the next 30 minutes I recounted the events of the previous night for Louie. He took some notes and seemed very interested in the descriptions of all seven of the thugs we had encountered. He was also mildly curious about people fitting our description stealing a patient from the hospital. I confirmed that we had indeed liberated Doc from that hell hole. He took very detailed notes when it came to the thugs. He also wanted to know if we still had the weapons we had taken from them. We did have them, and they were turned over to him.

"Mind if we go off the record?" he asked as he was looking at the pistol with special interest. Both Allan and I nodded our approval.

"I really wish you had put that bastard down last night," Louie said barely above a whisper. "This pistol belonged to one of my deputies. He was jumped and beaten to death by four guys yesterday. A 7-11 clerk was gunned down and the store was robbed by the same four guys two hours later. Every witness described the same four guys you described," the anger in his voice and eyes turned them as cold as ice. "While I do not condone vigilante justice, I would have looked the other way this time."

"Listen Louie, I know these guys already extended the offer of help and I just want to make sure you know we are serious about that," Allan said.

"I know you are serious about it and I may have to call in that favor. I'm down to seven deputies."

"Just say the word and we will do everything we can to help," Allan reassured him.

"I really appreciate that. You guys should also know that we have another problem," he paused to take a sip of the coffee Allan had given him. "Remember Marvin?" both of us nodded slowly. "He was out of town when you filed that report a couple of months back. His alibi was solid as a rock. I did have an inform- ant in town keep an eye on the guy when he got back though. He was very, very pissed at me, and pissed at the people of the ranch, Jill in particular. He felt that we all had it out for him. He moved out of his apartment and started squatting on some mining property a friend of his owned. That property is less than 20 miles from your doorstep." Allan and I shot each other a quick glance.

"He had hooked up with half a dozen turds from the L.A. area. Real outstand- ing citizen types if you get my drift. Like I said, we were watching him and his newfound friends but could never nail down anything concrete. If all of that is not troubling enough, Marvin has made a lot of weapons purchases in the last couple of months. Mostly cheaper weapons like AK-47's and some of the real cheap pis- tol caliber carbines. Again, nothing that we could nail him for. The bastard is slip- pery to be sure."

"Where is he now?" I asked.

"We don't know. I sent our informant out to his property three days ago and haven't heard anything back. Of course, a lot of shit has gone sideways since then."

"If he shows his face around here he is going to end up with a few new holes," I growled.

"Again, I would look the other way," the sheriff said. "All you would have to do is shoot, shovel and shut up. You would be doing a lot of people a huge favor."

"We will definitely be keeping an eye out for him. Can you give us the loca- tion of his camp?" Allan asked. Louie wrote down the directions and slipped them across the desk on a folded sheet of paper. Louie got up to leave and thanked both of us for our time. He paused in the doorway and turned to face us again.

"I have been a cop for 33 years and I learned a long time ago to listen to my gut instinct. It has kept me alive on more than one occasion. Right now, my gut is telling me two things. First, you are good people. You have a lot of secrets, but you are definitely good people. Second, it's telling me that there is going to be a lot of bad shit going down in very short order. Maybe not tomorrow or next month, but things are going to get a lot worse before they get better." He said as he put his hat on his head and walked out the door.

"Sooner or later we are going to have to deal with Marvin," I said to Allan. He let out a long sigh.

"Yes, we are. I'm also afraid Louie is right; it's going to get a lot worse before it gets any better."

After our meeting with the sheriff, I tried to go back to bed. Sleep never came. I ended up in the study going over the map of the area where Marvin had set up camp. It was basically on the side of a mountain. If he had any tactical motivation, it would be a position that was very easy to defend. There was a horizontal mine shaft, but I didn't have any information beyond that. I knew he had it out for Jill and that worried me. I knew he had extensive weapons training and from what Jill had told me, his specialty was long-distance shooting.

Jill had also told me that he had shown up at the range one time with a brand new .408 Cheytac that had cost him nearly three months' worth of pay. It wasn't that he showed up to show it off, he put rounds down range. The 1,200-yard range proved to be of no challenge and by the end of the day his accurate range was 2,500 yards. That terrified me. Knowing that he could take a shot at any of us from a mile and a half away and kill any of us, with or without body armor, was truly scary.

By noon I had finished the second pot of coffee and went to find Allan. He was still in the security shack when I walked in. I sat in the chair opposite his desk.

"You look like a man with a lot on his mind," he said as he looked over the top of his glasses.

"I think our problems with Marvin need to be dealt with sooner rather than later," I told him. "We need to get our own set of eyes on him, figure out what he is up to and take him out if we get the chance."

"I take it you didn't go back to sleep this morning," he said, standing from his desk, he walked to the map on the wall. He looked over his shoulder at me. "I wouldn't have gone to sleep either." He turned back to the map and was looking at Marvin's last known location.

"If that is where he is, he's got a good spot," I said.

"Yes, he does. Any ideas on how to get him out of it?" he asked.

"Right now? No, I've got nothing," I admitted.

"If I know Marvin," he began, "he won't try anything yet. Louie and his deputies are the only thing holding him back right now. Marvin may be an asshole, but he is also very calculating. If I were Louie, I'd be watching my back. For that matter, all the deputies are in danger and I would go as far saying the local government officials are at risk."

"You think he would go that far?" I asked.

"I know he would. The guy is a sociopath if I ever saw one. It doesn't help that he is also as narcissistic as anyone I have ever met in my life. You combine those two personality traits in one person and hold on. Getting him fired from the department only served to free him from the constraints of the system. Throw in the end of the world just for good measure and I can guarantee that he has taken a long walk off a short pier."

"Should we warn Louie?"

"Louie knows what Marvin is and has for a very long time," Allan said.

"That brings us back to the question, what do we do about him?" I asked.

"We need a meeting between our top security people and Louie's people. Jake, Mike, Jill, you and I need to get together with them and figure something out and soon. If things continue to deteriorate at this pace, Marvin will make his move in the next couple of weeks."

"Set it up," I said as I stood. "Let me know when and we will make it happen."

"You have security duty tonight, are you going to be okay to pull your shift?" he asked.

"Keep the coffee hot and strong, I'll be fine," I walked out the door and headed home. I needed a long hot shower and I needed to talk to Jill. She had to know the stakes of the game we were playing.

When I got back home, I stopped in the kitchen and poured two cups of coffee and took them upstairs with me. Jill was still sound asleep, so I just set her cup on the nightstand. I pulled some clean BDUs out of the closet and headed for the bathroom. Thirty minutes later I was dressed and ready for the rest of my day. Jill was sitting up in bed with her back to the headboard. Her coffee cup was held to her lips with both hands. She took a small sip and smiled at me.

"You sure know the right way to wake a girl up," she raised the cup up in a mock toast. "Did you sleep okay?"

"Yeah, both hours were great," I said sarcastically.

"What? What have you been doing all morning?" her concern was sincere. I sat on the bed next to her and walked her through my morning. By the time I was done recounting the events, it was hard to read the expression in her eyes. It was comparable to the eye of a Cat 5 hurricane. Calm in the center with unimaginable destruction everywhere else.

Jill finished her coffee and grabbed a shower. After she was dressed, she joined me in the kitchen and helped me make breakfast. We were washing the dishes after breakfast when Alex came in.

"Sir, ma'am, I have a message for you from Mr. West....."

"Go ahead," Jill urged him.

"Ma'am, Mr. West respectfully requests that, and I quote, turn your damn radio on and call him," his voice was quivering. Jill and I both started laughing. The poor boy looked like he was scared to death.

"Okay Alex, thank you for the message," she said as she got up and pulled her radio from her gun belt. Alex nodded and hauled ass. After he was gone Jill sat back down at the table with her radio in hand. "Allan has that poor kid scared of us, you know that, right?" she looked at me and winked. She turned her radio on and put it to her mouth.

"West, Butler. You called?" there was a moment of silence before Allan answered.

"Yes, I did. I need you in the security shack, I heard from your dad." Jill looked at me and blinked. An instant later she was out the door at a dead run. I knew I couldn't catch her, even on my best day. I closed the front door and trotted to the shack.

I went inside the shack a full minute behind Jill, so I walked in on the middle of a conversation. Both Jill and Allan had their fingers on the map.

".........north of Lovelock, it sounded like he said Imlay, that's the only thing that made any sense. He said he had couple of people with him but didn't go into details. It was then that we lost contact. Hopefully it was just the radio fritzing out again," Allan said.

"We have to mount a rescue party right now!" Jill said excitedly.

"We will but we only have one shot at this so let's get our shit together beforehand," Allan said.

"What happened?" I asked.

"I just heard from Bill on the HAM radio. He said that they were hit in an ambush on the highway north of Lovelock. The Jeep was a total loss, but he and two others were on foot and evading their attackers. Their portable radio had been damaged in the initial attack and he knew he was on an open channel so he wouldn't give any coordinates. His radio went dead after that," Allan told me. He turned to Jill. "Call Jake, Mark and Alex. Have them meet us in conference room one in 15 minutes," he ordered. Before he was even done with the sentence, Jill was on the radio.

"What can I do?"

"You can cover for me here for a little bit," Allan said. "Jessica and Mike are mobile right now, they just left gate two heading toward the range," with that he and Jill were out the door.

I had been in the security office for about an hour. Jessica and Mike were back inside the compound and finishing their loop of the buildings. To save on fuel, they were both on horseback. Not as fast as a Jeep but not nearly as slow as being on foot. Dale had arrived at the shack, so I filled him in on what I knew. He took over the shack duty for me and I headed to where all the vehicles were parked. I picked the two Jeeps on the end and checked all their fluids and tire pressures. I checked all the lights and radio equipment too. Once that was done, I pulled both medical kits and made sure they were up to standard. I pulled all the rifles one by one and made sure they were clean and in operating order. They were. I was in the middle of refreshing the drinking water when I saw the rescue party come from the barracks building. I topped off the last five-gallon can of water and replaced it on the Jeep. Jill was headed my way; her game face was on.

"How soon are you pulling out?" I asked her.

"As soon as the rigs are checked out and everyone gets their gear on board."

"I've already gone through the two Jeeps on the end, they are ready to go," I told her. We were walking side by side back to the house to get her gear when she suddenly stopped and spun to face me. She put her arms around my neck and pulled me close.

"I tried to get Allan to let you go, he wouldn't budge," she said quietly. "I really wish you were going."

"Jill, I knew I wasn't going as soon as he called the meeting. I also know that you wouldn't trust this mission to anyone if you were sitting here. You would be impossible to deal with," I said with a grin. "Go get your dad and bring him home," she smiled and planted a long, sensuous kiss on my lips. When she finally pulled back she had a tear in the corner of her eye.

"Jason, I haven't said what I'm about to say to you to anyone in a very, very long time," her voice was barely above a whisper. "So, know that when I say it, I mean it," she paused and locked eyes with me. The tear rolled down her cheek. "Jason Sterling, I love you."

I'm pretty sure my heart had stopped beating in my chest. Up until now, neither of us had said the words aloud.

"Jillian Renee Butler, I love you, too," I said. She smiled and kissed me again.

"Don't do anything stupid while I'm gone," she said.

"You know me, we're too good of a team to split up," I said, she grinned from ear to ear. "Now it's your turn to be in the right place at the right time," her grin got bigger. I smacked her on the butt. "Now get out of here!" she laughed and took off toward the house. The smile on my face must have been as big as hers as I walked back to the Jeeps.

As gear started arriving, I was throwing it onto the roof racks and strapping it down. Each Jeep was given an extra ammo can of 5.56 and .45 ammo. They were also given extra body armor just in case Bill's party had lost theirs. Spare radios and batteries were also loaded up. Fuel was a concern, but each rig was equipped with a hose and electric pump that could pull fuel from underground tanks. The last thing that was loaded was the NVG equipped helmets along with a slew of extra batteries. The rescue team assembled at 6pm and had their final briefing. There were three maps. One for each Jeep crew and one for the shack. Again, primary and secondary routes were laid out along with rally points and communications plans. They pulled out of the gate at 6:45pm.

I was officially on shift at six, but Allan allowed me to help send the rescue party on their way. It had already been a long day and it was going to get longer. After Jill and her team left, I went and found Allan in the security shack. He was parked behind the desk like he normally was. I sat in the chair across from the desk and he looked at me over the top of his glasses.

"Can I pick your brain for a minute?" I asked him.

"Of course. What's on your mind?"

"I'm just curious as to why you chose those particular people for the rescue mission."

"Well, there were many reasons but in the end I felt that it sent Jill into the field with a good crew and it kept a good crew here at home. Do you have a problem with that?" he asked.

"No, there's no problem. I was just trying to figure out your motivations behind the people you picked. I'm trying to learn something here."

"Okay, I picked Jill because she is the best we have, and she trained all three of those guys. She knows their limits and their abilities. Jake went because he has real-world combat experience and he has proven to be a pretty good medic. Mark went because he and Jake are like you and Jill, they are a damn good team. Alex was picked because he is young and strong and can take orders and follow them to the letter. He has also proven himself to be mechanically oriented. If something happens to one of the Jeeps, he will probably be able to fix it...... Does that answer your question?" I nodded my head. His choices made perfect sense.

"What about keeping Mike and me here? What was the reasoning behind that?"

"I kept you two here because I consider you my heavy hitters. Both of you are very well-rounded in your training and both of you can fill any position here."

"Okay, that all makes sense," I said as Jessica came through the door. She looked at me.

"Ready whenever you are. The boys just brought us fresh horses," she said. I stood from my chair and started to follow her out. I stopped and looked back at Allan.

"Thanks for filling me in," I said.

"Anytime Jason, anytime," I headed out the door behind Jess and we began to make our rounds. Jessica was going to pull a 24-hour shift and stay until 6:00 in the morning. The girl was tired, but she had tenacity. Mike had left to get some sleep. I climbed up on my horse and Jessica and I headed out.

The security team had debated using the horses at night but the choice to use them had proved to be the right one. They were sure-footed trail horses and they didn't care if it was light or dark outside. We just let them have their heads and they did just fine. It was a good thing too because I had far too many things on my mind to try and control a 1,000-pound animal.

The shift went without incident and Mike replaced Jessica at 6am. At shift change, Dale told me that so far everything was going according to plan with the rescue team. That news gave me a little bit of relief. According to the plan they had laid out, they should be about halfway to the ambush site. Their plan called for them to get within a couple of miles and then hump it the rest of the way on foot after dark. They would report in again when they were leaving their vehicles.

Thursday, July 7, 2016

Mike and I got fresh horses and Dale's boys took the other ones for brushing and feeding. Ben and Mike were really stepping up to the plate for a couple of young kids. They were making everyone proud. I don't know if it was the night shift or the lack of sleep or the fact that so much had happened in such a short time, but I had no idea what day it was. I had to ask Mike to make sure that it was Thursday the 7th of July. He laughed and told me that it was. My sleep-deprived brain was trying like hell to keep up. It was around noon when we spotted a vehicle moving down the main road. Mike called it in, and we kept an eye on it. When it made the turn onto the ranch road, Mike and I started riding toward the main gate. Mike was about to call Allan back and let him know we were going to have company when Allan called him.

"It's a sheriff's deputy, show him in please," when we got to the gate, Mike dismounted and opened it. It was the old Jeep we had seen at the hospital when we rescued Doc. The driver slowed but Mike waved him through before he could stop. I followed the little Jeep to the security shack and climbed down off my horse. I recognized the officer as Deputy Owens. I escorted him into the office. He quickly pulled a note from his pocket and handed it to Allan.

"A message from Sheriff Case," he announced. The young man was standing at attention. Allan looked from the note to the young deputy.

"At ease son," he said. "Take a seat please," he motioned for the young man to sit in a chair. Allan opened the note and read it. He looked up at the deputy and then to me and then back to the deputy. He then sat at the desk and pulled a notepad out and began to write. The next few minutes were spent in total silence. When Allan was done writing, he tore the sheet from the pad and neatly folded it. When he stood the deputy popped out of his chair like he was on springs. Allan handed the note to him.

"Deputy Owens."

"Yes sir!"

"Take this note to Sheriff Case as quickly as you can. Tell him that it will happen tonight, after dark."

"Yes sir!" the young man said as he snapped Allan a salute. Allan returned the salute and the deputy was out the door double-time. Mike was still at the gate waiting to open it.

"What the hell was all of that?" I asked Allan when I heard the little Jeep start.

"That young man is scared shitless. He was a Marine before he became a cop. He's reverting to what kept him alive in the past," Allan picked the note up off the desk and handed it to me. I read it and by the time I was done, my hands were shaking. Louie was down to three deputies. His men and their families were being targeted and eliminated. He wanted to use the cover of darkness to move his remaining men and families to the ranch. Sheriff Case wanted it to happen tonight before he could lose another man.

"What's our play?" I asked Allan. "That's too many people for me to pick up in one trip," I stated.

"You and Mike will ride escort in your truck, Jessica and I will bring the five-ton. Bring the AR's up from underground and make sure all of them are suppressed. Four for us and four more strapped in the back of the five-ton. Throw two more in the back seat of your truck. Ammo cans and eight spare mags per rifle. Spare body armor and helmets for the civilians. NVGs and comms for every vehicle crew. Now get it done!" he snapped. I nearly knocked Mike down with the door when I bolted out of the office. Mike quickly caught up to me and I filled him in on the run.

It took us nearly two hours to get everything loaded up for our rescue mission. When we had our pre-mission briefing, Susan and Dale were also present. Susan was instructed to be ready for casualties and she said that she was as ready as she could be. Dale would be pulling compound security solo and monitoring comms. His horse was saddled and waiting outside the security shack in case he had to get to the gate in a hurry. I was going to be driving my truck with Mike in the passenger seat. Allan was going to drive the five-ton with Jessica riding shotgun. We were going to pull up to the sheriff's office at 10pm, load everyone in the back of the five-ton and haul ass. We were to drive blacked out and let nothing stop us. Allan said that we were not expecting a fight but if we ended up in one, the bad guys would know that they had screwed with the wrong people. Everyone checked their own weapons and gear to make sure they were good to go. Comms were checked and the NVG's tested. Now all we had to do was wait.

I was in the shack right at dusk when Dale received the radio call from Jill and her team. They had reached their first objective and were departing for their second. All was well. I did not talk to her but hearing her voice made me feel better. So much for not doing anything stupid in her absence.

CHAPTER 10

We rolled out of the gate at 9pm. Trying to drive with NVG optics on your face was a different sort of challenge. Your brain was screaming that it was dark, and you needed lights. Your eyes were saying that they could see just fine in the green glow. Mike and I were calling out obstacles as we came across them. A stalled car in the left lane, one on the right shoulder and so on. We were traveling right at 60 miles per hour on the open road but that would change drastically once we were inside the city limits.

Once we reached the edge of town, Mike had his rifle up and his head on a swivel. I was sure Jessica was doing the same thing. All of us heard the gunfire coming from the direction we were heading to. Allan was trying to raise the sheriff on the radio but was having no luck. We slowed our pace but only slightly. When we eased around the last corner we could see the source of the gunfire. There were two dozen cars against the curb on the opposite side of the street from the office. Mike and I could see sporadic gunfire from there directed at the front of the building across the street. There were a couple of bodies lying in the street, not moving.

At this point we were still undetected in the black night. I stopped the truck and told Allan to have Jessica come up and drive my truck. Mike and I were going to go thin the herd a little. I grabbed my rifle and jumped out of the truck and Jessica jumped in the open door. Mike and I slipped silently into the dark. I had stopped the truck a full two blocks from the gunfight, so it did not surprise me that they had not seen us. There was no moon in the sky. Their night vision had been ruined by all the muzzle flashes and their hearing had to be in the toilet too.

We were working our way down the sidewalk at a 90-degree angle to the bad guys. It looked like ten of them. We were also using the stalled cars as cover should we be discovered. I would bound past Mike and then take cover between cars and cover him while he bounded past me. That got us to within a car length of the first thug. He had no clue that death was about to ruin his day. Mike waited until he was looking the other way. He stepped out of cover and crept up behind him, the suppressed barrel only two inches from the back of his head. Mike squeezed the trigger, the rifle making a quiet pop, and the thug went face down in the gutter.

Mike slipped into the thug's hiding spot. I was watching the other thugs but none of them looked in our direction.

It was then that there was a huge volley of gunfire from the sheriff's office. It dawned on me that Mike and I might become the victims of friendly fire. Mike waved at me and I sprinted past him to the next break in the cars. As I rounded the corner of the car, I came face to face with thug number two. The surprise on his face disappeared quickly. The suppressor of my rifle smashed into his chest and I pulled the trigger. I had the rifle set to a three-round burst, so he never stood a chance. He rolled backwards and fell halfway into the street. Two down, eight to go was the only thing I could think.

Mike ran up to my position and ducked in with me. Neither of us spoke, instead we used hand signals.

There were four taking cover behind a van two car lengths ahead. We agreed on a plan and waited for the gunfire from the office to slack off before we moved. As soon as the incoming rounds died down, the thugs all jumped up to return fire. Mike and I both stepped from our cover and ran down the sidewalk toward the bad guys. One of them spotted us but it was far too late for him. Mike put a three-round burst in his chest. Before he hit the ground the other three were also dead. Mike was working the targets left to right and I was working them right to left. Instead of stopping and taking cover, Mike and I picked up the pace and ran at the four remaining attackers. They may have seen us, but it was too late for them. It was over in an instant.

The gunfire from the front of the sheriff's office had ceased and was replaced by cheers. Mike and I both replaced our magazines and I started across the street. I got on the radio and told Jessica to bring the trucks up. A moment later I heard the diesels coming down the road. Mike went to picking up all the weapons and ammo from the thugs. He had to dispatch one with a round between the eyes. Allan pulled up in the five-ton and backed it up to the entrance. He was coordinating with a deputy to bring weapons and ammo, any working communications equipment and finally the families. He wanted them safe inside until everything else was loaded. Once everything of use was taken from the dead thugs, it was loaded in the back of my truck. We would sort it all out later.

Thirty minutes later, we were back on the road. We drove as fast as we dared to get back to the ranch. I didn't know if we had any wounded and I was also worried about more thugs picking up our trail. It was just best that we un-assed the area as quickly as possible. We pulled through the gate at 12:32 in the morning. I drove up to the infirmary and Susan was waiting with her gurney. Allan brought the five-ton to a stop and shut it down. Susan started to move with the gurney, but he waved her off.

Mike and I both moved to the back of the big truck and started helping the deputies unload their families. That's when I saw the body bag on the floor. A quick look around and I realized Sheriff Case was not among the living. That hit me like a ton of bricks. Once the women and children were herded into the clinic, the three deputies brought the gurney over and removed the black bag from the back of the truck. It was covered with a sheet and moved to the back room of the clinic. Jessica had excused herself about 20 minutes before and joined Dale at the shack. Mike and I were just about to do the same thing when Allan approached the two of us.

"Jill is going to kick my ass when she gets back here," he said to me with a grin playing across his face.

"What? Why?"

"She told me explicitly to keep you from doing stupid shit and you went and did it anyway!" Mike started to laugh when Allan looked at him. "After she kicks my ass, she is going to kick yours too!"

"It wasn't my idea!" he blurted.

"You really think that is going to matter?" Allan said. "Seriously though, you guys did a hell of a job tonight. If you hadn't acted when you did, that could have ended very differently. Nice work," neither Mike nor I knew exactly what to say so we both just said thanks and headed for the shack.

Friday, July 8, 2016

When Mike and I walked through the door, I could see concern on Jessica's face. I looked at Dale.

"Like I told Jessica, it is probably nothing to worry about, but the other team missed their midnight check-in. There are a million different reasons why that might happen, none of them are bad," he said. He was right. One missed check-in was nothing to worry about.

"It's okay Jess, they could be up against a mountain, they could be sneaking around and have the radio off. It could be anything," I tried to reassure her. "We can't let this get to us, it's normal on this kind of operation. Right now, we have to get back to work," she took a deep breath and blew it out.

"You're right, I'll go get the horses," she said and left the shack. I turned back to Dale.

"When is their next check-in?"

"6am, four and a half hours from now."

"All right, I'll be out patrolling with Jessica. Mike, go get some sleep. You have to be on duty in four and a half hours," I said.

Mike headed out the door muttering something about sleep. I didn't catch what he said and I'm not sure I wanted to.

Once Jessica and I were on the horses and making our rounds, my mind began to wander a little. It was Friday the 8th of July and in the span of four days my world had vanished. In a flash at 9pm on the 4th of July, my world was ripped from me in a blinding instant. In the past four days I had stolen a patient from a hospital and committed not one but two acts of breaking and entering. Technically that probably wouldn't stick since I was just helping a friend out. What else. I had the woman of my dreams tell me that she loved me and an hour later sent her on a rescue mission a hundred miles away. My brother and his family were, as of now, missing. I was party to a gunfight that left ten bad guys and the county sheriff dead. Now I was riding around in the dark, on a horse, wearing full body armor and a suppressed AR-15. Four days and this was what my life had become.

It just seemed strange how quickly our lives could be altered. I wasn't the only one who was trying to wrap my head around it all. Everyone here was dealing with the effects of the EMP in one way or another. I hated to even think it, but we were the lucky ones. We had prepared for this; we had trained for this. There were people out there dying on a massive scale because they had done nothing to prepare. We were pretty safe behind our ten-foot-tall wall of concrete. We had people like me who were willing to risk everything to make sure those inside these walls were safe. In theory, once everyone was accounted for, we would never have to leave the safety of these 21 acres. Everything we needed was here.

Unfortunately, I knew that was false hope. People like us always did everything we could to help those in need. We proved that last night. Other good people needed our help and we ran toward the sound of gunfire to help them. We never once questioned what we were doing. We just did it. We did not ask for anything in return, nor would we. I knew now, without a doubt, that any one of us would do anything for anyone else who lived within these walls. Up to and including lay down our lives. All of us knew that evil was lurking on the outside. It was there. It was palpable. I no longer feared it, but I did understand it. I understood that the lurking evil would stop at nothing to take what we had here. I also understood that we must be willing to stop at nothing to protect it. Maybe that was why I had no remorse for the killing that I was a party to last night. I found it regretful that it had to be done. I didn't enjoy it. It was just necessary. Like putting down a feral, rabid animal.

I was so distracted by my own thoughts that I failed to realize that Jessica had led us back to the shack. It was 5:55 in the morning. She and I both dismounted and the Butler twins took our horses to the barn. Two fresh ones were waiting for the day shift. I was trying to walk in the door, but my legs were just not working right. The exhaustion was catching up fast. Mike was right behind me and helped me through the door. He pointed me to a chair, but I opted to hold up the wall. It was 6am sharp and the radio crackled to life. The conversation was very short and one-sided. Jill reported that they had located the package wrapper but not its contents. She also reported that there was a herd of cows and had counted 22 that night. They would check in again at the regular time. That was all code. They had found the Jeep but not the people. They had also located the enemy camp and there were 22 combatants. At this point they had only observed and not made contact. Jessica and I both relaxed a little. The last thing I remember was sliding down the wall and everyone looking at me.

Saturday, July 9, 2016

I woke up in the pitch black. My muscles were sore, my arms and legs feeling like they were made of lead. It was too much effort to move so I just laid there for a while. I had no idea what time it was and at that point I didn't really care. I was pretty sure I was in my bed. I still had no idea how long I laid there but eventually the door slowly opened and Susan came in carrying a lantern and her small medical kit. She set the lantern on the nightstand and pulled her stethoscope and blood pressure cuff from her kit. I moved a little and it seemed to startle her.

"You're awake," she said with a smile. "You gave us all a bit of a scare there," she took my arm and began to take my blood pressure.

"What happened?" I croaked out.

"The short story is that your body shut itself down from exhaustion. We got you back here and got you into bed and I gave you a little something to keep you asleep," she released the cuff and took it off my arm.

"How long was I out?" I asked. She looked at her watch.

"Almost 18 hours," she said as she was repacking her stuff. "Don't worry, one of the deputy's is covering your shift. Jill and her team are fine," she smiled at me again. "Allan told me you would want to know that as soon as you were awake. He also told me to tell you that he would be up to see you after the day shift briefing." She slipped out the door but had left the lantern behind, turned way down. I must have nodded off again because the next thing I knew it was 5:00 in the morning. I was still sore, but my muscles were starting to move a little better. I slowly got out of bed and made my way to the bathroom. After a very hot and long shower I was starting to feel better. I got dressed and made my way to the kitchen. As always, the coffee pot was on. I poured myself a cup and headed out the door.

When I got to the shack there were four horses tied up out front. It was five minutes to six so I should be able to catch the morning call from the rescue team. I went through the door and was greeted by both the day and night shift. Two of the deputies, Owens and Hawkins were there. Owens was coming off of night shift with Jessica. Hawkins would be working day shift with Mike. Right on time the radio squawked, and everyone went silent. Jill reported that they had found two of the three packages and that they were going to put the cows to pasture before they returned. Allan and Dale shared a look of concern. Dale put the mic to his mouth and keyed it up.

"Please repeat the last," he said.

"You heard me; we are going to put the cows to pasture. Signing off!" she snapped at her older brother from a hundred miles away. Again, he and Allan shared the look.

"I haven't heard that one before, what is she saying?" I asked.

"They are going on the offensive," Dale said.

"Wait...What? Six people against 22? Call her back right now!" I demanded.

"It's 29 people and it won't do a damn bit of good to call her back. Even if her radio were on, which it's not, she wouldn't answer," Dale snapped at me as he threw the mic down and stood up. "She's hardheaded to begin with and now something has got her worked up," he looked up at me. "And you of all people should know that when she has her mind made up, all conversation is over!" he stormed past me and out the door. Allan spun and followed him out. Everyone else in the room was making themselves busy looking at the floor, the walls, and even the ceiling.

"Jill is his baby sister and she is my girlfriend," I explained to them to try and diffuse the awkwardness a little. That just made it worse. Since I wasn't assigned to patrol duty I sat behind the desk.

"Night shift, anything to report?" I asked.

It was about an hour before Allan returned to the shack. He looked a little surprised to see me sitting in the chair drinking my coffee.

"It wasn't anything personal, just that his brother, sister and father are all out there and someone has not been accounted for. Per protocol, Jill has not said who is missing. Now she has a wild hair up her ass and is going to take on five to one odds. He's just worried," Allan explained.

"I get it Allan, I'm worried too. Listen to me though. Jill trained everyone here, she is the best we have, that's why you sent her. Mike and I put her training to use the other night. We took on five to one odds and we came out without a scratch. She has the best tools and the best crew. Like you told us a few days ago, have a little faith," I got out of his chair and started toward the door but stopped short. "Some days faith is all we have to hang on to and if you're hanging on you might as well hang on like your life depended on it," with that said, I walked out the door.

I wasn't sure where I was headed but I needed to go somewhere. I ended up going to the clinic, figuring I would pay Doc a visit. When I got there, I found him sitting up in his bed reading a book. I sat in the chair next to his bed and we talked for about an hour. His spirits were high, and Susan said that he should be out of bed the next day. She had been taking him for afternoon strolls for two days now and his strength was improving drastically.

After I left the clinic, I went out to the cabins that were under construction. The ground floor was all enclosed and the outside walls were up on the second floor. They were both lacking the roof trusses and all of the roofing. It was my hope that when Jill's team returned, we could begin working on them again. No matter what, they were going to have to be finished now. I did the math and we now had 21 people living here, which included the kids. Sixteen adults and five kids. The Butler boys were the oldest at 16. The youngest, an infant, belonged to Andy and Diane Walker, a deputy and his wife.

We were going to have to do something about the housing situation and soon. Even though the new arrivals were happy to have a roof over their heads, I was sure the dorms weren't appropriate for a family. I was so wrapped up in my own thoughts that I didn't even hear Dale come up next to me. He startled me when he spoke.

"I'm sorry for blowing my top at you this morning, Jason. It was uncalled for and unprofessional."

"I'm over it, Dale, we're still good. You just have a lot of family hanging out there and you're worried and scared," I said.

"I didn't even think when I started yelling that you would be worried about Jill and your family. I just wasn't thinking....."

"Dale, it's okay," I insisted. It was obvious the poor guy felt bad, so I decided to switch subjects on him. "Are we going to have enough food to feed everyone here? We are up to what, 20 people?" I asked him.

"Twenty-one to be exact and yes, we will have plenty of food. As a matter of fact, we are going to have too much even after we can what we need and freeze the rest. We are going to have way too much for our storerooms," he beamed at his accomplishments. "We will begin harvesting in the next day or two."

"What do you plan to do with the extra?"

"We planted enough corn to feed the animals through the winter so a lot of that will be stored for our use. Other things we will keep the seed from for next year's crops and the winter crops for the greenhouses. Everything else we can share, I guess. No sense letting it go to waste."

"How are we set for hay for the horses?" I asked.

"We have enough to get through the winter and well into the summer but after that we will need to think about planting and harvesting our own."

"Do we have the seed for that?"

"Again, yes we do. Your father was very diligent about consulting his experts and he listened to what we told him," he smiled.

"Well, here is a big question for you. Once everyone gets back, are we going to have the manpower to finish these houses and build a couple more?"

"It's not my area of expertise but I think we should be able to resume construction and maintain security. It's just a guess on my part, you would have to ask Allan for a real answer," we talked for another half hour about his part of the ranch operations and the distraction did both of us good. I know that he gave me a lot to think about.

I wandered around for a while longer before I went to get lunch. I went back to my house and found Jessica at the dining room table. It was obvious she had been crying. I offered to make her a chicken sandwich and she accepted. I took the food to the table along with a pitcher of cold water. It took me a few minutes, but I finally got her to open up. She was very worried about Jake. The current situation reminded her all too much of when he was in the Marines and deployed to Iraq. She went on to explain that he lost the lower part of his leg in an IED explosion during his second tour. She went on to say that he was having trouble getting the help he needed from the VA. He couldn't find a job and was pretty much at the end of his rope when they left everything behind in San Diego so she could take a job at Bill's law firm. Bill found out about the trouble they were having and made a few phone calls. Within a week Jake was being fitted for a new leg and getting the counseling that he needed. All of it was paid for by Bill.

When Bill told them about the ranch, they jumped at the offer. Right now, they were very glad that they did. This was probably the safest place around. She was a little stressed about the gunfight the other night though. Not only had that been the closest she had ever been to a dead body, that was the first time she had ever witnessed an actual killing. She now had a comparison to what her husband had seen in Iraq. By the time we were done eating I had convinced her to see Susan. She had become the de facto counselor of the ranch.

Jessica went back to bed with the promise that she would indeed see Susan. After I took care of the dishes, I too went to take a nap. It was one in the afternoon and there was nothing for me to do but wait for the briefing at 6pm. My radio was on, but all had been quiet. I set my alarm for 5pm just in case my nap ran over what I intended.

I was up before my alarm went off. It was 5pm when I left the house, a full hour before the call from Jill should be coming in. Allan was parked behind the desk. I put my butt in the chair across from him. I was really glad that I was early, it gave me time to pick his brain like I had done with Dale. He told me that the construction should be able to continue and that we had enough timber to build two more homes like the ones already under construction. The problem was that we did not have the stuff to finish them. Most of it we could make but the roofing was the biggest problem. The plumbing, fixtures and appliances were next on the list.

When I sarcastically asked how they ever made do in the 1800s, I could see the gears in his mind kick into high gear. We also talked about the repairs to the electrical system. He told me that on day one they repaired the systems that ran the water pumps and communications equipment and while they had all they needed to repair everything else, they just did not have the time to do it. He said that it was going to be a priority as soon as everyone made it back. It was 5:50 when the radio started its squawking. Allan answered it right away.

"You're early," he said into the mic.

"Yep, we are getting ready to go mobile and we are leaving behind everything we don't need," Jill replied.

"Still putting the cows out?"

"Yep, also found some sheepdogs roaming around out here. They are going to help us even the odds."

"Copy on all of that. Godspeed," Allan said and was about to hang up the mic when Jill came back on.

"Tell my man that I'm in the right place at the right time. Tell him that I'm about to do something stupid," the personal message was a total breach of protocol, but Allan went along with it. He handed me the mic.

"Your man says to hang on tight and he says that he already did something stupid," I said and handed the mic back to Allan. We could hear laughter in the background when Jill keyed the mic again.

"Talk to you at 6am, out."

Allan hung the mic back up just as Dale and both shifts walked in the door.

"You just missed the call, they were early," Allan said to Dale.

"Everything okay?"

"Yes, they are leaving the Jeeps and heading out on foot. They left everything behind that they didn't need. Best guess is that she is going to hit them sometime tonight. She has picked up some local help too," Allan finished. He left out the personal message. Dale nodded and traded places with him behind the desk. The shifts traded information and day shift left to go home. Allan and I were walking back to our house.

"Can I ask what all of that was on the radio?" he asked.

"It's kind of a slogan between Jill and me. It's about making a difference in somebody's life, about being there when you're needed the most."

"I see," was all he said, and we continued to walk to the house.

After dinner was eaten, Allan and I both retired for the night. I was going to be working a day shift patrol the next day. I thought sleep was going to be a fleeting thought but was quickly proven wrong.

Sunday, July 10, 2016

I slept until my alarm went off at 5am. Jill was the first thing on my mind, but I was sure of her abilities and those of her team, so I let the thought slip from my mind. I got my shower and my coffee and was in the shack by 5:45am. Dale had reported another quiet night. My new partner arrived about five minutes after I did. He formally introduced himself as Dan Hawkins. He was one of Louie's men that we had brought to the ranch. Jessica and Jeff Owens walked in right at six and began their pass down. When that was done everyone was just kind of hanging out waiting to hear from the rescue party. It was 6:10 and nothing. There was a palpable tension building in the room. 6:20 and still nothing. It was 6:30 when the radio finally sounded but it wasn't Jill's voice. It was Mark.

"Mission accomplished. We are expediting our return trip. Inbound heavy with eight souls on board," there was a pause. "Hopefully we make it back with all eight. ETA is two hours," fear and panic were evident in his voice. I could hear the roar of the Jeep's engine and I could hear yelling in the background. It was impossible to make out what was being said or who was saying it.

"Copy that, let us know when you are close and we will clear the pad," Allan said. The only reply he got was the two clicks in acknowledgment.

"You heard him, they ran into trouble and are hauling ass home," he stood from behind the desk and grabbed a radio from the charger. Jessica, get to the clinic and tell Susan to prepare for casualties and give her a hand setting it up. Jeff and Dan, I want you to pull a quick patrol and be at the clinic when they pull up, we may need the extra hands. Dale, I know it's your family out there, but could you hold down the shack and communications? At least until they get here."

"Sure thing," Dale replied.

"Jason, you're with me! Move people!" Everyone scattered. Allan and I headed to barracks one. When we got there, he talked to Miranda Hawkins and

Diane Walker. They were the wives of two of the deputies. He pressed Miranda into service in the clinic. Diane was going to stay behind and take care of the kids. Andy Walker was still down sick, so he was allowed to stay in bed. Allan checked his watch and we headed to the clinic.

The clinic was a hive of activity. Jessica was lining up the four gurneys that we had. Susan was in the back room of the clinic setting up her surgical trays around her surgical table. It was actually one of Doc's stainless-steel vet tables, but it would do the job, if it was needed.

Doc was on his feet and moving around pretty well. His arm was in a cast and he had gotten rid of the sling. Miranda got there about five minutes after Allan and I did. Doc was giving her a crash course in bandages and surgical tools. She was a quick study and was going to help if surgery was needed. Allan excused himself and went to the security shack. When he returned, he had two pistols in his hand. He put one in a drawer in the surgical room and did the same thing in the waiting room. He made sure everyone knew where they were. He explained that there were only supposed to be seven people returning. Mark had reported that eight were inbound. It was just a precaution.

It was 8:21 when Dale got on the radio and let everyone know that the Jeeps had just turned off the main road and they were coming in hot. Jeff and Dan were at the gate and they pushed it open as the Jeeps closed the distance. As soon as both of them cleared the gate, they secured it and jumped on their horses. They headed to the clinic at a full gallop. They were pushing the Jeeps as hard as they dared through the turns of the driveway and both of them slid to a stop in front of the clinic.

Mark was driving the lead Jeep and he jumped out as soon as it had come to a stop. He was yelling for a medic as he threw open the back door. Jessica and I were rushing toward him with a gurney when he leaned in and lifted Jill's limp body from the backseat. Her BDU shirt and tank top were gone and there was a blood-soaked bandage secured to her chest. A woman that I didn't know emerged from the backseat with Jill. She held a nearly empty IV bag in the air and followed Mark to the gurney. When Mark laid her on the gurney, I could see that she actually had two bandages. I recognized the one on her chest as an occlusive dressing. It was used in the treatment of a sucking chest wound. The one on her arm by the armpit looked like it was wrapped as tight as they could get it and it was still

THE RANCH

bleeding profusely. The woman with the IV bag grabbed ahold of the bandage and squeezed as hard as she could.

The four of us rushed her into the clinic and Susan stopped us in the waiting room. The woman that I didn't know started talking rapid fire medical terminology to Susan. Everything around me felt like it was moving in slow motion and everyone sounded like they were muted. All I could see was Jill on the gurney with blood-soaked bandages. The blood was already beginning to soak the white sheet she was laying on and dripping onto the polished hardwood floor.

She was so pale, and the only movement was the shallow breaths she was taking. Susan pushed her way past me and felt for a pulse in her injured arm. Then she started packing more bandage material into her armpit. She pushed past me again and shined a small flashlight in Jill's eyes. Doc was standing by with the BVM (Bag Valve Mask) when Jessica inserted an oropharyngeal airway and took the bag from him. She started bagging Jill in an attempt to assist her breathing as her breaths were far too shallow. I could feel my heart sinking. Jess looked at me and we locked eyes. I could see her lips moving but I wasn't hearing the words. Jessica and the new woman traded places and Jess grabbed me by the arm. She forcibly pulled me from the room.

She basically dragged me out the front door, and once we were moving, she yanked me around the corner of the building, away from everyone else's eyes. She stopped pulling me and spun around to get right in my face. We were literally nose to nose.

"Jason, I need you to pull it together right now!" she growled. I just stared at her. "I won't bullshit you Jason and you know that. Jill is in rough shape. She's lost a lot of blood and they are going to rush her into surgery right now. Are you hearing me?" her voice was low, but I heard her. I nodded and I could see a change in her eyes, an angry change. She took a small step back and slapped me hard across the face. In that instant it was like someone had suddenly turned the volume back up. She leaned in close again, her voice still a growl. "Pull it together and do it right the fuck now! Jill did her job out there and she is still doing it! She is fighting for her life! Doc and Susan are fighting for her life. That paramedic chick fought for her life for two hours! Step up and do your job!" I took a deep breath and I started to feel renewed energy. I was getting pissed. Not because she was in my face but because she was right.

163

"You have about two seconds to get out of my face Jess!" I said it with way more anger than I intended. She took a step back and for a second I thought she might slap me again.

"Jill would have smacked you too. She would be pissed off at you for falling apart and you know it. She would tell you to get out there and do your job," she said. I stood fully erect and took another deep breath.

"Are we going to stand here and blow smoke up each other's ass or are we going to go sort this shit out?" I asked her. She didn't answer. Instead she spun on her heel and went back inside the clinic to treat the wounded. I was right behind her. She stopped at the door and turned to face me again.

"No, that's as far as you go for now. Jill is going into surgery and there is nothing for you to do in there. Go check on them," she pointed out to the grass area where everyone else was. "If anything changes, I promise, I **will** come get you," I nodded and slowly backed away from the door.

I went to see what I could do to help the others. I knew there were some other injuries but nothing as severe as Jill. The first patient I came to was Jake. He was leaning against the second Jeep holding his prosthetic leg. He wasn't hurt but the leg was missing everything below the ankle. I checked him over and as he said, he wasn't injured. All the blood on his hands and pants wasn't his. He explained to me that his prosthetic had been amputated by a guy wielding a double-bladed ax. I helped him get over to a shady spot on the grass and got him sat down.

I moved on and found Miranda cleaning and bandaging what looked like a cross between a cut and a burn on Mark's neck. He was flinching in pain, but he wasn't giving Miranda a hard time. He and I exchanged nods and I moved on. I found Alex sitting on the curb staring at the Jeep Jill had been in. I looked to see that he was staring at the bloody door panel and seat. There was also a wad of blood-soaked bandages along with Jill's ripped multi-cam shirt on the ground and medical gear scattered all over the backseat. As I walked past the Jeep, I picked up the bandage and shirt and threw it on the floorboard. I closed the door and put myself in Alex's line of sight. He looked up as I approached. I reached my hand down to him and he took it. I pulled him up off the curb.

"You alright son?" I asked him.

"Fine sir."

"You don't look fine; you look like someone kicked you in the nuts."

"Is Jill.......?" his voice faded away.

"Is Jill dead? Is that what you were going to ask?

"Yes sir."

"No. She is not dead. She is in a bad way; I won't lie to you. She is a fighter and she has the best team of medics working on her. Understand?" I asked.

"Yes sir," he replied.

"Now, I need you to get back to work. Can you do that for me?"

"Yes sir."

"Double time it to the basement of my house. In the storeroom is a set of crutches. Get them and bring them back here," I ordered.

"Yes sir!" he said and bolted for my house.

I turned around and found Jeff and Dan. I waved them over. Once they were standing in front of me, I told them what I wanted. "Get these Jeeps out of here. Take them to the pole barn and strip all of the gear out of them and off of them. Take the garden hose and wash all of the blood out. There is nothing in them you can hurt so be generous with the water. Radio me when you are done."

"Yes sir!" they both said and were gone with the Jeeps within seconds.

When I started to walk back to Mark, I saw Bill Butler walking out of the clinic. He looked like he had gone ten rounds with Mike Tyson. He was shielding his one good eye from the sun when he spotted me walking toward him.

"Jason!" he said, his hand outstretched. I took it and the old man still had the iron grip.

"Damn Bill, you look like shit."

"I feel like shit too," he quickly replied. I could see that he had some stitches in his forehead and scalp. His nose had been broken and his lips looked like he tried to kiss a meat grinder. There was what I guessed to be antibiotic ointment caked all over them.

"Miranda, I think that was her name, told me to find a place and park my ass. The seating arrangements around here suck." He tried to smile but it was too painful. I walked him to a place in the shade and helped him to the ground. "Has anybody said anything to you about Jill's condition?" he asked.

"Just what Jessica told me, but at this point you probably know more than I do," I told him.

"She will pull through this Jason. If anyone can, she will. She is a fighter and don't ever forget that," he tried to reassure me.

"I'd love to stay and chat," I told him. "But I have other things to attend to. If you need anything just yell, okay?" he nodded and leaned back on his elbows in the grass. Alex had returned with the crutches and I had him take them to Jake. He had returned to my side as I had asked him to do.

"Alex, there is a case of water in the fridge of the shack. Go get it and bring it back here. Make sure everyone gets some please."

"Yes sir!" he was gone a second later. I really needed to keep that kid busy and keep his mind off Jill. I headed back over to talk to Mark and found him laid out on the grass in front of the clinic. I kneeled down next to him.

"How's Jill?" he asked.

"I don't know, I've been banned from the inside of the clinic. Want to give me a rundown on all of the people you brought back?"

"Sure," he said as he sat up. "The two who were with dad are Marcus and Contessa Thompson. He was a welder/fabricator, she was a dental assistant. That fiery redhead is Amanda McHale, a paramedic from the UK. Other than that, I can't tell you much about them."

"Trust them?"

"The Thompson's I do. My dad handpicked them. We grabbed Amanda before the shitheads who had dad could have their way with her. I'll say that she's spunky."

I looked at my watch and it was approaching 9:30am. It had only been an hour since this shitstorm had begun. I saw Allan come out of the clinic and I headed toward him. He met me halfway.

"Marcus and Contessa are both going to be okay. Miranda and Amanda are getting them bandaged up and they should be out shortly," he said. He didn't say anything about Jill, and I didn't ask.

"I was thinking, we need to get everyone together for a debriefing as soon as possible. We need to find out what went right and what went wrong, and we need to do it while it is still fresh," I said.

"You're right. Where and when do you want to do it?"

"Noon in the conference room of barracks one."

"All right, I'll spread the word," Allan said.

"Put Alex to work moving enough chairs in there for everyone. He needs to be kept busy," I told him. "I've got him getting water for everyone right now."

"I'm sure I can find something for him to do. Is this meeting an all-hands or do we leave someone in the shack?" he asked.

"Bring everyone. If the medics are still busy, leave them alone but I want everyone else there."

"Okay, I have some things to take care of. I'll take care of Alex too," he left, and I was standing alone in front of the clinic taking everything in when Marcus and Contessa came out the front door. He was limping a little and she had a bandage on her left hand. They introduced themselves to me and asked if there was anything they could do to help.

Everything was going as well as it could so there was really nothing left to do but wait until noon for the briefing, so I told them to find a shady spot and try to relax a little.

By 10:30 most of the people had dispersed. All of them knew about the meeting at noon. Jeff and Dan had cleaned out the Jeeps and returned them to the parking area. They both walked up to me and I could see that Dan was holding a plate carrier in one hand. It was still wet from being washed off, but I could still read the name plate on the front. J. Butler. All of the magazines were gone, and the left side of the fabric was torn away. He handed it to me.

"That is why we wear this heavy shit. If she had not had this on, we would be planning a funeral right now," he said. "Look close at the impact site," I lifted the heavy carrier up so that I could get a better look at the damage. It quickly became obvious that the round did not hit straight on, there was an angle to the damage of the plate. I couldn't get a real good look at it, so I pulled the plate out. I set the carrier on the grass and took a closer look at the plate. Even with the angle of the impact, there was significant deformation. The initial impact was about two inches from the upper left corner. Instead of skipping off the plate, the round actually creased it and penetrated about a half-inch from the edge and broke a chunk off.

"Shit," was all I could mutter.

"If that round had hit head on, the impact trauma alone would have killed her instantly," Jeff said.

"Any idea on caliber?" I asked.

"Bare minimum, .308 at fairly close range. Has anyone said what went down?" Dan asked.

"No, we will get the play-by-play at the briefing," I picked up the carrier and put the plate back in it. I handed it back to Dan and told him to bring it to the meeting. They left within a couple of minutes and I was alone with my thoughts. That was a bad place to be.

My truck was about fifty feet from the door of the clinic, backed into a parking spot. I walked over, dropped the tailgate and sat on it. At 11:15 Amanda McHale came out of the clinic. She walked around the corner and lit a cigarette. She was about halfway through it when she spotted me. She started walking toward me.

"Those things will kill ya," I said and started laughing at the irony of it all. Here I was, sitting there in full body armor, a pistol strapped to my leg and a military grade AR laying on the tailgate next to me. Her blue jeans and white t-shirt were covered in dried blood. When she got close, she reached out her hand and introduced herself. I shook her hand and returned the introduction.

"Are you the only Jason here?" she asked.

"As far as I know I am. Why do you ask?"

"In the Jeep, right after Jill got hit, I was trying to stop the bleeding and she kept saying that Jason was going to be pissed. Before she went unconscious, she started asking for you. She kept telling Mark to drive faster," she said. Her Irish accent was thick. I took a deep breath and tried to hang on to my composure. I needed to change the subject.

"You're a paramedic, right?" I asked.

"I am, been one for seven years now."

"Mark told me you were from the UK but that is an Irish accent if I've ever heard one."

"I've been working in the UK, I'm originally from Cork," she said.

"What the hell brought you all the way over here?"

"My ex-husband," she laughed a little. "I signed the divorce papers with that cheating bastard a month ago. Our flat in London sold three weeks ago so I decided to spend my half of the money on a road trip across the States. That seems to have ended like my marriage, badly," I couldn't help but laugh a little. She shot me a sideways look.

"It's not funny but look at the bright side, it could have been worse," I said.

"How the bloody hell could it have been worse? I'm stranded on the opposite side of the world, a world that seems to have come crashing down around our ears!"

"This morning you were in the right place at the right time," I said as I looked at my watch.... 11:45. I slid off the tailgate and stood there for a minute.

"What's that supposed to mean?" she asked.

"Ask Jill," I started walking. "If you are free, we are going to have a meeting with all of the people that were involved in your rescue, you are more than welcome to attend."

"Actually, I can't. I have to get back to your clinic. Thank you though."

CHAPTER 11

The only people who did not attend the meeting were Susan, Doc, Amanda and Diane. I was the last one to arrive and I took the only empty chair, at the head of the table. Allan had seen to it that everyone had a notepad and a pen. I cleared my throat and began.

"Sometime between 6pm last night and 6:30 this morning, something went very wrong. We are here to find out what that something was so that we can prevent it from happening again. We are NOT here to place blame or point fingers. As the guy sitting in the big chair at the head of the table, I am ultimately responsible for our successes and our failures. Is everyone clear on the objective of this meeting?" I asked. I made eye contact with everyone in the room. There were nods and yes answers from everyone.

"Since Mark was the Executive Officer on this mission, I would like to turn it over to him so that he can walk us through the mission from the time they left here to the time they returned. Please do not interrupt him. If you have questions or comments, write them down and we will address them in a Q&A forum when he is done. Mark, the floor is yours." he nodded and stood.

"When we left here Thursday night, it was slow going. We really weren't sure of what we were going to come across. There were a few people still camped out on the highway, but they gave us no trouble. For the most part the roads were actually clear. Most of the cars had simply coasted off to the side of the highway. We made it about halfway the first night and camped out during the day. It was Friday night when we got to about five miles from where we thought Bill and his team had been ambushed,"

"We stashed the Jeeps in some tall brush and pinion juniper trees. From there we packed up and humped it along the side of the mountains that parallel the highway." He paused and showed us the route they took on the wall map. "There is that huge truck stop at Imlay and it was our objective to be in position to watch it during the day. We tried to call in, but the mountains were interfering too much. We watched the truck stop all day and it was obvious some bad shit was going on there. At dusk we moved farther south and scouted along the road. That's when we found what was left of the Jeep. It was obvious to us, even from a distance, that someone had followed protocol and destroyed it and its contents. Bill said that they had thrown half a dozen lit road flares into it as they were leaving."

"We could also see someone was ambushing travelers. We put that on our list of things to take care of before we left the area. I'm going to gloss over a lot of stuff because everything up until this morning went exactly by the book. We found Marcus and Contessa hiding in the trees about a half mile from the ambush spot. They had told us that Bill had been captured and taken to the truck stop. We knew at that point that we were going to be going on the offense. We spent a lot of time watching how they did things. Where were the guards, when did they do shift change and so on."

"Saturday night we thought we were about to be ambushed so we took up positions to defend. After a very tense hour of sneaking around we discovered that we had some new friends. Six cowboys from a ranch not far from where we were. One of theirs had been killed by the assholes at the truck stop. It didn't take us long to form a plan to work together. Everyone would be in position to hit them at midnight last night," he took a long drink from his bottle of water and began again.

"It was straight up midnight when all hell broke loose. We hit them from one angle and the cowboys got them from the other angle. Before they even had a chance to react, we had cut their numbers in half. With our suppressed weapons and night vision we pushed right into their camp and it quickly turned into a knife fight in a phone booth. Eight minutes later, it was all over. Thirty-two assholes had been removed from the gene pool."

"Our only casualty was Jake's leg. It got chopped off at the ankle with an ax. We freed eight people. Bill and Amanda were going with us and the other six went with the cowboys. Jill and Alex humped it back to the Jeeps and brought them to the truck stop. We spent some time looking around to see if there was anything useful but there wasn't much. We topped all of our fuel tanks off from the underground tanks and we were getting ready to radio in. This is the point at which everything went shit sandwich on us."

"Jill and I were talking about pushing all the way back to the ranch or taking our time. She was just starting to turn away from me when it felt like a red-hot poker had hit the side of my neck, but I heard it as much as I felt it. The sound was a high-pitched whistle. I also heard a distinct CLANG. Jill stopped and turned back toward me. I'll never forget this. She pulled her hand up to look at something and there was blood running off of her fingers. Both of us just stood there looking at the blood dripping on the ground. Then I heard the crack of a gunshot. Jill was starting to collapse so I scooped her up and shoved her into the open back door of the Jeep. I was yelling at everyone to de-ass the area. Amanda jumped in on top of Jill and we all hauled ass. We were about ten miles from the truck stop. Amanda was screaming at me to pull over. We found a dirt road and cut off the highway before we stopped."

He continued, "Amanda had a death grip on Jill's upper arm, trying to get enough pressure on it to stop the bleeding. We parked the Jeeps side-by-side and pulled Jill out onto the ground. Alex got the medical gear and Amanda went to work. At this point Jill was still conscious and talking to her. We took off her body armor and cut her shirts off. Once Amanda got most of the bleeding stopped, she started an IV. We loaded Jill back in and hauled ass here. Amanda held pressure the entire time. The bleeding wasn't stopped but she had gotten it slowed way down. We were around Carlin when Jill finally went unconscious on us. There were stretches of road where we were doing 120 mph and then some. It still felt slow," he paused for a moment then turned it back over to me.

"Thank you, Mark. I saw that a couple of you were taking notes, so I'll open it up to questions now," Dan Hawkins was the first with his hand in the air. "Yes, Dan?"

"Mark, first, thank you for the account. Can you tell me how long after Jill was struck that you heard the shot?" he asked.

"I honestly don't know. My best guess is three to five seconds."

"How far apart were the two of you standing?"

"About eight to ten feet I guess."

"This may seem stupid, but how tall are you?"

"Five feet ten inches, why?"

"I'm trying to do the math on this shooting. Jill is what, five eight?"

"That's pretty close to right," Mark answered. Dan was listening but he was writing furiously on his note pad.

"Where were the mountains in relation to you? In front of you? Behind you?"

"They were behind me," Dan took some more notes and walked over to the wall map. It was a topographical map, so it showed the elevation contours. He was in the middle of scribbling more notes when there was a knock on the conference room door. Amanda peeked in.

"Sorry to interrupt, but I need you Jason," she said. Allan looked at me and waved me out of the room

"GO!" he said. I bolted out of my chair and everyone cleared a path. We were moving quickly, Amanda right behind me. I hit the front door of the barracks and took off at a full sprint. When I burst through the door of the clinic, both Doc and Susan stopped me from entering the surgical room.

"Slow down!" Susan demanded. She was blocking the door. "Jill is holding her own right now. We repaired the damaged artery in her arm, and we repaired her damaged lung. That was the easy part. The next few days will be critical. Every hour that she hangs on, her chances improve but it will be a while before she is out of the woods. She is heavily sedated, and we will keep her that way for a few days. We need to give our repairs a chance to take hold. I'm going to let you in there, but you have to be quiet and you have to be prepared for what you are going to see. Most of her chest is black and blue. We have her on an IV and whole blood to try and replenish what she lost. Talk to her, she can hear you. Do not, under any circumstances, lose your shit in there. Are we clear?"

"Yes ma'am," I said. She slowly moved to one side and let me pass. I pushed the door open and walked into the dimly lit room. All of the blood-soaked sheets and bandages were gone, and Jill was in a semi-sitting position on a hospital bed. She was covered in a white sheet and an off-white blanket. Her bandage wrapped around her chest, shoulder and upper arm. Her breathing was still a little shallow but way better than when she had arrived. I sat quietly in the chair next to her right side. It took me a while to come up with something to talk to her about but eventually I was blabbering away.

Every hour on the hour Susan would come in and quietly take her vital signs and check her bandage for bleeding. She did that for the first four hours that I was there. After that it was Doc's turn. A little after 6pm, Jessica brought me dinner. She spent about ten minutes there, wanting to see how her friend was doing. I think it was around midnight when I finally fell asleep in the chair. I didn't sleep well by any stretch of the imagination.

Monday, July 11, 2016

It was 5:30 when Allan brought me breakfast and coffee. He visited until I had eaten and then he left. Doc and Susan had both taken the time to tell me that she would remain sedated for a few days. They did not want her to wake up until she was a little stronger. They urged me to go take a shower and get some decent sleep. I refused.

When Jessica had brought me dinner that evening, she commented that Jill's color was improving. Since I had refused to leave, Doc and Susan had made me a deal. Go take a shower and when I got back, they would have a bed made up next to Jill's. I conceded and went to the house. After a real fast shower and a change of clothes, I was back in the clinic. They had indeed made up a bed for me right next to Jill.

I slept better that night and awoke the following morning feeling a whole lot better. Jill was still unconscious, but her breathing and her color were back to normal. They changed her bandage that morning and I got a good look at the damage that had been done. They had me glove up and assist them because they knew that I would be the one doing it when she came home. It was a little after 1pm when Dale slipped into the room. He visited for a little while then asked to speak to me outside. Reluctantly, I went with him.

"We've been harvesting from the greenhouses the last two days and we have everything we need for our own needs. I think it is time to figure out how we are going to get the rest of it to town," he said.

"Why don't you work with Allan on that?" I asked him, just a little annoyed.

"He told me to talk to you. He wants you to be in charge of that."

"Tell Allan to come find me," I said. I turned abruptly and went back in the clinic. It was only ten minutes later that Allan came into the room.

"How's she doing?" he asked.

"Better. Her vital signs are getting stronger. They've got her on some heavy-duty sedatives and antibiotics."

"I'm glad to hear that she is doing better. Can I speak to you please? Outside," I followed him to the waiting room.

"Dale tells me you had something to say to me. What's on your mind?"

"How about we start with the fact that my girlfriend is laying on a bed in there recovering from a gunshot wound. I'm not going anywhere!" I told him.

"If you think it is healthy to sit here and hold a vigil until she is well again, you're wrong. We have things to do and Jill would want you to do them. What was its Jessica said to you? Do the damn job!" he growled. I had never seen Allan angry, so this was uncharted territory for me. I averted my eyes and looked at my boots. "It's one thing to be worried and scared. It's another thing entirely to withdraw from everyone who needs you, who is counting on you. Jill would be up and off of that bed if she could hear you. You know it too. If the roles were reversed and that was you laying in there, she would do her job," he took a deep breath and changed tactics.

"Jason, this place is all Jill has known for the last five years. She didn't see this coming but if she did, she would have thrown herself in front of that bullet to save it and the people who live here. You need to go into town and start forging a relationship with the townsfolk. If the Mayor is there, work with him."

"If you want a diplomat, then you really should talk to Dale. If you want someone to broker a deal, you need Bill. Not me."

"You may not think so Jason, but you are the leader of this outfit. You have stepped up more than you will ever realize and now I'm asking you to do it again," he said. I looked around and sat in one of the chairs.

"Listen to me, Allan. I can't lead these people. I do what needs to be done. That doesn't make me the leader."

"Jason, you couldn't be more wrong. The other night when we went to get the deputies, I watched you do something, and I couldn't believe my own eyes. Mike told me that there was no plan to take out those thugs, but you blazed the way and he followed. Not because he had to, but because he trusted you. He also said that he had never in his life seen anything like that. Every hour that you have spent training with these people came together in a few fleeting moments and YOUR decision to act saved lives," he sat in the chair next to me.

"Allan....... Right after Jill was shot, she was worried that I would be pissed off at her. Amanda told me that she kept saying it over and over again. Just before she passed out from blood loss, she was asking for me," I had to stop for a minute before I totally lost my shit. "I have to be here when she wakes up. I have to tell her that I'm not mad."

"She will be under sedation for at least three more days. Have you already told her that you are not mad at her?" he asked.

"Over and over again. I have gotten on my knees and prayed to God that she will recover. I have prayed more in the last two days than I have in the last two years."

"She heard you. She may not be able to let you know right now, but she heard you. I'm pretty sure God heard you too," Allan said. There was a long period of silence, at least five minutes, before I spoke again.

"I assume this mission to town has to be done tomorrow?"

"It does. The five-ton is already loaded and ready to go."

"We are not just going to give the food away. I want something in return from whoever is leading those people down there."

"Jason, we have always donated the extra food and....." Before he could go any farther, I cut him off.

"I'm not going to ask for anything they need. I will not take away from those that have little to nothing and the deal that I'm planning will benefit all parties involved. They get what they need, and we get what we need," I said sternly.

"Okay, I trust your judgment."

"I pick the team and the equipment that goes. I want to send a crystal-clear message. If I have to lead, let me lead."

"You got it. Just tell me what you need from me," he said. I got up and got a notepad and pen off the front desk.

"Come see me in an hour. I'll have a list for you," with that I went back into Jill's room. I sat next to her bed and began to talk aloud about my plan as I scribbled furiously on the pad. It helped me to voice my thoughts and I could almost hear Jill in my head pointing out things I had missed or forgotten.

It was almost three when Allan returned. I gave him the two-page list and he checked it over. He looked over the top of his glasses with a raised eyebrow.

"Seriously?" he asked.

"Faith Allan, have a little faith."

"I'll put this together tonight."

"Make it so, Number One," he smiled at my TV show reference. It was corny but it helped break a little of the tension between us.

"Aye Captain," he threw a smart salute, did an about face and left. It actually made me smile a little. I went back to writing on the notepad. This time it was a letter to Jill. I didn't stop until just before dinner arrived at 6pm. Jessica brought it in again. She waited for the dishes and started to leave. I followed her out the door, letter in hand.

"Jess, wait up," I said. She stopped and I handed her the letter.

"What's this?"

"I need you to promise me something as Jill's best friend."

"What?"

"If anything ever happens to me, I need you to give that to Jill," she looked at the letter like it had just grown horns and tried to give it back.

"Jason, no, this.... I can't....." she stammered. I pushed her hand with the letter back toward her.

"We live in a very dangerous world now Jess and I cannot bear the thought of something happening to me and Jill not having some last thing to cling to. That is as much for her as it is for me so please hold onto it. Just in case," she kept looking between the letter and me. Finally, she relented and said she would keep it safe for me. I thanked her and sent her on her way.

Doc had been sitting in the office when Allan and I had talked, and he was sitting there for this conversation. Up until now he had said nothing, but I caught his stare as I turned to go back in Jill's room.

"What Doc?"

"Sit for a minute while I tell you a little tale from my youth," he said. I sat in the chair across from his desk, and after putting his feet up on the corner, he started talking again. "When I was just a young lad, I went off to fight a war in a foreign land. I left behind a beautiful woman. My best friend in the world wanted to go with me but couldn't because of some health issues. Anyway, I gave him a letter just like the one you gave to Jess. In that letter I professed my eternal love for her and that basically if I came home in a box, she was to move on and live her life. Love would find her again. Correct me if I'm wrong, but that was the basic gist of the letter you wrote, right?" I nodded. "It was this crotchety old Staff Sergeant that took me under his wing and taught me how to survive a war. Do you want to know what he told me?"

"Yes, I would."

"He said, "Son, fight like you are already dead. Once you start to think that you won't live another day, you fight harder. When you think you're going home in a box, you start to think about how many of the bastards you can take with you. Pretty soon, you're the only one left standing," What I'm getting at Jason is that if you find yourself in the middle of a fight, don't worry about surviving, worry about how many of the pricks you can take with you."

"Damn Doc, that's some heavy shit," I said with a grin.

"You were right you know."

THE RANCH

"About what?"

"About it being a dangerous world. Without the rule of law or the fear of repercussions, men will do unspeakable things to each other. Make no mistake my young friend, for a good while to come, we will be fighting for our lives so every one of us has to fight like today is our last day on this rock," he pulled his feet down and stood up. It was time to check on Jill.

Tuesday, July 12, 2016

The next morning, I was up at 5am. I kissed Jill on her forehead, told her I loved her and left the room. After a shower and breakfast, I changed into the multi-cam fatigues that had been left for me. My black plate carrier had been changed out for a tan one. Instead of all black, now I was in head to toe multi-cam or tan. The black cover had been removed from my helmet and replaced with a tan one. I grabbed my gear and headed out the door. The mission briefing was at 7:00 in the parking lot.

I arrived to find my team and the requested vehicles. There were two Hummers and the five-ton. Mike Taylor and I would be in the lead Hummer, Alex and Dan would be in the middle in the five-ton, and Mark, Marcus and Amanda would be in the last Hummer. All of us were wearing the multi-cam.

I stopped about twenty feet from the vehicles. "Everyone in a line right here, right now!" I shouted. It caught everyone off-guard, but they formed up in front of me quickly enough. I cleared my throat and began to speak loudly. "Today we are going to town to make a trade deal with whoever is in charge down there. We will make a deal, or we will bring all of this food back here. We will not be giving it away to an ungrateful city leadership. Expect anything and everything that may come our way. IF we get in a fight, we fight to win but let me remind you that there ARE innocents down there. All of you have been briefed by Allan this morning and I hope you paid attention. We only get one chance to make a lasting impression. I want that impression to be one of awe and fear. Are we clear?"

"YES SIR!" everyone answered in unison.

"Mount up! We leave in five!" I said. Everyone scrambled to their assigned vehicle. I walked to the lead Hummer and climbed in on the passenger side. Mike had it running when I got in. My AR was laying across the center console alongside his. Every member of the team was issued one of the military grade, suppressed AR's. Mike looked at me and I nodded to him. He dropped it in gear, and we rolled out.

CHAPTER 12

The drive to Elko went fairly well and really quiet. Our little convoy drew some attention and that was exactly what I wanted. Once we made the turnoff from the little two-lane highway onto I-80 we had to slow a little because there were quite a few stalled cars. On our previous excursions to town we had taken the back roads. This time we were making no effort to sneak in. One thing I noticed once we were on the highway was the significant amount of semi-trucks that were abandoned. Most were box-type trailers but there were a few with tarped loads on flatbeds. We passed one that was fully loaded with plywood. Mike and I looked at each other and I'm pretty sure we had the same idea at the same time.

"Don't we need plywood at the ranch?" he asked with a smile on his face.

"Yup, and it looks to be left there just for us!" I said. We continued on our way to town and made it to about a quarter mile from the first exit when we came to our first test. There were cars turned length ways across the road. They went off the side of the road and through the median and across the southbound lane. I could see four guys manning the roadblock. They were armed with a couple of deer rifles and shotguns. I told Mike to roll up to about 100 feet from the blockade and stop. I squeezed the transmit button on my throat mic and told everyone that it was show time. I switched my radio from PTT, (Push to Talk) to the voice activated position. Anything I said from here on out would be heard by everyone. I pulled my AR off the center console and clipped it to the single point sling around my neck.

Mike slowed the Hummer to a stop and angled it across the two lanes of traffic. The five-ton stopped about 50 feet behind us but stayed in the center of the road. The rear Hummer also angled across the road. I sat there for a second surveying the situation. There were only four guys manning the roadblock and I don't think the oldest was a day over 22 years old. All of them had their guns aimed in our direction. Mike and I both got out at the same time. He walked to the front of the truck and laid his rifle across the hood and I knew it was locked on the target he felt to be the biggest threat. I left my rifle hanging and started walking toward the roadblock. When I was close enough to hear them talking to each other, I stopped right in the middle of the road.

"Which one of you is in charge here?" I bellowed. There was some chatter among the four and finally the one on the right end spoke up.

"I... I am," he sounded scared shitless. "We are not letting anyone through."

"You mean to tell me that you retards are going to try and turn us around?"

"Um, well.... The Mayor told us to close the road."

"Son, we are on official business here and you got until I walk back to that Humvee to get that damn road clear or we are going to ram our way through it!" I started to turn, and he spoke again.

"Sir, the Mayor told us..."

I spun around to face them again. "When I talk to your Mayor the conversation is going to go one of two ways. Either I'm going to tell him he has four idiots out here taking a nice long dirt nap or I'm going to tell him what good boys you are by thoroughly checking us out. The choice is yours," I spun back around and walked back to the Hummer. When I climbed back in and had the door shut, Mike then jumped in. I looked in the direction of the roadblock and could see them arguing.

"As soon as you get this thing pointed at their blockade, aim for the center car and firewall the throttle."

"You got it boss," Mike said as he turned the steering wheel and lined us up. As soon as they heard that diesel start spooling up they started pushing the car out of the lane. We blew through with inches to spare. Once all three rigs were clear I looked at Mike and his grin was huge.

"Like I said, act like you know what you're doing and act like you own the place. People generally won't try to stop you."

"I'm pretty sure at least one of them pissed their pants," he said with a laugh. We could have gone farther before we got off the highway and had a more direct route to the Mayor's office, instead we got off at the first exit and took the long way. Again, I wanted to make sure we were seen. I was surprised to find that a lot of the cars that were blocking the streets on our first visit had been pushed to the side of the road. That told me the small city still had some operating vehicles.

We drove all the way to the Mayor's office without having to re-route because of traffic jams and there were a lot of people that had seen us. I had Mike pull the convoy up right out front and park right in the middle of the street. Both Hummers were again angled across the road. Everyone got out of their vehicles and stood positions around them, rifles at the low ready. Mike stayed with our rig, Mark joined me and the two of us walked up to the front of the building.

Here we found four guys standing guard. Two had deer rifles slung on their shoulders, one had an AK-47 leaning against the wall next to him. The fourth guy was a beast. He had to be 6'-4" and pushing 300 pounds. He was holding his Mini-14 at low ready and he looked like he knew how to use it.

Both Mark and I had our rifles, but we made no move to point them at anyone. I walked straight up to the giant and looked him square in the eyes.

"You have to be about the biggest son of a bitch I have ever laid eyes on! What the hell are they feeding you?" I looked back at Mark. "Butler, have you ever seen anything like this?" I asked him.

"No sir can't say that I have," he said as he eyed the three other men. I turned back to the giant and could see a grin playing at the corners of his mouth.

"Can I help you gentlemen?" The big man asked in his deep bass voice.

"I hope so, I am here to see your Mayor. I have urgent business with him," I said.

"May I tell the Mayor who is here to see him and what this business regarding?"

"Tell him that Jason Sterling is here and I have a truck load of food out there that I need to deliver," all four of the men looked from me to the truck and back again. By the look on their faces, they were all a little hungry. "If you would please direct us to him or fetch him for us, we need to get that truck unloaded," big guy pointed at a guy and told him to tell the Mayor that he had a visitor. He took off through the glass doors.

"Thank you," I said as I extended my hand. "You know my name, what's yours?"

"Harold, Harold Anders," he shook my hand. We exchanged pleasantries for a couple of minutes before the other man returned. He spoke directly to Harold.

"Harry, the Mayor and Tom will see them, but he said that they are to leave their weapons outside."

"Did the Mayor say that or did Tom say it?" he questioned.

"It was Tom."

"Screw that fool," he muttered and motioned us through the door. Harry and the guard with the AK escorted us to the second-floor office of the Mayor. There were two more guards outside of his door. They opened the door for us and tried giving us hard looks as we passed. The Mayor and another man were standing at the big bay window looking out at our small convoy. The Mayor was a stately gentleman. He wore a navy-blue suit and polished black shoes. His hair was almost all white.

The little man next to him instantly gave me a bad vibe. He looked to be younger than me but almost completely bald. He wore wire-rimmed glasses perched on his pointy, beak-like nose. His suit looked about two sizes too big for his 5'-4" frame.

While the Mayor greeted us with a warm smile and a firm handshake, Tom scowled at us and gave a limp, clammy handshake. I had to stop myself from wiping my hand after I shook his.

"Dammit Harold! I told you they were to leave their guns outside! Do you want me to fire your ass from the security team?" Tom berated the big man. "I'm sure we could put you to work clearing streets!" Harold started to speak but I beat him to it.

"Tom, was it? Harold here demanded that we leave our weapons, but I told him that if our weapons leave, so do we and we take that truck load of food with us."

"We do not allow anyone to have a gun in here that is not a part of the security team. That's the way it is," Tom said belligerently. I pushed the talk button on my throat mic and began to speak, all the while staring him down.

"Squad, team lead..... Butler and I will be there in three minutes..... Affirmative, we will be taking this food to the next town....." the Mayor finally stepped between Tom and me.

"Mr. Sterling, please, there will be no need for that. Tom is just very protective of me. You and your guns can stay," I keyed my mic again. "Squad, belay the last, stay ready," I released the button and looked at the Mayor. "Sir, I understand protecting those around you, but I also understand identifying real threats from perceived threats. If we were a threat, we would have already taken the building," the Mayor did not catch the double meaning of what I was saying but Tom sure did. The Mayor waved Mark and me to the chairs in front of his desk. I sat but Mark remained standing behind me.

"Mayor, I'll be quick with what I have to say, my time is very precious, and I assume yours is too," the Mayor nodded, Tom glared. "I have a truck full of fresh produce sitting out there that needs to be distributed to the people of this town. While I know that it will not feed everyone, it will help. If this meeting goes as planned, we will be delivering a truck load once every three to four weeks. There are stipulations on whether or not you will receive this gift."

"Always a catch isn't there!" Tom interrupted.

"Actually Tom, there are two catches," I turned my attention back to the mayor. "First, this food will go to the people who need it the most. If I catch any government official hording food for themselves the consequences will be, shall we say, severe. Second, your city has a couple of big chain hardware stores that we need access to. If we are to continue to supply your town with what food we can, we need supplies to help with the production of that food. Questions?"

"It seems like a win for everyone," the Mayor stated, when Tom broke in.

"What happens after you take what you want from the hardware stores? You people always want something else after you have exploited what you already took," he sneered. I was getting ready to lose my cool with this prick.

"Tom, let me be very, very clear. My men and I could roll in here anytime we please and take anything we want. We could operate in your city anytime we want, and we already have. When you couldn't protect your sheriff and his men, we did, and you had no idea what happened. The six people in my squad could wreck your day if we wanted to," I growled at him. I could see Harold beginning to get really nervous. Tom had a look of surprise on his face as he realized that we were the ones who left a pile of bodies in the street in front of the sheriff's office.

"We have no intention to do that though," I said as I again turned my conversation to the Mayor. "We need supplies, you need food more than you need building supplies. Right? We can also show you how to get the fuel from the underground tanks for your vehicles and we would be willing to take on a couple of your security people. We can train them for you, and they can train the others. Your hospital is probably in complete shambles by now and you have probably lost most of the staff. We can also train your security guys in proper first aid," I paused to let it all sink in. "The ball is in your court now Mayor and I need a decision."

"Like I said Mr. Sterling, It's a win for everyone. You have a deal," he said. "I hope a handshake is good enough," he rose from his chair and extended his hand. I stood and took it. Tom looked like he was ready to blow a gasket but kept his mouth shut.

"We will unload the truck here this time and this time only. On our next trip, please have a place to bring it that is centrally located and make sure the people know in advance that we are coming," I told the Mayor and he agreed. We worked out a couple smaller details and then Mark and I were escorted out. Tom followed behind us. He and Harold showed us where to unload the five-ton and with the help of Harold's men, it was empty in about 30 minutes. We were all back in the trucks and getting ready to pull out when Tom walked up to my door.

"That old fool up there doesn't know who you are, but I do," he hissed. "I know you're not military, you're from the ranch up the road. Jack Sterling's old place. Heard you people have had some trouble over the last few months," The sneer on his face almost got under my skin. Instead I elected to play the game with him.

"Again, Tom, you should probably get your facts straight before you start letting shit fall out of your mouth. I never said we were military; however, we are military contractors. Come to the ranch sometime and I would be glad to show you the contract," I smiled at him. "Things at the ranch couldn't be better, but thank you for your concern," I started to tell Mike to take us to the hardware store when Tom said something that made my blood turn to ice.

"Not what I heard. In fact, I heard you and that bitch girlfriend of yours had a pretty big argument a little while ago. That's what I heard anyway, gossip travels fast," he had a sickly-sweet smile on his face.

"That's the problem with gossip Tom, most of the time you can't believe what you hear," I said struggling to keep my voice even. "Mr. Taylor, take us out of here, we have things to do," I told Mike and we pulled away from Tom.

The fake fight that Jill and I had put on had been witnessed and that Tom asshole had some tie to whoever was watching us. I doubted it was him. He was too prissy to be sneaking around the desert in the middle of the night and he was too short to be the person we had caught on video. He did know something though and I was going to feed him some bad Intel. I smiled a little as a plan was beginning to form in my head.

Fifteen minutes later we pulled into the lumber yard of the hardware store. We had to cut the lock on the gate to get in, so it was a good bet that the place hadn't been looted, yet. Our original plan was to grab as much plywood as we could but that had changed when we saw the loaded semi on the highway. Instead we got all of the steel roofing material we could get our hands on. We also grabbed felt paper and insulation material. Once we had the trucks filled to capacity, we put a new lock on the gate and left.

On our way out of town, I spotted something we were going to need so I had the convoy pull over next to a bunch of semi-trailers. Sitting in front of one of the trailers was a set of wheels with a fifth wheel plate mounted to the top of it. The hitch mated up to the pental-hook on the back of the five-ton. The five-ton was also equipped with air and electrical hookups next to the hitch. Once we had the wheel set secured to the rear of the five-ton, we headed back down the highway.

We stopped at the broken-down truck and trailer that contained the full load of plywood. After releasing the brakes on the tractor, we cranked the landing gear down, pulled the fifth wheel release and dragged the dead semi out of the way. With a little assistance, Dan got the fifth wheel plate backed under the load and got it all hooked up. It took the five-ton a couple of minutes to build enough air pressure, but finally the brakes on the trailer released and we were able to start moving again. Dan couldn't turn very sharp and he was so overloaded that he didn't want to get it over 30 mph. We took our time and pulled into the compound a little after 6pm. Allan was waiting when we dismounted the vehicles. I could tell that the contractor in him was happy with our haul. I handed him my rifle as I walked up to him.

"Could you stow that for me? I'm going to run in and see Jill then I'll be at the house for dinner. We have a lot to talk about," I told him. I didn't wait for an answer, I just headed to the clinic. Once inside, I found Susan taking her vital signs. She greeted me with a smile. The first thing that I noticed was that the IVs were gone. The needle was still in her arm, but it was secured and capped off.

"That's got to be a good sign," I said to Susan.

"It's a great sign! Her vital signs are strong, and Doc wants to start weaning her off the sedative tonight. I just gave her a half dose. The hope is that she will begin to wake up by morning," I kissed Jill on her forehead and told her that I had to go talk to Allan, but I would be back in a little bit. I thanked Susan and went to the house. Allan was in the living room. I pulled my body armor off and dropped it by the front door where he had put my rifle. After grabbing a bottle of water from the fridge, I joined him.

"The Mayor is pretty reasonable to get along with, but he has a guy working for him that is a real prick!" I started in. "Guy's name is Tom, never did get a last name. The little bastard tried to bully us around and I had to shut him down on more than one occasion. Here is the kicker Allan, he knew about the fake fight that Jill and I had after the last incident with someone lurking outside the fence. He didn't come right out and say it but I think he knows about the shooting too."

"So, your hunch that we are being spied on was right?"

"It was and I think we need to assume that we are still being watched. We also have to assume that whoever is watching us has a high-powered rifle. I think Jill was the target and I think that they believe they succeeded in taking her out of commission. We need to make them think that they took her out for good."

"What are you saying?" Allan asked.

"Jill is going to be bed ridden for a few weeks. We need to make whoever is watching us believe that she is dead. That's the only way they will back down a little, maybe even make a mistake. That's the only way we can get the target off her back," I told him. He laughed a little.

"She's going to hate this plan. You know that, right? She would much rather be out there kicking someone's ass than playing dead."

"I know that she's going to hate it but right now she doesn't have much choice. Even after she wakes up it's going to be a couple of weeks before she is up and moving," I said. "And when she is up and moving she is going to need a job to keep her from going nuts. We can let her run the shack from the underground. All of the cameras should be operational by then and that will free up a body to help with the housing situation."

"I am liking your plan Jason, when do you want to put it into action?" Allan asked.

"The day after tomorrow. Jill should be waking up tomorrow and I want to be here when that happens. Once she is awake, I'll be freed up for my acting role," I told Allan. We worked out a few more details over dinner. After he and I finished up the dishes, I headed back to the clinic. Susan had once again made me a bed right text to Jill's.

Wednesday, July 13, 2016

I was awake at 5am. Susan had come in to give Jill her antibiotic, but no sedative. She reassured me that she should be waking up this morning. Allan brought my breakfast in at 6:00 and sat with me for about an hour. He told me that the crew was going to spend the day unloading our haul from the day before. He was already putting together a list of what we needed to pick up the following day. He also told me that the new guy, Marcus, had drawn up a plan to use parts from the trailer we brought home to make a new fifth wheel plate to haul behind the five-ton. It would have a longer hitch and have double axles instead of a single axle. It should be able to handle the weight a little better. All conversation stopped when Jill let out a small whimper and stirred slightly.

"Allan, I know that there are going to be a lot of people that want to come see her when she wakes up, that's fine, just have them use the underground. We don't want any suspicion of our upcoming plans."

"Already thought of it, everyone has been told." He stood from the chair he had been sitting in and walked to Jill's right side. He squeezed her hand for a moment. When he was done he collected my plate and left. I sat in my chair right next to her bed and held her hand. Every so often she would whimper again. It was a little twelve when I felt her squeeze my hand. I stood so that I could see her face and I could see that her eyelids were trying to flutter open. I continued to hold her hand and I put my free hand to the side of her face. She opened her eyes about halfway and I could see that she was trying to focus. Finally, her eyes settled on my face and the confusion and fear started to leave her face.

"Hey kid," I said quietly.

"Jason...." she croaked out in a hoarse voice.

"Shhhh, Don't talk," I told her. I held her gaze and that was enough for her for the moment. It was about 20 minutes before she tried to talk again. I could see the cobwebs clearing out of her eyes as she overcame the lingering effects of the sedative.

"How long...." her voice trailed off again.

"How long have you been out?" I asked. She nodded slightly. "You have been out for three days," her eyes widened a little.

"Shot?" she asked as she pulled her good hand from mine and gently touched her shoulder.

"Yeah babe, you got shot. Doc and Susan have got you all patched up," she put her hand back in mine and relaxed a little. She closed her eyes for a few minutes, and I thought she had gone back to sleep. I was still standing by her side when her eyes opened again. The fires in her brain had been stoked up a little and she was more alert now. She lifted her head a little but winced in pain and put it back on the pillow.

"Holy crap that hurts," she said.

"I bet! That's what happens when you do something stupid without me," I said with a smile and a wink. That warranted a slight grin on her part.

"Are you mad?" she asked.

"I'm not mad! I am just very thankful that you are here talking to me now," I told her. It was about then that Doc and Susan came in and took over for the next few minutes. They checked motor function in her left hand and wrist. They gave her vitals a once over and had about a million questions to ask her. She told them that of course it hurt like hell, that she was hungry, and she was thirsty. With the promise of food and water, they left the room.

It was after Jessica brought her soup and water that we were finally alone again. Jess had come and gone using the underground. We had to keep up appearances. I told Jill of everything that had happened since they had left the ranch almost a week ago. She was very interested in the night we rescued the deputies and asked me to go back over some of the finer points. She seemed satisfied that Mike and I had done excellent work.

When I got to the part about meeting with the Mayor and Tom, she told me that she knew Tom. He was one of Marvin's beer drinking buddies and that those two went way back. That was the missing piece that I needed to tie the two together. Marvin was the muscle and Tom was the brain. She seemed almost amused when I told her of our plans regarding her demise. She wanted to hear all about the funeral we were going to have for her. It seemed rather morbid, but she did want to know. More importantly, she agreed with our plan.

By the time Jessica brought dinner back that evening, Jill was fully awake and alert. She insisted on sitting up and Doc finally let her. Her appetite was back, and Jess had to sneak back to the house for seconds. I let Jess and Jill visit for a little and I met with Allan to finalize the details for tomorrow. It would be an award-winning performance by everyone when we returned from town. Everyone knew their roll. After Jess passed us in the underground, I headed back to the clinic. Jill was tired by now, so I set my bed up next to hers and we went to sleep for the night.

Thursday, July 14, 2016

THE RANCH

I was up again at 5am. Jill was still sound asleep on the bed next to me. I slipped out the front door and went for a shower and breakfast at home. The small convoy was set to roll out at eight. Allan had given me the list of stuff we needed, and I gave copies to all of the team members. Everyone knew the drill and we were not expecting any problems. We were ready for anything that came our way though.

We rolled past the highway blockade at 8:30 without even slowing down. They saw us coming and had the lane clear. We drove straight to the hardware store and pulled into the yard. The lock that we put on the gate had not been tampered with. By 12:30 we had everything that we had come for loaded on the truck and in the backs of the Hummers. We had decided to take the long way out of town. Many of the people that we passed on the street waved as we went by. We went past the hospital and the place was a ghost town. The ER looked like it had burned.

When we got to the highway we went east instead of west. There was no hurry for us to return to the ranch, so we decided to do a little sightseeing. I had to laugh at some of what we were seeing. The truck that had been loaded with big screen TVs had been looted. The truck that was full of lumber had been left untouched. We repeated the process of hooking the trailer to the five-ton. Once we were attached, we headed back to the ranch at 30 mph. That should put us back there at a little after 5pm, perfect timing.

We parked the rigs just as we had after the last trip to town. I got out of the lead Hummer and started walking toward the clinic. Jessica burst from the door, screaming hysterically. She nearly knocked me down when she threw herself in my arms. Allan came through the door and ran to where Jessica and I were. He put his hand on my shoulder. From a distance it would look like Jessica was racked with grief and Allan was trying to console me. In reality, they both told me that Jill was fine, and they were getting ready to move her through the underground. I didn't wait for more. I dropped my rifle in the grass and took off at a run toward the clinic. My team was gathering around Jessica and Allan.

I slammed the door to the clinic behind me and smiled at Doc and Susan. Both were standing there in their blood-soaked surgical gowns and gloves. The Butler twins were in the surgical room with their Aunt Jill. She was standing with the help of both the boys. All she had to do was make it down the stairs and there was a wheelchair waiting there for her. It was obvious that she was in pain, but her face lit up as soon as she saw me. I helped the boys get her down the narrow stairs and into the chair. After a quick kiss, I went back up and closed the secret entrance behind me.

Susan told me to stick my hands out and she poured me a handful of pig's blood. I smeared it all over my hands and forearms. I winked at Susan and headed out the front door. I staggered a few steps and collapsed to my knees. People were surrounding me from every direction. Everyone was laying it on thick and it was perfect. We continued to put on a show in the grass for about 20 minutes. At one-point Doc and Susan came out and threw off their bloody gloves and gowns. All in all, I would say it was an Oscar-worthy performance by everyone.

Allan and Dan helped me back to the house and as soon as the door was closed, we all relaxed. We congratulated each other on our performances, and I headed to the underground to see Jill. Allan was going to bring us dinner a little later.

Friday, July 15, 2016

We were going all out for this one. We needed whoever was watching us to back off a little. Allan had ordered the flag to be flown at half-staff. A little after 9am, Alex and Dan came from the clinic, each holding one end of a black body bag. They loaded it into the back of a Hummer and all, but the security team loaded up into vehicles and drove to the meadow. Allan officiated the funeral and we buried her body next to her mentor, Walter Jenkins. Her plot was between Walter's and the plot for the old miner. It was about halfway through the service when I noticed something I had not seen before.

The headstone for the miner was a marble cross that stood about five feet tall and 6 inches thick. In the center, where the vertical and horizontal parts of the cross met, there was an intricate carving of a shield. It had the minor's name, Mitch McCall, and the date of his death, September 11, 1911, etched into it but nothing more. Neither of those things were remarkable. What caught my attention was that the horizontal end of the cross was also etched with something that I couldn't quite make out. I spent the last half of the service inching my way toward it. When I got to about five feet away, I could see that the etching was that of my family crest surrounded by a circle. The circle was about 2 inches in diameter and was perfectly centered on the 6- inch by 6-inch end of the cross. From where I was standing, I couldn't tell if there was one on the other end.

When Allan finished his speech, I was handed a shovel to throw in the first shovel full of dirt. I did, but when I passed the shovel off to the next person, I positioned myself so that I could feel the crest on the end of the cross. It was tall enough that I didn't have to bend down. I was shocked to find that the circle around the cross was not an etching but rather a seam in the marble. There was nothing to grab on to but when I pushed on it with my finger, it easily slid in. I heard something thump softly in the dirt behind me. I had to fight the urge to whip around and look to see what it was. I very slowly and gradually turned to see what hit the dirt.

I had pushed the crest in on my side about two inches and laying on the ground on the opposite end was a two-inch marble slug. It was the same diameter as the one that I had pushed in. My heart leapt when I saw the small flash drive lying next to it. I knelt down and picked up both pieces. The flash drive quickly went into my pocket and I palmed the piece of marble. Once work began in earnest to bury the body bag, I slipped the marble back into the hole that it came from. It took another 20 minutes before the graveside memorial started to break up. Allan and I were walking back to the Hummer that we came in. Once we were in the backseat, I showed Allan what I had found.

"Do you think it survived the EMP?" I asked him.

"More than likely. Where did you find it?" I told him the tale and he laughed a little. "Your father was a spy, I guess it only fitting that he would use a dead man's cross as a dead drop to feed you information."

We made the drive back to the ranch in about 45 minutes, all the while speculating as to the contents of the drive. We still had working laptop computers in the underground. As long as the drive itself was not damaged, we should be able to find out what was on it. I had been up to the meadow at least a dozen times in the past year and I had never seen the etching on the cross. I must have just been at the right angle and in the right light today. Once we were back at the compound and the vehicles were parked, Allan and I headed to the house. We went straight downstairs to the underground. The security office and the clinic were in the same room and I could see that Jill was awake when we walked in.

"How was my funeral?" she asked with a smile.

"Oh, you know. Lots of crying and wailing. It was gloomy, very, very gloomy," I told her. Allan had retrieved a laptop and brought it back to Jill's bedside. I handed him the drive and started to explain to Jill where I had found it.

"Looks like there are two files on here....one is data and it looks like the second one is a media file," Allan said. He clicked on the data file. It opened and it was a Word file, but it was nothing more than numbers. 40.829342,-115.761354. 40.861446,-115.733360.

"GPS coordinates?" Jill asked.

"That's my guess," Allan said as he went to get a map from the security office. He returned a moment later and unfolded it on the bed next to Jill's. "Read me those coordinates again," Jill read them off and he studied the map intently. His expression gradually went from curiosity to frustration.

"What is it?" I asked as I moved to look at the map.

"This first set of coordinates are not even on ranch property," he pointed to a location that was in the city of Elko. Jill read off the second set of coordinates and Allan located them. "Same thing with this set, just on the other end of town."

"Road trip?" I asked.

"Tomorrow. We need to let everyone be sad and somber today," he said as he winked at Jill. She flipped him the bird and winked back.

"What's the second file?" Jill asked. Since the laptop was sitting on her lap, I told her to go ahead and open it. Allan and I stood on either side of her bed to see what came on the screen. It was a video file. The screen filled with a video of my father. He was seated on the corner of a desk but there was nothing to indicate where he might have been.

"Braden, Jason," he began. "If the two of you are watching this, it means you have been successful in decoding what I put in your journals. Well done boys. By now you have undoubtedly discovered many of the treasures that the ranch has hidden from prying eyes. I'm sure that you have been informed as to how many of those things have been brought here legally and with all of the proper channels followed."

"If it is still a perfect world when you see this, please do not allow anyone outside the compound to see what is at the coordinates that you have been given. There are agencies out there that would love to nail someone's ass to the wall over a lot of the stuff that is there. If the world has gone to shit, I trust you will use what you find wisely. It's not that I didn't trust the others enough to let them know what was there, I just didn't want them put into a position to have to explain it."

"Both of you have grown into fine, honorable men but I must warn you that there are people out there that will try to destroy everything that you have. It does not matter if the world is rolling along or if it has come crashing down around your ears. Some people are just born evil. Remember that and it will serve you well."

"If the world has tanked and you are using the ranch as the haven that it was designed to be, defend it with everything you have. If you have to fight for it, fight hard, fight mean, and most of all, fight to win. Those that would take it from you are not bound by such words as honor and truth. They are not bound to help their fellow man, instead, they will enslave and use those that are weaker to serve their own purpose. I honestly hope this ranch never has to be used for its intended purpose."

"Instead I pray that the two of you can come together and live out your lives in the luxury that it has to offer. Jason, hopefully you can find yourself a nice girl and settle down here. Braden, I hope your girls will find the ranch to their liking too. They can live here as long as they wish and hopefully one day you and Jason can turn it over to the next generation."

"I know I was far from a role model of a father. I hope you understand why I did the things I had to do, and I pray that the two of you can forgive me. Everything that I did here, I did for the two of you. I hope it was enough. I love you boys more than you will ever know," the camera turned off and I was left speechless and shaking. Jill took my hand in her good one and squeezed. I didn't trust my voice, so I just squeezed back. Allan was the first to break the awkward silence.

"We roll out tomorrow morning at 5am. All available hands go on this one," was all he said. He turned off the laptop and handed me the flash drive.

Saturday, July 16, 2016

I stayed the night in the underground clinic with Jill. Susan poked her head in the door a couple of times that night just to check on Jill. She slept most of the night, only waking up once from pain. Susan gave her something for it and she was quickly back to sleep. I, however, did not sleep well at all. My thoughts kept drifting to my brother and his family. We were 12 days into this disaster, and I had no idea where they were or even if they were okay.

By my crude calculations, it could easily take them four months to walk here if they could make ten miles a day. There was no way to mount a rescue operation like we had done for Bill, the distance was just too much and there were far too many unknowns. The biggest unknown was the route they might take. Braden could be a pretty clever guy when he needed to be. Hopefully he had kept his wits about him, and they were headed towards us.

I was also trying to envision what my father had stashed off the ranch property that was so important. Judging by the way he talked about it, my guess was weapons of some sort. That was the only thing that I could think of that might cause Bill and Allan to get their panties in a wad, in a normal world anyway. In a post-apocalyptic world, weapons would seem to be something high in value. I had no idea what kind of weapons they might be though. Here at the ranch we had some pretty high-end firearms. I guess we would find out for sure in just a few hours.

Rather than lay there and brood about everything, I decided to get up at 3am and go hit the gym. When I got there, I found Dan and Jeff hitting the weights. I elected for the punching bag. Whenever I had a lot on my mind, I found that the bag could help me re-focus. This morning was no different. I was so focused in my assault on the bag that I did not notice that I was drawing a crowd. By the time I was done, not only were Dan and Jeff watching me, but Marcus and Jake had joined them. Jake was back on both feet after Marcus had managed to repair the main shaft of his prosthetic leg. As I began to wipe the sweat from my face, all four of them started clapping.

"I hope to God that I am never, ever on the receiving end of any punches or kicks you may throw!" Dan said. "Some of those hits were just savage!"

"Who the hell taught you to fight like that?" Jake asked.

"Jill has spent a year teaching me to fight. You should see some of our sparring sessions!" I laughed. "If you didn't know any better, you would think we were trying to kill each other!" I spent a few minutes telling them about what Jill had taught me. I explained that the actual sparring sessions were part Krav Maga, Jujitsu and good old-fashioned street brawling. They were all in agreement that they wanted to start learning hand-to-hand combat from Jill.

At 4:15 I ran upstairs and took a hot shower. I quickly dressed in my Multi-Cam uniform and ate a quick breakfast. After grabbing my gear from by the front door, I headed to the assembly area in the parking lot. The only ones who were not present were Doc, Susan, Miranda, and Andy Walker, who was still not feeling well. Bill was also going to stay behind. He felt that with his injuries still healing, he would be a hindrance to the mission. We were going to take two Jeeps, two Hummers and the five-ton. Every vehicle would have three people with the exception of the five ton, which would have two.

Allan briefed everyone on the objectives, rules of engagement and the communications plan. As with all the other missions, we had rally points, evacuation routes and a medical plan. This would be the first time we went with this many vehicles and people. It would be a learning experience. Our convoy call sign was Tiger and each vehicle was assigned a number. The lead Jeep was Tiger One, the next vehicle in line, a Hummer, was Tiger Two and so on down the line. Once everyone was briefed, we climbed into our assigned vehicles and rolled out the gate at 5:15.

We wasted no time in getting down the road and we made it to the town's roadblock at 5:50. They must have been asleep because we were baring down on them at 60 miles per hour and the center car was not being moved out of the way. I was sitting in the passenger seat of the lead Jeep and Alex was driving for me. Contessa was our medic and she was riding in the seat behind me. I told Alex to lay on the horn when we were about a quarter of a mile from the barricade. Four heads popped up from the other side of the car and they had to hustle to get it out of our way. Alex started to let off the gas but I told him to keep his foot on it and not to slow down. Once again, we cleared the roadblock with a scant few inches to spare. As soon as we exited the highway, we made a hard right and only slowed to about 45 mph. We were about four blocks from the first objective when my radio crackled to life.

"Tiger One, Tiger Five," Jeff called from the last vehicle in the convoy.

"Tiger Five, Tiger One," I replied.

"Looks like we might have a tail on this Tiger. He is hanging way back and hiding behind the corners. Looks like a black muscle car but I can't get a good look."

"Copy Tiger Five. If he decides to get bold let me know. We'll deal with him then."

"Roger that Tiger One, we will monitor the situation."

We made the last turn and I could see our objective about halfway up the street on the left-hand side. It was a mini storage complex and there was a large chain-link gate across the entrance. To the left of the gate was a parking area and a mobile home that had an "Office" sign on the front door. I motioned for Alex to pull up in front of the office and told Allan to hold the convoy on the street while I tried to get us easy access through the gate. Alex brought the Jeep to a stop and I promptly got out and walked up to the front door and knocked. I had left my rifle in the Jeep as I didn't want to be over the top on the threatening scale. I knocked a second time and the door finally opened about six inches.

"What do ya want?" came a gruff male voice through the crack.

"Good morning sir. I am hoping that you might be able to help me find a storage unit that belonged to my father. I'll make it worth your time if you can help me," I said with a smile. To my surprise the door quickly closed, and I could hear the chain latch being removed on the inside. When the door re-opened I was staring down both barrels of a 12-gauge shotgun. The old man behind it looked as if he had not ventured outside since the EMP attack nearly two weeks ago. The body odor almost made my eyes water.

"Jack always told me that someday one of you boys would come around. Which one are you? Tim or Robert?" the old man asked.

"Neither, my name is Jason," I told him. He eyed me for a second over the top of his old coach gun and finally lowered it.

"Good answer son, I would have hated to blow that pretty head of yours all over the parking lot," he set the shotgun down just inside the door and stepped out onto the porch.

"How did you know I was Jack's son?" I asked him.

"Hell boy, you look like a mirror image of him," he laughed a little and started walking toward the gate.

"Really?"

"Shit no! I have a picture of you and your brother on the back of the door! Jack made sure I was taken care of and he made damn sure I knew what the mission was. Now that you boys have shown up, I am relieved of my duty to your dad," he said as he pulled the gate key from his pocket.

"Wait...what?" I was totally confused now.

"Let's get you guys off the street and I'll explain it a little better," he unlocked the gate and threw it open. I waved the convoy in. Once all five rigs were inside the fence, he locked the gate behind us. He pointed me down the alleyway that the convoy was sitting in and we started walking.

"Many years ago, your dad saved my life. There were some very bad hombres that were after my ass and he made me disappear. Faked my death and gave me a new identity. He gave me one last mission to complete as a way to repay him. That mission was to wait for you and your brother to show up here," when we got to the end of the alley, we took a left and kept walking. The entire time the convoy was creeping along behind us.

"What if I had never figured out that this was here?" I asked him.

"Then this is where I would have eventually died. Lucky for me, you're smart like your old man," as we neared the end of this row he stopped and pulled another set of four keys from his pocket. He handed them to me. "The two storage units on the end of the RV storage section are yours. When you get to the other storage yard, look for the same thing. If you get lost, the unit number is on the back of each key. Since I have fulfilled my promise to your father, I will be taking my leave very shortly. I'll leave the front gate unlocked and I'll leave the key in the lock. Take it, you will need it at the other lot," he stuck his hand out and I took it.

"I didn't catch your name," I said

"Mitch McCall," he said.

"If there is anything I can do for you Mitch, let me know."

"Everything was taken care of a long time ago, but thanks for the offer," he walked away and was about halfway back to the front when it dawned on me that it was his name on the miner's cross in the meadow. I couldn't help but laugh out loud.

I walked all the way to the end of the alley and could see that the RV storage units were about 50 feet deep by about 15 feet across. Big enough to pull a big RV into. I found units 19 and 20. I got on my radio before I unlocked the door.

"All Tiger units set security and let's see what Santa brought us today," it took them all of 30 seconds to set up a perimeter. Those not on security joined me at the big roll-up door. I twisted the key and threw the door up. Just barely inside the door was the front of another five-ton like the one we already had. I looked down between the five-ton and the wall and could see yet another six-by-six parked back there. Both of them had the covered stake side beds on them. I pointed at Allan and Mark to check them out while I opened the second storage unit. I found the same as the first unit. Two five-ton six-wheel drive trucks. Why all the cloak and dagger for this I thought to myself. I was a little lost in thought when Mark stepped from the first unit.

"You are not going to believe this Jason, you gotta see this for yourself," he said as he motioned me to follow him. He squeezed between the two trucks and used the barrel of his rifle to lift the canvas cover off the rear of one. It was filled three quarters of the way to the top with ammo cans and there were a couple of wooden crates taking up the last quarter.

"More guns and ammo?" I asked.

"Not just guns and ammo, those are .50 caliber ammo cans and look at the stenciling on the crates, it says M2HB!" he said excitedly.

"You mean like fifty caliber machine guns?"

"Hell yes!" Allan said from behind me. "The other one seems to be full of 5.56 ammo and a half dozen M249 Saws."

The three of us checked the second storage unit and both of the trucks that were there appeared to be loaded exactly like the first two. All four trucks were pulled out and given a quick once over. They were put into the middle of the convoy and we shuffled people around so that everything had a driver. We were joking about hoping the next objective didn't have any vehicles. We were running out of drivers!

It was 6:30 when we pulled out of the storage lot, right behind Mitch and his tan 1967 Ford Bronco. He quickly pulled away from us and made the turn to head to the highway while we stayed on the surface streets. It only took us about 15 minutes to reach the second storage yard and to my relief there were no large RV units. We quickly found the two units we were looking for and got them open. Inside each unit was an 18-foot-long enclosed utility trailer. Rather than take the time to go through them there, we elected to hook them up behind the Hummers and get the hell out of town.

Within 15 minutes of arriving we were getting ready to leave but there was a black car blocking the driveway. Tom from the Mayor's office and two of his goons were standing between my Jeep and their car. The goons had AK-47's leveled at my windshield. I slowed to a stop.

"All Tigers, heads up, we may have trouble," I said over the radio as I got out of the Jeep. I left my rifle in the rack and walked casually toward Tom and his men.

"Well, well, well Mr. Sterling. What are you down here stealing today?" Tom sneered.

THE RANCH

"Again Tom, I thought we talked about you getting your facts straight. We are simply here to clean out my storage units. Is that a problem?" I said with all of the sarcasm I could muster. I had closed to about five feet from Tom when goon one put his rifle to my chest and told me I was close enough. I could see that his safety was off, and his finger was on the trigger. "Better back your dog's down Tom or things are gonna get really stupid really fast," I said to Tom, but I was staring down goon number one.

"I really hope it does Jason. I know these boys would love to see you planted in the ground next to your girlfriend. You killed a whole mess of their buddies in front of the cop shop a few days ago," Tom said. I shifted my glare to him.

"Here is what's about to happen, Tom. I am going to take this asshole's AK-47 away from him. I am going to shoot this other asshole right in the gut, so he dies nice and slow. Then I am going to wrap my fingers around your throat, and I am going to squeeze, and you know what, Tom? I am going to enjoy it," I said in a dead level voice. All three of them started to laugh. I heard someone in my ear-bud ask if I needed help. I reached up with my left hand and squeezed my throat mic. It was on VOX, but the motion put my hand about four inches from the barrel of the AK. "Negative, stand down. I got this."

I was still staring at Tom but could see goon one in my peripheral vision. He glanced over my shoulder when I spoke into the mic. That was all I needed. With my left hand I grabbed the barrel of the AK and shoved it toward goon two. As I predicted, goon one pulled the trigger and he shot goon two right in the gut and he went down hard. I spun 180 degrees to my right with my left hand still controlling the barrel and I smashed goon one in the head with my right elbow.

That dazed him and when I spun back around, I shoved the barrel of the AK straight up with my left hand and punched him hard in the throat with my right hand. I felt the cartilage in his neck collapse from the impact. He immediately let go of the AK. The whole ordeal had happened in under a second. Tom did not even have a chance to comprehend what was happening. When I had his neck in the grasp of my right hand. I pushed him back against the car as he clawed at my gloved hand with both of his.

I had no intention of killing him, but he didn't know that. I was allowing him to have a little air, just enough to keep his mind in panic mode. I got right up to his face and just stared into his eyes for what had to be thirty seconds.

"I'm only going to tell you this one-time Tom, so do us both a favor and listen very closely to me. You need to call your boy Marvin in and get a leash on that dog. If I find him anywhere near my ranch, I'll kill him with my bare hands. Hopefully now you will understand that I do exactly what I say I'm going to do," I paused and looked at both of the bodies on the ground. "I told you this was going to happen, and it did. Call Marvin off or I will kill him and when I am done, I will come for you. Do you want me to hunt you down, Tom?" he tried to shake his head from side to side. "Good boy, Tom. Now, I'm going to let you go. You're going to get in this car, and you are going to haul ass out of here," I had heard foot steps behind me and knew I had three of my guys standing back there. I slowly let Tom go and he started gasping and gagging and he jumped in the car and burned rubber out of there. We collected the weapons and ammo from the dead guys and dragged their bodies out of the driveway.

After leaving the second storage unit, we had no more issues in town. We arrived back at the ranch a little after 9am. The new trucks were pulled up to the warehouse along with the trailers. Everything was unloaded on to the floor inside. After everything was taken from the trucks and trailers, the inventory began. I left the warehouse and checked in on Jill. Doc and Susan were there changing her bandages. The bruise covered half of her upper torso from front to back. The flesh around both wounds looked healthy and Doc gave her an excellent prognosis.

It would be one hell of a scar, but she should regain nearly all function in her arm. I gave her the rundown on how our morning had gone. She laughed when I told her about the name on the miner's cross being that of the man who was hired to protect the assets at the storage yards. I gave her a basic idea of what we had brought back with us. When I told her about my run-in with Tom, she surprised me and told me that I should have snapped his neck when I had the chance.

I told Jill that I had to get back to the warehouse and she sent me on my way with a kiss. The warehouse was still a flurry of activity. Everything was being sorted through and a physical inventory was being done. There were four new .50 caliber machine guns, 12 M249 Light Machine guns. We had counted 250,000 rounds of .50 and 450,000 rounds of 5.56mm. That's just what came out of the five-ton trucks. The two trailers contained a total of four PRG7 launchers and 300 of the actual rockets. We also found about 500 pounds of C-4 explosives and a couple thousand detonators for it. There were dozens of cases of claymore mines, fragmentation grenades, and flash-bang grenades.

The final numbers were given to me at dinner that night and they were pretty staggering. The one thing I had not seen earlier were the two footlocker sized crates that were full of gold and silver coins. Allan put its total worth at about $5,000,000 before the world ended. After Jill and I had eaten, I gathered up the plates and took them upstairs. I helped Allan wash up and told him that I wanted an all-hands meeting for dinner the following night. The only place big enough was the underground dining hall and we would still have to move tables and chairs down there. No one was to miss this meeting. When he asked me about the children and manning the security shack, I told him again that I wanted everyone there.

CHAPTER 13

Sunday, July 17, 2016

We spent all of Sunday putting away everything that was brought back from town the day before. All of it had to be moved underground so it was very labor intensive. I had noticed throughout the day that people were starting to look at me a little differently. Every once in a while I would catch people looking my direction and speaking in low voices. I couldn't take it anymore and finally stopped Mark and asked him what was going on.

"What's up with everyone looking at me like I've sprouted horns?" I asked him. He chuckled.

"The tale of you single-handedly taking on three men, two of which had AK-47's pointed at you, has gotten around!"

"What?"

"Yeah, there were a lot of people who think you carry your big brass balls around in a fur-lined five-gallon bucket," his grin was from ear to ear. "You have become the ranch's resident bad ass!" he laughed.

"That's bullshit!" I said incredulously.

"Jason, listen man, these people need a person with a pair of huge swinging nuts to lead them, and they need someone to show them that we can stand against whatever is thrown our way. You did that yesterday."

"All I did was defend myself against three turds with no training. All I did was send a very clear message that we will not be screwed with," I told him.

"You stood up for everyone here as soon as you stepped out of that Jeep."

"They were not going to shoot anyone; they were just trying to intimidate us a little. Tom knows he's not the big dog on the block anymore and he was just posturing," I insisted.

"Sure, he was. You proved to him, without a doubt, that you were capable of taking him out at any time and you have that jackass shaking in his boots. I have no doubt that he will call Marvin in because he wants to keep a guy like that close. He needs Marvin at his side to defend himself from you."

"I hope you're right about that. Just do me one favor though...."

"What's that?" he asked.

"Tell everyone to knock off the hero worship. I'm just a guy. I don't have a cape or a big S on my t-shirt," I said with a smile. "And I definitely don't wear tights under my BDUs!" Mark gave a hearty laugh and said that he would see what he could do.

By five that evening everything had been properly stored in the underground and all of the vehicles had been fueled and parked.

The Butler twins had set up the dining area downstairs so that everyone had a seat. Now they were helping with all of the cooking. It was about 5:45 when everyone else started showing up. The security team, led by Bill, were the last to arrive. I was still getting some of the strange looks but not nearly as bad as earlier in the day. Miranda, Diane and Susan had made a feast of pot roast, fresh bread, vegetables from the garden and mashed potatoes. The twins were going to sit with the younger children, but I asked them to stay at the big table with the adults. Doc wheeled Jill in right at six and parked her to the right of my seat. Once everyone else was seated, I remained standing. I picked up my glass of water and began to speak.

"I would like to propose a toast," I raised my glass and everyone else did the same. "In under two weeks we have faced a lot of adversity and we have overcome it. Two weeks ago, many of us were strangers and we have come together to form a big family. Everyone here has gone above and beyond every expectation I could have ever had, and I want to thank every one of you!" I said and I raised my glass a little higher. There was a round of clanking glasses and "Hear, Hears." I remained standing to signal that there was still something I had to say. I set my glass down and put my hands on the back of my chair. Everyone quieted down and all eyes were on me.

"I'll try to keep this short because I know all of us are hungry and are dying to dig into this feast....... At 9pm tomorrow, we will pass the two-week mark since our civilized world fell apart in a flash. We have all done things that we never thought we would have to do. Speaking for myself, I have killed people. My best guess is six people have had their lives ended by my actions."

"I'm not the only one at this table with that weighing on my mind. I'll tell you this, and maybe it will help you come to terms with what we have done," I paused and made eye contact around the table. "We will have to continue to do things that we never wanted to do if we want to keep what we have here at the ranch. We will not go looking for a fight, but we will rise to the occasion if one comes looking for us. We will continue to help those that we can, when we can but I for one will not sacrifice our well-being for those that will do nothing to help themselves. We have adopted many militaristic traits in the past two weeks, and I believe that will continue to evolve."

"Mixed in with that, we have brought the strongest of our family traits to the forefront. I believe that we will continue to blend the two together and it will only continue to help us strengthen our bonds. Everyone here has picked a role and filled it better than I would have ever imagined. Miranda, you and Amanda have stepped up to help Doc and Susan. Dan and Jeff, you have been of significant help to the security team. Marcus and Contessa, you are the newest members of our family, yet both of you have found a niche and filled it. Everyone here has done that, and I want to thank each and every one of you from the bottom of my heart," I finished my little speech and started to sit. Applause started with Allan and quickly spread to the rest of the tables.

Everyone enjoyed the dinner and the conversation around the tables lasted until almost nine. Diane Walker excused herself early to put her infant son to bed. Andy, her husband, had stayed behind but he mostly stayed to himself, listening in on the conversations around him. He seemed withdrawn. I had not had the chance to really get to know the guy. He'd been down sick since he arrived here. I went into the kitchen and grabbed two beers from the fridge. When I returned, I pulled up a chair next to him and offered him one of the cold bottles. He graciously accepted. I carried most of the conversation for the next half hour while he just listened and offered short answers. He wouldn't hold eye contact and it was like he couldn't relax.

"Jason, is there somewhere that you and I could talk in private?" he asked. It caught me by surprise.

"Sure, come on," I said as I stood from the table. He followed me out of the room, and we went to the underground clinic. Jill was still enjoying herself in the dining room. Once we were in the clinic, I stopped to pull the hatch closed behind us. When I turned around, Andy had his pistol out of its holster and pointed at me. He took two steps back because he knew he was in range for me to do some dam- age. I looked at the pistol and then at him. I never made a move to put my hands up or any such nonsense. I had my pistol and while I was quick on the draw, this was a no-brainier for me. I sat in the chair that was at Doc's desk and crossed my arms across my chest. Andy was shaking and sweating profusely even though it was not hot in the room.

"Andy? Care to explain this?" I asked evenly.

"It's complicated."

"Then please un-complicate it for me. You have a captive audience," I said, motioning to the gun in his hand.

"They want me to kill you," was all he said.

"Who, Andy? Who wants me dead?"

"Tom and Marvin want me to kill you. They think Jill is dead and I haven't told them any different."

"Why didn't you tell them that Jill is still alive?"

"Because she's not a threat, she never was....." his voice trailed off.

"Am I a threat?" I asked him. There was a long period of silence before he finally started talking again.

"I was just trying to protect my wife and my son. I never wanted anyone to get hurt. They said they would kill them and make me watch if I didn't do what they wanted....."

"Andy, Diane and Justin are safe here, they are safe behind these walls," I told him.

"NO! Nobody is safe from them. They will pick us off one by one until they decide to attack this place and kill everyone here!" he said, raising his voice slightly.

"Andy, everyone here will do everything in their power to make sure your family is safe."

"It won't be enough. I have to kill you, that's the only way to keep Diane and Justin safe," he said.

"You're wrong Andy, and you know it. That's why you haven't shot me yet. You know deep down that they're not the kind to keep their word. They will use you for what they want and then discard you. It's what they do," I said. Andy was really quiet and staring at his gun. The shaking in his hands was getting worse. "There is a way that we both can walk away from this, but I need you to trust me."

"There is no way out for me."

"You're wrong again Andy. You could shoot me right now and walk out of this room. I doubt anyone out there would even hear the shot. You walk out of here and pretend nothing ever happened. Then in a few weeks, Tom and Marvin rally their men and attack this compound. With enough manpower, they overrun our security and kill everyone here. You and your family included. That's option one. Option two is that you put the gun away and both of us walk out of here and together we figure all of this out."

"When I let my guard down, you kill me and throw my family out and they die out there anyway. Both options suck!" he said.

"You help me nail both of those assholes to the wall and none of this ever-happened Andy. Nobody will be thrown out of here. Put the gun away and we will figure this out," he stared at me for what felt like forever. Finally, he lowered the pistol and tried to hand it to me butt first. "I said put it away, I don't need two pistols," I motioned to his holster. Reluctantly he put it away. I pointed to the chair across from the desk and he sat heavily in it.

"I have your word that nothing will happen to Diane and Justin?" he asked.

"Your family is part of my family, Andy. You have my word."

He nodded and sagged in the chair. We talked until almost eleven when Doc and Susan brought Jill back and got her to bed. I told Andy to go home but I wanted to meet him for breakfast at six at my house. He agreed and went home. When Jill asked me where I had been, I told her that Andy needed to talk. I didn't mention the gun or Marvin and Tom. We got her settled in bed and she was quickly asleep. I, however, found myself wide awake.

Monday, July 18, 2016.

Andy was in my kitchen at 6am. I poured four cups of coffee just as Allan and Bill walked through the front door. A look of concern came over Andy's face. I reassured him that everything was going to be okay and pointed him to the table. All four of us took our seats and I began the conversation.

"Andy and I had a long talk last night and I felt that there was a lot of infor-mation that you guys needed to hear," I took a drink of my coffee. "Andy came to me last night after dinner because he and his family had been threatened by Tom and Marvin. They told Andy that if he didn't do what they wanted him to do, they would kill his family and make him watch before they killed him." Allan and Bill looked at each other. Then back to me. "They wanted him to kill me. They wanted him to leave the gate open so they could slip a dozen fighters in here one night and kill the rest of us. Andy chose a different path though."

"He chose to come to me last night after dinner and give me a heads up," again, I chose to leave out the part about him pulling a gun. Over the course of the next hour and a half, Andy told Allan and Bill everything that he had told me from the night before. All three of us learned that he had an FRS radio and that was how he was being contacted by Marvin or Tom. They always contacted him, but he had not heard from them since the day after Jill's funeral. He handed the radio over and wrote down all of the contact information and the time that he was told to wait for their call. He assured us that he had not heard from them since I threatened Tom. Both men had questions for him, but they were satisfied that he had indeed told them everything that he knew.

After Andy was dismissed, the three of us discussed our options. Andy had given us an approximate location of where Marvin could be watching us from, so it was decided that we would start patrolling outside the wall on horseback and we would get a team of two people to sneak around on foot. It was decided that Mark and Mike would be the two that lurked around on foot. They were the two best people we had when it came to field craft. They were to stay out for a minimum of five days.

Jake, Jeff and Marcus were going to be the first mounted patrol outside of the compound. They would be out for three days before returning. Everyone that was going out drew a full five days rations and extra ammunition for their weapons, along with radios and first aid gear. Mike and Mark were going to slip out under the cover of darkness and the mounted patrol was going to leave at dawn the following morning. Not only were they going to patrol the ranch property, they were going to search the surrounding properties up to two miles from the ranch.

Everything went fine for the next two weeks. None of the patrols found anything, not even where Andy suspected Marvin might be hiding out. Work continued on the two new cabins and the plans were coming together for another one. It was August 1st and we had another load of food ready to go to town, so we made plans to take it the morning of the 2nd. Jill was healing well, just going nuts from being relegated to the indoors. She spent a lot of her time in the underground security office which was a big help.

One of her duties was to monitor the HAM radio that we had. Unfortunately, there had been very little to hear over the airwaves. It had been strangely quiet.

Marcus had been able to repair one of the drones that we had purchased. He had scavenged parts from the other two to do it. Jill was becoming quite the pilot. The little drone had a range of just over a mile and could stay in the air for almost four hours. Marcus said that he might be able to find the parts to fix a second one at an electronics parts house in Elko.

I asked if the parts he needed would have been damaged by the EMP and he said that as long as they were still in the Mylar bags, they should be fine. He also told me that he might even be able to fix our heavy equipment if he could find the right parts. The guy was proving to be a treasure trove as far as our mechanical and electronic needs went. His wife, Contessa, had become a regular at the clinic. Doc and Susan had both taken the young woman under their wings and were teaching her a lot about the medical side of things.

The one that really surprised me was Andy. After his confession, it seemed like a weight had been lifted from his shoulders. We had decided to keep him off of security duty just because he had been compromised. Instead we put him to work with Dale tending to the crops. Come to find out, he had a green thumb.

Tuesday, August 2, 2016

We had loaded all of the food in the back of a five-ton the night before and we were all set to roll out of the compound at 7am. The small convoy was to consist of the big truck and two Hummers. Mike and Amanda were with me in the lead, Alex and Bill were in the five-ton and Dan, Jake and Miranda were in the rear Hummer. As with every trip to town, we were all decked out in our multi-cam BDUs, helmets, body armor, weapons and comms.

Everyone met for the briefing at 6:30 and we left right on time. The drive was uneventful until we reached the roadblock. We bore down on them like we did the last time but this time they made no attempt to move the car out of the way. Instead of four guys, there were 12 and all of them had their rifles leveled at us as we began to slow our approach. I could see that several of the cars had burned since our last visit and they were all riddled with bullet holes. These guys were clearly on edge, so I had Mike stop the truck about a hundred feet from the barricade. He angled it across the road per our protocol.

"Be ready for anything," I said into my throat mike as I opened the door to get out. Mike and Amanda did the same thing but took up covered positions behind the Hummer. Both had their rifles trained on the roadblock. I had my rifle hanging by its sling as I started up the road. I could see that one of their guys had stepped out from behind a car and was walking towards me. He had an AK-47 cradled in his arms and a red bandanna tied around his head. He met me at the halfway point, and we stopped about ten feet from each other.

"Don't get any ideas mister, my men could cut you to ribbons before you get that rifle up," he said.

"Is this the part where I tell you that we come in peace and to take me to your leader?" I grinned. That seemed to relax him, if only slightly. "No hostile intentions here, I can assure you of that," I told him.

"Are you the guys from the ranch? Are you Jason Sterling?" he asked.

"Yes, to both questions. We have a truckload of food that we need to get to town."

"Okay, the Mayor said to keep an eye out for you guys. He said that you need to go to the Wal-Mart parking lot. It has become a sort of trading center. I'll radio ahead and let them know that you are coming," he turned slightly and waved to the guys still behind the barricade. They relaxed a little and started pushing the car out of the way. "Is there any chance we could have you leave a little bit of food here for these guys? They've been standing a post for three days now, most of them on empty stomachs," it was more of a plea than a question.

"Tell me what happened, and we could work something out."

"Deal!" he smiled. "Three days ago, a bunch of guys rode in here on motorcycles. When the four guys at the gate refused to open up for them, all hell broke loose. The bikers shot the shit out of everyone and everything. They threw a few Molotov cocktails and then roared their way into town. Straight up to City Hall. They shot the crap out of that place too."

"Did your security there stop them?" I asked.

"No, Harold stopped them. Dude went ape-shit and got nine of them singlehandedly."

"How many guys did you lose?"

"Three of the four that were manning this post were killed, and we lost five more at City Hall. We also have two critically wounded. Our doctor doesn't expect them to make it," he said sadly. I just shook my head.

"Sorry about your losses," I said.

"Yeah, me too."

"About that food," I reached up and squeezed my mic. "Alex, would you grab one case of MREs from each rig and bring them up here please," I could hear him answer in my earbud and he was standing next to me five minutes later with three cases. He set them on the asphalt, and I dismissed him. "It isn't the greatest food, but it will help."

"Thank you so much!" he said as he picked up the cases and started back to the opening in the barricade. I walked back to my rig and climbed in. Once Amanda and Mike were back in, we were on our way.

Twenty minutes later we pulled into the parking lot and could see that it had been set up as a trading outpost. There was a wide assortment of stuff being traded but I saw very little food. One of the Mayor's men directed us where to unload everything. It only took us about 30 minutes to unload the truck. The food was being distributed almost as fast as we could get it off the truck. A lot of people offered to trade for it but in every case we declined any form of payment.

After the truck was empty, Mark, Amanda and I walked around the swap meet. We drew a lot of strange looks with our uniforms and weapons. Folks were cautious but not unfriendly. The one thing that really stuck in my mind was the fact that everyone was armed. It had been a month since the balloon had gone up and people had realized that their safety and security were their own responsibilities. There was no help coming from a government that had been totally silent.

Amanda had found a young girl, maybe 18 years old, who was trying to trade her collection of music CDs and not having any luck. For most everyone, they were totally useless. Amanda took a gold necklace with a gold cross on it from around her neck and made a deal with the girl. She could use the necklace to trade for something she needed, and Amanda wanted the CDs to play in one of the laptops from the underground. She said that she had missed her music the most in the apocalypse.

Once we had returned to the trucks, we took shifts and let the others wander around in small groups. I figured it would be good for morale to let them interact with others outside the compound. I had counted 22 men that all had red bandannas tied around their right arm or forehead. They milled around in groups of two to four and were not interested in bartering or anything. I surmised that they were the security guards for the swap meet. I confirmed it when I stopped a pair of them that were walking by us.

Most of them seemed genuinely friendly but there were eight of them in two groups of four that acted differently. They were studying us from a distance and every time I caught them looking, they would look away. As soon as the last of our people got back from their shopping trip, all of us mounted up and left at about noon. Instead of going back to the ranch, I decided that we needed to go see the Mayor.

It only took us about ten minutes to get to City Hall and what we found shocked me. The neatly manicured lawn out front was now home to gallows and there was a body swinging from the noose. A crude sign was hanging from the body that simply said "THIEF". From the looks of it, the body had been there for a couple of days in the August heat. As Dan and I made our way to the entrance, we passed four different and distinct pools of dried blood on the gray concrete.

The front of the building itself was pockmarked with bullet holes and just about every ground level window had been broken out. The entrance itself was now ringed with sandbags and the glass doors were completely gone. There were six guys manning the entrance. All of them had the trademark red bandanna. They were all trying to give us hard looks. The apparent leader stepped from behind the barricade and leveled his shotgun at us. This had a very different feel to it than the roadblock.

"Stop right there!" the leader said, much louder than he needed to. "What's your business?"

"I'm Jason Sterling from the ranch and I need to see the Mayor."

"I know who you are, what's your business?" he snarled.

"I told you, I have to speak to your Mayor," I said with a smile. "Are you going to take me to see him or are we going to do this the hard way?" he stepped forward and held the barrel of the Mossberg 500A shotgun just below my belt. I looked down at the weapon and knew I had a total rookie on my hands. He still had the safety lever in the rear position, the safety was on. Dan sidestepped and brought his rifle up to his shoulder but pointed it at one of the other men.

"We can do this my way asshole. I can blow your nuts off and then we will see just how tough you really are!" he laughed a sinister laugh.

"You seem to be forgetting one thing," I said calmly and evenly.

"What? Looks to me like I got you by the balls!"

"You are forgetting that while you might indeed blow my balls off, there are people behind me that have all of you in their sights. One wrong move on your part and your brains will be all over the concrete. In that same instant, every man here will join you in hell," I could see the look in his eyes change. I could also see the other five men looking at each other. He looked over my shoulder and was looking down the barrels of multiple AR's. All of my people had taken covered positions and each one had chosen a different target. If this went sideways, they wouldn't hesitate to put these good ole boys down.

"I want you men behind the sandbags to listen very closely to me. If you do not lower your weapons and stand down, those people behind me will ventilate your heads. If you so much as flinch when I take this shotgun from this asshole and beat him with it, they will put you down before you even have the chance to think about it. Do you understand what I've just told you?" I asked, all the while staring at the man in front of me.

I could see them exchanging glances and their resolve wavered as the first guy lowered his weapon. The eyes of the man in front of me quickly changed to reflect his fear. He was suddenly alone and knew it. It was time for me to give him a way out.

"You can lower that shotgun, stand aside, let us pass and retain some of your dignity as their leader, or I can take it from you, beat you half to death with it and pass anyway, you choose," I told him. He looked at his men and back to me and my men. The barrel of the 12-gauge began to lower, and he took a step back. I started to walk past him but stopped. "You just saved your life and quite possibly the lives of your men. You chose well," I said and then walked into the building.

The last time we were there the place was still pretty clean and kept up. Now was a totally different story. There were scraps of paper littering the floor and I could smell the restrooms as soon as I walked inside. Dan and I went upstairs and directly to the Mayor's office. The heat on the second floor was brutal. It had to be over 100 degrees in there and the smell was terrible. The two guards were still outside the Mayor's office, but they made no move to stop us as we pushed the door open. There was a third guard just inside the office.

The Mayor was seated at his desk going through papers. Gone was his stately appearance. His suit was the same one that he was wearing at our first meeting. Except that now it had stains on the front of it and the breast pocket was slightly torn. His tie was loose, and the white shirt was now a dingy off-white from sweat stains. His hair was disheveled, and his eyes were not quite right. Dan and I exchanged glances, both of us thinking something was off. He had looked up from his papers only long enough to acknowledge our presence. The paperwork that he was shuffling through looked like it had been shuffled from pile to pile hundreds of times.

"Mr. Mayor?" I asked. Again, he looked at us but went right back to his papers.

"Looks like someone checked out," Dan stated.

"Looks like you're right," I said. We heard someone come in behind us and turned in unison to see who it was. There was a young woman dressed in jean shorts and a tank top. She had a tray of food and stopped short when she saw Dan and me.

"Who are you?" she demanded.

"I'm Jason and this is Dan," I said pointing my thumb at Dan. "And you are?"

"Jackie Tanner, Mayor Tanner's daughter," she said as she approached the desk and set the food tray down. The Mayor looked at first the food then at his daughter. There was no recognition in his eyes. She encouraged him to eat but he went back to shuffling papers.

"Excuse me Miss Tanner, can you tell us what is going on here?" Dan asked. She looked at the two of us and motioned us into the hallway.

"The doctor thinks he snapped from the stress. It's like his brain has shut itself off," she said, looking back into the room at her father.

"Is there anything we can do to help?" I asked.

"Not unless you can get him to eat and sleep. The doctor said he didn't want to waste the sedatives that he had. He said that eventually he would either snap out of it or just die," she said. She turned slightly and wiped a tear from the corner of her eye. Dan and I shared another look and he took a couple of steps down the hall and spoke quietly into his throat mic.

About two minutes later Amanda and Miranda came up the stairs with their medical packs. Dan quickly explained the situation to them. Jackie was looking at the two women curiously.

"They might be able to help your father, with your permission of course," I told her.

"Please!" she said quickly. Amanda and Miranda went in and began to talk to the Mayor. Within minutes they had his jacket off and they were assessing his vital signs. He was not cooperating with them, but he was not actively resisting them either. After a few minutes Amanda returned to the hallway.

"He is very dehydrated and from the looks of it, he hasn't eaten in a few days. All of his vitals are elevated to dangerous levels," she gave her report.

"Can we help him at the ranch?" I asked.

"We certainly can," was Amanda's immediate response.

"Miss Tanner, with your permission, I'd like to take you and your father to our ranch," Jackie instantly started nodding her head in the affirmative. I told Amanda to get him ready to travel. They would have to ride in the back of the five-ton, fortunately we had brought one that had the covered bed. I was a little concerned about people seeing the Mayor leave in the back of one of our trucks, so I had the convoy pull into the parking lot. I wanted to shorten the exposure time.

I'd asked Jackie Tanner if she had any other family that we needed to pick up. She informed me that her mother was in Carson City and her older brother was on a Navy ship at sea. It looked like her father was all that was left at the moment. It took all of the coaxing of the three women, but they finally got the Mayor on his feet and moving. He moved like he was intoxicated so Amanda and Miranda were assisting him while Dan and I carried their gear out to the trucks.

We got the Mayor and his daughter loaded in the back of the five-ton. Amanda and Miranda were about to join them when Dan told me that we had company approaching from behind us. I turned and could see the two guys who were pulling security outside the Mayor's office coming up the walkway. Neither had their weapons up yet they were moving with a purpose and they kept looking back toward the building. Jackie jumped out of the back of the truck and pushed her way past Dan and me. I could hear her telling the two guards that it was going to be okay. We would take the Mayor for medical attention and return with him as soon as possible. The taller of the two leaned in close to Jackie and spoke so quietly that I couldn't hear what was said.

Jackie talked to the pair for a couple of minutes before walking back to the convoy. Both guards stayed where she had left them. Jackie walked straight up to me.

"Mr. Sterling, I know that you have already done a lot, but could I ask one more thing of you and your people?" she questioned.

"You can ask but only if you call me by my name. You say Mr. Sterling and I want to turn around and look for my father," I said with a smile. "My name is Jason."

"Okay, Jason, those two guys are the only two left from my father's security detail. The other two are in the infirmary back there," she motioned with a thumb over her shoulder. "Both are in critical condition and probably won't make it....." I didn't let her finish.

"Dan, take Jake, Mike and Alex with you. Grab those two guards and have them show you this infirmary. Get the wounded and get them loaded in the back of the five-ton."

"You got it boss!" Dan said as he moved off to get the people he needed. I turned back to Jackie.

"We will see what we can do but I won't make any promises."

"Thank you so much!"

"When they get back, tell the two that are still on their feet that they are welcome to come with but if they do, it's my place and it's my rules," I told her, and she was okay with that. While we waited on the team to bring them from the infirmary, she told me that all four of the guards were single men. Two of them were former military, which branch she didn't know. The other two were corrections officers.

It took about 15 minutes before Dan appeared. He was pushing a gurney and it was quickly obvious to me that the man on it was the big guy we had met on our first trip to town, Harold Anders. I didn't recognize the man on the second gurney that was being pushed by Alex. Instead of trying to transfer them to the bed of the six-by-six, they just lifted both gurneys into the back. Both of them were secured and Miranda and Amanda began their assessment. Jackie had a quick word with the two remaining guards, and they were happy to accept the offer to go to the ranch. Once they were all loaded, we quickly left.

It was hard to say exactly what it was, but something was changing quickly in this little town. The guys running around with the red bandannas was something that was troubling me. I understood the need for a security force and that's exactly what a lot of them seemed to be. The troubling part were the ones that seemed more like enforcers. The group at City Hall for example. They were all worked up before we ever got there and fortunately, they had enough sense to back down before they got killed. The gallows in front of City Hall was also a disturbing development. Here we were, a month into the apocalypse and we had already reverted to roaming gangs, the gallows and a government that had been totally silent since day one.

THE RANCH

I couldn't even begin to imagine how many people in this town of 19,000 had already perished. Whether it was from violence or natural causes, I had to imagine that the number was staggering. I remember reading something in the government sponsored EMP commission report that in the first year after such an event that the mortality rate would be roughly 90% dead. The sad thing was, that report came out the same day as the 9/11 report and went largely unnoticed by the public and the media. It was yet another case of media sensationalism that put this very important information on the back burner and then swept it under the rug completely.

We were very, very lucky at the ranch. We had good food, clean water and all of our sanitation needs were covered. Our security needs were ever evolving but we had competent people on top of it. It just went to prove that all of our planning and training had not been a waste of time and money. Sadly, it took the end of the civilized world to prove that truth. I knew there were other preppers in the area and I also knew that there were some that referred to themselves as patriot groups. I was worried about the individual preppers; how long would they be able to hold out on their own?

The patriot groups were a different concern entirely. Their vision of the way things ought to be could be disturbing to say the least. I figured at the end of the day; those groups would prove to be trouble down the road. Not all to be sure, but some of them espoused the very things they allegedly stood against. Racism, tyranny, and just plain brutality against those who did not fall in line. I had to ask myself if that was beginning to happen here in Elko.

All of those things and more were bouncing around in my head as we made the drive back to the ranch. As we pulled through the gate and up to the parking area, I noticed a bright yellow Volkswagen bus. It was painted with flowers and slogans from the early seventies. When we came to a stop and began to unload our patients, Doc and his daughter, Sam emerged from the above-ground clinic. Susan was walking out with two people that I could only describe as Hippies.

They looked the part to be sure. The woman, probably in her mid-sixties, was wearing an off-white sundress with no shoes. Her gray hair was frazzled but it looked almost like she meant for it to look like that. The man, about the same age, was wearing bell-bottom blue jeans and a button-up tan shirt with a huge collar. His gray hair was longer than hers and pulled back into a ponytail. He had flip-flops on his feet. All of them were jovial and Doc was walking with his daughter under his arm.

Before the five-ton came to a complete stop, Amanda bailed out of the back and yelled for Susan and Doc. Both of their moods visibly changed, and they started for the big truck at a sprint. They were followed closely by our new guests and Sam. I climbed out of the lead Hummer and started back to where everyone was congregating. Susan had climbed into the bed of the truck and was beginning her assessment and relaying information to Doc. We helped the Mayor and his daughter out of the truck and Sam immediately took them toward the clinic.

The hippie woman was right there with them. Harold was the next to be unloaded and I could see that someone had started an IV and dressed his wounds with clean gauze. Doc and Amanda wheeled him into the clinic next. The third casualty was unloaded but there seemed to be no sense of urgency. Miranda checked his pulse and put a stethoscope to his chest. The look of defeat was evident on her face. She shook her head and pulled the sheet that was covering him all the way over his head. She took a step back and waved at Alex and Dan to wheel him into the clinic also.

I walked up next to her and put my hand on her shoulder. She instantly broke down and started sobbing. I pulled her into a hug, and she buried her face into my shoulder. We stayed that way until Dan returned and then he took over comforting his wife. I looked into the back of the truck and the floor was littered with bloody bandages and a couple of empty IV bags. One look at Mike and he knew what to do. He took the rest of the gear from the truck and put it on the sidewalk.

Once he was satisfied that it was empty, he took the rig to clean it out. I turned to walk to the clinic and came face to face with Jill. Most of her face was covered with a *shemagh*, but I would recognize those eyes anywhere. They were filled with relief. She had pulled on a BDU jacket and wore it with only one arm in the sleeve. Not wanting to make a spectacle, she turned and strode back to the clinic. I took a few seconds but eventually followed her inside. I no sooner had the door closed when she threw her good arm around me.

"You asshole!" she blurted out. "You scared the hell out of me!" I chuckled a little and that only seemed to make her mad.

"We didn't go do anything stupid without you!" I laughed. "Just trying to help some other folks out."

"Well.... Good! You have to wait for me to heal up before you go starting shit!" she proclaimed.

"Deal!" I told her. Today was only the second day that Doc had allowed her out of bed without supervision. No longer were her arm and chest bound together by the bandage, instead both wounds were bandaged separately. She had a tan tank top on and was wearing her BDU pants and boots. Her left arm was still in a sling, but she looked happy to be up and moving around. She leaned in close and pulled my face to her level.

"I was worried that you had gotten hurt. I saw the medics jump out of the five-ton, but I hadn't seen you yet. You really scared me for a second," she said so only I could hear.

"It was nothing like that. I'll do my best to stay out of trouble, but I can't promise you anything. Things are getting bad out there," I told her seriously. "I can promise you that I won't go looking for trouble without you though," I said with a smile and a kiss on the forehead.

"Okay, just be careful," she said, and she returned the kiss. Doc came up to us and interrupted the moment.

"Sorry you two. Jason, the big guy is going to go into surgery right now. I don't give him very good chances to be honest, but we will give it everything we got. Amanda is going to work on the other guy. Physically he should be fine in a day or two, mentally, I don't know. He went over the edge and hopefully getting his physical state right will help his mental state," he said flatly as he spun and headed for the surgery room. Jill told me that she had to get back to the security office. She pulled the *shemagh* off of her shoulders and wrapped it around her head again. I helped her get her jacket back on and she left. She was going to use the underground entrance in Dale's house so as not to attract attention to herself. Amanda left Jackie and Mayor Tanner in Jessica's capable hands and came over to talk to me.

"He's talking now and actually making sense," she said as she nodded toward the Mayor. "Another day, maybe two, and he would have been dead from dehydration. After seeing him and the other two, it was like they had been left for dead."

"What?" I asked.

"The two wounded guys both had very treatable wounds, but nobody had done shit for them! They didn't even change the bandages or give them fluids. The guy that died, had that happened to one of our guys, he would have survived! That's what upset Miranda so much, he didn't have to die!"

"Okay, find out what you can about their so-called doctor from Jackie. We need to get a feel for what's going on down there," I told her. She said she would find out what she could and went back to her patient. I turned to leave and came face to face with Allan. He and I went outside because it was crowded in the clinic.

"Place is getting busy all of a sudden!" he said with a smile once we were standing by the flagpole.

"Not to be rude, but where did you find the hippies?" I asked with a chuckle.

"They were teachers at the school Sam was attending."

"Medical school?"

"Yeah, he is a psychiatrist and she is an oncologist. Mitchell and JoAnne Olsen. They won't be staying with us for very long though. They were headed this way and Sam tagged along."

"They're leaving?" I asked incredulously.

"Yeah, they are headed to a commune or some shit in northern Utah. From what they said there are a lot of people there and I guess they are pretty well-stocked."

"Then I guess the least we can do is make sure they have enough provisions. They brought one of ours home and we need to take care of them for doing that," I told him.

"You bet; I was thinking along the same lines. I just didn't want to make the offer without your consent," Allan said.

"I appreciate that, but I think you know how I feel about it; I would have been fine with whatever decision you came to. Why don't you invite them over for dinner tonight?"

"Will do boss. See ya at six," he said and started back to the clinic. I went back to my Hummer and grabbed my rifle off of the console and headed to the house. It was almost four in the afternoon and I was hot and tired. I walked through the front door and dropped my body armor and rifle on the kitchen counter. After downing a bottle of cold water, I plopped on the couch and started to nap. It felt like I had just dozed off when I heard my radio squawking in the other room. With a hefty sigh I got up and got my radio. Jill was calling me, and I could hear excitement in her voice.

When I answered it, she told me I needed to get to the security office as fast as I could. I took my radio and ran downstairs into the underground. It only took me about a minute and a half to get there and when I burst through the door Jill was listening intently to the headphones for the HAM radio. She was also scribbling on a notepad. She unplugged the headset and I could hear what she was listening to.

CHAPTER 14

".....esident Wilcox will address the nation on this frequency at 7pm, Pacific Standard Time on August 2nd. We encourage you to gather as many people around your radio sets as possible. President Wilcox wants all Americans to know that your government is working tirelessly to restore the power and communications......... President Wilcox will address..." the message began to repeat itself and Jill turned the volume down.

"I was scanning the channels and that popped up. It's new because it wasn't there when I scanned through three hours ago," she said.

"Who the hell is President Wilcox? That name doesn't ring any bells."

"I guess we'll all find out at seven tonight," she said with a shrug.

"I guess you are right," I laughed. "Get ahold of Allan and let him know that we will all meet at the main security office above ground at 6:55. All non-essential personnel are to be there."

"Will do," she said as she picked up her handheld radio. I left the room and went back upstairs. After looking at my watch, I decided to go ahead and start dinner. Beef stew tonight.

Mitchell and JoAnne joined me, Allan, Jill, Jake and Jessica for dinner. They were very pleasant people to be sure. They both volunteered to stay on for a couple of days. Mitchell wanted to see if he could help the Mayor regain his hold on reality and JoAnne wanted to see if there was anything she could do to help Harold. Doc and Susan were still in surgery trying to patch him up.

They had nothing but good things to say about what we had here at the ranch. Both of them commented that it was like life was still normal here. We had power, running water and plenty of food. They also commented that while they did not believe in guns, they understood the need to have them. After a short while the conversation turned to their commune in Utah.

They had about 100 people who had signed on to show up if things went to hell, about 30 of those were there full-time. They did have a small security force but nowhere near the firepower that we had. They also did not benefit from a wall around their compound. The main mission of the place was to help the local communities with food and clean water. There were several doctors to see to the medical needs of the locals. They had given Jill the frequency to connect with them via HAM radio, but as of yet were unsuccessful in making contact. There could have been any number of reasons for that and neither of them was even willing to look at the worst-case scenario.

Allan voiced his concern about their small security force but was quickly rebuffed. He was told that it was a very different type of community and they had no fear of raiders. Theirs was an open community and anybody that needed help was welcomed with open arms. Jake brought up the raiders that hit Elko on motorcycles, but he was also shut down by Mitchell. He was told that if the community had been welcoming, the raiders would not have used violence to get what they wanted. Jake pressed the issue and told him that if the residents had not been willing to resort to violence, the raiders would have done a lot more damage and killed many more people. He was dismissed with a wave of the hand.

I changed the conversation when I could see that there would be no reasoning with their logic. It was an argument that just wasn't worth it. We turned our attention to the upcoming presidential address. Joanne knew that the new President was a guy by the name of Martin Wilcox. He was 15th in the line of succession and the former Secretary of Education. Apparently, she had met him a little over a year ago at a conference for higher education. Even with all of her glowing comments, I could tell that I would not like our new President. He sounded like a raging liberal and I wanted no part of that. I had been very conservative my entire life and I could not fathom the mental disorder known as liberalism.

I liked Mitchell and JoAnne, but their political views were as foreign to me as the Chinese language. These two were about as far left as it got. They believed in the all-knowing, all powerful, all intrusive government helping us citizens get safely through life on a daily basis. That was something I could not stand for. Don't get me wrong, I wasn't against helping people that really needed it, but the system had become so corrupt and top heavy that it was destroying those that made every effort to be self-reliant. That seemed very wrong to my way of thinking.

We continued to make small talk until it was about 6:50 and all of us made our way to the above-ground security shack for the President's address. Everyone but Susan and the Mayor was there by the time the address started.

"My fellow Americans. I come to you this evening as a humble man seeking your help. As you know, nearly a month ago, our great nation was brought to its knees by an unprecedented act of terrorism. Sadly, we were not the only ones to suffer this fate. All of Europe, China, Russia and Australia were hit with the same type of attacks that we were. It was a coordinated attack that has left most of the globe without modern conveniences and, by initial estimates, has left millions of people dead."

"There is no assistance being offered by any other country, nor are we offering any. I have issued an order that will withdraw all of our military assets from abroad and re-deploy them here at home. Our primary concern is what is happening within our own borders. Many cities are experiencing looting and violence on a level never seen before. This MUST stop. That is why I have signed several Executive Orders authorizing the military and National Guard to lock down all of the border crossings leading to and from our country. They will also be putting a stop to any and all interstate travel. Many major cities will be cordoned off and relief centers will be set up as soon as humanly possible."

"I would ask all Americans to shelter in place during this time of national crisis and to help your neighbors. Effectively immediately, there will be a sun-down to sun-up curfew in place and the military has orders to use whatever force they deem necessary to enforce it. All state and local law enforcement will answer directly to the regional military command. As of now, this country is in a state of martial law. These are not steps that I have taken lightly, but in light of the recent violence, they were necessary steps. If we all work together to quell the looting and violence, we should be able to remove these measures soon."

"Be assured that your government is working very hard to restore power and communications throughout the country. We are working tirelessly to restore law and order and we are doing everything that we can to get supplies distributed to those who need them the most. Please be patient."

"There will be a radio address on this frequency every Sunday at 7pm to keep everyone informed on our progress. Please pray for your nation and indeed the world. Thank you, goodnight."

The address ended and the silence in and around the security shack was deaf-ening. You could have heard the proverbial pin drop. Dan, Andy and Jeff all shared a quick look before Dan broke the silence.

"Jason, I think I can speak for Jeff and Andy on this one. We will not comply with any order to report for duty as either sheriff's deputies or as members of the Army National Guard," he said quietly. Jeff and Andy both nodded in agreement. "As far as I know, I'm the senior deputy and a staff sergeant in the Guard and right now my duty is to my family and my friends. This government and the Elko city government left us swinging in the wind when we could have made a difference, when we had a chance to get out in front of this thing. I owe them nothing, but I owe everything to my wife, my kids and my friends here at the ranch," Jeff and Andy were still nodding their heads in agreement. I was about to say something when JoAnne spoke up. Her face was in a scowl, like she had just bitten into a lemon.

"I for one, think the President is doing the best that he can under very bad circumstances. He has some very tough choices to make and I'm sure that no matter what path he takes, some of you will still frown on it," she said directly to Dan. "And people like you who refuse to do their duty are not helping matters."

"Listen here lady, you have not earned the right to use a word like "Duty" in your vocabulary. You know nothing about what I've done for my country or my community and until you do, keep your mouth shut!" He snapped. Miranda put her hand on her husband's arm to try and calm him a little. "I have buried men and women, my friends, who lived by the words Duty, Honor, and Courage. They died believing in words that you and your ilk use at your snooty dinner parties when you talk about your socialist agendas. Agendas that get good people killed because you use those same words to castrate us every time we try to defend the wall that protects you! Let me tell you something else, this new world out there, it's gonna kick your ass and leave you dead on the side of the road somewhere. You may preach love and peace, but outside of these walls all you will find is hate and brutality and that's just for starters," when Dan paused to take a breath, I jumped in. Miranda had moved between Dan and JoAnne; both of her hands were now on his chest. I could tell that this wasn't the first time she'd had to back him down.

"That's enough! Instead of standing here fighting among ourselves, we need to figure out how this is going to affect us and our operation!" I paused and looked around the group. Dan was still glaring at JoAnne. "Bill, as a military contractor, how does martial law affect us?" I asked. Bill stepped forward so that everyone could see him.

"It could go a couple of different ways for us. First, we could probably get away with a few things the average citizen couldn't get away with. As long as we are conducting humanitarian missions, we could stay out after dark. If we are enforcing the curfew, we could be out after dark. If we are working in a law enforcement capacity, we can stay out after dark. All in all, in that case, it wouldn't affect us much."

"A second scenario is that the military could decide that they want their hardware back. That is to say, the hardware that they know about," he said with a slight grin. "That's not likely to happen though. As I see it, they are going to have a surplus of hardware and a shortage of soldiers. Dan said it a minute ago, most of them will be trying to help their families and friends, and I would imagine the desertion rate will be pretty high. My suggestion is that every time we are outside of these walls, we act like a military unit. It goes back to the old saying, act like you know what you're doing, and most people will never question you. If someone questions us, we are just a contractor, we are not regular military," Bill and I could see Dan, Jeff and Andy starting to squirm a little. Dan started to say something, but Bill waved him off. "I know what you're about to say Dan, and like I said, we will not impersonate a military unit. If we are asked, we are a military contractor and we do have the documentation to prove it," he finished and that seemed to appease the three of them.

"Thank you, Bill. Allan, how are we sitting on supplies for the long run and do you have any suggestions for security needs?" I asked. Allan stepped forward and cleared his throat.

"I would put us in the top half of a percentage point on all of our supplies. Even with all of the driving we have done, our fuel reserves are still above 97%. We have not touched the freeze-dried food yet. We have been operating on what we have in the freezers and what comes from the garden. I would suggest that we keep the cattle down here on the lower pasture where we can keep an eye on them. The feed for the livestock will last well into next year's growing season. Our medical supplies have seen a lot of action, but we are still very well stocked."

"Again, just a suggestion, any trip we make to town we need to be on the lookout for medical gear. Weapons, bullets, powder and batteries are still in excellent shape. We could use a full-time hand with the reloading but as of now we are staying ahead of the demand. Security patrols outside the fence have turned up nothing out to two miles so I would like to pull them back to a one-mile perimeter and I would like to discontinue the foot patrols outside the wall. Just a side note, all of our fuel here has been treated with a stabilizer but there is a lot of fuel out there on the roads and in underground tanks that will, in time, start to go to waste. First, I think that whenever possible, we use that fuel. Second, I think we need to get some scout teams out to find us some fuel tankers and we can bring them back here for our use. They could also be on the lookout for other supplies and bring us back intelligence on what is out there," Allan finished and stepped back into the crowd.

"Thank you, Allan. If you would draw up a plan for the scout teams and a list of what they need to look for, I'd appreciate it. Doc, your turn. Can you give me an update on the medical side, please?"

"Sure. As Allan mentioned, our supplies have gotten a pretty good workout. About the only thing we are beginning to run low on is whole blood. That has gotten far more usage than I would like. I would highly recommend that we start a blood drive to replenish those supplies. Most of us have already had our blood typed but we do have a lot of new people here. If you don't know what type you are, don't worry about that, we have the technology to figure it out."

"I would also like to remind everyone to keep yourselves clean and sanitary. We are living in a semi-closed environment here and a cold or anything else could spread like wildfire. Don't blow the small scrapes or cuts either. Make sure you clean any small wounds and use the antibiotic creams we have available. If you get an infection, left untreated, it could be deadly. Take care of your feet too. Fresh socks and foot powder can go a long way during long days. I can't say this one enough, hydrate, hydrate, hydrate. This is the hottest month of the year and with all the gear you guys wear, you could dehydrate in nothing flat. Take care of yourselves because you don't want me to!" he said with a laugh.

"Thanks, Doc," I said as I returned my attention to the crowd. "As far as the President's address goes, it tells us a couple of things but leaves a whole lot more unanswered questions. It tells us that there is indeed a government running this country, or at least trying to. It tells us that this is a worldwide event, not something local that will go away in a short period of time. If everyone was hit with EMP weapons, the grid will be down for a very, very long time. Not weeks or months, but years."

"One other thing that I found interesting was the fact that he made no mention of the cities that were attacked with dirty bombs. So far, most people have kept their wits about them but this may be the catalyst that drives a lot of them over the edge. There is no hope of rescue from the government and what help they do provide will more than likely be too little, too late. These relief centers that he talked about will probably be over-run by desperate people."

"From the sounds of it, most of the major metropolitan areas have already devolved into chaos. Many of the small towns will try to hold their own but if the wrong element takes control, it's going to get ugly fast. I think that is something that we will have to worry about in Elko. Those of us that went to town last time were starting to see the beginnings of it," I went on to explain my thoughts on the red bandannas and gallows.

We stood around for another half hour discussing our plans before the group split up. After having Dan jump down her throat, JoAnne Olsen was very quiet for the rest of the meeting. Mitchell did offer some insight into what might be going on, but he too was very quiet. It was obvious to me that they were not a good fit for our group. Sadly, if they left the confines of our walls, they probably would not fare well in this brutal new world.

As the group dispersed, I spotted Dan talking to the two security guys that we picked up at the Mayor's office earlier in the day. They introduced themselves as brothers, Pat and Eric Teller.

"This is quite the set-up you have here Mr. Sterling," the older brother, Pat said. "Eric and I were pretty new to the prepper thing but it looks like you guys have been at it for a while." Amazement evident in his voice.

"We did have a bit of a head start," I shrugged. "I have some questions about what is happening in town, would you guys mind telling me what you know?" Both of them nodded quickly.

"I just have one request first...... Could I get a glass of water?" Eric asked sheepishly.

"Didn't you guys get taken care of when we got here?" I asked. As soon as the words were out of my mouth, I knew the answer just because I too had forgotten about them in the hustle. "I am so sorry! Yes, follow me. We'll get you something to eat and all the water you want," I motioned for them to follow me to the house. The pot of beef stew was still on the stove and it was still hot.

I had them drop their gear by the front door and showed them where the bathroom was. While they were washing up, I got them two big bowls of stew and some fresh bread. There were two glasses of ice water and a pitcher of water on the table when they returned. Both of them looked totally shocked by the ice water. They sat at the table and began to eat. I could tell that it had been awhile since either of them had eaten a good meal. Instead of interrupting them with my questions, I let them eat. As they neared the bottom of their bowls, I put the pot of stew and the half loaf of bread on the table and told them to eat what they wanted.

After three pitchers of water and finishing off the pot of stew and bread, they finally seemed to be getting full. I went to the fridge and pulled three cold beers out and I motioned for them to follow me out to the front porch. I opened their beers and handed them over. Both of them thanked me profusely for the hospitality.

"I apologize guys, I had assumed someone had taken care of you when we got here," I said. "What can you tell me about what's going on down there in Elko?" Pat was the first to speak.

"It was about a week after all this started that they started asking people to help with security around town. They wanted people to stand posts at the roadblocks and at other vital places. At first both of us were assigned to the roadblock on the north side of town. It was day four if I remember right, there had been a big gunfight in town the night before. We were told that all of the sheriff's deputies had been killed and a bunch of gang bangers were dead too," Pat paused for a drink of beer and Eric picked up the story.

"We went and checked out the sheriff's office that day, but things didn't add up compared to the story we were being told. It was obvious that there had been a big gun fight, but we couldn't find any dead cops. All we did find was a bunch of dead thugs. They had been stripped of everything useful and so had the sheriff's office. Everything of use was gone and that struck us as odd. Dan told us tonight that you guys were responsible for saving their asses and kicking the shit out of the thugs. One mystery solved," he laughed a little. Pat picked up the story again.

"That was the day that Harold picked us for the Mayor's security detail. It was a couple of days later when you guys showed up with the food. We were the guys standing security outside of Mayor Tanner's office when you showed up," he smiled a little. "You had both of us scared shitless. We knew if things went sideways, we didn't stand a chance against you and your men."

"What? Why?" I interrupted.

"It was obvious that most of you had some serious training. Eric and I, we've had to train ourselves. We bought videos and spent a lot of time scouring

YouTube," both of them chuckled a little. "Over the course of the next couple of weeks, things more or less stayed steady," Pat said. "It was a couple of days before you showed up again that we were hit by the biker gang.....," he paused for a few seconds. "That whole thing stinks to high heaven. They hit us in broad daylight and the Reds all conveniently faded away in the middle of the attack."

"Reds?" I asked.

"The guys with the red bandannas. There were only about a dozen of them before the attack. All of them buddies with Deputy Mayor Tom Perry and all of them real shitheads. They figured that since they were Tom's private security force, they had free run of the town. They took food, fuel, vehicles and there were even a couple of rumors about them having their way with some of the women in town. Couldn't prove it though because we could never find any living witnesses."

"Harold was our boss and he was in charge of the Mayor's security. He hated Tom and his men. Tried like hell to find something to pin on them, but they were very good at covering their tracks. The day of the attack, they were guarding City Hall, which was unusual in itself. When the shooting started, they all took cover inside the building and left Harold and Garry on the outside."

"Garry was halfway across the front lawn and running for all he was worth for the front door. He was caught in the open with no cover at all. That's when he took two to the chest. The shots were fired from inside City Hall! Harold came from the back of the building and went full on medieval on those guys. He shot seven of them, stabbed one and killed the ninth guy with his bare hands. Jason, all of the bad guys were dead, and he was on his way to check on Gerry when he was shot in the chest. Again, both shots came from inside City Hall," he paused, and Eric picked up the story again.

"The Reds were more concerned about getting the motorcycles, guns and ammo than they were about getting help for Gerry and Harold. Both of us ran down and started first aid but nobody would help us. The one bystander that helped us get them inside and helped us treat their wounds was strung up on the gallows that night. The Reds said he was a thief. They had been keeping the two of us, the Mayor and his daughter locked in a storeroom until just before you showed up today. No food, and the only water that we had was in our canteens. That ran out a day and a half ago. Just before you got there, they ushered us back to where we were supposed to be. They told us that if we did anything stupid, we would be the next to go."

"After you took Jackie and her father out of the building, Eric and I decided to try and make a break for it. I broke the neck of the asshole that was guarding us and we hauled ass out to where you were. We knew they wouldn't come after us if we made it to you and your team," Pat continued. "We also knew we had to get Harold and Gerry out of there and get them some help," he finished the story and took the last swig of his beer. I stood and collected the empty bottles and took them inside. I returned a moment later with three fresh bottles and took my seat again.

"Why are there so many Reds in town now?" I asked.

"My best guess is that they have started to recruit people for a new security team for the town. Those of us that really know what happened that day are either dead or here. That left them there to spin their own story. After they locked us away, who was there to tell the townspeople anything different?" Eric said. I simply nodded. "A lot of the new guys, we had never seen before, but I think they were convicts. My guess is that they were probably from the prison in Lovelock. They are the ones who make up the core group, the hardcore ones."

"There are also a lot of Reds who are just well-meaning citizens. They are allowed to carry their guns, but they are not allowed to have any ammunition. If there is a problem, they are to call in the other Reds and let them settle things," we talked for another hour and I learned that Tom was using a small mansion on the town's golf course as his own headquarters and that the leader of his group of Reds was a guy known only as Marv. It was about 10:00 when Alex and Jessica came by on their patrol. I made introductions all around and asked them to escort Pat and Eric to the barracks where all of the bachelors were staying.

After the four of them had left I went back inside and collected their gear from the entryway. I laid it on the table and started with the rifles. Both of them were AK-47's and while they both had magazines seated in the mag-wells, they were devoid of rounds. I went through their spare magazines and every one of them was empty too. I picked up their pistol belts and found that they too had been stripped of ammunition. Both canteens were bone dry. I returned their gear to the entryway and headed up to bed.

Wednesday, August 3, 2016

I was up at 4am and in the gym by 4:30. I had not slept well at all that night. There was still a lot of information that I was trying to process. It would seem that we were going to have trouble from Tom and Marvin sooner rather than later. All of the information that I had gotten from Pat and Eric seemed to jive with everything else that I had learned in the last month. What really bothered me was the fact that they were duping the good citizens into following a bad plan. If we had to go in there and sort it out, it was going to get ugly. We needed a plan to separate the good guys from the bad guys and it was something that we were going to have to do soon. We couldn't allow the Reds to assume too much power. If they did, it could spell disaster for us here at the ranch.

It was about 6:30 when I went upstairs and got my shower and dressed for the day. Jill was already up and had breakfast going for the house when I got back to the kitchen.

"You tossed and turned all night. Are you okay?" she asked as she set a plate of bacon and eggs in front of me.

"Not really," I told her. "I learned last night that Tom and Marvin are working very hard to assume control of the whole city. They have a new security force that is headed by Marvin and made up of gang members and convicts," I told her.

"What are we going to do about it?" she asked as she sat next to me.

"I need to talk to the Mayor and his daughter. After that, I'm not really sure."

"We're going to have to deal with them, you know that, right?"

"Yeah, I know that. The biggest problem right now would be the collateral damage. There are a lot of good people mixed in with the bad guys right now and we don't have a way to tell them apart. If we go in there now, a lot of good guys are going to get hurt. That's not something we can afford," I went on to tell her everything that I had learned the night before from Pat and Eric. She agreed that I should confirm their story with the Mayor and his daughter. She also suggested that we send a team in to keep an eye on things in town. We needed first-hand intelligence as to what was happening. She looked a little disappointed when I asked her to get Dan Hawkins and Mike Taylor for the mission.

She was chomping at the bit to get back to her full duties and I couldn't blame her. I would have lost my mind spending all my time locked in behind a desk all day. Her wounds were healing extremely well but Doc had not given her the all-clear yet. Against his wishes, she had been spending some time in the gym.

THE RANCH

It was almost eight by the time she and I finished talking and cleaning up after ourselves. She headed up to get ready for her day and I headed over to the clinic. I slipped in through the front door and caught Susan napping behind the desk. She was leaning back in the chair with her feet on the corner of the desk. The door made the slightest click when I eased it shut and Susan's eyes popped open. She let out a big sigh and pulled her feet from the desk.

I spent a few minutes talking to her and she filled me in on Harold's condition. He had made it through the night, which was a start. She also told me that the Mayor and his daughter had been given one of the rooms in the barracks where everyone else was staying. I spent a few more minutes chatting with her and made sure she knew how much all of us appreciated what they were all doing at the clinic.

When I got to the barracks, I found Pat and Eric sitting at the table eating breakfast and sipping coffee. Both of them looked a lot better than they had the night before. I greeted both of them and asked them which room the Mayor was staying in. They both pointed to the first door down the hallway. I could tell that both of them were still doing their jobs. Pat was positioned so that he could see the bedroom door and Eric was sitting so that he could see the front door. I thanked them and walked down the hallway. I paused for a moment to listen. When I heard low voices from inside, I gently knocked on the door.

"Come in," Jackie Tanner said from inside. I opened the door and walked in, closing it behind me.

"Good morning," I said to her and Mayor Tanner. Both were sitting on the edge of the bed. While Jackie looked like she could use some rest, the Mayor looked like a broken man. He had been given clean clothes and his suit had been cleaned and was hanging on the bathroom door. Jackie stood and extended her hand.

"Thank you so much for bringing us here Mr. Sterling. Your hospitality has been more than gracious," she said.

"Please, call me Jason. You're more than welcome Miss Tanner. You and the Mayor looked like you could use a hand. Good food and good rest go a long way."

"How is Harold doing?" Mayor Tanner asked quietly.

"I just came from there and he is still holding his own. I can assure you that our medical staff is doing everything in their power to help him. Doc says he has fifty-fifty odds at this point but every day that will improve a little," I told him.

"And his men, Pat and Eric? Are they okay?"

"They are fine. They are right outside the door having breakfast. Are you two hungry?" I asked. Both nodded in unison. "Come on, let's get some eat," I motioned them to the door. Jackie led the way and I followed the Mayor to the breakfast table. Pat and Eric were still sitting there finishing off their coffee. Both of them stood and pulled out the chairs for the Mayor and his daughter. They grabbed their empty plates from the table and took them to the sink. I grabbed two coffee cups and the coffee urn. When I poured their coffee, Jackie looked a little surprised.

"Is this real coffee?" she asked with wonder in her eyes.

"Of course, it is," I told her. She held the cup to her nose and just smelled it for a long time before she took her first sip. Eric and Pat had washed their dishes and were just kind of standing around. I cooked up some scrambled eggs and a slice of ham for my guests and followed that up with some homemade bread on the table. While Jackie dug in, Mayor Tanner seemed to take his time, just pushing his food around on the plate. I kept quiet and let them eat. As they finished up, Pat moved in to clear their dishes and refill their coffee mugs. When he was done he stood against the counter next to Eric. I stood and motioned for both of them to follow me into the hallway.

"Would you two mind waiting outside? I have some delicate information that I need to discuss with the Mayor," I said. Both of them looked hesitant but they stepped out the front door onto the deck. I went and sat back down at the table.

"I had a long conversation with Pat and Eric last night. They told me some pretty interesting things about what is happening in town," I started. Jackie looked in my direction, but the Mayor just stared off into space. "They told me about your captivity for the last few days and I just need to get your version of the story," Jackie was the only one who replayed what had happened. Her story was very similar to the one that Pat and Eric had told me.

While Pat and Eric had glossed over a few of the details where the Reds were concerned, Jackie had some graphic particulars. Things she had witnessed with her own eyes. A store owner and his family murdered because he refused to do business with them. After they were killed and the store stripped of everything, it was burned to the ground with the bodies inside. Men were beaten for refusing to give up their weapons or ammunition. Women had disappeared after refusing their advances. The more I listened, the more rage I felt inside.

THE RANCH

She also confirmed that it was a core group, probably 30 to 40 men. The rest of the Reds were allowed to carry weapons but with no ammunition, and they were being watched. If any of them stepped out of line, they disappeared. She filled in a few more details for me too. They were using the sheriff's office as their main headquarters while Tom and Marvin were using big expensive houses on the edge of the golf course. They had kept the Mayor around to use as a figurehead for their plans because the people liked the Mayor and usually listened to him.

The one other piece of information she had was that there was another group like ours, smaller to be sure, but just as prepared as we were. That group was on the opposite side of town on a small ranch that was owned by the previous Mayor of Elko, a guy by the name of Jim Calvert. Apparently, the Reds had decided to go after him but came back with their tails between their legs and four less members.

"I played dirty in the election," the Mayor said quietly. Both Jackie and I looked at him in surprise. "He should have won. He was the better man and I paid off some people to make sure he didn't win. I cheated," he said, still staring off into space. By the look on Jackie's face, she was just as surprised as I was.

"Dad....It's...." she started but was silenced with a wave of his hand. He looked at me for the first time since being at the table.

"Mr. Sterling, what are you planning to do about Tom and his men?" he asked frankly.

"Honestly sir, I don't know yet."

"Kill them. Kill every last one of them," he said with conviction then pushed himself away from the table and went back to his room without another word. Jackie and I were both speechless. It took her a full minute before she too left the table and returned to their room.

CHAPTER 15

I sat at the table for another half hour, lost in my own thoughts. My radio crackled and brought me back to reality. It was Doc asking me to come to the clinic. I pushed away from the table and went out the front door. I had completely forgotten about Pat and Eric waiting outside. I stopped long enough to tell them both to carry on with their duties to the Mayor and Jackie. Both looked relieved to be allowed back inside. I quickly walked to the clinic and was greeted by Doc when I went through the door.

"Harold?" I asked.

"No, he is fine. It's the Olsen's we got a problem with," he said as he headed out the door. He directed me to their van which was at the far end of the parking area. The motor was running but there was a Humvee blocking it in its parking space. Andy and Jeff were standing at the driver's door arguing with the Olsen's.

"What's going on?" I inquired as I approached.

"We want to leave and these goons of yours won't let us!" JoAnne Olsen shouted from the passenger seat. Andy and Jeff moved to the side as I stepped up to the door.

"Mr. and Mrs. Olsen, I need to make sure you want to do this, and I have to make sure you are aware of the dangers out there."

"We WANT to leave, and we want to leave NOW," Mitchell said.

"I'm not going to stop you. You are aware that the situation outside of the wall is very dangerous right now, right?" I asked.

"It's not that bad," JoAnne fired back.

"Mrs. Olsen, we cannot and will not be responsible for your safety once you leave here. Once that gate closes behind you, you are on your own."

"It can't be as bad as it is here! Neither of us can live under your jackboots or your warmongering ways. You damn people and your guns!" she nearly screamed. I stepped back from the door.

"Jeff, move the truck and escort the Olsen's to the gate. Show them out!" I ordered. He and Andy jumped into the Hummer and moved it forward. As the

Olsen's backed out of the parking space, both of them shot me the middle finger. I waved and that did nothing but agitate them further. They left with the Hummer following closely behind.

"What the hell was that about?" I asked Doc.

"Follow me, I'll show you," he said as he spun and headed back to the clinic. We went into the operating room and there was a black backpack sitting open on the table. Doc reached in and pulled out a big bag of white powder and a second one that I recognized as pot.

"I caught them snorting cocaine on my steel countertop!" he bellowed.

"Seriously?" I asked in disbelief.

"Yup, snorting blow right there where I prep my surgical packs. Dumb asses tried to offer me some if I would keep quiet," he said.

"For shits sake," I muttered. Doc put the bags back in the backpack and threw it over his shoulder. "What are we going to do with it?" I asked him.

"Believe it or not, there are some medical uses for both of them. For now, though, I'll lock this pack up in the security office downstairs."

"Your call Doc, good catch too. We don't need that kind of crap going on around here," I said and made my way toward the door.

I stepped out of the front door and just stood there for a few minutes trying to get my head around everything that had happened this morning. First I had confirmed that the town was being run by a warlord. Second, the Mayor had stolen the election and third, two doctors were snorting cocaine in the operating room. What the hell else was going to happen today I thought to myself?

I was standing there going over everything I had learned so far that morning when I saw Dan Hawkins and Mike Taylor come from the security shack. They were headed toward the barracks when they spotted me. We walked toward each other and met halfway.

"Gentlemen," I said in greeting.

"Hey boss," they said in unison.

"Did Jill talk to you two yet?" I asked.

"She sure did. There is only one thing we are not clear on though," Dan said.

"What's that?"

"Is this mission strictly eyes on the targets for intelligence gathering? What do you want us to do if shit goes down? Do we intervene?"

SEAN LISCOM

"We really need the intel that much is for sure. We need an accurate count of bad guys and their habits. To be honest, I hadn't given the rest of it much thought," I told them.

"Tell ya what boss, we will get you what you need but we need the leeway to take care of any trouble before it gets out of hand," Dan said.

"Don't compromise yourselves. If you can do it discreetly, then do what you have to. Just don't put yourselves in a bad spot. Got it?"

"Yes sir."

"I talked to the Mayor and his daughter a little while ago and she gave me some insight that you guys might find useful and we might be able to exploit for our benefit," I began as we once again started walking toward the barracks. "From what she told me, the real red bandannas probably number between 30 and 40. The rest are conscripts, forced to act like the friendly security force. We need to separate the two groups. The conscripts are armed but they are not allowed any ammunition."

"You think we could start an insurrection?" Mike asked.

"I think we could definitely get some assistance if we could find a way to get the right people some ammo and let them know that we will be there to help them take their town back."

"What if we get a clean shot at Marv or Tom?" Dan asked.

"Again, if you can do it without blowing your operation, do what you have to," I told them as we walked in the front door and headed to the stairs. We went downstairs and into the conference room. Allan and Jill were already there. I sat at the far end of the table, opposite of the "Big Chair" that Jill occupied. I sat back and listened to the four of them plan the mission for the next two hours.

Dan and Mike were going to be leaving the compound under the cover of darkness this same evening and be in position by sunrise on Friday, August 5th. They were planning on traveling on foot so they could remain hidden the entire time. They would both carry their standard suppressed rifles, but Dan would also take one of the M40a5 sniper rifles that we kept. Dan was known for being able to hit a dinner plate sized target at 930 yards with it. He would also take a suppressor for it just in case he needed it.

Both of them would have enough food and water for a seven-day excursion even though the plan only called for five days. Both would have radios capable of reaching the compound. The entire time they were outside the wall, there would

238

be a quick response force ready to go at a moment's notice. That team was made up of Jill, Amanda and me in the lead Hummer. Mark, Jake and Susan would be in the second one. Both rigs would have the big .50 caliber machine guns mounted in the turrets just in case we ran into some real trouble.

The one standing order that would be given to everyone involved was to only shoot at people that were shooting at you. If it came to that, hopefully it would keep the collateral damage to a minimum. If everything went according to plan, Dan and Mike would be back home by the morning of the ninth. With any luck at all, they would have the intelligence that we so desperately needed. Once the meeting had adjourned and Jill and I were alone, I finally spoke up.

"Doc is going to be a little pissed when he finds out that you're back on duty," I said with a smile.

"I don't really give a damn," she said in her all-business tone of voice. "If it comes down to brass tacks, I can drive, and I can fight if I have to. Hell, you know that I'm better one-handed than most people are with two!"

"Hey, you don't have to defend yourself to me. You are the head of security and you know your limitations. I was just pointing out that he won't be happy if you screw up his handy work on your shoulder," I said as I stood and walked the length of the table. "I trust your judgment where your mission capabilities are concerned." I stopped right next to her chair and turned it to face me. I put one hand on each arm of the chair, my face only a couple of inches from hers. She smiled slightly, remembering the little game we used to play.

It was almost ten that night when Mike and Dan slipped out one of the side gates. There was absolutely no moon to be seen in the night sky, so it was rather easy for them to vanish. Jill watched them on the infrared and night vision cameras but within an hour they were gone from those too. With everyone briefed on what to do if an emergency call came in, there was nothing left to do but go to bed for the night. It was almost midnight before Jill, and I retired to our room and it only took a few minutes for both of us to fall asleep.

I awoke at a little after 5am on the morning of the 4th. Even though I had only had about five hours of sleep, I felt refreshed and ready to start the day. I slipped out of bed and headed to the bathroom. After a quick shower, I dressed in clean Multi-Cam and quietly walked back into the dark bedroom. I grabbed my radio and sidearm from the nightstand and slipped out into the hallway. Jill didn't have to be back on shift until eight, so I was trying very hard not to wake her. Her healing body could still use all of the rest it could get.

I fired up the coffee maker and while I was waiting on it, I strapped on my battle belt and slipped the Sig Sauer into its holster and the radio into its pouch. With a hot cup of coffee, I headed out the front door to the security office. Bill was seated behind the desk and looked up as I came through the door.

"You're up early," he said.

"It wasn't much sleep, but I guess it was enough," I shrugged. "Have the boys checked in yet?

"Not yet but I expect their call at any time now. Starting to see some hints of daylight," he said, sipping from his own cup of coffee. I sat in one of the chairs across from him and just kind of enjoyed the pre-dawn silence for a few minutes.

"Can I ask you a question, Bill?"

"What's on your mind?"

"What would have happened if I had told you to get the hell out of my office last year?

"Honestly, I don't really know. I was praying you would come with me and scared to death that you wouldn't. I knew deep down that Braden wanted nothing to do with this place and you were our only hope," he said. The mention of my brother was like salt in an open wound. I had tried very hard to reassure myself that he and his family were okay, that they were headed here, and everything was going to be all right. Today marked one month since the EMP and still no sign of Braden...... I was beginning to get worried.

"Come on Bill, you guys would have held this place together and you would have done the same things that I have done," I said, pushing my brother back into his place in the back of my mind.

"If we followed the protocol that we had planned on, without you, this place would probably be very close to failing. You and your ideas have given us what we so desperately needed to keep and defend this place."

"Ha, I'm just one guy with absolutely zero experience with anything like this Bill, I'm making this shit up as I go along,"

"Then I must say that your improvisational skills are pretty good," he said as he took another sip of coffee. "Believe it or not Jason, you are the glue that is holding this place together. You have shown the same leadership skills your father had. Most of the time I think he made shit up on the fly too. That's why he was so good at what he did. He took one look at the rule book and tossed it out the window. He had people skills. The kind of skills that could talk a man in the desert out of his last drink of water. The kind of skills that instilled confidence in everyone he associated with. You two are not as different as you would like to believe."

I sat quietly for a few more minutes letting his words sink in. I was about to speak again when the long-range radio came to life.

"Nest......Authenticate, Sierra, Sierra, Romeo, Whiskey......" it was Dan's voice. Bill picked up the microphone and opened his notebook.

"Raptors....Authenticating.... Juliet, Oscar, Charlie, Zulu."

"Copy that Nest. Raptors are at drop point one nine three."

"Copy that Raptors, get some rest," he said as he hung the mic back up. He looked at the map on the wall and pinpointed their exact location. "Damn, they made it over halfway last night."

"Boys are in pretty good shape! That would have killed me!" I laughed.

"You and me both," Bill chuckled as he sat back in his chair.

"I have another question for you," I said. "What do you know about Jim Calvert?"

"That's easy. Former Mayor of Elko. Stand-up guy. Runs a ranch on the other side of town with a couple hundred head of cattle. Last I heard it was him and his four sons that ran the place full-time. Why do you ask?"

"Elko is going to need a new Mayor, Tanner is not up to the task anymore. He has pretty much checked out if you know what I mean. I'm thinking about making a trip over to his ranch and having a talk with him."

"Be very, very careful with that. Last I heard he was pretty pissed off about losing the election to Tanner. He was positive there were some shady things going on, but it was just a hunch. He couldn't prove a thing and bowed out gracefully."

"His hunch was right, I heard it straight from Tanner yesterday. I also heard that he and his boys handed the Reds their asses a few days ago. They put a few of them down for good."

"No shit? I always thought Tanner was a little slippery."

"Yeah, typical politician. I think Calvert would be a good guy to have on our side."

"Well, why don't you take the response team over there tomorrow and see what you can do to make some new friends. Just a word of advice, he is a whiskey drinker so don't go empty handed. Don't show up in full force either, intimidation tactics won't work with him," Bill said.

I chuckled a little. "Got it, take him a bottle of our finest and don't come on too strong. Any other sage advice?" I asked.

"Yeah, if he tells you no, let it go and move on. Once his mind is made up about things, it tends to stay made up. He is a hard but fair man, but I honestly think you two will get along just fine," he said with a smile.

We talked until shift change at seven and after the morning briefing, I headed back to the house. I spent the rest of the day just sort of hanging out. With nothing to do but monitor the radio, I started reading the other journals that were kept in the study. Starting with volume one, I managed to read six of them before lunch. Every time I came across some of the coding, I would write it down on a note pad on the big desk.

It was obvious to me that there was a lot more information to be had, I just needed to decode all of it. There was a total of 43 journals, and I wanted to read all of them before I even attempted to decode the messages that were hidden within them. One other thing that had become painfully obvious was that my father did indeed spend a lot of time thinking about his two sons. I could sense a lot of regret in his writings.

The rest of the day was very mundane. By all rights, it was downright boring. After dinner I went back to the guard shack and waited until the "Raptors" checked in. Everything was fine on their end and if they stuck to the plan, they would be in place before dawn the next morning. After I left the guard shack, I made the rounds to let everyone know that we would be going to town in the morning. Doc was a little miffed that Jill was going but he let it go with a shake of his head and some muttering under his breath.

Friday, August 5, 2016

The Raptor team had checked in at 4:30am and reported that they were in position and had eyes on the sheriff's office. Their initial report was that there was very little activity, but they would report in around noon or if anything changed. The QRF (Quick Response Force) was assembled in the parking area a little before eight and they were ready to go. Since Amanda didn't know much about manning

THE RANCH

the turret position in the lead Hummer, we added Marcus Thompson to the group. We pulled out of the gate at eight on the dot. Jill was wasting no time and quickly got us up to 65 mph and held us there.

It was right after we passed the small housing subdivision that the Raptor team called in. They reported that everything went from all quiet to chaos in nothing flat. The Reds were scrambling for their two running cars and six motorcycles. They hauled ass for the highway and headed westbound. If I was right, they were sending out a welcoming committee to meet us at the roadblock. I consulted my map for a couple of minutes trying to find an alternate route. I found a dirt road that paralleled the highway and quickly gave Jill instructions on how to get to it. A quick radio call to the second Hummer and we were all on the same page.

"What do we do if they have this dirt road covered too?" Jill asked.

"We blow through, do not stop for anything," I told her. She smiled a smile that held no mirth. She put the throttle pedal to the floor and opened the diesel motor all the way up. Before long the 7,000-pound truck was hurtling down the two-lane road at nearly 80mph. As we approached the highway, Jill started to ease off the throttle a little. We would blow past the on-ramp, go under the main road and take the dirt road that was about 100 yards to the other side.

Once we made the turn, Jill was back on the throttle. It was a well-traveled road and looked to have been well-maintained. There were only a couple of spots where we managed to get a little air under the tires. The second Hummer closed the distance between us so that they wouldn't get choked out by our dust cloud. They were literally only 20 feet off of our rear bumper at 70 mph.

I again consulted my map and found our next turn about five miles ahead. This would put us back on the blacktop and inside the city limits. As we tore down the dirt road, I could see the roadblock on the highway to my right. Sure enough, two older sedans and six motorcycles were just pulling up to it. It was obvious that we had thrown a wrench in their plan to intercept us. The lead car locked up the brakes and slid sideways. The second car nearly hit him and in turn, the motorcycles nearly crashed into that car. They were all over the place trying to get turned around so they could follow us back to town.

We were quickly approaching the turn ahead and Jill radioed the second Hummer and told them what to expect. They backed off a little as Jill started braking and scuffing off speed. We made the hard turn and as soon as the tires met blacktop they started howling. The truck fishtailed a little, but Jill quickly corrected with the heavy application of throttle. I was calling out directions and she was deftly handling all of the maneuvers. It was working to our advantage that most of the stalled cars had been cleared from the roads.

We raced all the way through town and caught another dirt road that again ran parallel to the highway. Jake called from the turret of the second Hummer and said that the two sedans had appeared back on the highway and were racing to get alongside of us. There was no sign of the motorcycles. When we passed the road-block on the east side of town, both sedans gave up on the chase. That did nothing for Jill's lead foot. She stayed on it hard and we quickly put distance between us and town.

It was about 15 minutes later that we reached the turnoff for Calvert's ranch. Jill eased off the throttle and we slowly made our way up the main road. As the main gate to his property came into view, I had her stop about 100 yards shy of it. I got on the radio and told Marcus and Jake to keep the .50s pointed away from the gate. I had Amanda dig into my pack that was in the back seat and pull out a fifth of Jack Daniels. I opened my door and stepped out. I took my helmet and body armor off and put them on my seat. I left my battle belt on with the Sig securely in its holster. Picking up the bottle of whiskey, I closed the door and started walking toward the gate.

Both sides had what appeared to be sandbagged foxholes with three-gun ports in the front side of both of them. There were two-gun barrels pointing at me from both emplacements. When I got to about 50 feet from the gate I stopped in the middle of the road.

"Hello at the gate!" I yelled.

"What do you want?" came the reply.

"I'm here to speak to Jim Calvert."

"What about?"

"Listen, my name is Jason Sterling. I think we might be able to help each other out and I brought a fifth of Jack Daniels to discuss it over," there was the murmur of hushed voices from the foxhole.

"Stay right there and don't even think about reaching for that piece on your hip," the voice yelled.

"You got it," I yelled back. I crossed my arms across my chest and waited. It took about five minutes but finally two guys crawled out of the foxhole on the left side of the gate. They cautiously made their way toward me. The resemblance between the two was remarkable. Definitely brothers I thought to myself. They closed to about ten feet and stopped.

"Put the bottle on the ground and put your hands on your head," the older one said. I did as he asked and did it slowly. The younger one came closer and took my pistol from its holster. He dropped the magazine and ejected the round from the chamber.

"Sorry for the inconvenience Mr. Sterling, just can't be too safe these days," the younger man said.

"As long as I get it back when we are done here, it's all good," I told him. He put the magazine and loose bullet in his pocket and tucked the .45 into the back of his pants. He picked up the bottle of Jack and motioned me toward the gate. As we walked through the gate two more men rode up on horses. They dismounted and quickly filled the empty places in the foxholes. The two brothers escorted me to the ranch house that lay a quarter of a mile from the gate.

When we got there, I stayed on the deck with the older brother while the younger one went inside. About two minutes later he returned with his father, Jim Calvert. I expected a retired politician, but what I got was a cowboy in every sense of the word. The boots with spurs, the Levi jeans, the big belt buckle, the western style button-up shirt with a blue bandanna tied around his neck, the Sam Elliot mustache and the Stetson on his head. He looked like he had just stepped right off the stage of a Hollywood western. It was almost amusing. He walked through the door and stood a couple feet in front of me. I could tell he was sizing me up just as I had him moments before. Finally, his hazel eyes locked with mine.

"So, Mr. Sterling, what is it that brings you out here this morning?" he asked in a gravelly voice.

"It would seem that we have a lot in common Mr. Calvert. We have a compound on the other side of town. There is your compound on this side of town, and it looks like we have a whole lot of trouble brewing in the middle. I think it would benefit all of us greatly if we could come up with a plan to work together and stomp on the neck of the troublemakers," I said, holding his eye contact the entire time.

"If trouble comes this way again, we will deal with it again," he said simply.

"Begging your pardon sir, they are getting stronger every day and they are getting bolder every day. It won't be long before they try to roll in here in force. While I have no doubt that you and your men would fight valiantly until the end, it would indeed end badly for you. I don't want to see that happen," I noticed a slight smile around the corners of his mouth and eyes.

"Straight shooter just like your old man. Why don't you come inside, and we can discuss this," he motioned me through the door and into his dining room. Over the course of the next 45 minutes we forged the basic alliance between our groups. I wasn't really concerned about asking him to become Mayor again. I was, however, very concerned about getting him on our side. The Mayor thing could be discussed at a later date. By now my team with the Hummers had been escorted inside their compound and they were hanging around in front of the ranch house.

I learned that Jim had his four sons here plus his six hired ranch hands. All of them were single men ranging in ages from 17 to 73. They were all armed with Mini-14 rifles and they had plenty of ammo and magazines to go around. They had plenty of food put away and they had a working water well with the old-style hand pump. While they were not as well off as we were, they were doing quite well at holding their own. Before we left, I had Marcus give them one of our spare portable HAM radios. This would give them the ability to talk to us should the need arise.

It was with a handshake that the alliance had become reality. In another week, Mark Butler was going to come over and spend some time at their ranch and give them some tactical training. We were also going to deliver them some body armor and some night vision equipment. They had none of either. We finally left the Calvert ranch just before noon. Jill asked if we were going to take the same route back. I told her no. Jim had told me about an old county road that ran down next to the river. He said that if we were to take that road, we could be in downtown Elko before anyone would even realize it.

We took the route that Jim had given us, and we were happy to discover that it did indeed put us only a couple of blocks from the Mayor's office. Instead of leaving, I instructed Jill to take us to the Wal-Mart parking lot where the trade center had been set up. When we got there, the booths and tables were still set up but there was nobody around. It was like a ghost town. The entire town was like that. Very few people were on the streets. Those that were, quickly ducked into open doorways or around the corners of buildings. The townsfolk were scared, and it was starting to put me on edge.

"Get us out of here Jill. This place is giving me the creeps," I told her.

"You can say that again," she said as she pushed down the throttle and spun the steering wheel. She pointed us to the parking lot entrance. We spotted the black sedan at the same time they spotted us. The black car fishtailed into the parking lot and blocked that driveway. Jill never let off the throttle when she cranked the wheel back to the right and pointed us toward another driveway. That driveway was quickly blocked by the second sedan. There was only one more driveway and we could see motorcycles congregating there.

"Marcus! Put some rounds over the heads of the bikers!" I yelled into my throat mic. An instant later the big .50 caliber gun started barking in short bursts. Jill knew what to do. She pointed the Hummer at the bikers and gave it all the throttle it had. As the bikers dove for cover, Marcus started concentrating his fire on the bikes themselves. The heavy rounds tore through them, igniting a couple of the fuel tanks on fire. In my earbud I could hear Jake telling me that the sedans were starting to give chase again. I told him to put a couple rounds into the engine blocks.

Jill smashed the truck into the wrecked and burning bikes sending parts and fire flying in every direction. The collision was bone jarring. We hit the main street and she pointed us back toward the dirt road that we had come into town on. I looked in the side mirror and saw that the other Hummer was right behind us. I could also see that both sedans were stopped dead in their tracks with white plumes of steam coming from under the hoods. We made our way out of town at a high rate of speed with no further confrontations. I don't know if we had taken the fight out of them or if they just didn't have anything else to pursue us with, but I was happy they had backed off. Jill stayed hard on the throttle all the way back to the ranch. We didn't want to give them the chance to regroup and chase us down. -

The gate was opened for us by Jessica and Alex and closed behind us as soon as the second Hummer was through. Jill finally slowed down and took us to the main parking area. Instead of pulling into a parking spot, she simply parked the truck in the drive lane. The second Hummer pulled up alongside and everyone climbed out. I instructed Marcus and Jake to take both rigs and refuel them. They were also going to give them the once over and make sure there was no damage to them before returning them to the front parking area.

Jill and I were greeted by Allan and I proceeded to tell him about our trip to town. That debriefing lasted almost half an hour. By the time it was done, both rigs had been returned to the parking area and their crews were relaxing in the shade by the clinic. Allan headed back to the security shack and Jill and I went to be with our crews. She gave me a quick kiss on the cheek and told me she had to go see Susan in the clinic for a minute. I kissed her back and continued on to the grass area where everyone was lounging around. It was about 20 minutes later when Susan came out of the clinic and motioned me to come inside. I was immediately concerned and made my way inside as quickly as I could.

Jill was sitting on the exam table. Her body armor was sitting on the floor and her Multi-Cam shirt was laying on top of it. She also had her sports bra off and was covering most of her chest with a sheet. Piled on the bed next to her were some bloody bandages and an open suture kit. She looked pissed.

"What the hell?" I said. "Did you get hit?"

"No, I just popped a couple of stitches. I'm fine," she said through clenched teeth. It was obvious that she was in pain.

"She popped six stitches. I've got her patched back up, but I am going to pull rank as Medical Officer and pull her from duty. She needs a couple more weeks," Susan said flatly as she was cleaning up her tools and trash. Jill looked like she was fighting back tears. I knew it was hard for her to be deemed unfit for duty. She spent so much time training and honing her skills, and staying physically fit and strong, and all of it was for naught right now. Granted, she was healing much faster than anyone had expected but it just wasn't fast enough for her.

I put my arms around her and pulled her into a tight hug. She squeezed me back with her good arm and whispered an apology into my ear. After holding her for a few more moments, I let her go and took a step back.

"Come on, let's get you dressed and back outside," I said as I handed her her sports bra. After she got that back on, I gave her the multi-cam top she had been wearing. The left side under the armpit was stained red from the blood-soaked bandages that had been there. She was a little unsteady on her feet from the pain meds that were finally taking affect. I picked up her body armor and helped steady her. We walked out the front door and everyone that was on the grass went silent.

"Jill has been pulled from duty by medical. That confrontation we had on our way out of town caused her to rip some stitches out and Susan has given her some painkillers. Jake, go find Alex and tell him that he is taking her place on the response team. I'm going to take her and get her to bed before she falls down," I said, and with that Jill and I turned and headed to our house. Once I got her settled in on the couch in the living room, I went back to where the QRF was hanging out. The rigs had been backed into their parking spots after they were refueled. Alex was quickly brought up to speed on the mission plans and what had happened on our previous trip to town.

CHAPTER 16

Tuesday, August 9, 2016

Since our trip into town the Thursday before, everything had been quiet. The Raptor team had slipped out on Sunday night and made it back to the ranch at four Tuesday morning. Both men were exhausted, and Allan decided to let them get some sleep before they gave their briefing.

Jill and I had been up since 3:30am. I helped her wrap her chest tightly with an elastic bandage and was helping her in the gym. After getting pulled from active duty, she had redoubled her efforts to maintain her strength and conditioning. She had taken over the underground guard shack again and spent a lot of her time surfing the channels on the HAM radio. The address that was supposed to come from our new President on Sunday evening never came. There was a lot of speculation as to why, but nothing concrete.

It was ten in the morning when Mike and Dan met with Jill, Allan and me in the conference room. They had hand-drawn maps of the defenses around the sheriff's office and the residences of Marv and Tom. They had counted 49 true Reds. The good news was that most of the time they hung out around the sheriff's office or the two residences. The best news was that they had contacted some of the locals and were setting up the basic plans for an insurrection. I had also learned that we had destroyed half of their vehicle fleet and that is why they did not give any further pursuit.

Mike and Dan were going to go back and continue their surveillance on Saturday the 13th. They were going to use the same tactics as the last time. When they met with the resistance this time though, they were going to finalize a plan to overthrow the Reds.

The QRF team had stood down and everyone had gone back to their regular duties and everyone was allowed to unwind and relax a little before the Raptor team went out again. It was the afternoon of the 12th when Jill called on the radio and said that her drone had spotted six men on horseback coming up the main road. She had the drone a half mile from the gate and she said they were about a mile from there. The approach was slow, and she tracked them with the drone until we had a visual on them from the gate.

Mark and Alex had pulled one of the Hummers up to the gate and Alex had them covered with the fifty caliber. All of them had rifles but they were in scabbards or slung across their backs. They made no hostile moves and the sight of the machine gun-equipped Humvee seemed to have no effect on them. They rode right up to the gate before the lead man held up his fist and signaled them to stop. He dismounted his horse and walked the last few feet to the gate. I was watching everything unfold from the security office video feeds. Mark ran up to the gate and had a few seconds of conversation with the man. I watched him lift his radio to his mouth and begin to speak.

"Jill! It's the cowboys from Imlay!" he said.

"Copy, what's their status?" she asked.

"They are in rough shape Jill, permission to bring them up to medical, they have a couple of injured here."

"Affirmative Mark, escort them to medical. Break, Jason and Allan, meet me at medical please," Jill said. Allan and I both acknowledged her and headed for the clinic. All three of us arrived at the same time. We were greeted by Sam and Doc. They were waiting patiently for the cowboys to arrive. Jill made one more radio call for the Butler boys, Ben and Mike, to take their horses and tend to them. Once the group arrived and dismounted, I could see what Mark had meant when he said they were in rough shape. They looked like they had been on the run for days. Their clothes were filthy, their faces were dirty, their eyes were sunken in and they all looked exhausted. One young man had a blood-soaked bandage around his head. Another had his arm in a sling and a third had a bloody bandage around his thigh.

We helped them to the grass where Sam and Doc began assessing their injuries. The Butler boys gathered the six horses and led them off to the stable where they too would be cared for. It took about ten minutes, but all of our medical people had come out and were treating different injuries. It looked like a mass casualty incident. Dan, with the help of Mark, relieved them of what weapons they still had on them. Instead of taking them away completely, they just stacked them against the building after making sure the chambers were empty. Jill was talking to the young man with the head injury as Amanda and Sam worked on him. When they loaded him on a gurney and took him inside, Jill came to stand with me and Allan.

"That was Darren, he is the one who helped us out in Imlay. Most of these guys were the ones who helped us. He told me that the ranch they were using as a base was attacked and overrun six days ago. Out of 32 people, these six are the only ones who managed to escape. They had nowhere else to go Jason," Jill told us. I waved Dan over as she was finishing her sentence.

"Dan, what was the status of their weapons and ammo?" I asked.

"Shit, I think between the six of 'em, they might have had 25 rounds total. They had no food, one canteen of water and not much else," he reported.

"Thanks Dan, make sure to secure all the weapons from their horses too please," I told him. He nodded and left for the barn.

"You trust these guys Jill?" Allan asked.

"With my life!" she replied without hesitation.

"That's good enough for me," I said. I spotted Mark and waved him over.

"What's up boss?" he said as he jogged up.

"Mark, would you make arrangements to move these guys into one of the barracks buildings as soon as they are released from medical? We need to get them someplace to relax and we need to get some food going for them. Would you see to it, please?" I asked.

"Absolutely boss!" he said and jogged off. I turned back to Jill and Allan.

"We need to go somewhere and talk," I said to the two of them and started toward the main security shack. Both of them fell in behind me. Once we were in the shack with the door closed behind us, I began to speak.

"Jill, you said that there were 32 people at their ranch?"

"That's what Darren told me," was her reply.

"Can I assume it was men, women and children?"

"I didn't ask but I would assume so."

"Did he say how many attackers hit their settlement?"

"No, all he said was that there was a lot of them. They had dirt bikes, quads, dune buggies and a couple of old pickup trucks. They were hit just after dark, so it was impossible to get a count," I looked out the window as I was putting my thoughts together. I turned back to Allan and Jill.

"Jill, I want the guards doubled for the next few days. They either escaped their attackers, or they inadvertently led them here. We will continue at condition one inside the compound and as of now I want a Hummer patrolling the grounds too. Lock this place down and keep your eyes peeled day and night. Jill, keep the drone in the air as much as possible. Train someone else to fly it if you have too and keep it out at its maximum of its range."

"What do you want to do about the Raptor team's upcoming deployment?" Allan asked.

"Go ahead and deploy them. Just make sure they are aware that there may very well be hostiles roaming around between here and town," I told him. "Jill, I want you and Mark to act as the liaisons between us and the group of cowboys. Make sure they know that if they stay here, it's our house and it's our rules," she and Allan both nodded in agreement.

"They really are good people Jason, I'd bet my life on it, again," Jill said.

"I have no doubt that they are good folks. You are a pretty damn good judge of character, but I need them to understand the pecking order around here. This place is beginning to overflow with people, and we cannot have any lack of communication among any of us. When Darren is out of the clinic and feeling up to it, I'd really like to talk to him. We really need to glean as much information from them about the attack as we can," I told Jill.

"I'm sure they won't have any problem working with us Jason. They just had their asses kicked and lost everything. If anything, they will probably be up for some payback," she said.

"Oh, I have no doubt that they would be up for some of that, but I need them to understand that we do not do shit freestyle around here. When we get to that point, we will have a plan and the assets in place to pull it off."

"Okay," she said.

With their assignments clear, both of them left the room and left me with my thoughts. I was shocked at just how fast things had gone crazy in the world. A month had gone by and civilization had already reverted to this. I also had no doubt that the day would come when we would have to defend the ranch. The question was, how dearly would it cost us? Would we end up like these poor bastards? Beaten and on the run with nothing but the clothes on our backs? I again vowed to myself that I would die before letting it come to that.

Saturday, August 13, 2016

All of the cowboys had spent the night under the care of Doc, Susan, Sam and Amanda. The leader, Darren, had a head wound but it was not overly serious. The medical team just wanted to keep an eye on him. One guy had suffered a dislocated shoulder and a third one had impaled his thigh on a steel fence post. Everyone was malnourished and dehydrated but I was told that they would all make full recoveries.

I spent the day with Allan and Jill. We were going over all of our security protocols and then going over them again. I told them of my fear that we would one day have to defend this place. Both of them agreed. Not only did we work on our perimeter defenses, we revisited all of our plans for inside the compound defenses. It was Jill that suggested we booby-trap the living spaces, medical and the guard shack. Allan and I both thought she had lost her mind, at first anyway. Once she explained what she wanted to do, we both quickly jumped on board.

"Listen to me," she started. "If this place is infiltrated, we need to be able to take away anything that they could use against us. This security shack has access to ALL of the video feeds. Even the ones from underground. We cannot allow that to fall into enemy hands. Sure, we could cut the feeds, but this will still be one of the first buildings to be stormed. Wire the shack to blow and we can take that away from them and quite possibly take out a few of the attacking force. All of the heavy weapons are stored in the underground, so that is not a concern. If we have to go down there to defend this place, we will have the advantage because we will still have our eyes and ears. That is until they destroy the cameras. I suggest that we wire medical to blow and set booby traps at the entrances to all of the living quarters and all of the other buildings on the ranch property. We can cut off all of the power and water from the underground and we can rig all of the explosives to a computer down there so that we can detonate any of them anytime we please. They could walk through a doorway ten times and we could decide to blow it on the 11th," she finished. Allan and I were both very interested in her plan and after a couple of minutes of thought, Allan was the first to speak.

"Let's take it one step farther. If this place were to fall into enemy hands, let's have a scorched earth policy in place for the worst-case scenario. Let's rig all of the buildings so that we can actually blow them into splinters and leave nothing standing."

"Jesus...... "I whispered out loud.

"Jason, I know you don't like it, but if it's a last-ditch effort, then we need to be able to pull out all of the stops and leave nothing standing. Leave nothing for them to use against anybody else," Jill said.

"It's not that Jill. You two are right. I just can't believe that we are being forced to think like this."

"Trust me Jason, I would hate to see it come to that, but it would kill me to see this place fall into the wrong hands," Allan said.

I put both of my hands on the table and leaned over the maps that were laid out. So much work would go up in flames if we ever had to burn this place to the ground, but Allan was right. I guess the consolation was that if it came to it, I wouldn't live long enough to see that happen. My head was starting to fill with dark thoughts, and I didn't like it. Then an idea came to me.

"Jill, how big are the caves?"

"What?"

"The caves up by the meadow, how big are they?" I asked again.

"I don't really know, I've never been more than a few feet inside of them," came her answer.

"They are massive once you get about a hundred yards inside," Allan said. Jill and I both looked at him. "Your dad and I explored them a few years back," he explained.

"Are they big enough to house everything from the warehouse?" I asked.

"Absolutely. Why?" he asked.

"We need to transfer as much as possible from the warehouse to the underground. What doesn't fit in there, we should move to the caves. Separate baskets for our eggs so to speak."

"I get that, but why go through all of the trouble to move everything?" Allan asked.

"We need to have an alternate plan. If this ranch falls, it's a good bet that all of us are dead or under siege in the underground with no way to escape. We need to let Calvert know about the cave and the underground. If it comes to the worst-case scenario, we need to have someone to come bail us out or at least give them the tools for a fighting chance," I said. Allan and Jill were both giving the notion some thought. We discussed a few different plans and options. In the end, we settled on a course of action that we felt gave us the highest probability of survival.

"When do we want to do all of this?" Jill finally asked.

"Why are you two still standing here?" I said with a wink. Both of them chuckled and Jill started folding up the maps of the compound.

"Allan, would you mind spreading the word to everyone that we are going to start enacting some new protocols. Get everyone up to speed, please," I said.

"I'll handle it, Jason. If it comes to it, we will be ready," he reassured me as he was walking out the door. Jill had her maps tucked under her good arm and she walked around the table to stand in front of me.

"Something's got you spooked," she said quietly.

"Am I that easy to read?" I asked.

"Like a damn good book."

"The cowboys.....they lost everything in the blink of an eye. Everything including 26 of their own people. I cannot allow that to happen here," I said with a sigh. She put the bundle of maps back on the table and stepped even closer to me. She wrapped her good arm around me and pulled me in close.

"Listen to me, hon, we've got much better defenses and much better training. We have the tools and the talent to defend this place. Even if the walls are breached, we will defend this ranch," she said, her face only a couple of inches from mine and our eyes locked. "We also have the advantage of seeing this coming. We have an idea of how they operate now, and we can defend against that."

"If it comes to that, babe, I'll die to defend this place and the people who live here. Of that I have no doubt."

"I'll kick your ass if you let that happen!" she said, as she pulled me in and planted a long kiss on my lips. When she finally pulled her face back, I could see tears in the corners of her eyes. "Don't you dare die on me Jason Sterling! I couldn't stand to lose the love of my life, again...." she whispered. I wiped the tears away with my thumbs.

"Jill....."

"Stop," she said. She took a deep breath and let it out slowly. "Let's get to work on these security measures and make damn sure we never have to use them." She started to pull away, but I held her firmly.

"Jill I love you and I'll do everything I can do to grow old with you," I said with a slight smile before I let her go. She stepped back and wiped her eyes. Once her maps were tucked under her arm again she started to leave but stopped and looked back at me.

"Right place, right time?" she asked.

"Right place, right time," I responded.

"Promise me Jason, if someone is trying to kill you, you will try to kill them right back."

"I promise babe."

"Good. I love you too, Jason," she said and then she left the shack.

I spent the next few hours in the shack covering for Bill who usually had the day shift. He was busy working with Allan and Jill on the plans that we had come up with earlier in the day. It was around 4pm when there was a knock on the door of the shack. I stood from behind the desk and opened the door. Darren was standing there. He had a clean bandage wrapped around his head and he had on clean black BDUs.

"Come in," I said as I took a step back and let him pass by me. I pushed the door closed behind him. I motioned to one of the chairs and he seemed more than happy to sit down.

"Jill said you wanted to speak with me," he said.

"I do. I assume she already told you the rules of the ranch?"

"Yes, and let me assure you that all of us are very grateful for your hospitality and we are all on board with following your orders. We owe you our lives."

"Darren, you don't owe us anything. We saw people in need, and we jumped in and helped. It's kind of what we do around here. Are all of your people going to be okay?"

"Thank you, Mr. Sterling. Yes, my guys will all be all right. Your doctor is a little worried about an infection in Junior's leg, but I've seen that guy heal from a lot worse with a lot less medical attention," he said with a slight grin.

"As much as I would like this to be a social meeting, I really need to get some information about what happened at your place. Are you up to telling me what went down?" I asked.

"I'll tell you everything Mr. Sterling."

"Please Darren, call me Jason."

"Okay, Jason, it all started about two weeks ago. There were five guys riding around on dirt bikes. They would ride up to the main gate and when they were confronted, they would speed off. A couple hours later they were spotted riding along our western fence line. We gave chase on horseback but there was no way we were going to catch them. No sooner would we get back to the house, they would be on the eastern fence. Same thing. This went on for two days. On the third day they again approached the main gate and by now I'd had enough. I dropped one of them from 300 yards with my old ought six. Dude was dead before he hit the dirt."

"Do you think they were testing your defenses?"

"I think that's exactly what they were doing. Anyway, after I dropped that guy they all hauled ass and we didn't see hide nor hair of them for almost 24 hours. I had given my men permission to drop them if they could get a shot, but the bastards were keeping their distance and watching us from the hillsides, well out of our range. This went on until last Saturday evening. There was another farm about three miles up the road from our place and it sounded like all hell was breaking loose up there."

"I'd known the Drake family all my life, hell, I had dated his oldest daughter when I was in high school. Anyway, eight of us grabbed our guns, jumped on our horses and hauled ass in that direction. That left ten of my men to hold down our place. I thought that was plenty for a rear guard. Boy was I wrong. We got to the Drake place, but it was obvious that we were way too late to do any good. The whole family was dead in the driveway. Lined up and shot. We could see two dirt bikes hauling ass away from us."

"All of a sudden I had a really bad feeling. I looked back to where my ranch was, and I could see an explosion that completely leveled my house. When we finally heard it, we could also hear the gunfire," he paused and took a deep breath. After he let it out, he continued.

"We rode as fast and hard as those horses would take us, but it was almost over when we finally raced through the gate. There were only two of my guys left and we got there just in time to see both of them go down. There were bodies and parts of bodies lying all over the place. It was obvious we were too late; everyone was already dead."

He went on, "We still hadn't slowed down, and my horse went down and threw me hard. It rang my bell when I hit the ground. I watched my baby brother take a round right between the eyes. My guys were returning fire, but they had us dead to rights. We were in the open and had no cover to speak of. Junior's horse went down, and he jumped for it. That's when he rammed that T-post right through his thigh. Gabe and Don pulled him off of it but Don took three or four rounds to the chest. He was done. Joe bailed off his horse and grabbed me by the collar. He helped me onto Don's horse, and he got Junior onto a horse and we retreated.

There were six of us left and we rode as hard as we could. I swear, we almost killed those poor horses before we stopped that night."

Continuing, he said "We were in sad shape. Half of us were all screwed up physically and all of us were messed up mentally. They slaughtered men, women and children....... They couldn't have been after our food; they blew it all up with the house. They weren't after the women; they were killed right along with the men. It just seems that they were hell bent on burning everything and everyone to the ground. We were going to go back the next morning to see if there was anyone left or anything left to salvage, but they were still there. There had to 30 or 40 dirt bikes. They had four of those four-seat dune buggy things, quads, and a couple of old pickup trucks."

"How many men would you say they have?" I interrupted.

"It's just a guess but I would say somewhere in the neighborhood of 50 to 60 men and women."

"Women?"

"Yeah and from what I saw, they are just as vicious as the men, if not more so."

"What about weapons?"

"Mostly AK's, some of those cheap plastic rifles, but mostly AK's," he said.

"Do you think you were followed here?" I asked.

"I don't think we were. We headed out cross-country and crossed some pretty rough terrain."

"How did you know about our ranch?"

"Jill and Mark told us that they were from a ranch up in this neck of the woods. After the raid on the truck stop in Imlay, I told my pops about Jill and her guys. I told him about the way they were dressed, their weapons and gear, and the Jeeps. I told him everything only because he kept asking questions. I guess my pops did business with your pops at one time or another. He also told me that if we ever needed help, find Jack Sterling and his ranch," he finished.

"Well, Jack may no longer be with us, but you are still welcome here, Darren. I know you and your men have been through a lot, but as soon as all six of you are well enough to ride again, I have a mission for the cowboys," I told him.

"The cowboys?" he asked.

"Blame Jill and Mark. They told us all about the cowboys when they got back from Imlay."

"Fair enough, what's this mission you have for us?" he asked.

"I've got a 100 head of cattle scattered over 3,000 acres and I need them brought back down here for safekeeping," I told him. He chuckled a little.

"Sounds like a good mission for a bunch of cowboys."

"When that is done, I want you and your men to start working with Jill and Mark. They will bring you up to speed on our daily operations around here," I said as I stood from my seat. He also stood and extended his hand.

"We will not disappoint you, sir, you have my word on that," he said. I took his hand and yet another deal had been brokered with a handshake. After he showed himself out, I was again left alone with my thoughts. That was beginning to be a dangerous place to hang out. Something was nagging at me, lurking around the fringes of my mind's eye. I knew things were going south in town but for right now everything was actually fairly stable. We would see Calvert and his men on Tuesday, they were doing okay and had not had any further trouble from the Reds. Whatever it was that was bugging me would not show itself. On the surface everything seemed to be going as well as it possibly could under the circumstances.

There was the subject of my brother and his family that was still rubbing me raw. We were a month into the apocalypse, and things were starting to get bad. Violence, starvation, dehydration, Illness......so many ways to perish in this new world and I had to wonder if any of these things had claimed my family that was trying to make it here. It was nearly six in the evening when Dale came into the shack to relieve me. I gave him the pass-down and told him to call me when the Raptors decided to head out. He told me he would and sent me on my way.

I met Jill at home and found that she had already made dinner. She gave me her usual smile when I came through the door and told me to get washed up. Jake and Jessica were going to join us, which was not uncommon, Jill just seemed a little happier about it than normal. She and Jess had become the best of friends and could often be caught hanging out when they were off duty. Once everyone was seated at the table and Jake had said the prayer, Jessica stood.

"Jason," she began. "When we were invited to come live and work at your ranch, we were literally hanging on by our fingernails. Our hope was that living here would give us a new lease on life and indeed, it has. While life here for the last month has been a little chaotic and even a little scary at times, life HAS continued," she paused when Jake stood up next to her. I was a little confused about what was going on. Jake began to speak.

"Sir and ma'am, with your blessings, we would like to name our child after you. Jillian if it's a girl and Jason if it's a boy," he said, grinning from ear to ear. Jill squealed and jumped from her seat to give Jessica a huge hug. It took my guy brain a second to catch up. When it did, I stood and extended my hand and congratulations to Jake.

CHAPTER 17

Tuesday, August 16, 2016

The Raptor team had slipped out of the ranch compound the night of the 13th as planned and had set up their observation post in the city on the morning of the 15th. They reported that things were a lot quieter than they were the first time. Even fewer people were on the streets and even the Reds seemed to have toned it down a little. We decided to go ahead and go to Calvert's ranch as we had planned. Mark was going to stay there for a week and help them with their defenses and training. We were also going to be bringing them some much needed gear. Mark just wanted us to drop him off, but I insisted that we take three Hummers to Calvert's and leave one there with him. He finally relented and accepted it as fact.

The three-rig convoy pulled out of the gate at 8am and I instructed Alex to drive it like he had stolen it. He was a little more timid than Jill, so he kept it under 70. Again, when we drove past the subdivision, the Raptor team called in to report an increase in activity. Only this time they were digging into defensive positions instead of trying to go on the offensive. This had me a little puzzled. I instructed Alex to take the highway and he did. As we roared up to the roadblock, it was unmanned and the car that normally blocked the road was pushed off to the side.

Something was wrong....... Very wrong.

"STOP THE TRUCK!" I shouted. Alex locked up the brakes and turned the wheel slightly. We came to a stop sitting across the two eastbound lanes. Both of the other Hummers slid to a stop.

"What's up boss?" Jake asked from the turret of Hummer Three.

"Gut feeling man, something is really wrong here," I told him through the throat mike. Marcus kept traversing our turret from left to right. I could tell something had him spooked too.

"Hang on boss, we're going to pull alongside," Jake replied. A couple seconds later their rig was parked on our left side. Jake climbed out of the turret to stand between the two rigs. He leaned in Alex's window.

"What's setting off your spidey senses boss?"

"I don't know!" I almost yelled at him in frustration.

"All right boss walk me through it. Is it the fact that the Reds have gone defense or is it the empty roadblock? Is there something that you see up the road that looks out of place? Are you thinking about an ambush? Gimme something to work with," he said. I scanned the road ahead for a couple of minutes when it donned on me what was different.

"Look, at the semi-trailer that's up by the exit," I said to Jake and handed him the binoculars.

"The one that forces all traffic to take that exit?" he asked and handed the glasses back to me.

"Yeah, and if you take that exit and are forced to make a right turn, you eventually end up at the sheriff's office! They haven't gone defensive; they are trying to herd us or anyone else that comes down the road!" I said. I put the high-powered binoculars back to my eyes and scanned the dirt road that we used last time. The spot where it turned back to the pavement had been clogged with stalled cars.

"Shit," I muttered.

"They are getting smarter, adapting to our strategies," Jake said. I sat for about a minute while I decided what to do. "What's our play boss? We're sitting ducks out here in the open," he said. I pulled the radio mic from its clip on the dash and put it to my mouth.

"Calvert...Sterling...." there was about a 30 second delay before the response.

"Go ahead Sterling."

"Listen Jim, we are going to have to rethink the visit today. We are having a hard time finding a route to your location."

"Copy that Jason, let us know what you come up with."

"Will do my friend, stay safe," I said and hung the mic back up. "Alex, take us home."

"Yes sir," he said as he slipped the truck back into gear. Jake climbed back into his turret and we headed back the way we came. The farther we got from Elko, the angrier I became. They had managed to turn us back without ever firing a shot. Jake was right, they were adapting quickly.

As we blew past the subdivision again, the Raptor team reported that the Reds were standing down. We were going to have to deal with that problem. Whoever was ratting us out was giving the Reds 15 minutes early warning and we couldn't have that. I did not know how we were going to figure out who it was though.

There had to be 70 or 80 homes in there and short of going door to door..... I just didn't know.

We pulled through our gate and everyone unloaded in the parking area. Alex and Jeff took care of refueling the rigs. I went into the clinic with the intention of using their passage to the underground but stopped short when I saw that Harold was awake. Since he was, I didn't want to compromise the entrance to the stairs, so he and I just shared a short conversation. That did help with my mood a little. After about ten minutes, I excused myself and went to my house. Going straight downstairs, I slipped into the passageway and went straight to the security office that Jill was using.

I stepped inside and pulled the bulkhead closed behind me. Jill was at her desk with the earphones for the HAM radio over her ears. I sat on the corner of the big desk and she pulled the earphones off.

"Trouble on the way in?" she asked.

"Yeah, they had us all blocked. They were trying to herd us into an ambush. I told Jim that we would have to figure something else out."

"Any chance at all that Jim would grab everything and bring his men over here?" she asked.

"I really doubt it but I guess I could ask him," I told her. "I just have to figure out how in the hell I'm going to get there," I sighed and stood up. I walked to the giant map that she had on the wall. Every alternate route that I could come up with was a day's drive one way and that's if everything went right. Jill was standing next to me looking at the map too.

"You do realize that they have effectively cut us off if Jim gets in trouble? They have also cut us off from the Raptor team," she said.

"Yeah and if I were them, I'd take out all of the small fish first. I think that's what they are planning. They have disarmed most of the population, they have deposed the leadership, they have sealed off the town and they are dug in for a fight."

"Walter told me that the problem with most fixed defenses is that they are only designed for a one-way fight. It's the same thing we were looking at a few days ago with our defenses," she chimed in thoughtfully. I turned to look at her. "We need the Raptor team to do some recon. We need to find out what they have in mind. Are they guarding their strongholds, or the entire town? Can we move freely once we are past the outer defensive line? Is this a line in the sand defense or a 360-degree defense? All things we need to know before we go in and deal with them."

"I think we are still a long way from that Jill. Best case, they have us outnumbered three to one. Those are not odds that I'm willing to go head to head with..."

"DAMMIT JASON! We are past the point of having to deal with them!" she said hotly. "If we don't do it soon, they will outnumber us five to one, then ten to one! The odds only continue to get worse! They will never get better!" I stood looking at her. That was the first time I had ever heard real anger in her voice that was directed at me. When she spoke again, she had softened her tone a little.

"I'm sorry Jason. I'm just sick and tired of sitting here on my ass waiting for the next fucking shoe to drop. There is no Cavalry riding in to save the day, there is nothing out there, but violence and brutality and I want to keep it outside of these walls, it's my job to keep it outside the walls. I want to hunt it down and destroy it wherever it may hide. I'm sick of this pussyfooting around!" her voice was on the rise again. "There are more two-legged predators out there than you can shake a stick at and here we sit! Make it open season on them, no fucking bag limit. If you want to defeat evil in the world, you got to be ready to get your hands bloody. You got to fight dirty and most of all you got to fight to fucking win. Hiding behind these walls ain't going to get it done! It's only a matter of time before they decide to take out Jim and his men, and when they have done that, they will come after us!" she slammed the headphones down and she stormed out of the room leaving me in open-mouthed shock. I heard the door to the hallway slam shut behind her.

That was the first time that I had been the object of her anger and it left me shaken. While it had rattled me to my core, it also gave me the balance that I was looking for, the balance that I so desperately needed. It took me a few minutes to realize it but my mind had slipped into overdrive as I tried to formulate a plan to take out the Reds.

The Raptor team checked in at 7pm and I was in the security shack to take the call. After the routine authentications, I gave them their new orders. Allan was sitting at the desk and his eyes got a little wider when he heard what I told them. If they were shocked, it was undetectable in Dan's voice. He sounded just as calm and cool as he always did. When that radio call was done, I placed a second one to Jim Calvert.

"Jim, I'll dispense with the pleasantries and get to the point. I'm going to send you some ranch hands to help out around there. They will be bringing you a message and Christmas will be coming to your place early," I told him over the airwaves.

"I'm not sure if I should thank you or curse you but I guess I'll figure it out," he chuckled.

"I'm sure you will curse me, but I can live with that," I told him in a serious tone. When I was done with that call, Allan's eyes were just a little bigger.

"Mind if I ask what you're up to?" he questioned.

"Follow me and you can find out just like everyone else," I said as I headed out the door. I headed straight to the bachelor pad. The six cowboys and Mark were at the dinner table finishing up their supper when I burst through the door, Allan right behind me. All conversation ceased and all 14 eyeballs were on me.

"You boys ready to earn your keep?" I asked loudly. Every head at the table began to nod in the affirmative. "Good, here is what I want you to do….." I spent the next hour going over the plans that I had laid out. I also gave Mark a handwritten message to give to Jim Calvert. When the meeting was over, all seven men at the table stood and followed Mark out the front door. Allan had still said nothing when I turned to him.

"Spread the word Allan. I want every able-bodied fighter at the security shack at eight in the morning. Everyone. No exceptions," I told him. He nodded and headed out the front door, too. I followed him out but turned and headed for the clinic. I was relieved to find Harold still awake. I spent a few minutes explaining to him what was about to go down. I asked him for his permission to use Pat and Eric in my plans. He agreed, like he had a choice. I thanked him and left the room.

It was nearly ten when I finally went through the front door of my house. I had not seen Jill since our blowout that morning, a little over 12 hours ago. The ground floor was dark except for the sliver of light coming from under Jake and Jessica's door. I crept up the stairs and came to our door. There was a very faint light seeping out from under it. I slowly turned the handle, and found it wasn't locked as I had feared it would be. I eased the door open and slipped inside. There was a lone candle burning on top of Jill's nightstand. I could see her still form under the sheet and did my best sneak to my side of the bed.

THE RANCH

I un-holstered my Sig and set it on the nightstand. The battle belt came off and I hung it on the bed post at the foot of the bed. I stripped down and slipped into bed. I laid on my back, proud of myself for not waking Jill up.

"I thought I heard an elephant come in the room," she said as she rolled over to face me. She draped her arm over my stomach and put her head on my chest.

"Are you still mad at me?" I asked her. She propped herself up on her right elbow and looked at me in the dim light.

"I was never mad at you, Jason. I was, and still am, pissed off about the sad state of humanity. I'm pissed because people have to act like animals, and they are dragging the rest of us down to their level. That's what's eating at me. Why can't they just leave everyone alone and let us get on with the business of trying to put the world back together?" she asked softly. Her blue eyes were almost luminescent in the candlelight.

"You really rattled my cage babe, made me rethink the way I've been acting. The way I've been leading," I told her as I stroked her arm that was now on my chest.

"I'm sorry for yelling at you, hon."

"Don't be. That was exactly the kick in the ass I needed, and I don't ever want you to hold it in, Jill. You were frustrated and needed to vent, I'm cool with that babe. Hell, I was frustrated, and I needed someone to slap me out of my funk," I said with a smile. She leaned in and kissed me on the lips.

"I heard you on the radio to the Raptor team and I heard you when you called Calvert," she said when she pulled back. "I take it you've decided on a plan?" she asked.

"I have, and hunting season opens bright and early Friday," I said. I lifted my head and kissed her lightly on the neck. She closed her eyes. I could feel the goose-bumps on her arm, and I could hear her breath catch. She slipped her leg over me and pushed herself on top of me. She pressed her naked body against mine and spoke in a raspy whisper.

"Enough office talk. Make love to me Jason Sterling."

Wednesday, August 17, 2016

Surprisingly, Jill and I were both up early. After she took her shower, I helped her wrap the healing wounds on her chest and arm. It had become practice to wrap them as tight as she could stand with an ACE bandage. The hope was that it would keep the stitches from tearing out again. It was a little after 6am when I headed to the security shack and she headed to the underground security office. Both of us opted to skip breakfast and went with just hot coffee. I walked through the front door and found Bill seated at the desk. He looked over the rim of his glasses at me and picked up his coffee mug. I closed the door and took my seat across from him. His eyes followed me the whole way. Once I was seated comfortably, I again made eye contact with him. He just stared at me and me at him. He caved first.

"We could just bring everyone inside the wall, build some guard towers and defend this place," he said.

"That will never work, and I think you know that, Bill," I retorted.

"Are you sure about this plan of yours?"

"Hell no!" I blurted out. "I told you, I'm making this shit up on the fly, man. If I were sure about it that would make me a fool."

"Good," he replied.

"Good? Seriously?"

"If you were sure about your plan, not only would that make you a fool, it would make me one for following you," he smiled. "It's a sound plan, Jason."

"There are a lot of variables to account for and we are probably going to get bloody," I said flatly.

"There is a good chance of that, make no mistake on that one. If we don't do anything, we will get bloody, that's a guarantee."

"Do I need to tweak anything?" I asked.

"Nope. Hit them hard, hit them fast and hit them with everything you have. Show no mercy and expect none. If we fail, we won't live long enough to regret it and if we win, we will get to regret it forever," he said.

"Here's to regrets," I said as I raised my coffee cup.

"To regrets." It was a couple of minutes later when the Raptor team radioed in. We were on the radio with them for nearly 90 minutes while they relayed the info that I had asked for.

"Dan, Mike, this mission will be a GO at 1:10 Friday morning. Remember, stay mobile because the situation will be fluid. I just need you to keep them off-balance once we get there. That's when the shit will really hit the fan," I told them.

"Copy that boss," was Dan's reply. I hung the mic back up and took a look at my notes. The large whiteboard on the wall had a hand-drawn map of the sheriff's

office and the surrounding area. Bill had been busy updating the map with all of
the defensive positions that had been put in-place. When he was done, he stood
back and looked at it.

"This plan of yours might just be crazy enough to work," he acknowledged. I
didn't get to answer him because the radio crackled again. This time it was Mark.

"Hey boss. We pulled in here about an hour ago and briefed Jim and his men.
We copied everything from the Raptors for our part of the mission. All of us will
be in position Friday morning."

"Sounds good Mark. Did Jim like his new toys?" I asked.

"He loved the toys and he says screw you for the chance to try them out." I
could hear laughter in the background. I couldn't help but chuckle a little myself.

"Copy that. See ya Friday."

At exactly 8am, Bill and I stepped from the security shack to address the
members of the ranch. The only people that were absent were those that were already on the mission, and Harold and Mayor Tanner. His daughter, Jackie, was
present but he had elected to stay in his room. I stepped in front of everyone and
cleared my throat.

"Six weeks ago, our world changed forever. Six weeks ago, about half of us
were strangers and had no idea that our lives would collide. Six weeks ago, the
biggest decisions we had to make were what to have for dinner or what to watch
on TV. Six weeks ago, the biggest danger we faced was maybe getting into a car
accident."

I continued, "Every one of us has ended up here today because of different
circumstances. I came here because my father was killed in a plane crash. Some
of you came here because thugs and punks were trying to kill you because you
wore a badge, or you were family of someone who wore the badge. Some of you
came here because you thought you had something to offer. All of you were told
the same thing. If you want to be a part of our small community, you had to earn
it and be ready to defend it, right?" I asked. Every person in the crowd was nodding
yes.

"Today I am going to call on all of you to step up to the plate. It's time to pay
the piper. Out there, outside of these walls in the little town of Elko, there is a
group known as the Reds. They are trying to gather enough men to come here and
take this ranch from us. Make no mistake, if we give them enough time, they will
do just that," I paused for effect and made eye contact with as many people as I

could. "I will not let that happen. I will fight with everything I have to protect my girlfriend and her family. I will fight to protect Jessica and her unborn child. I will fight to make sure the Butler boys get to raise their families here. I will fight to protect every single one of you. I would expect nothing less from each and every one of you."

I went on, "In 41 hours, we will take the fight to them and we will not stop until we have either killed them or driven them from our sight. If anyone here thinks I'm wrong, or if anyone here is not willing to fight, I ask you to step forward right now," I paused again, again making eye contact. I was a little beside myself when Jackie Tanner finally stepped forward. She turned to face the crowd and cleared her throat.

"You people have taken me and my father in and cared for us, you didn't have to do that. You have given food to the people of Elko; you didn't have to do that either. You took the cowboys in and cared for them, once more, you didn't have to. You cared for my friend Harold, again, you didn't have to do that. Jason is asking you to put yourselves in harm's way to protect people you will probably never know......and yet again you don't have to. I didn't see any of you stepping forward, so I wanted to step up to say thank you for everything you have done and to say thank you for what you are about to do," she finished. She turned to face me. "Mr. Sterling, thank you," she stepped back into the crowd and Amanda put an arm around her shoulders.

"If we are all in agreement, please see Allan and he will give you your assignments," I said and motioned Allan to take my place. I stepped off to the side and watched as a circle formed around the man. Jill walked up and stood next to me, a smile all over her face.

"Your old man would be proud of you, Jason."

"I hope so," was all I could say.

"I'm proud of you, Jason," she said with a wink. I knew what she was referring to and felt my face flush a little.

"I'm pretty proud of me too," I teased. She chuckled a little to herself.

"I'm going to get back to the office. It's time to get the drone in the air," she said as she started to walk away.

"Aren't you going to get your assignment from Allan?" I asked.

"What?" she asked as she stopped in her tracks.

"Susan cleared you for duty as long as you can keep your stitches wrapped," I told her.

"Really?" she asked excitedly.

"Yep, you're back in the saddle kid. Just don't screw up the Doc's handiwork again or it'll be my ass in a sling this time!" I laughed. She ran up and gave me a really big bear hug that lasted about a half a minute. When she let me go, she thanked me again and trotted off to see Allan.

After the meeting that morning, I caught up with Marcus and went over a couple of projects that I needed done. When I had showed him what I needed, he assured me he could put something together in time for our trip to Elko. When I finished up with him, I went to meet with Dale, Susan, Amanda and Contessa in the clinic. They were the four that would be using my pickup as an ambulance if we needed it. I showed Dale how to start it since it could be a little tricky for the uninitiated. When I left them, they were loading their gear in the bed of the truck.

Doc was going to be manning the clinic and waiting for any wounded to arrive. The Butler boys were going to be manning the gate and the security monitors. They were 16 years old and had shown themselves to be very responsible young men. Dale and Susan came to me later that day and asked if I had a problem with them strapping on their own pistols. I knew that they had been trained in all the basics by their Aunt Jill and Uncle Mark, so I took no issue with it.

The one that did surprise me was Jackie Tanner. She stopped me just after lunch and wanted to know why Allan did not have an assignment for her. Honestly, I hadn't given it any thought. She and her father were more or less our guests, not fighting members of our group. She spent ten minutes trying to sell me on the fact that she needed to go, wanted to go and exact a little revenge for what they did to Harold and that she could handle herself. In the end, she and I caught up with Allan and got her assigned as a medic to my assault team.

The ranch had been a hive of activity all day long and well into the night. There would be no radio check-ins tonight unless something drastic had changed. In this case, no news was indeed good news. The next check-in was going to be 7pm Friday night. Six hours before the assault.

Thursday was spent with each assault team going over all of the plans. I was team leader for the eight-person Alpha team and Jill was team lead for the seven-person Bravo team. My team would be the first ones in the line of fire with Bravo jumping in right behind us. Charlie and Delta teams were made up of the cowboys and Calvert's guys. They had their own mission objectives. The Raptor team would be the ones to kick off the party. They had been sneaking around and leaving little party favors.

By 4pm everyone had the plan committed to memory and I cut everyone loose to spend time with their loved ones if they needed it. Jill and I retired to our room and tried to get some sleep. Call it pre game-jitters or whatever you want but both of us were too amped up to sleep.

At 11pm, we decided to get up and get dressed. At 11:30 both of us were in full battle gear and ready to go. She checked my gear and I checked hers. We shared a long passionate kiss before we walked out of the house. We walked to the parking area where all of the vehicles were already assembled. Two Hummers and two five-ton trucks were parked on the tarmac. Tonight, I would be driving my own Hummer, so I put my rifle on the driver side of the center console and started walking around it. Alex showed up moments later and climbed up into his turret to make sure everything was the way he wanted it. He checked the big .50 caliber machine gun like he had done it a thousand times. Samantha arrived and put her medical gear and weapons in the back-passenger seat. Bill and Jessica arrived and put their stuff in the front seats of the five-ton. Everyone else loaded their gear in the back. When Andy arrived, he climbed into the back of the big rig and started going over his .50 cal.

Alpha team was made up of me, Alex, Samantha, Andy, Jessica, Pat, Bill and Jackie. Bravo was Jill, Jeff, Marcus, Jake, Eric, Allan and Miranda. Everyone had arrived by midnight and was making themselves busy checking and rechecking their gear. Everyone had night vision equipment mounted to their helmets and IR (Infrared) flag patches in the front and back of their plate carriers. That would make identification of friend or foe easier in the heat of battle.

At 12:30am I announced that we would be jumping off in ten minutes. A couple people ran into the clinic to use the bathroom. Amanda slipped around the back of her Hummer to smoke a cigarette and I caught Jake and Jessica stealing a quick kiss. Jill was behind the wheel of her Hummer when I walked up to the open window.

"Right place," I said.

"Right time," she said. We held each other's gaze for a few moments but neither of us said anything else. I took a step back and looked at my watch.

"MOUNT UP!!!!!" I shouted and went to the driver side of my rig and climbed in. All four trucks started up and we began rolling toward the gate.

CHAPTER 18

We were barreling down the road in the pitch-black night at 72 miles per hour. That was as fast as the five-tons could go, even after Marcus had reset their throttle governors. That was all right, we were going fast enough to be in town on time. All four trucks were in blackout mode, no lights at all. Once again, we were relying on our night vision equipment to guide us. We flew past the subdivision and I was waiting for the Raptors to report any activity. Nothing changed. Apparently, we had managed to sneak past our first obstacle. We made it to the freeway at exactly 1am, right on time.

We blew through the abandoned roadblock and hurtled toward the exit that would take us to the sheriff's office. Bravo team swerved off the highway, through the barbed wire fence and cross county for 1,000 yards until they again caught blacktop. This would put us on two different approaches to the objective with Alpha team arriving just a minute or so ahead of Bravo team. We got off the freeway and we were back on the throttle. I could see where they had blocked off the side roads with abandoned cars and I could see the roadblock ahead that marked the perimeter of their compound. We were about 500 yards away and I could see the first muzzle flashes. I swerved to the side and slammed on the brakes just long enough to allow Bill to pull alongside of us with the five-ton. Alex and Andy unleashed the big .50 caliber machine guns and started shredding the cars and defenders alike. It only took a few seconds of sustained fire from the big guns to silence any return fire from the barricade.

I could hear Dan and Mike on the radio calling out targets on the buildings on either side of the street. Andy and Alex would direct their fire at the window or rooftop where the bad guys had been spotted. With the withering amount of lead being thrown in their direction, the Reds started trying to fall back to the sheriff's office. Most of them never made it. The booby traps that had been set by the Raptor team triggered and, in most cases,, blew chunks of bad guys all over the place.

I slammed the accelerator pedal back to the floor and yelled for everyone to brace themselves. I had picked a point just to the left of center in the roadblock.

Two small sedans were parked trunk-to-trunk and I figured that was going to be the easiest way through. The huge bumper on the front of the Hummer slammed into the small cars and spun them out of the way like toys. The five-ton followed me through with no problem. As the two-story brick and concrete structure came into view, Alex began to fire at the visible windows and doors. Just as we made the turn in front of the building, I watched two RPGs (Rocket Propelled Grenades) slice through the air. Andy and Pat had fired them from the back of the five-ton and their aim was impeccable. Both rockets had gone through shattered windows and penetrated deep into the building.

Alex was concentrating his fire on the sandbag emplacements at the front doors. I could hear Andy calling out targets behind us and I could see his .50 caliber rounds pouring through the second-floor windows. Pat was firing the third RPG and this one slammed into the sandbagged front doors. I had just watched four guys take up position there too. An instant after that explosion, a pair of explosions blew out a chunk of the second-floor wall and I had to swerve hard to avoid the falling debris. Bravo team had arrived, I mused to myself. They were making a strafing run up the backside of the building as we were wrecking the front of it.

I heard Alex shout for more ammo as we went around the corner of the building. Sam hoisted another can up and he grabbed ahold of it and quickly reloaded his weapon. We made another left turn and began our run up the backside while Bravo was now on the front. We were taking next to nothing as far as incoming rounds so I radioed Bravo team to go to phase two of the operation. It had been confirmed that there were prisoners being held in the basement of the building and it was time to get them out.

I stopped the Humvee and bailed out with Alex right behind me. Pat and Jessica had jumped from the bed of the five-ton and all of us stacked up outside the rear entrance.

We burst in and started moving as quickly as we could. The place was totally wrecked inside. I heard Jill in my earbud. They had breached the front of the building and were going to clear the north end of the first floor. The plan called for Alpha team to sweep the south end and then get to the basement to free the prisoners. Bravo would watch our six from the top of the stairs. Alex was on point and I was right behind him as we made the first left at the tee intersection. Some poor guy made the mistake of stumbling out of a side room and pointing a sawed off 12-gauge in our direction. Alex and I both hit him with a three-round burst.

We made our sweep and found nothing else living on our end of the first floor. From what I was hearing on my radio, it was going about the same for Bravo team. Mike and Dan were picking guys off the roof and they were trying to hurry the entry teams. The second floor was turning into an inferno and they were starting to see signs of the fire spreading to the ground floor. Alex and I bounded down the stairs and were immediately assaulted by the odor. It was a combination of smoke, body odor, urine and fecal matter. It reminded me of the hospital when we liberated Doc.

There were ten cells down here and all of them looked to be crammed with women of all ages. There was a nude body of a young woman tied to the top of a desk. It became very obvious to me what had been going on down here. All four of us flipped our weapon-mounted flashlights on and a man in his early 30's stood up from behind the desk. He dropped the pistol he was holding and raised his hands. I was in his face in an instant with the muzzle of my rifle.

"Keys asshole!" I yelled.

"What?" he mumbled. The reek of alcohol on his breath was staggering.

"The keys to the cells, where are the keys?"

"Uhhh, I think she's laying on them," he said as he pointed to the body that was laying between us. I held my rifle on him with my right hand and slid my left hand beneath the warm body. I found the keys under her shoulder and pulled them out. I tossed them to Alex, and he began to open the cell doors.

"Did you do this?" I asked the man.

"We were just havin' some fun man, that's all."

"Did you kill her?" I growled. The rage inside of me was getting hard to control.

"Naw man, it wasn't like that! We were just foolin' around," he mumbled as he took a step back from the desk. I sidestepped around it so that there was nothing between the two of us. He kept backing up until he was against the wall. I stopped and picked his revolver up off the floor. I cracked open the cylinder and extracted five of the six rounds. I spun the cylinder and flipped it closed. I had let my rifle hang and now I had his pistol in my hand and it was pointed at his chest.

"I am going to ask you again; did you kill her?" I said, the tone of my voice startled even me.

"I don't know man..." he started. I pulled the trigger. Click.

"Did you kill her?"

"Listen man..." Click.

"Did you rape and murder the woman laying on that desk?" I nearly shouted.

"It was an accident man!" Click.

"A FUCKING ACCIDENT? YOU CALL THIS A FUCKING ACCIDENT?" I yelled as the rage began to win out. He just stood there trembling, a stain beginning to appear on the front of his pants. Suddenly a calm came over me.

"I tell you what asshole. I'm going to pull this trigger one more time. If I kill you, call it an accident. If I don't kill you, I'll give you the gun back and you can have a shot at me. Sound good?" I asked as I raised the pistol again.

"No, no, no...." Click.

"You really must be the luckiest piece of shit on the planet!" I said as I started to toss him the pistol. Jessica reached out and clasped her hand over the top of mine. It was only then that I became fully aware of everyone watching me, civilians included.

"Come on Jason, stand down, please?" she asked quietly.

"Jess, let go of my hand."

"I'm not going to let you kill him in cold blood," she said, standing her ground. I turned to look at the scared women that were huddled at the base of the stairs.

"Did any of you see this piece of shit over here kill this young woman?" I asked. Nearly everyone nodded their head yes. "Did all of you hear the confession from his own mouth?" Again, they nodded their heads yes. "Will all of you make sure justice is done?" Every single head was bobbing up and down. I turned back to Jessica and let her have the gun. "Cuff that pile of shit and drag his ass upstairs," I told her. She de-cocked the pistol and stuck it in the thigh pocket of her BDUs and did as I told her. I cut the ropes that were holding the body to the desk and after a very quick search, I found a jacket to cover her with. I carried her body and we quickly escorted the women up the stairs and out the back door.

"Alpha one is clear of the building on the backside. Can we get both five-tons back here?" I asked as we cleared the door.

"Copy Alpha one, Bravo two and Alpha two will be there momentarily," it was Allan's voice. True to his word, both big trucks came around opposite ends of the building.

"Bravo one, status?"

"I'm not sure Alpha one, I think it's a clean sweep here. No hostile fire at all," Jill responded.

"Alpha one, Raptors concur, we got nothing but friendlies moving down there."

"Copy that. Raptors come on down and hook up with us. We are going to escort the friendlies to the drop point."

"You got it boss," Dan said into the mic.

After we got all of the former prisoners loaded into the back of the five-ton trucks, we formed the convoy up on the main road. What used to be the sheriff's office was fully engulfed in flames. Mike jumped in with Jill, and Dan climbed into the back seat of my Hummer.

"What do you think Dan?"

"If we didn't get all of them, we got enough of them. We counted 16 dead at the roadblocks, you and Alex got one more inside. Mike and I accounted for eight more on the rooftop and we heard six of the booby traps go off. That's 31 dead and one prisoner," he said from behind me. I slipped the Hummer into gear and led the convoy out. We were headed to the Wal-Mart parking lot where the civilians were going to be off-loaded and reunited with their families. As we were pulling into the parking lot I got a call on my radio.

"Alpha one, Charlie one," it was Mark.

"Go Charlie one."

"Yeah boss, we are all done over here but we have something that you need to see," he said.

"Copy that, let me secure the civilians and we will head to your location," I told him.

As we came to a stop in the parking lot, Jill pulled her Hummer up next to mine and climbed out. She walked up to my door. "Leave us Alpha two and we can handle things here," she said.

"You sure?" I asked.

"Yeah, we got this. Go see what's up with Mark," she said as she slapped the door on the truck and stepped back. I nodded and we pulled out. As we pulled past the five-ton, Jessica stepped out and waved me down. I stepped on the brakes and she walked up to the window.

"Before you say anything, Jason," she started. By the tone in her voice, I could tell that she was still heated over the incident in the basement of the jail. "I gotta know, were you really trying to kill that bastard and were you really going to give him a loaded gun?"

"Jess, let me see the gun please," I held out my hand. She was still scowling at me but she started fishing around in her thigh pocket. She handed it over butt first. I popped the cylinder open and pointed it at the ground so that she could see the back of the single casing. "How many bullets do you see Jess?"

"One," she said sternly.

"Wrong, you see a bullet casing," I said as I ejected it. I held it up and it was simply an expended shell. "No Jess, I wasn't going to kill that scum-bag, I wanted him to know a little bit of terror. I wanted him to know fear. I wanted the women that were still there and saw the whole thing to know that they do not have to put up with these assholes preying on them. They can fight back, and they should fight back," I told her. She stared at me for about ten seconds before she spoke again.

"Really? Jason, I am so glad you are on our side. Remind me to never play poker against you!" she smirked and took the pistol from me. She stepped back from the Hummer and allowed us to pull out of the lot. We were still running lights out using the night vision to navigate the streets. The houses that Tom and Marv were using were side-by-side at the end of a cul-de-sac. The back side of the houses opened up to the golf course. The roadblock to the entrance of the street was still in place but the four guys that were standing the post were dead on the ground. I stopped the Hummer so that it was facing out to the main street.

"Dan, you're with me, everyone else stay with the truck," I said as I opened the door. I grabbed my rifle and Dan and I made our way around the stalled cars and dead bodies. As we approached the houses, we could see flashlight beams bouncing around inside. All of the windows were shot out and the front door had been blown off its hinges. From the shrapnel damage, my guess was a grenade had been used to breach it. Through my night vision goggles I could see four men on horseback patrolling the outside grounds. There were more horses standing on the asphalt in the cul-de-sac. I flipped my goggles up away from my eyes and turned on my flashlight.

"Charlie one!" I called out as we approached the shattered door. Mark stepped out and pointed his flashlight in our direction.

"Come on in boss, place is secure," he said as he motioned us inside. The first thing I saw was four dead bad guys in the front room. One of them must have been standing by the door when they breached. His head and both arms had been blown off and he had chunks of door embedded in his torso.

"Sit-rep?" I asked.

"Eleven dead shit-heads, including one heavy," heavy was the code word for leadership. "We have one casualty, just a minor wound. One heavy and one of his bodyguards escaped on dirt bikes. We have recovered a huge weapon and ammo stash, both garages are full. It all went down fast and hard just like you predicted," he said.

"Which heavy got away?" I asked.

"Marvin got away but you really need to see this," he said as he pointed to the back deck. We walked through the shattered sliding glass door to find another pair of bodies, one of which was Tom's. He was flat on his back with a bullet hole in his forehead. Dan knelt down next to the body and shined his light on the wound.

"That's a contact shot," he stated clinically. He moved to the body that was right next to Tom's. This one was face down. "Two to the back of the head.....both of these men were executed," Dan said, standing up and looking at Mark.

"They were dead when we made entry. This wasn't any of my people!" Mark said defensively. "There were four guys out here, one was Marvin. He and another guy shot Tom and his bodyguard, jumped the railing and hauled ass on a couple of dirt bikes that were sitting right there," he said and pointed to the ground below the deck. "My guys gave chase but couldn't get a good shot off at a full gallop in the pitch dark. They lost them at the north end of the golf course."

"It's all right Mark, you guys did a fantastic job. We broke the back of the Reds and that's what matters. We can hunt Marvin down during the daylight," I told him and patted him on the back. It was then that Calvert joined us on the deck. He was limping and had a bloody bandage tied around his left thigh.

"How did you guys fair?" he asked.

"Thirty-one dead, and one captured," I told him.

"I think saying that we broke their back is an understatement," he said with a grin. I looked over at Mark.

"Mark, you and your men secure everything here. I need to get back to the rest of the team. Good work!" I told him. "Jim, you want to walk me out?" he nodded, and we followed Dan out the front door. Jim and I were walking slow and let Dan get ahead of us.

"Jim, this town is going to need a new mayor and I hope you are up to the challenge," I said flatly. He stopped in his tracks.

"Tanner wanted the job so bad he was willing to cheat to get it, let that bastard deal with it!" he growled.

"Tanner has checked out mentally. He's done. This town needs a strong leader and you have proven you can handle it."

"What if I say no?"

"You won't," I said with a grin. "You have the same problem I have, an over-inflated sense of duty," he looked me in the eye and held the stare for a few seconds.

"Fine, but I'm doing this my way. No interference from you or your crew at the ranch."

"It's your town to run and I have all the faith that you will take care of business. I know that you will not let this kind of shit happen again. We don't want anything from you or your town," I told him. He didn't say anything for a few seconds. Finally, he stuck his hand out. I took it.

"Thank you, Mr. Mayor," I said and released his hand.

"Screw you," he said with a grin. He turned and walked back toward the cul-de-sac.

Friday, August 19, 2016

It was almost ten in the morning when we got back to the ranch. After all of the stress and adrenaline, everyone was exhausted. The Butler boys gave Allan and me the briefing of how their night went. We were both impressed with their attention to detail and professionalism. They agreed to stay on shift for a couple more hours while everyone else stowed their gear. Weapons were cleaned, trucks were refueled, and everyone attended an impromptu de-brief on the lawn in front of the clinic.

Everyone was relieved to find out that one of the leaders of the Reds had been eliminated and they were happy that we had managed to put an end to their reign of terror. The only person that seemed out of sorts about the results of the mission was Jill. I thought I knew what was bothering her and would ask her about it after the group dispersed. She and I both volunteered to relieve the Butler boys while everyone else got some rest. After the meeting broke up, Jill and I walked to the security shack in complete silence. I put my arm around her shoulders, but she pulled away. I let it go until we were out of sight inside the shack.

"What are you all pissy about?" I asked her.

"Pissy? You haven't seen pissy yet!" she said as she flopped into the chair behind the desk. "The one bastard I really wanted to get, got away," she growled.

"He hauled ass with his tail between his legs. He will have too big a target on his back to come around here again," I told her.

"Is that what you think? Seriously?" she asked.

"Jill, relax. We broke their backs......."

"No Jason, I won't relax. That bastard did this to my shoulder and he won't hesitate to do it again. He is a coward and he has no problem killing from a distance or shooting someone in the back. He is a coward and now he has a grudge. He will not let this go and you are a fool to think he would."

"Jill....."

"No, I'm not done. The only thing we did last night was take out his thugs, the bottom feeders of his troops. We did him a favor by taking out his useless eaters. He gave us Tom on a platter and slipped away into the dark. This is not over, it's far from over. It won't be over until he has a bullet in his brain!" her voice was starting to crack. I knew she was mad, but experience had taught me that she wasn't mad at me. She was venting like I had told her to. I let out a long sigh and chose my words carefully before I spoke.

"You're right, Jill. I am irritated that he got away. As soon as we can get regrouped and get Jim firmly in power, we will begin hunting him down. We will be just as relentless in our pursuit of him and the remainder of his men. You have my word on that," I told her. She nodded and wiped the tears of frustration from her eyes with the *shemagh* that was wrapped around her neck. "We will find him and deal with him."

"I know Jason. I'm just pissed off that he won't do us all a favor and just die already! He's like a cockroach."

Jill and I spent the rest of the day in the shack. We went over everything we knew about Marvin. We knew that at one point he was squatting on a piece of property about 20 miles from the ranch. When we had guys actively patrolling outside the wall, which was one of the places the horse teams scouted out. Their search had turned up nothing. Both of us agreed that in light of last night's developments, we needed to re-visit the place.

A little before six in the evening, the cowboys and Mark rode up to the gate. They dismounted in front of the security shack and Mark was the first one through the door. Once all of them had filed in, I could see that all six of the cowboys were sporting shiny badges and huge grins.

"Jason, Jill, I'd like to present you half of the new deputies for the city of Elko," Mark said and stepped to the side. I stood and began to shake their hands.

"Our new Mayor moves quick!" I said. "Congrats guys, I know you will do the job."

"If it's all right with you and your people Jason, we would like to keep the equipment that you have loaned us. We really could use the night vision goggles and automatic weapons," Darren said.

"Under one condition Darren," I stated. "If you guys get a lead on that bastard Marvin, you let us know."

"It would be my pleasure sir."

"Okay then, everything you guys left with the other night is now yours. Tell your boss Merry Christmas," I said with a grin. "You guys are more than welcome to spend the night here and let your horses rest up."

"I'm afraid we will have to pass this time sir, we just wanted to make sure Mark got home. We actually have a mission just up the road tonight."

"Well thank you and know that our gate is always open to any member of law enforcement," I said. "Can I ask what your mission is for tonight?"

"We are conducting a raid on the little subdivision up the road. Rumor is that someone there was working to feed the Reds information whenever you folks were headed to town. We are going to go put a stop to it," he smiled.

"Then I'll tell you thank you again."

"We have to get going sir, you and your people have a good night," he said as he tipped his hat. His men walked out and before the door could close behind them, I saw Amanda come up and embrace the tall cowboy turned lawman. I chuckled to myself a little. I thought there might have been something there, but now I was sure.

CHAPTER 19

Friday, September 2, 2016

It had been two weeks since our raid and life at the ranch had become more or less normal again. Morale was the highest I had seen it since before the EMP almost two months prior. The work crews had been working on the new houses full-time and they were nearing completion. Everyone had put it to a vote, and it was unanimous that Jake and Jessica be given their own house. She was just starting to show her pregnancy.

Jill had been totally released to active duty and all of her stitches had been removed. She was back in the gym every morning trying to get full strength back on her left side. Her workout and sparring sessions were downright brutal. The one benefit was that she and I got to spend a lot of time in the hot tub nursing sore muscles.

Amanda had left the ranch to live in town with Darren. One of the first things Jim Calvert did was to get an emergency room working at the hospital and she was pretty much running the show there. They had found equipment in the basement of the hospital that still worked, and they had rigged up a hybrid solar/wind generator that would power most of the ground floor. Jim had also put together a construction crew to start re-building the emergency room.

We had made a run to town a couple of days ago and we were surprised at the progress that was being made. Jim had re-constituted the sheriff's office using the six cowboys and his six hired men. Darren was the head man and the job seemed to suit him. The hospital was open for business again and they even had a running ambulance. It was an old Jeep, but it did the job. They were also forming a city defense force and those people were issued weapons and ammo from the stash that was found at Marvin and Tom's places. Marcus had been able to repair a couple of dozen handheld-radios for them and they were using them all over town. They had taken the solar panels from the highway signs and were using those to keep the batteries charged. Jim had moved back to the city hall building full-time. The building also doubled as the new sheriff's office.

THE RANCH

The coolness was already starting to seep into the evening air. It was fore-shadowing of a cold winter that was coming. Everyone was worried about how many people the town would lose over the course of the winter. Jim had told me that before the EMP, the population of Elko was right around 19,000 people. The results from the census that he had just taken only accounted for 10,112. The town had lost 9,000 people in two months. Not all were dead to be sure. Some left to find their families in other locations. Some just left because they felt there was nothing for the town to offer them and still more left because they couldn't deal with Jim's rules. One of which was that every able-bodied person was to work. Some folks didn't like that, so they left.

There had been no sightings of Marvin since the night of the raid. He had vanished and left no trace. The group that had attacked Darren and his people had been harassing ranches and travelers all along the I-80 corridor up until just before the raid, then they just stopped and vanished too. I found the coincidence too fishy. My hunch was that Marvin had ties to them and when he bailed, he took them with him. There were rumors that the gang had around a hundred members and all of the stories surrounding their attacks made them some of the most hardcore and brutal that we had heard. A group like that didn't just vanish.

We had been monitoring the HAM frequencies 24 hours a day and things in the rest of the country were only getting worse by the day. There were small pockets of civilization left. Usually small towns and cities like Elko that got the upper hand and kicked the troublemakers out.

The rumor regarding the new government was that it had died a crib death. There had apparently been a coup followed by another coup. Ultimately all those that were seeking to assume control of the United States were so busy infighting that they proved to be totally inept. Most of us knew that once the beast that was our government was toppled, it would never regain its footing. What the politicians didn't realize was that a new age was upon us and had they studied their history; they would have known how to right their ship. Sadly, they had no clue what they were doing and proved it over and over again. Their own self-interests came first and in the new era, that just wasn't going to fly anymore.

I was personally devastated when one of our contacts in Colorado had told us that winter had already come to the Rocky Mountains. He was in Boulder and he was reporting that they had received six feet of snow in 24 hours. Boulder was in the general path of where my brother and his family would be traveling. I didn't know if they had already made it that far or if they had already cleared the mountains, but I knew this couldn't bode well. I knew that they had left Hutchinson, Kansas with Alex's parents and sister about a week after the EMP. We had a contact there and that was the last time they had been seen. I knew they were coming; I just didn't know if they would make it.

The American southwest was having a hard time with the gangs coming up from Mexico. We were hearing about skirmishes between them and regular military units. From what we could gather, the gangs had seized most of New Mexico, Arizona and southern California. Texas was pulling itself together and fighting back and winning. They had their own Army, Navy and Air Force and a functioning government. Even though San Antonio had been nuked, they were getting it together, and fast. After many dinner conversations with Allan and Bill, we all felt that the new United States would be born not back east, but in Texas. The politicians in Texas had studied their history.

I was in the study of my house reading the journals again. I had made it to number 27. My radio crackled; Jill was calling me from the security shack. "Jason, could you come to the shack please. I have Mayor Calvert on the horn for you," she said.

"On my way," I replied. I returned the journal to its proper place on the shelf and double-timed it to the shack. Once there, Jill picked up the mic and handed it to me.

"Mayor Calvert, Sterling here."

"Good morning Jason. I hope you are not too busy this morning. I have some folks here that would like to speak with you," he said rather cryptically. I looked at Jill and all she offered was a raised eyebrow.

"Ummmm, okay, I guess. What time would you like us there?"

"Actually Jason, they are insisting that they come to see you, at your place........." Jim said, but when he finished his sentence, he left the mic keyed up and I could hear the background conversation. "..............listen to me Major, Sterling and his people at the ranch have been nothing but helpful to this town and never once posed a threat. One thing that I can tell you is that they won't respond well to threats or posturing. You play it cool with them and they'll play cool with you....." Jill and I exchanged looks and she bolted out the door to get Allan and Bill.

"It's not a problem Mayor. You know our gate is always open to you. We will have the coffee on and ready," I said cheerfully.

"Thanks Jason, they will see you in about an hour," I stared at the mic for a second before I hung it up. My mind was racing when Jill, Allan and Bill burst through the door.

"Bill, do we have anything here that is not covered by our military contract?" I asked. I could see his mind begin to race too. After about 30 seconds he finally spoke.

"I don't think so. Our contract calls for us to be combat ready and deployable within seven days. Why do you ask?"

"Jim is talking to a Major and they are coming here within the hour. I don't know what he wants but it sounded like this Major likes to puff his chest and throw his weight around."

"Shit," he muttered. "We need to posture and puff our chests right back. I was worried that this day would come. Put your game face on Jason, we're going to need you to pull all the stops out on this one. We gotta convince this guy that we are not going to take any crap. While we technically don't answer to him, we need to get the impression out there that we got it together," he said.

"All right, what do we need to do?"

"Get everyone in uniform and armed. Post guards at the gate with two of the Hummers. Make sure the .50s are manned. Move two of the five-tons up to the parking area, one at each end and again man the .50s. Everyone answers with yes sir or no sir. Everyone not assigned to a vehicle has their sidearm and those that are assigned are in full rattle. We show them around the grounds, answer their questions and hopefully they leave satisfied," he spoke rapid fire. "If he tries to throw his weight around, you are going to have to back him down, get him off balance. Just be careful, most of their command and control is probably gone. If you get the feeling they have gone rogue, it's going to be a whole new ball game. Play it by ear and go with your gut feeling, Jason," I looked at Allan and he must have been reading my mind. He pulled his hand-held radio from its belt and switched to the channel for in-compound comms.

"Attention all hands. Attention all hands. This is not a drill; I want all personnel to the security shack now. I repeat this is not a drill. All hands to the security shack immediately!"

It took all of three minutes and everyone was standing on the lawn in front of the shack. Jeff and Andy were holding the reigns to their horses while they munched on the grass and Diane had her infant son on her shoulder. Allan and Bill spent the next five minutes lining everyone out. When they were done, everyone scattered. There was a flurry of activity for the next 40 minutes. Jake and Jeff were manning one of the Hummers at the gate, Marcus and Alex were manning the second one. The two five-tons were manned by Pat and Eric who had decided to stay on with us after the raid. Allan had the idea of bringing up some of the sandbags that we kept out by the barn and using them to barricade the security shack and the clinic. Both of those positions were manned by Dan and Mark. Both of them had M249s.

Everyone was in uniform and full battle gear. I thought that another nice touch was added when Bill put Samantha, Mike and the Butler boys on horseback. They were roaming the grounds in pairs. Everything was set and we were as ready as we would get. I was standing outside the shack when Jill yelled out to me that they were turning up the road.

"Jason, Jake here. Looks like three four-by-four Cougar MRAP's (Mine-Resistant Ambush Protected) and one six-by-six Cougar MRAP. All of them have turrets on top."

"Copy that, play it cool. We are all one big happy family," I told him. "Showtime," I said to Jill from the doorway. I turned and grabbed one of the two horses that was tethered behind the shack. I jumped up in the saddle and rode to the gate. I arrived at the same time the MRAP's did. I dismounted and walked to the gate but made no move to open it. My right hand was on the grip of my AR, but I also made no move to raise it. The turret on top was manned and I was looking down the huge barrel of a .50 caliber machine gun. It felt like forever before the passenger door opened and a soldier stepped out and approached the gate.

"Sergeant," I said. The poor guy looked scared and I don't think he was a day over 21 years old.

"Sir, Major Jackson requests that you stand aside and allow him access to this installation."

"Does he now? Please kindly tell the Major that I allow access to no one who I cannot look in the eye. Also, tell the Major to kindly have that fifty pointed somewhere other than my head," I said and nodded at the turret. The sergeant looked totally beside himself. This must have been the first time someone didn't bow to the Major's request.

"Yes sir," he finally said, and trotted back to the door of the MRAP. It took about 30 seconds but the guy in the turret finally turned it to face 90 degrees away from me. The passenger door on the second, larger MRAP opened, and another soldier stepped out. He walked like he had a fire under his ass, and I assumed this must be the Major. I confirmed it when I spotted the golden oak leaf on his uniform. He strode right up to the gate.

"You must be Sterling?" he said with force.

"Was it the name-tape that gave it away?"

"Calvert said you could be an asshole."

"I think the correct term you were searching for is cocky prick," I told him with a straight face.

"Are you going to open this gate and let us in?" he demanded. The irritation in his voice was evident.

"State your business and I'll think about it."

"Shit...." he sighed. "We need your help. You may have information on a biker gang operating in the area and we need to know what you know," I looked at him for a few seconds then I looked at his convoy.

"How many men do you have?" I asked.

"What does it matter?"

"Do you want to stand here and continue to irritate me, or do you want to come in and talk?"

"Twenty men including myself," he said shaking his head.

"Thank you Major. Here is what is going to happen next. My man Thompson over there is going to open this gate to allow you in. All four of your rigs will park on the grass right over there," I said as I pointed to an area between the gate and the security shack. "Those turret-mounted weapons will be pointed anywhere but at my people. Once the vehicles are parked, all of your men will dismount and stay where we can see them. If I get even the slightest hint of hinky shit going on, all hell is going to break loose. Do we have an understanding?" I asked him. I could tell that I had him off-balance by not automatically bowing to his request.

"I get it. Your base, your rules," he said with resignation. The man looked like he was exhausted, and he was in no mood for a confrontation. Something had already taken the fight out of him and I didn't think it was Jim Calvert that did it.

Something else was going on here. I stepped back from the gate and motioned for Marcus to open it. The Major walked to each truck and said something to each driver before he returned on foot. I had pulled my horse to the side and motioned the trucks through. The turrets were now un-manned, and the weapons pointed skyward. The Major walked back and stood next to me. All four rigs pulled in slowly and parked where they had been told to park. All of the doors opened, and 19 soldiers dis-embarked their rides. The only weapons they had on them were their side arms. Man, they all looked so young, scared and tired.

"Major, with your permission, I'll have some coffee brought out for your men," I asked as we started walking toward the shack.

"That would be fine," he said. I nodded and squeezed the transmit button on my throat mic.

"Would someone be so kind as to bring these men out here some coffee please?" Diane acknowledged and again I squeezed the button. "Bill Butler, Allan West, and Doc Williams, please meet me and Major Jackson at the security shack," all of them copied and said they would be there. I escorted the Major into the security shack, and we were greeted by Jill.

"Sirs!" she said as we walked through the door. I motioned the Major to one of the chairs. I poured him a cup of coffee and handed it to him. A second later Bill, Allan and Doc came through the door.

"Major, I'd like to introduce you to my command team. This is Allan West and Bill Butler; they head up Operations. That young lady is Jill Butler, head of Security and that Is Doc Williams, head of Medical Operations," after all of the hands were shaken and everyone had settled into seats, I got the meeting under-way.

"Major, first of all I would like to apologize for the heavy security presence. You just cannot be too secure these days. Second, I can speak for everyone here when I tell you that we would like nothing more than to see that renegade biker gang put down. They have been nothing but trouble since the EMP. Now, what is it we can do to help?"

"Thank you, Mr. Sterling," he said as he stood again. "My men and I have been dispatched to deal with this gang and we have been trying to run them down for almost a month. Unfortunately, they are always one step ahead of us," he moved to the wall map. "We know that they are operating out of this general area," he pointed to a spot on the map. It was an area that we had yet to explore. "The problem is that the area is littered with mining operations and we just don't have the manpower to search all of them. We have found remnants of their camps starting out here and then here and here," again he was pointing to the map. Jill pulled out a box of pushpins and handed them to him.

"Could you please mark those spots, sir?" she said and sat back down. He obliged her and continued.

"Originally three teams like mine were dispatched because regional command deemed this particular group extremely dangerous. Over the course of the last three weeks, we have lost all contact with the other two task forces."

"Wait, what do you mean lost contact with?" this was Jill again.

"Task force two was the first one to go dark. Their last known position was right here," he said as he put another pushpin in the map. "That was August 22nd. Task force three went dark on August 31st. Their last position was here," another pushpin in the map. Jill was writing on her paper tablet as fast as she could. "When I say that we lost contact with them, I mean that they made their routine check-in and then there was nothing the next day. All of our calls have gone unanswered. We went to their last known locations but were unable to locate anything. No shell casings, no tire tracks, nothing. They simply vanished."

"Sorry for all of the interruptions sir. How were Task forces two and three equipped?" Jill asked.

"They were equipped the same way that we are. Four MRAP's, and 20 men."

"I assume that you are loaded for bear, right?" she asked.

"That would be correct," was his answer. Again, she was scribbling furiously.

"Regional Command wants this gang nailed down but I'm afraid we have lost the initiative here," the Major said.

"No shit," Jill blurted out. She quickly realized what she said and looked around the room. "Sorry sir," she said sheepishly.

"Quite all right Miss Butler," he chuckled.

"If you don't mind my asking Major, can you tell us a little about the Regional Command? Who do they answer to?" this was Bill chiming in.

"Sure, Regional Command has been set up in Salt Lake City and is in charge of the seven western states. California, Nevada, Arizona, Utah, Oregon, Washington and Idaho all fall under their command. It's also known as Region 1 now. It's made up of a mishmash of Guard and regular Military units. Right now, they are answering to the government operating out of Austin, Texas. They seem to be the only ones who could un-fuck themselves and start putting shit back together."

"How did you know about the ranch?" Bill asked.

"Before we pulled out of Salt Lake, we were given a list of friendlies in our AO (Area of Operations). You guys were the closest outfit but to be honest, we didn't even know if you would be up and running. That's why we stopped in Elko and gathered a little intelligence before we made the trip."

"What made you think that we wouldn't be running?" I asked.

"Your contract went active on January 1st, 2000, but you have never been deployed, or even called up for that matter. We were worried that it would be a ghost town when we arrived."

"Well, as you can see, we are here, and we are active. What can we do to be of assistance?" I asked.

"I don't want to impose but my men have been on the move for the last ten days. The only time we would stop was when we needed to pull fuel. The other two Task forces went dark after stopping for the night, we kept on the move. My men need to stand down for a little bit and our equipment needs some maintenance. Would it be possible for us to bivouac inside your walls tonight?"

"I'll do one better than that Major. You and your men can stay in the barracks building tonight and we will get you some real food. Tomorrow we can see about getting your rigs fixed up. You have been out for a while now and I'm sure you could use some supplies too. We will see what we can do to replenish them for you."

"It would be very appreciated Mr. Sterling. The other thing I need is some intelligence from you and your people. I have heard that you had a skirmish with these biker assholes a couple of weeks ago in Elko and I also heard that you handed them their behinds on a silver platter. I want to know how you did it and what you know about their current operations," he queried as he sat back down. Over the course of the next hour and a half we told him everything about the fight in town and what we suspected regarding Marvin. We went on to fill him in on our current operations to try and find the biker gang. It was his turn to write furiously on his notepad. The meeting ended and the small talk began. I let it go on for a few minutes then cleared my throat loud enough to get everyone's attention.

"I want to thank all of you for taking time out of your day for this impromptu briefing, but right now I'd like to have the room with the Major," I said. Everyone took that as their cue to exit the shack, even Jill stepped outside and closed the door on her way out.

"Major, permission to speak candidly?"

"Please Mr. Sterling, say what's on your mind," he said.

"Major, we have enough space for you and your men to stay here for a day or two. Let your men get some much-needed rest and let us handle the watch. Let them get some decent food and a good night's sleep before you push on."

"I appreciate..." he started.

"I'm not done Major. My suggestion to you is that after you have let your men rest, push back to your Regional Command and inform them that you are going to need a lot more manpower. My fear is that this gang has not only killed the soldiers from the second and third Task force, they are now in control of their equipment too. That is bad news for all parties involved. You need to come in here with superior firepower and superior numbers. We will stand ready to assist but right now, this mission is FUBAR," I told him.

"Calvert also said you were a straight shooter. He was right."

"Major, please consider what I have told you," I was basically begging him now.

"One leader to another, I'll consider it," he replied and extended his hand. I shook it and walked him out the door.

The Major and his men were shown to the second barracks building. We made them burgers and homemade French fries for dinner and even brought a couple of cases of beer out of storage. The Major was used to coming off like a hard-ass officer, but I could see that even he appreciated the chance to relax a little.

Jill and I finally went to bed at 11:30 that night. Both of us were exhausted but had too much on our minds to sleep. She curled up next to me, her head on my shoulder and her arm draped across my chest. "We are in for a shit-storm if the Major and his men can't put that gang down," she whispered.

"Yeah, to say the least," I muttered.

"How do we defeat eight of those armored MRAP's? How do we defeat 100 two-legged animals?" she asked. I could hear the worry in her voice. I was silent for a few minutes.

"I don't have a clue, babe. Tomorrow we need to sit down with Dan, Jeff, Jake and Andy. All four of them are combat vets, maybe they can give us some insight," I said. It was her turn to be silent. Both of us laid there in silence with our thoughts.

I wasn't about to admit it out loud, but I was scared shitless. The day had finally come when they had us out-manned and out-gunned. If they came after us right now with a full-frontal assault, we were going to get our collective asses kicked.....

I don't think either of us really slept that night. I heard Allan leave his room around 2:30am. He must have been having trouble sleeping too. Every time Jill would nod off, she would jerk awake a few seconds later. It was a horrible night for sleep. It was 3:00am when she finally slipped from under the sheet and padded into the bathroom. After a quick shower she came out and got dressed in the dark. I too decided that laying there staring at the ceiling was doing nothing but causing my mind to run wild. I threw the sheet back and went and got my shower.

After getting dressed, I went downstairs and found Jill and Allan at the table sipping coffee. After pouring myself a cup I sat at the table. All of us exchanged looks but said nothing. After about five minutes of silence, I finally spoke up.

"Who's on duty tonight?" I asked.

"Bill's in the shack, Jake and Dan are mounted patrol, and Marcus and Andy are foot patrol," Jill answered,

"Good, five of the six people we need to talk to," I replied. I stood and went to top off my cup and headed out the door. A moment later Allan and Jill followed. When I walked through the door of the shack, I found Bill staring at the wall map of the compound.

"Morning," he said without turning around.

"Morning," I picked up the mic for base communications and squeezed the transmit button. "Mounted patrol, foot patrol, finish your current rounds and report to the shack," within seconds both groups responded in the affirmative. I walked back around the desk just as Allan and Jill walked through the door. Without a word, Jill pushed past Bill and me and pulled the plastic covered map from the wall. She moved some things off of the large desk and laid it flat.

"We have a huge problem," Jill began. "We need to figure out a way to defeat a superior attacking force. We must assume that they have the means to breach our walls. We must assume that they have the means to defeat most of our weaponry. That leaves us with unconventional warfare. We must assume that they will also use unconventional warfare against us....." she paused when Dan and Jake stepped into the room. They looked a little confused at first. "We must assume that at the very least we will have to defeat six of the four-by-four MRAP's and two of the six-by-six MRAP's. We must also assume that the enemy will also have a numbers advantage. We must assume that they have at least 100 fighters." She paused again when Andy and Marcus came through the door.

During the pause, she wrote the size of the attacking force in the margin of the map. Once everyone had a place around the desk, she resumed speaking. "We do not know when the attack will come but we must assume that it is imminent and we must assume that we will be on our own, no cavalry coming to our aid. I need some thoughts on how we defeat the armor and how we make up for the number's deficit. What do you have for me?" she asked as she stood up. Everyone intently studied the map for a moment before Dan broke the silence.

"There are three approaches to the compound, here, here and here," he said pointing to the vehicle gates. "We need to narrow that down to one, the main entrance. We block these other two off so that they cannot be breached by vehicle and we force the MRAP's to come at us head on. We turn the area around the outside of the main gate into our primary kill zone. We set up secondary and tertiary kill zones with overlapping fields of fire inside the gate, say here and here. Assume that they will over-run the primary and secondary positions fairly quickly. The tertiary position will be the final stand and will most likely be hand-to-hand combat," again he was pointing to the map.

"Do you really think that they will breach the main gate?" this was Marcus.

"Count on it. If one of those rigs gets a decent run at it, it will blast right through that gate and take part of the wall with it. If they can figure out how to use the MPATS, you can bet the farm that they will breach the walls too," Dan replied.

"MPATS?" Marcus asked.

"Man-Portable Anti-Tank System. It's a shoulder-fired weapon," Dan replied. Jake leaned in and studied the map closer.

"We should wire this culvert that runs under the main road to blow too. If we can trap the convoy, or at least most of it, between there and here, we can set up RPG teams in the wash and ambush them from the backside. That will give us three angles to hit them from. It will also give the RPG teams an escape route when they need to rabbit out of there," Jake said.

"That may stop the MRAP's, but we also have to assume that they will be bringing their off-road vehicles with them. The wash probably won't even slow those down," I chimed in.

"That's true," Jake conceded.

We stayed in the security shack until nearly ten that morning. We were eventually joined by Dale, Jeff and Doc. By the time we filed out of the building into the morning air, we had devised a plan that might just give us a fighting chance. We ordered a stop to all internal patrols and brought everyone up to speed on what we were expecting to come our way.

The Major and his men enjoyed a homemade breakfast, hot showers and most importantly, some restful downtime. The vehicle crews spent some time doing much needed maintenance on their rigs. Jill had befriended most of the young men and spent a couple of hours learning about the Cougar MRAP's, or more specifically, their weak points. She also spent some time learning about how the task force was equipped. She was very interested in the weapons load-outs and with a little flirting, batting of the eyes and flipping of her sandy blonde hair, she had all of the information she needed. I'm sure the unzipped BDU shirt and ample cleavage didn't help the poor boys keep any of their secrets.

By three in the afternoon, Marcus had managed to resurrect the Case backhoe. It had been on his project list since he arrived, but it had been deemed a lower priority. Until now that is. Within an hour he had dug six foxholes from the security shack all the way up to the pond. The Butler boys began filling sandbags from the dirt pulled out by the backhoe. Once they had all six fighting positions sandbagged, Jake went to work with his stash of C4 explosives. After our meeting that morning, I had placed a radio call to Jim Calvert. He wasn't in his office, so I had to wait for him to call me back. That happened at 5pm.

"Jim, listen buddy, I need some help," I began. I spent 20 minutes relaying information to him and at the end, I had his word that he would help us out. His word was good enough for me. I leaned back in the chair behind the desk and rubbed my eyes. My lack of sleep was starting to catch up. The door to the shack opened and the Major stood in the doorway.

"Permission to enter?" he asked. I nodded and waved him in. He sat in the chair across from the desk.

"What's on your mind Major?" I asked tiredly.

"First of all, thank you and your people for your hospitality. I, for one, forgot just what a real bed felt like. Second, with your permission of course, we would like to stay on for a couple of days and help with your preparations," he said evenly.

THE RANCH

"What about your mission?" I asked. He looked uncomfortable all of a sudden.

"Sir, do you really want the truth?" he asked. It was my turn to be uncomfortable.

"Let's hear it, Major."

"The truth is that we lost contact with Regional Command two days ago. Our comms are working just fine but they are not answering our calls. Even with the loss of the other two Task forces, we decided to stay on mission, for now anyway. You need to understand that we have been granted a lot of leeway in accomplishing our mission and I intend on getting the job done," he paused for a moment. "I was thinking about linking up with other units in the western sector or even trying to make a run for Texas but now I'm not sure what to do. My fear is that if we find this biker gang, we will suffer the same fate as the other two Task forces. If we could link up with some other units we might stand a chance but I'm having a hard time finding units willing to get into the fight," he said.

"What do you mean? They don't want to get into the fight?"

"Well, for example, there is a unit up the road in Winnemucca, but they have taken over the town security. Most of the guys have family there and they don't want to leave it open to attack. Same thing in Wendover. It's like the old fort mentality. They stand a post on the wall of the fort and everything outside of that is fair game for lawlessness."

"I see," was all I could say.

"Sir, it's not like we would be derelict in our duty if we stayed on to help you or the city of Elko, we would just be setting up another fort," he tried to reason.

"I see your point Major......" I let the silence hang in the air for a few moments. "Mayor Calvert will be sending some men out here in the morning, and he will be coming with them. May I suggest that you and your men take another night to relax and we will discuss it with him when he gets here? Maybe he can give us some insight into the situation," I told the man. He seemed to be okay with that and took his leave.

I knew that we really could use his men and equipment here at the ranch, that was a given. I also knew that the city of Elko was just as much of a target as we were. One big soft target to be more accurate. I knew that Jim would be thinking along the same lines. He was probably a step ahead of me already.

CHAPTER 20

Saturday, September 3rd, 2016

Jim and six of his deputies arrived a little after eight in the morning and were escorted to the security shack. It was comical because all seven of the men were riding in and on the old Jeep that doubled as the ambulance. With all of them in full battle gear, it was amazing that none of them fell out of the rig. Jim was the only one that joined Jill and I in the shack. After the pleasantries, we got to the meat of the reason that I wanted him there. Jill and I filled him in on the developments of the past 24 hours and he was not pleased.

"So, what you're telling me is that someone stepped on their own dick and now those bastards have military grade hardware?" he bellowed.

"Pretty much" was my reply. He launched into a tirade that lasted a full minute. Jill and I let him get it out of his system.

"Here is the thing, Jim, you can pretty much bet the farm that they are going to hit either the city or the ranch, or probably both. We are bolstering our defenses, but we are worried about yours and we need to move some equipment out of here," I told him. "Once the attack begins, we won't be able to come help you and you will be cut off from helping us."

"Do you really think they could pull off a simultaneous attack?" he asked.

"Why not? We pulled it off and we pulled it off without the heavy armor that they now possess."

"When do you think that this is going to go down?"

"I don't know, but I'm sure that it will. If I were Marvin, I would do it sometime after the weather turns. Winter's coming and he is probably assuming that we will get lax when it gets cold," I said.

"Okay, how would you do it if you were in charge of the operation?" he asked

"I would hit the ranch first. We are better prepared, and we have better firepower and training than Elko. If they can contain or destroy the assets here at the ranch, they can take their time coming after the assets in the city. Their biggest fight will be here, and Marvin knows that. They will need their best fighters and assets to take us out. I would also send a smaller force to Elko to harass the defenders there. It would keep them occupied and out of the way while they concentrate on the heavy hitters."

"Sounds like a good strategy."

"Yeah but if they take this ranch, they are going to pay for every square inch of the grounds in blood," Jill said in a low voice. "Whatever they have left, they won't have much fight left in them."

"Alamo defense?" Jim asked.

"Modern day Alamo with high explosives mixed in," she said with a look of determination on her face.

"Jill, you do know the Alamo didn't end well for the good guys, right?" he asked.

"Here is the thing Jim, if the ranch falls and you manage to defeat whatever is left of Marvin and his men, we need you to come here and rescue the non-combatants," I told him. He looked at me with a puzzled expression. I motioned for him to follow Jill and me. We left the security shack and went to our house. I stopped at the top of the stairwell.

"I have to say this Jim. What you are about to see and hear must never leave the confines of this compound. I need your word."

"Of course, Jason. You know that I won't spread your secrets around," he said.

"In the worst-case scenario Jim, every building on the property has been rigged to blow. Nothing will be left standing. You will have to come in here and dig out the survivors," his confusion was even more evident. I led him downstairs and to the secret door to the underground.

Jill and I spent the next hour giving him the tour of the underground and he finally understood why there would be survivors. He swore that they would come and get our people out if it came to that. When we exited the underground by the horse barns, we took him over to the warehouse. While the majority of the supplies had been moved out, there were two five-tons and two Hummers parked inside. Both of the five-tons had been loaded down with an assortment of heavy weapons. Jim was told that when he left here today, he would be taking all four rigs plus two of the Jeeps with him. He was also told that the Major and his men were going to help him defend his city.

"Jason, this is too much. You will need all of this to defend the ranch. I can send some of my best men to help you."

"The best thing you can do to help us is to take the equipment that we are giving you. Take the Major and his Task force and solidify your defenses. We will hold out as long as we can and we are going to need you guys to come in and mop this place up after you have taken out the second prong of the attack," I told him. "Jim, you have a working hospital, you have vehicles, and now you will have the superior force garrisoned in Elko. All of those things are probably going to be needed here when the fight is over. You're going to be our rear guard now. We will hold them off for as long as we can. Hopefully until you can get here to bail us out."

"But....." he started, and I waved him off with my hand.

"There is nothing else to say, Jim. Take the men and equipment. After you have defeated Marvin's men, come swooping in here to save the day. Can you do that?" I asked. He was silent for a moment as he held my eye contact. He looked to Jill and she simply nodded.

"Yeah. Yeah, we can do that," he said with a heavy sigh. We worked our way back to the security shack and for the first time I can remember, Jim didn't have much to say. He sat heavily in one of the chairs across from the desk. Jill had left us to get the Major. The two of them returned within five minutes.

"Sir, Miss Butler said you wanted to see me?" the Major said.

"Yes Major, I have made your decision for you in regard to your orders."

"Yes sir?"

"I want you to assemble your men and your equipment and follow the good Mayor back to Elko and help him and his men turn the city into a fort. Mayor Calvert will be your new commanding officer," I told him.

After the Major and his men left with Calvert, his men and all of their new equipment, our preparations continued at a fevered pace. Marcus had installed an alarm system that had a panic button in both security shacks. When the button was pressed, an array of horns blasted nonstop and they were loud enough that they could probably wake the dead. In addition to the horns, every security light inside the compound and on the walls would come on and stay on. We began running readiness drills at all hours of the day and night. It was the 17th of September when Jackie Tanner returned to the ranch. She and her father had left two weeks earlier to return to their family home in Elko. She said that there was nothing left for her there after her father, the former mayor suffered a massive stroke and passed away. She began training as a medic and quickly became a part of our family.

The first snow fell on the 10th of October and it had been bitterly cold in the two weeks preceding that. Even though it had been over a month since we began our preparations and nothing had happened, we stayed vigilant and on-point. We had continued with our drills and we continued to refine our defenses. It was 1:30 in the morning on October 21st when all hell broke loose.

Jill and I were sound asleep in our bed when the alarm klaxon sounded. Both of us bolted upright and started pulling our boots and gear on. We had taken to sleeping in our clothes when the weather had turned bitterly cold, not because it was cold in the house but because we didn't want to waste time in the event of an attack. Jill beat me out of the bedroom door by two steps. As we reached the bottom of the stairs, Jessica flew past us and headed downstairs. Jake bolted out of their room and hit the front door just ahead of Jill. As the three of us burst onto the front deck, a huge explosion lit up the cold, dark sky. It had come from the direction of the front gate. In the dying light of the explosion I could see that the gate was still standing but the gatehouse had been reduced to rubble. I looked left and right and could see my people pouring from the buildings and running for their posts.

The M249 that was in the first foxhole by the security shack started firing. In short order the machine gun nest on top of the clinic opened up and began pouring hot lead toward the gate. Jill and I both had our NVGs pulled down and the entire area was bathed in the green light. Jill was running full speed for the second foxhole when rounds started coming at us through the gate. Jill was in the line of fire and she threw herself to the ground and returned fire with her AR.

I jumped into my foxhole and squeezed the firing paddle on the big fifty caliber. It was enough cover fire to allow Jill to scramble into her foxhole. I heard Dan yelling in my earpiece that they were starting to come over the walls. They were using grappling hooks and ladders to get over. Dan and Mike were engaging the people coming over the walls with their sniper rifles. I spun my machine gun and engaged a half dozen people coming across the grass from the gate at the east end of the compound. I could still see their ropes hanging from the wall.

I couldn't tell how many I got, but when I turned my attention back to the gate, they were all down. I could see four big vehicles coming up the road heading for the weakened gate and my heart skipped a beat. They were bearing down on the gate at a high rate of speed. There were fighters pouring through the hole in the wall where the gate house used to be. I unleashed the fifty and started thinning their numbers.

The fifty that was on top of the lead MRAP started returning fire at my position. Several of the sandbags to my left exploded when the big rounds slammed into them. The MRAP's were almost to the wash when the culvert detonated. Jessica and Jackie were running the explosives from the underground and their timing couldn't have been better with that one. The lead MRAP couldn't stop in time and ended up nose first in the smoking crater and the second one veered to the left and ended up sliding on the icy, snow-covered road. It slid broadside into the first one. In the glow of my night vision, I could see the crews climbing out of the trucks and they began running toward the wash. Just as they reached the edge, the claymore mines blew and shredded every one of them.

I was starting to think we might have a chance when there were two huge explosions, one on either end of the compound. I looked to the east end of the compound and could see a gaping hole in the wall that had to be ten feet across. Dirt bikes and quads began to pour through the hole. The roar of dirt bikes began to overpower the barking of automatic weapons. Within seconds the air was sizzling with gunfire from every direction. There was nowhere safe to hide.

Jill's M249 ran dry and she was reloading when I saw a biker headed straight for her. His AK-47 was firing full auto. I sighted him in with the fifty and let three rounds fly. His whole torso evaporated, and his bike came to rest just outside of her foxhole. I watched her take the heavy weapon and jump out of the hole. She ran toward a group that was firing toward the houses. The one guy that was wearing night vision was the first one in her sights.

My fifty ran dry when I spotted Eric bailing out of foxhole number one. He only made it a dozen strides before he went down in a hail of gunfire. I pulled my AR to my shoulder and started firing three-round bursts at anyone that crossed my sights. I wasn't really concerned about a kill shot, I just wanted to take the fight out of them. Two men jumped in Eric's foxhole and started to spin the M249 back toward the buildings. Both of them vanished when the explosives inside it were detonated. Another case of perfect timing. Two more guys jumped in the foxhole that Jill had just vacated and it too exploded.

For as much as was going on, there was not much chatter on my earbud. That told me that everyone knew their jobs and they were busy doing them. The security shack was about 100 feet ahead of me and in the green glow of my night vision, I could see two guys kick open the door. There was an exchange of gunfire and both of them went down. Jeff crawled out of the door a second later. Two more were closing in on him and I put both of them down. I leapt from my foxhole and sprinted as fast as I could toward the shack.

I dropped three more before I got to Jeff. I dragged him from the doorway and pulled him up onto my shoulders in a fireman's carry. He was shooting his pistol as we were making a mad dash for medical. Around the halfway point I started yelling in my mic for Jess to blow the security shack. The enemy was starting to use it for cover. I no sooner got the words out of my mouth when a massive explosion sent Jeff and me to the ground. There was a searing pain in the back of my left thigh when I rolled onto my back and got back to my feet. I picked Jeff up again and continued to make a run for it. The door to the clinic was thrown open just before we got there, and it slammed shut right behind us. Jeff and I both fell to the floor and slid halfway across the room. Doc was there and grabbed Jeff by the drag handle on the back of his plate carrier and dragged him toward the back room. When I tried to stand again, I felt the pain in the back of my leg. Contessa was the other medic in the room, and she pushed me back to the floor.

"Hold on Jason!" she said as she tore open a large bandage. "This is gonna hurt!"

"What....." was all I could get out of my mouth before she ripped a six-inch long shard of wood from my thigh. I clenched my teeth and swore under my breath as she slapped the bandage on and tied it securely in-place. When that was done she helped me back to my feet. I swapped out magazines on my AR and threw the door open.

I ran full speed into a woman that was racing toward the door with a hatchet in one hand and a small pistol in the other. My rifle and her pistol went off at the same time. The three-round burst put her instantly in a heap on the sidewalk. Her round tore a chunk out of the meaty part of my right bicep.

I spotted Dan fighting with three men out by the dock on the pond. As I was running across the parking lot, I shot one attacker but the other two were too close to him to take the chance. I flipped my rifle around to my back and slammed into the second attacker. It was a hit any NFL linebacker would have been proud of. When we hit the ground, I could feel his bones break and I could hear the air being forced from his lungs. I pushed myself up and drove my gloved fist into his face with all the force I could muster. The bones in his face and skull gave way and his fight was over.

I rolled off of him only to find a wood ax coming for my face. I jerked my head to the side and the blade buried itself in the frozen ground next to my ear. I kicked up with my legs and the shin of my right leg connected solidly with his groin. He screamed but it was cut short when the top of his head exploded in a spray of brains and bone. As he collapsed, I could see Dan standing behind him with his pistol drawn. He reached down and pulled the body off me and helped me get to my feet. My left leg was aching, and I was a little slow getting to my feet. He slapped me on the shoulder and took off running for Dale's house. There were half a dozen guys trying to break down the front door and he was going to go put a stop to it.

The bikers were having all kinds of trouble breaching the living quarters. One of the preparations that we made was to bolt one-inch thick plywood over the windows and all of the doors had been reinforced with braces from the inside. We were going to hold them off as long as we could. I saw Pat go down, less than ten yards from me. I don't know if he was dead or not. I didn't have time to check. I double tapped the woman that shot him, and I just kept shooting. There were just too many targets to keep up with and I was burning through magazines. The air around me was sizzling and cracking with bullets from every direction.

I wasn't rushed and I wasn't scared. Everything was automatic. Bang, bang, bang, next target, bang, bang, bang, next target, bang, bang, bang, change mags, next target.... I was on my eighth and final mag and I had no idea how many bikers I had sent to hell but there were bodies everywhere. Some were moving, most were not. The next thing I knew, my right leg felt as if it had been hit by a baseball bat and I was going down on my right side. There was blood spray all over the white snow in front of me and I could see the blood stain growing on my right pant leg. I had been hit from behind and there was a man running at me firing wildly with his rifle. Still laying on my right side, I raised my rifle but saw that the bolt had locked back on an empty chamber. I rolled onto my back and grabbed my pistol. It was slippery from all my blood that was coating it and as I brought it up and fired, a round slammed into my chest. The AR500 plate stopped the round but a fragment of the bullet sliced through the flesh on the right side of my face.

The gunman dropped and was still. The 230-grain jacketed hollow point had done its job. I rolled on to my stomach and struggled to get back to my knees. I tried to stand but it was impossible. I stayed on my knees and found two more targets before my Sig went to slide-lock. As I was fumbling for another magazine with my bloody hands, I was thrown forward into the snow. The blow was devastating, and I was gasping for air. My back felt like it was on fire and I couldn't get any of my limbs to work. Everything except my spine was going numb. I couldn't move and breathing was near impossible.

I heard footsteps drawing closer and someone rolled me onto my back. Time stopped and it felt like my heart did too when my eyes focused on Marvin. He was standing over me with a huge .44 magnum pointed at my head. I could see the animal rage burning behind his eyes. His smile was that of a predator about to make the perfect kill. I could see his finger pulling back on the trigger. Click.......click, click, click... the pistol was empty, and he threw it to the side. He stepped back and delivered a hard kick to my side. There was nothing I could do to stop the blow. The tip of his boot hit just above the side plate and below my armpit. I felt the stabbing pain of ribs breaking.

"I'm going to enjoy this!" he sneered as he grabbed the shoulder strap of my body armor as he dragged me out onto the boat dock. I tried to swing a fist in his direction, but my arm felt like it was moving in slow motion and he easily batted it away. We were about three-quarters of the way out when he dropped me. He reached for the buckle that held my rifle in-place. Again, I tried to land a hit, but he managed to pin one arm under his knee and he pulled my rifle free. He used the butt of the rifle to smash a hole in the ice. He again grabbed my shoulder strap and with one hand, he half hoisted, and half shoved me into the icy water. He held me just under the surface for what felt like forever. My lungs were burning, and my vision was getting dark around the edges and there was nothing I could do to fight back. He pulled my face above the surface and he put his just inches from mine. I gasped hard trying to get some useful air in my lungs.

"Don't worry buddy boy, when I am done with that fucking bitch girlfriend of yours, I'll make sure to share her with every one of my men," he growled. "It will take her days to die. It's too bad that you won't be around to watch....." something caught his attention and he turned away from my face. His expression changed and I could see surprise flash across his face as he let go of me. Just before I slipped beneath the ice with the weight of my gear dragging me under, I heard what could only be described as the howl of a banshee straight from the depths of hell. As I slipped deeper, the last thing I caught a blurry glimpse of was the screaming banshee attacking Marvin with supernatural speed and ferocity.

Then there was nothing but darkness and the icy cold. My last thoughts were that I was descending to a watery grave and the only sound I could hear was the beating of my racing heart. I felt the muscles in my body begin to spasm. I gasped for a breath and I felt the cold water fill my lungs. The beating was beginning to slow down. Then there was nothing, the beating simply stopped.

CHAPTER 21

My thoughts were a jumbled mess. I couldn't process any words and it seemed like I was only hearing parts of the conversations going on around me. Everything sounded like I had cotton stuffed in my ears......... Someone opened my eyes and shined a bright flashlight in them.... *Crap that hurt......Everything hurt....Why was there a woman screaming and sobbing..... Who the hell was punching me in the chest.....Sooooo cold........*

........more mumbling..... The beeping.....beep.......beep......beep.......... Beeeeeeeeep....... more screaming and sobbing........ An explosion of light in the darkness and more screaming........ Another explosion of light and this time it brought so much pain.......beep.......beep........ Beep........

.....*warmth....it was getting warmer but why couldn't I move or see? Why did I feel like I was choking all the time?.........* *Why was there so much crying? Who was crying? It was a woman; I was sure of that.....* There was the beeping again......beep......beep.......beep.... beeeeeeeeeep....... more screaming and yelling......

...I could start to make out words in the mumbling.... *Jill....* that one was important..... *why?......beep......beep.... beep.......*again with the light in my eyes......*stop it that hurts........*

".........I don't know how long Jill, I don't know if he will ever wake up," that was a man's voice..... I understood it...... "Please Doc there has to be something you can do?" the woman's voice again.... *Jill, that was Jill's voice.........*

.... *warmth.....warmth and pressure......something was lying next to me and it was warm...it smelled nice too.....*

...the pressure and the warmth were gone but the smell was still there.... I felt my hand move.... someone was holding my hand..... soft, quiet crying.... Jill was crying. She was holding my hand and crying... *was I dead? No, wait, I am alive but something bad happened.......doesn't matter, I'm alive.........*It took every ounce of my being and the pain was tremendous, but I forced my hand to move. It wasn't much but I was sure it moved. The crying stopped.

"Jason!!!!" Jill yelled.

THE RANCH

Now that I knew I could do it and how to do it, I forced my hand to move again.

"Jason! Oh my God! Jason, if you can hear me do it again......squeeze my hand."

I did it again and managed to hold on to her finger this time.

"AMANDA!!!!!" I heard her yell.

"What's wrong Jill?" I knew that voice too, the Irish accent.

"He's squeezing my hand, Amanda! I asked him to squeeze my hand and now he is holding on to my finger!" Jill said excitedly.

"Let me in there, Jill!" Amanda demanded.

Ughhhhh the light in my eyes again..... The light was gone but I could see....it was blurry but there were shapes...... Everything hurt so bad.........

"Amanda! Look, his eyes are open and moving!"

"Jason, don't try to talk. If you understand me blink your eyes twice," Amanda ordered. It was a struggle, but I did it.

"Jason, can you squeeze my fingers?" again, the Irish accent. I squeezed both hands through the pain. I felt like I was going to black out again.

"That's great Jason! Can you wiggle your toes for me?" I tried the best I could but stopped just before the darkness returned. I don't know if they moved or not.

"Good job my friend! Jill, I'm going to go put in a call and see about getting the Doc down here. Just stay with him," Amanda said and left the room. I could hear Jill crying again. I squeezed her fingers tighter and she pulled my hand up to her face. I could feel her skin on the back of my hand. It was rough. I tried to focus my eyes on her face. Both of her eyes were black and blue. There were stitches across the bridge of her nose and under her left eye. The knuckles of her right hand were scabbed over and black and blue. When she lifted her left hand to push the hair from her face, I could see that it was in a cast up to her elbow and the knuckles of that hand were also scabbed and bruised.

It all started to flood back into my mind as if someone had opened a set of floodgates. The ranch, the gun battle, getting shot, getting drowned in the icy water........Marvin. I swallowed hard and managed to croak out a one-word question.

"Marvin?" I asked. It surprised me to hear my own voice.

"Dead, just be quiet and rest."

It was the next day that I discovered that I had been in a coma for three weeks. It was November 11th. I could muster a scratchy voice when I needed to but most

308

of the time, I just listened to what everyone had to say. Apparently, the battle at the ranch had been a win against all the odds.

When it was all over, they had counted 129 dead from the biker gang. We lost both of the Teller brothers, Eric and Pat. Contessa had run from the relative safety of the medical clinic to try and drag Andy to safety and both of them perished when a grenade had landed between them and exploded.

Allan......... I couldn't believe that Allan was gone too. That one made my heart hurt the worst. He had been my mentor and friend since day one at the ranch. Jill told me that he had fired his AR until he had run out of ammo and then he used it as a bat. He fired his pistol until it had also run dry then he used it to smash a few skulls. He was eventually overpowered by six bikers who beat, stabbed and shot him. He did not go quietly into the night, just the way he would have wanted it. He pulled the pin of a grenade and took all six bikers with him. He went down fighting.

Doc, the Butler boys, Jessica, Jackie and Diane had been the only ones to escape injury. I found out that Dan had fought like some crazed Norse Berserker. A machete in one hand and a camp axe in the other. He had been shot in one leg, stabbed in the other and then shot again in the shoulder but he didn't go down until after the fighting was over. The only reason he went down then was from blood loss. He was trying to help Jill pull me from the water when he finally collapsed.

The shot that I took right between the shoulder blades was from a very close range from Marvin's .44 magnum. Not only did it knock the wind out of me, it bruised my spinal cord which caused the instant paralysis that I had suffered from. Jill told me that I had been in the frigid water for almost 30 minutes while she battled it out with Marvin. In the end, she drove her combat knife through his neck and watched the life leave his eyes and spill out onto the snowy dock in a crimson puddle. She was the one who dove into the water to pull me out.

She also told me that I had been clinically dead for an hour while they tried to warm me enough to try and restart my heart. They had gotten it going and I had arrested three more times before they got me to stabilize. In the end, I had been shot in the right leg and right arm, I'd had a huge piece of wood penetrate my left leg, been shot in the chest and back, had four broken ribs, a bruised spine and a four-inch long laceration on the right side of my face and I had been drowned.

Doc later told me that if it hadn't been for Marvin throwing me in the water, I would have passed out and probably bled to death within minutes of being shot in the leg. He said that if I hadn't drowned, I would have died. He chuckled at the irony of what he said. In essence, Marvin actually did me a favor by throwing me in the icy water.

Jill had taken the title as the most savage fighter on the ranch. Jessica had watched the whole thing unfold on one of the security cameras and when I asked her about it, she told me every detail. Jess had seen Marvin shoot me in the back as she watched helplessly from the safety of the underground bunker. It took her a couple of minutes to raise anybody on the radios and when she finally did, it was Jill. She told me that Jill was back by the horse barns and had to race all the way up to the pond. Jess said that was the fastest she had ever seen anyone run 100 plus yards.

As she was running, she dropped two more bad guys and butt-stroked one so hard she actually separated the upper and lower receivers on her rifle. When she got to the pond and saw what was happening, she raced full speed toward Marvin. He had caught sight of her out of the corner of his eye but didn't have much chance to do anything except brace for the impact. Jill had launched her 130-pound body at Marvin who easily had a 100 pounds on her. She caught him square in the chest and sent him flying backward. Jill managed to stay on top of him and land a half dozen solid blows to his face and head before he threw her off. Both of them got to their feet and he wasted no time coming at her with a right hook. She stepped outside of the swing and once his fist went past her face, she stepped back in and smashed her open palm against his ear. She followed that up with a right jab to the face and shattered his nose. As he staggered back a step, she caught his right knee with a shin kick fired from her left leg. He recovered his balance quickly and took a couple of steps away from Jill.

He sized her up again and with lightning speed he closed in and had Jill in a bear hug. He was lifting her off the deck and trying to carry her to the edge of the dock. While her arms were pinned, her legs were not. She raked one of her combat boots down across his knee cap. He yelled in pain and released her from his grip as he went down. Jill managed to stay on her feet and wasted no time delivering a savage kick to the side of Marvin's face. The blow rolled him onto his side, and she came in for another kick. The second one hit him firmly in the side of his ribs. She came in for a third one and he deflected the blow with enough force to cause Jill to lose her balance. She fell to her side but quickly rolled away. She was back on her feet and so was he. Marvin was moving a little slower and favoring his right knee.

He came in with another right hook and Jill set up to defend against the blow. It was a fake and she ended up taking a left jab to the face. The blow had enough power behind it to stun her and that was all the opportunity he needed. She took a half step backward and he stepped in and grabbed her by the shoulder strap of her plate carrier with his left hand. She never had a chance to defend against the brutal punch that caught her square in the face. There were three blows total before he let her go. She went to her knees and swayed back and forth. Blood poured from her shattered nose and she looked like she was finished. Marvin came in with a kick and Jill surprised him when she deflected it. She drove her left fist into his groin with every ounce of strength she had.

He clutched his groin with both hands and went to his knees. Jill was back on her feet and she stepped in closer and drove her knee up and into his face. He flipped onto his back and she pounced. She was straddling of his chest again, landing punch after punch into his face. His arms were flailing, and his legs were kicking but he couldn't get her off his chest. Blow after blow and he could feel his strength starting to fade, the panic beginning. She was driven by a primal rage and was showing no signs of letting up.

His hand found the knife that was strapped to her right calf. He was fighting to free it from its sheath before he lost consciousness. He finally got it free and pulled it back to strike. The only place he could stab her was the thigh and he did just that. She didn't flinch and she didn't stop the beating. He pulled the knife back for another thrust into her thigh, but he never made it that far.

The look in her eyes was like nothing he had ever seen in his life and he knew it was the last thing he would ever see. The wild rage had won out over sanity and mercy. She was only hitting him with her right fist now. He was sure he had heard the bones in her left arm snap from hitting him so hard. Her face was directly over his and the blood was running off her nose and dripping on his face. With all the blood, the snarling lips and the wild look in her eyes, she looked like something right out of a nightmare.

Her right hand grasped his hand that was holding the knife. With a power that he couldn't understand, she twisted his wrist until the blade was pointing at his neck. She was overpowering him at every step. She forced the blade against the side of his neck, and he could feel it slowly penetrate his skin. He felt it slip all the way through. He had been right; those eyes were the last thing he ever saw.

Mayor Calvert came by to see me that day too. He recounted the events that went on in his town when the biker gang launched the other half of their assault. Compared to our story at the ranch, it was pretty anti-climactic. They had ambushed their attackers before they ever made it off the highway and they had forced a surrender. Major Jackson had come up with the plan and they had executed it to perfection. Once they were secured and their MRAP's seized, the Major had led the charge back to the ranch. By the time he and his men had arrived, most of the fighting was over. It was what he called a mop-up operation.

He and his men stormed the gate on foot and finished off the few attackers that remained. Lucky for me, they had a working AED (Automatic External Defibrillator) in one of their rigs. Once he saw what was going on with me, he sprinted all the way back to the truck to retrieve it and then sprinted all the way back to the clinic. If it hadn't been for him and his defibrillator, I would not be alive today.

The Mayor vowed to help us repair and rebuild at the ranch. I told him that we could handle it but he insisted. He had already posted a security force to stand posts at our breached walls and already had a construction crew out to help with the clean-up. The majority of my people were out of commission with various wounds. Dan, Mike and Mark were also in the hospital with me. Alex had insisted on returning to the ranch to help Marcus get the work crews organized.

I was finally allowed to leave the hospital on the eighteenth of November. I was the last member of the ranch to leave. Doc wanted me to ride out in a wheelchair but I was having none of that. He stopped the chair in the lobby and helped me to my feet. My balance was all screwed up and I was still having issues with my motor skills. Doc assured me that as the swelling and bruising continued to go down, the more function I would regain. With Jill under one arm and Doc under the other, I walked out the door to the waiting Jeep. As soon as I stepped from the building, the crowd that had assembled started cheering and clapping.

There were six sheriff's deputies on either side of the walkway, all of them standing at attention. I found it all a little overwhelming. As we approached the passenger door of the Jeep, Major Jackson stepped from the crowd and opened the door. He snapped a smart salute and held it until I returned the gesture. After I was helped into the seat and the door was closed, he stepped back and called his men to attention. All of them saluted and again I had to salute them back before they stood at ease. Jill climbed in the driver's door and fired it up. She slipped it into gear and pulled us out of the hospital parking lot.

As soon as we pulled out onto the main street, a Hummer pulled out in front of us, and escorted us all the way back to the ranch. The main gate had been heavily damaged by a shoulder fired missile, but Marcus and his construction crew had already repaired it. They had also repaired the crater that had stopped the advancing MRAP's. While we were waiting for the gate to open, I reached over and shut the ignition off. Jill looked at me. I looked at my watch.

"What are you doing?" she asked.

"Help me out of the car," I said and threw the door open. She climbed from the driver side and assisted me in getting my feet on the ground. I leaned against the Jeep and walked to the front of it.

"What the bloody hell are you doing Jason?" she asked again. I reached my hand out to her and she took it. I pulled her closer to me.

"It was the 9th of July 2015, at 8:30 in the morning. Do you remember it?"

"Remember what? What are you talking about?"

"We were parked right here. Your dad and brother had just climbed back in the Jeep and were getting ready to leave. You and I were standing right here. It was the day you changed my life, Jill," I looked her in the eyes and pulled her in close for a kiss. I had to be gentle, her face was still pretty sore.

"You have a near-death experience and now you get all sentimental on me?" she asked with a half grin.

"Technically, I was dead. Not only have you changed my life for the better Jill, you saved my life," I said as I sat on the bumper of the Jeep. She leaned against the fender and sighed.

"Jason, you died on me four times that night. When I saw you slip into the water and I saw no signs of fight coming from you, my world came apart. I felt the rage exploding within me. That bottle didn't uncork, it exploded. It was the same rage that I felt the night my mother and Joshua were killed. I've spent years trying to push it away, to hide it, to turn it into something positive,"

"When I thought you had died, I lost all control of that rage. The only thing that mattered was the object of that rage, of all my rage. When Marvin smashed my face in, the only thing that kept me from going down was the rage. By all rights he should have knocked me out, but the rage wouldn't let me quit. When I had him on the ropes, I was hitting him with a strength I didn't know I had. I felt the bones in my arm break, but I didn't feel any pain. When he stabbed me in the thigh, I felt the knife go in, but I felt no pain. When I watched the life drain from his eyes, the rage was finally appeased. The need for vengeance and the blood-lust drained from me as his blood pooled on the dock,"

"I still felt no pain in my wrecked body. When I dropped my body armor and dove into that freezing water, I still felt nothing. It was like my mind had severed all of my pain receptors. That water was pitch black and I knew you were all the way at the bottom. Somehow, I knew exactly where you were, something was guiding me. Something that I cannot explain helped me get you to the shore and it helped me drag you halfway across the parking lot," She paused for a second and took a long breath.

"I saw the look on Doc's face when he and dad dragged you into the clinic and got you on that table. I had seen that look on the faces of the paramedics that worked on mom and Joshua. Every medic we had available was in the room and doing everything they could. I don't know how long I had been standing there or how long they had been working on you but when I saw my mother and Josh standing at the head of your bed, I lost my shit. I came completely unhinged. Jessica told me later that I started screaming hysterically that they couldn't have you. When they hit you with the AED for the final time, they left. I looked up and they were gone," She paused again.

"It was sometime after they got you semi-stabilized that Jess stabbed me in the ass and pumped me full of sedatives. She told me later that it was twice the normal dosage and it took me twice as long to pass out as it should have. They put me on a bed in the same room as you and patched me up while I was out. I had a vivid dream during that time. Mom and Josh came to me. It was then that I understood that they were the ones guiding me in the water. They were the ones who helped me swim you to shore. They were at your bed not to take you but to make sure you stayed with me," she stopped and wiped a tear from the corner of her eye. "They brought you back to me....." her voice cracked, and she started crying. I pushed myself off the bumper and hugged her. I could feel her body tremble with each sob as I held her tightly.

We were out there for almost an hour before Jill helped me back into the Jeep and we drove up to the parking area. The majority of the snow had melted and all of the debris that had been the security shack had been cleared away. The crew had been busy cleaning up and making repairs. What damage had been done had been mostly repaired and the place was almost back to normal. Jill parked the Jeep and was helping me get out when Bill walked up.

"Good to have you back Jason," he said as he extended his hand. I shook it and as always there was that iron grip.

"You have no idea how glad I am to be back Bill. Hospital food still sucks," I said jokingly.

"Well, let's get you two settled in and I'll see what I can do about rustling up some good ole home cooking," He said as he got under one shoulder and started toward the house. He and Jill helped me up the stairs and into our room. Once I was seated on the edge of the bed, he excused himself. Jill helped me get my boots off and got me laid down. She kicked her boots off and curled up next to me. About a half hour later Bill returned with a tray and two plates stacked with bacon, eggs, thick slices of ham and toast. The two of us ate voraciously then resumed our cuddling on the bed. There was no need for words. Just being together was enough.

We stayed up there for two days, rarely leaving the comfort of each other. It was the third day when I started physical therapy with Jill as my trainer. Most of the swelling in my back was gone but I still had a massive black and purple bruise. After a two-hour session of stretching and very basic exercises, I was exhausted. Jill and I spent another 45 minutes in the hot tub and then she helped me back to our room. For the next week, this was our daily regimen. Then she added light weight training to the routine. I was blown away by how weak my muscles had become, and she told me that she had the same problem when she had been shot and confined to a bed for three weeks. That was some consolation. The irritating thing was having to walk with a cane. Doc said I might need it for a while. I told him not to bet on it.

It was January 17, 2017, when I had finally been cleared for full duty. The majority of the bruising on my back was gone except for a slight yellowish color right at the point of impact. That too would fade away. There were days that I still needed the cane but for the most part I could do without it. I was still weak compared to what I was before the attack, but we were working on that.

Jill's injuries had healed, and she was left with two small scars on her face. She would bear the physical and mental scars of her fight with Marvin for the rest of her life. The day after the attack, Marcus had driven the backhoe up to the meadow and dug the graves for our fallen comrades. There had been a very brief ceremony and then the bodies had been laid to rest. He used that same backhoe to dig a mass grave for the attackers out by the main road. Their bodies had been stripped of everything useful. Polaroid pictures were taken of their faces and then they were loaded into the bucket and unceremoniously dumped in the grave and dirt pushed over them.

When that grisly task was done, the rebuilding had begun. By the time I had returned to duty, the breaches in the walls had been repaired and the new security shack had been rebuilt on the site of the old one. Every member of the ranch community had healed physically, but all of us would bear the mental scars of that night forever. Every one of us swore that we would never allow the enemy inside our walls again. Marcus had thrown himself into his work. Doc said that he was grieving the loss of Contessa and that we needed to leave him be, let him work it out. He would work around the grounds from sunup 'till sundown and then he would go to his workshop in the warehouse where he would stay until midnight some nights.

He was responsible for many of the upgrades to the security of the ranch. He erected six guard towers in the compound. One at each corner, one at the main gate and a taller one in the center. All of them had thick wood timbers that would stop most bullets and they had a fireman's pole in the middle that could be used for a fast exit. He built steel shutters and doors for all of the buildings out of 1/2" thick AR500 plate for every building on the grounds. He had scavenged the plate from a local mining outfit that used it to line the buckets and blades on their heavy equipment. He also custom-made armor for the doors, windows and turrets of the Hummers and five-tons. When he wasn't doing that, he was repairing radios for the town and for the ranch. He had found everything he needed in a warehouse and he proved his technical aptitude.

On the morning of February eleventh, Major Jackson showed up at the gate leading a convoy of nine 4×4 MRAP's and three of the six-wheel drive rigs. All of the rigs that had been taken by the gang had been confiscated and the two that had been damaged were repaired. They were allowed through and they took up most of the parking area in front of the clinic. I greeted the Major as he climbed out of the lead rig.

"Major, good to see you," I said.

"It's good to see you too sir, you look well."

"So, to what do we owe the honor of your visit today?" I was in the middle of saying when I noticed all of his men disembarking their vehicles. Most of them were civilians.

"Got somewhere we could talk?" he asked. I looked from him to his men and back.

"Yeah, let's go in the house," I told him and started walking that way. When we walked into the kitchen, Jill was there putting a roast in the crock pot for dinner.

"Major!" She said excitedly and ran over to give him a hug. She would forever hold him in reverence as it was his crew that had shown up with the AED that was credited with bringing me back from the dead.

"Ma'am," he said simply and returned her hug. I sat at the table and motioned him to do the same. Jill grabbed three coffee cups, filled them and sat at the table with us. He looked at her and back to me.

"This concerns her too. As head of security, she needs to know what we are up to," he said.

"Head of Operations, Dan runs security now and dad stepped down as operations," Jill corrected him.

"Even better then."

"What's on your mind Major? I'm sure you didn't drive all this way just for the coffee?" I asked. He leaned back in his chair and crossed his arms. Jill and I shared a quick look.

"I have been talking to Mayor Calvert and Sheriff Watson, Darren......."

"This can't be good," I said half-jokingly. He didn't smile.

"We have come up with a plan to start securing the area and rebuilding. As you know, Elko had a population of 19,000 before the EMP. That population is projected to be in the neighborhood of 3,000 by the time we hit the one-year mark. There have still been reports of roaming bands that are attacking and harassing the outlying ranches and refugees that are trying to make their way down the highway corridor," he paused for a drink of his coffee and my thoughts jumped to my brother and his family who were still missing. "Anyway, we need your help to put this plan into action...."

"I'm not sure how much help we can be Major. We are still licking our wounds from the last engagement and I know that most of these people want nothing to do with going out and looking for trouble," Jill said.

THE RANCH

"Ma'am, we are not asking you to do that. You and the people of the ranch have paid their dues in blood and tears. We are, however, going to ask the people of Elko to step up and provide for their own security."

"Get to the point Major, what do you want from us?" I asked.

"The point? We want you to train the new security forces," he said.

"I don't know if we are the right people for that kind of thing," I started but he cut me off.

"Jason, what you people did here at the ranch the night of the attack was, by all metrics, outstanding. We want you to teach others how to do what you did. We want you to teach them about weapons, hand-to-hand combat and wilderness survival. Those are all things you have plenty of experience with."

"Most of you think that we won when they attacked us but that's not the truth. We lost five people that I would sell my soul to get back," I said looking into my black coffee.

"Yes, you lost five outstanding people and you will miss them for the rest of your days on this planet. Listen to me though, do the damn math. For every one of yours that they killed, you killed 29 of theirs. You withstood an attack from a numerically superior force, and not only did you repel them, you destroyed them. By all rights, they should have rolled over this place like a steamroller and killed everyone here, but you fought them off."

"I did the math Major! I still come up with five of my own that are dead!" I said heatedly. Jill reached over and put her hand on mine.

"Jason, Jill, I am very sorry for your losses. Believe me when I say that I know what it's like to lose people. Friends. From the bottom of my heart, you have my condolences. Please, consider this though, let the loss of your friends mean something in the bigger picture. Take the lessons of their loss and the lessons of how to prevent it and teach it to those young men out there. Help them put a stop to all of the senseless killing," he implored. I was silent for quite some time. I didn't know what to say. Jill squeezed my hand and began to speak.

"Major, speaking as the Operations Manager for this ranch, we will help you under one condition," she said slowly.

"Name it."

"Every group that comes through here will be limited to 20 people and we reserve the right to hand-pick one student to offer a position here at the ranch. All of the students will live here and work here for the duration of their training and we will have total control over who graduates and who does not....."

"Done!" he said. She held up her hand.

"I'm not through yet, Major. We will need supplies to train these people. I'm not talking food or uniforms. I am talking about weapons, ammo and fuel. Those are finite resources and we are not willing to part with what we have here. We will also tell you at the time of graduation what the student's specialty will be. Not everyone is cut out for combat and I expect you to abide by that," she finished.

"Ma'am, we will abide by your skills assessment of the students and we have already given this group all the weapons and ammunition that we could scrounge up. The fuel tanks in the city of Elko are free for you to draw from. Will that suffice?" he asked. Jill looked at me and I nodded. I knew by the look in her eyes that she was up to something and I knew enough to give her the lead on this. She stuck her hand out across the table and the Major took it.

"We have a deal Major," she said. She withdrew her hand and finished her coffee in one gulp. She stood up and jogged upstairs leaving the Major and me sitting there. We made light conversation and Jill returned five minutes later. She was dressed in her black fatigues and black cap and she had her gun belt strapped on. She pulled her radio from her belt and put it to her mouth.

"Dan, Mark, meet me in front of medical in five. Wear your best black fatigues and gun belts," she said with a grin. Both men acknowledged her.

"You two just going to sit there or are you going to come help me welcome Class 1 to the ranch?" her grin was getting bigger and she slipped her black sunglasses over her eyes and headed for the door.

CHAPTER 22

Jill strode down the sidewalk and stood in front of the flagpole. She was quickly joined by Dan and Mark. She said something to both of them and then turned to face the group of civilians. Dan and Mark were on both sides of her and a step behind. She cleared her throat.

"Form up! Five across, four deep!" she yelled. They started moving to form lines in front of her. It wasn't fast enough. "What part of form up did you not understand? Move your asses!" she bellowed. Now they were hustling to find a spot. They lined up as she told them, five across and four rows deep. They were all standing ramrod straight. She silently walked up and down each row. She made eye contact with all 20 young men. Not one of them could hold her gaze for more than a few seconds. When she was done intimidating them, she moved back to the front.

"I don't know what they told you to get you to come out here and I for one don't give a rat's ass. You are here and for the next six weeks, your asses belong to me! I will tell you when you sleep, I will tell you when you eat. Hell, I will even tell you when to take a shit. This gentleman to my right is Dan and the one on my left is Mark. You will address each as Sir! You will address any member of the ranch as Sir or Ma'am! Am I clear so far?"

"YES MA'AM!" they shouted in unison.

"Good. While you are here, you will learn to shoot, you will learn to move and communicate, you will learn basic first aid, you will learn to farm and build things. You will learn to fight and destroy things. In six weeks, 19 of you will leave here and one of you will be given an invitation to join the ranch. If you want to be the one who stays, you have to earn it! Am I clear?"

"YES MA'AM!" they shouted again.

"I'm going to grind your asses down to nothing and I'm going to take great pleasure in doing so," she took a long pause. "I will take even more pleasure into building you up into the protectors of the future. Am. I. Clear?" she asked again.

"YES MA'AM!"

"You have one minute to grab your shit out of the Major's vehicles and pile it right here in front of me and get back to your spot information. GO!" she shouted. They scattered as Jill made a show of holding her arm up and looking at her watch. Backpacks, weapons and ammo cans started to pile up in front of her. She started counting down from ten and by the time she got to one, they had re-formed in front of her. What they didn't know was that she had been watching them during the whole exercise. She had been looking for four people who naturally took the lead. The ones who helped the others and kept them moving. Once again, she walked up and down the rows and she picked one from each. She told them to move to the left end of the line. When she was done with that she moved back to the front.

"The four of you standing on the left end are now squad leaders and you will be until I find someone better. Now for your first exercise, squad leaders take your men for a run around the fence perimeter! GO!" she shouted. They bolted from the parking area by squad. It was kind of comical to watch as how about half of them were wearing cowboy boots and jeans. Once they were clear of the parking lot, Jill filled Mark and Dan in on what was going on. When their conversation was over, Mark took off to the warehouse where the recruits would be given uniforms and gear. Dan stayed with Jill.

The Major and I had been watching from the sidelines. Jill and Dan approached and both of them had grins on their faces. The Major had the same one on his face.

"I knew we picked the right people for this!" he said as he reached out and shook Dan's hand.

"We will take care of them Major. You won't recognize them when you get them back," Jill told him. We talked for a couple more minutes and I could see that Jill was back in her element. Maybe this was the distraction that we needed. The Major took his leave, but he only took four of the four-wheel drive MRAP's with him. The rest were left for us to use at the ranch.

Jill made the recruits run the fence line a total of three times and by the time they returned from the last trip around, they looked like they had been whooped. They had formed up again and she had them all drop to the ground and then she had them all belly crawl the 100 yards to the warehouse. The ground was still wet and muddy in spots so by the time she had them formed up inside the concrete building, they were a mess.

Each man was issued an Alice pack that contained all of their basic gear and two sets of uniforms. They were also given plate carriers, helmets and sized for boots. They were told to put their packs on and carry their boots and plate carriers. Their helmets were strapped onto their heads. It was about 50 degrees inside the building and almost all of them were shivering from being wet. She made them run the fence one more time. When they came stumbling back into the warehouse, Jill was gone and replaced by Dan. He stepped to the front of the formation.

"You all look cold," he said. "Are you?"

"Yes sir!"

"You look tired too. Are you?"

"Yes Sir!"

"I bet you're getting hungry too," he said as he looked at his watch. "Are you?"

"Yes sir!" they replied. A knowing grin flashed across his face. He pointed to two open cases of MREs that were sitting on the floor.

"You have until I count to ten to get your lunch. ONE....TWO...." they scattered, and everyone got a meal and got back into formation. Dan led them outside and had them form up standing in an ankle-deep water puddle. Their packs and gear had been left on dry ground.

"Sit where you stand!" he ordered. They sat cross-legged in the cold water. "You have five minutes to eat that food. The clock is running!" all of them were shivering hard and fumbling with the bags that contained their food. Dan was circling the group like a vulture.

"You're freezing your asses off. You're exhausted. You're hungry. Many of you are probably asking yourselves what sort of hell you signed up for. Some of you are probably even ready to walk out the gate," he saw a couple of heads nod slightly. "Look at the man to your right and then look to the man on your left. Look at all of the men around you," they did as instructed while they were shoveling food into their mouths. "Those men are going to put their lives on the line for you. They will be your brothers for the rest of your lives."

"Today is only the beginning of the experiences and lessons that you will share as brothers. Some of those men will even make the ultimate sacrifice for you. Any one of those men will be there when you need them the most. I have seen it firsthand. I watched Jason Sterling run into a hail of gunfire to pull one of his brothers to safety. He had no regard for his own safety, no regard for his own security. The only thing that mattered was getting his brother out of a bad spot. He killed eight men to get the deed done."

"I watched a sister beat a man, nearly to death with her fists. He outweighed her by a 100 pounds. She drove a knife through that man's neck and then dove into an icy pond to save a brother from drowning. She did that with no regard for herself. Those people are heroes. Those people are who you should strive to be like. Fuck the cold! Fuck the pain! Do what you have to do for your brothers and eventually your sisters. This is not a boy's club and you will be joined by the fairer of our species. Make no mistake, they can and will fight just as hard as you," he said as he continued to circle the group. He could start to see something shift in the group's attitude. He glanced at his watch; time was up.

"On your feet!" he shouted. All of the men sprang up. "Police your trash and put it in the trashcan over there. There is a toilet in the warehouse, you have five minutes to answer the call and get your asses back online. MOVE!" all of them ran their trash to the can and about half of them went to the bathroom. Once they had formed up, Dan ordered them to get their gear and form a single file line. He led them on a tour of the grounds so that they would have a reference as to where and what everything was. It was four in the afternoon when he formed them up again in the parking area. The pile of personal gear was still there. He had each man come forward to retrieve his stuff. Each man stopped in front of him and presented his weapons while the others stood shivering in the cold.

The whole ordeal took an hour and the sun was beginning to set. Another storm front was moving in and the cold wind was starting to blow. He finally led them into the barracks building next to Dale and Susan's house. When he got to the landing at the top of the steps, he pointed to the door on the right.

"Squads one and two, that's your new home," he pointed to the door on the left. "Squads three and four, you're in there. Squad leaders I need to speak to you after you have settled your men in. You have five minutes," the men all hustled for their dorms and five minutes later the squad leaders were standing in front of him. He looked at his watch again.

"It's 5:30. Get your men cleaned up and into uniform. Chow is at six. If you're late, you don't eat. Chow hall is downstairs. After chow, lights out is at seven and you will have your men up, fed and in the parking lot by 4am. Are we clear?"

"Yes sir!" the four men answered.

Over the course of the next six weeks the new recruits were transformed. They spent hours and hours with Jill in the classroom and on the range. They spent time with Mark learning how to forage, build shelters, track game and survive the elements. Dan taught tactics, map reading and communications. Even the Butler boys got involved and taught them everything they knew about how to properly care for animals. Dale taught them about farming and canning. Doc and Susan gave them lessons in first aid. Marcus showed them how to repair small electronics and how to build windmill generators from scavenged car parts.

Their instructors were hard on them, but they had to be. There was a lot of information to learn and a very short time to learn it. They were usually up by 3am and many didn't go to sleep until 10:00 or 11:00 at night. By the time they all graduated on March 25th, they appreciated everything that they had gone through to get to that point. They were as ready as we could make them for the hostile world outside of our compound and the little city of Elko.

We held a graduation dinner for them in the pole barn. The Mayor and the Major were among the honored guests. We treated them to a full-on BBQ, and they had to sit through my congratulation's speech. When it was all over, they all shook their instructor's hands and they all stopped to say a few words to me.

I learned from the Major that this group would be the first to venture out on a road trip. They were planning on leaving on the 1st of April and driving to Hawthorne, Nevada. There was an Army Depot there and the Major was hoping to find some remnants of the military personnel and he was really hoping to gain access to some of the hardened bunkers that were on the sprawling reservation. He was going to take his 20-man team and add the members of Class 1 to give him a 40-man team. What would have normally been a four- or five-hour drive was going to take them a couple of days.

They were planning on contacting the small towns along the way and hopefully coming back with some new contacts. He was very optimistic about their upcoming mission. The day that the Major and his men embarked on their new mission, another group of 20 green recruits were dropped off at our gate. They arrived in an ancient, faded yellow school bus. Sixteen men and four women comprised this group. They ranged in age from 10 to 36. Jill formed them up in the parking lot and the training of Class 2 began in earnest. She was a little out of sorts when Class 1 graduated. She was proud of each and every one of them to be sure, but she was sad to see all 20 leave the ranch. The one that she, Dan and Mark had handpicked to stay had graciously declined the offer. The young man wanted to go forth with his brothers and change the world for the better. Nobody could fault him for that.

On the afternoon of April 8th, I was in the study reading the last journal when I received an urgent call from Alex in the security shack. I put the journal down and ran to the shack. He had one of the cameras facing the main road and I could see a convoy of semi-trucks and MRAP's parked out there. A lone Hummer had turned onto our road and was making its way toward the gate.

"Ranch Security, this is Major Jackson, do you have a copy," the radio crackled. Alex picked up the mic and answered him.

"Ranch Security, we copy you Major Jackson."

"Good afternoon Alex. Would you mind letting Mr. Sterling know that I'm about a minute from your gate and I need to speak with him?" Alex looked at me and handed the mic over.

"It's good to see you back in the neighborhood, we will have the gate open for you, come on in," I said. I was genuinely happy that they had made it back from their road trip. I handed the mic back to Alex and trotted out the door. The lone Humvee pulled through the gate and wound its way up the driveway. It parked in a parking spot and the young man driving stepped out. Major Jackson climbed out from the passenger side. As I approached, the young driver snapped to attention and saluted me. It caught me a little off guard, but I recovered and returned the salute.

"At ease," I said as I passed by him. As I came around the front of the Humvee, the Major greeted me with his usual handshake.

"So, what's on your mind Major?" I asked.

"I'll get to the point; I need to store a few items here for a little while."

"Can you be a little more specific?"

"Our trip to Hawthorne was far more productive than we could have ever hoped," he said with an ear-to-ear grin. "We made it to the base on the morning of the third and we were greeted by eight guys from base security. They had locked that place down, but they were doing everything that they could do to help what was left of that little town. By the time we got there, only 16 residents remained. The security guys had moved them on base...."

"Wait, what happened to the town?" I interrupted.

"Sorry, I skipped ahead. Back in August, a lightning storm kicked off a half dozen fires in the area. About half of the population left right after the EMP and after the wildfires burned the town off the map, most of those that survived decided to leave too. There were two dozen civilian holdouts who refused to leave. They were living in cars and tents. The guys from the base moved them inside the fence line and took care of them in return for help guarding the grounds. Fast forward a little to our arrival on the 3rd. During the winter they had lost eight of the civilians to illness and injury so there was a total of 26 people left."

"We had a few tense moments at the gate, but we got it sorted out and we were allowed on base. Once we explained what our mission was and what we were looking for, all of them were on board and wanting to work with us. They had scrounged up six working big rigs and we found a lot of abandoned 53-foot trailers. Over the course of the next three days we loaded 24 of those trailers from front to back, top to bottom with everything needed to keep a small army running. Without the DOT or the highway patrol to muck things up for us, we made land trains like they used in the Australian outback. Each semi was pulling four trailers with the MRAP's and Hummers running security for them."

"We stopped in every little town on the way back and offloaded some supplies. Radios, MREs, guns, ammo, fuel, small generators and medical supplies were given to the townspeople. Many were worried that we would want something in return. They were shocked to learn that the only thing we wanted was information. They are now on a regular radio schedule and they have already started to relay information about any trouble spots so that's paying off in spades. We got back to Elko this morning and offloaded half of the supplies that we had left. We need somewhere to leave the rest of the supplies and the semi-trucks and we thought this was the most secure place. We will be back in a day or two to get them. We are setting up a distribution center for everything," he finally finished.

"Hell, why didn't you just say so!" I said laughing. "Bring them here and have them line up out by the greenhouses," he thanked me and leaned back into the Hummer and spoke into the radio for a moment. When he was done, he came back over and stood next to me. We waited a few minutes for the rest of the convoy to come up the road. Each semi was pulling two of the 53-foot-long trailers and there was no way they were going to negotiate the driveway. The Major went to talk to each driver, giving them directions to get to where they needed to go. As the last semi pulled in, he waved me over.

THE RANCH

"Jason, the contents of these two trailers are a gift from Mayor Calvert. Where would you like them parked to make it easier for your people to unload. I was a little shocked but told him to have them parked in front of the warehouse. I had no idea what was in the trailers, but I was sure they would be a welcome gift. After all of the rigs were parked, the MRAP's and Hummers all parked in the parking area. All of the Class 1 graduates were present, so Jill brought out the students of Class 2. The squad leaders from Class 1 stepped forward and addressed their counterparts in Class 2. It really was a magical moment for the Class 2 students. All of the instructors also came out and congratulated them on their first successful mission. Jill looked like a beaming mother of 20 kids.

The next day, the recruits unloaded and inventoried the contents of the trailers. There were enough uniforms and gear to take care of the next six classes of recruits. There were M4 rifles and almost a half million rounds of 5.56 ammo for them. Hundreds upon hundreds of thirty round magazines. There were 250 Beretta M9 pistols and yet hundreds more magazines for those. They counted 380,000 rounds of 9mm ammo. There were 500 cases of MREs and 24 field radios. Half a dozen small generators and ten 55-gallon drums of gasoline were also unloaded and counted into inventory. There were spare parts for our Hummers, MRAP's and five-tons. It was quite a gift to say the least. I called Mayor Calvert on the radio that night to thank him. I was told that it was the people of the ranch that were owed a debt of gratitude.

The Major and his men returned on the morning of the 9th and took the big rigs back to town. They had set up a distribution center and were going to get the generators, radios and fuel from the remaining three rigs to the people of the town. It would be a huge boost to the morale of the dwindling population. The Major and his men were set to leave again on the 11th. They were going back to Hawthorne, but they were taking more semi-trucks and trailers with them this time. This was going to become the new normal for a while. The Major and his team would go out and gather supplies to distribute to the towns on their return trip. It was a huge step in pulling civilization back from the brink of the abyss.

On April 15th I called a staff meeting and we discussed the future endeavors of the ranch. It was Marcus who suggested that he start traveling with the Major and his team. He wanted to start teaching the small towns how to produce their own wind power. He had perfected his windmill generators and he wanted to get that information out. There was a vote taken and it was unanimous to let him go do his thing. He would be missed at the ranch, but everyone understood why he wanted to leave.

Dale brought up a new subject. He wanted his sons, Bill and Mike, to be a part of Class 3 when the time came. They would turn 17 during the class and both of them had asked if they could be a part of it. Jill, Mark and Dan had a quick pow-wow and they agreed that they would up the class count to 25 to accommodate the twins.

We discussed the upcoming growing season and we also discussed our supply levels. When the meeting had adjourned, I asked Bill to stay behind for a few minutes. He and I talked for another hour in private.

On the morning of May 13th, Jill was manning the security shack as usual. Today was the day Class 2 was to graduate. We were set to have their graduation dinner at 5:00 that night. It was becoming a tradition for them to eat their last meal at the ranch as our equals, no longer students. It was also the night that I had a special plan for dinner. Only one other person knew what I had up my sleeve.

It was a little after 9:00 when I heard her call Mike and Dan on the radio. There was an edge to her voice. She ordered them to get a squad of students and meet her in the parking area. It was when she ordered them to be there in full battle rattle that I ran out of the house and intercepted her as she got to the parking area. Dan was running for the parking area with a squad of students hot on his heels. Mike galloped up and dismounted his horse before it came to a stop. She ordered them to mount up in two of the MRAP's and one of the five-tons.

"Jill, what's happening?" I yelled across the parking lot. She trotted up to me.

"It's probably nothing but we just got a call from the town of Wells. Their security force just stopped some suspicious travelers and they want some back-up. Major Jackson is down in Ruby Valley and he is going to dispatch two squads, but we are closer!" she said in rapid fire.

"All right, be safe out there," I told her and gave her a quick kiss. She started to turn away but stopped and turned back.

"Right place!" she said with a coy smile.

"Right time," I replied. As she turned again, I slapped her on the butt. "You better be back in time for dinner!" I yelled at her back.

"Yes dear!" she shouted over her shoulder. I stood and watched the small convoy pour the power on as they rolled out of the gate.

THE RANCH

We had to use one of the pole barns for the last dinner, so I went about my morning helping to set up the BBQs and the tables and chairs. The lighting was put up and it was hooked up to the solar generators. It was noon when Jill and her team checked in. They had made it to Wells and the situation was well in hand. She had turned the Major's team back; their assistance was not going to be needed. She assured me that they would be back in time for the graduation dinner. They had some injured civilians that they were going to bring back to the medical center in Elko so they would be out a bit longer.

It was 4:45pm when her convoy rolled back through the gate. I was busy cooking the steaks on the grill and putting the finishing touches on the tables. All of the staff from the ranch sat on the left side and the new graduates sat on the right. The graduates filed in single file by squad. All of them were in clean, pressed Multi-Cam uniforms. The squad that had gone with Jill had not had the chance to change into their pressed uniforms and they stacked weapons and body armor in the corner of the barn. They quickly found their places and joined the other three squads in standing behind their chairs, waiting for their mentors to enter the dining area. I was standing behind my chair at the head of the table as all of the members of the ranch began to file in. They too stood behind their chairs. Jill was the last one in and she had a grin on her face that I didn't quite understand. She gave me a kiss on the cheek and moved to stand behind her chair.

As recruits, they were made to wait to sit until their mentors had taken their seats. As graduates, the roles reversed, and they were allowed to sit first. Once they were all seated, their mentors finally took their seats. I was the only one that remained standing. I cleared my throat and began my speech.

"I'd like to welcome all of you to the graduation dinner for Class 2. Six weeks ago, you joined us here as wide-eyed recruits. Today you share a table with us as our equals. Tomorrow you will go out into the world to try your best to make our little corner a better place. There is no more noble cause than to be of service to your fellow man and you take on the responsibility of that cause with the strength of a Brotherhood. Today you are joining the ranks of an elite team and we welcome you to our family!" I said as I raised my glass. There were cheers and back slapping all around.

Now normally this is where I would have sat down and let the eating begin but I had a different plan tonight. I picked up my fork and tapped it against the side of my glass. Everyone quickly quieted down, and I cleared my throat again.

"Jill Butler, would you please stand?" I said. She looked at me with a puzzled look on her face but slowly stood.

"Jill, you and I have been through a lot since we first met. We witnessed the end of the world in a flash on the fourth of July. We have both nearly been killed. We have seen the worst and the best that mankind has to offer. Would you say that is a good summary of the last few months?" I asked her.

"Yeah….." she said hesitantly.

"Would it also be fair to say that you and I have grown pretty close since I moved here?"

"It would," she was looking around the room trying to figure out what was happening.

"You know that I have fallen madly in love with you, don't you?" I asked. Her eyes locked with mine and she just nodded her head. Her eyes were glistening as she was on the verge of tears. She had figured out what was about to happen.

I stepped to her side of the table and dropped to one knee. Her eyes were as big as saucers. I reached into my pocket and produced a ring that she instantly recognized as her mother's. Her trembling hands went to her mouth and tears started rolling down her face.

"Jillian Renee Butler, would you do me the honor of being my wife?"

"OH MY GOD!" she squealed. "YES! YES! YES!" she almost shouted. She held her hand out and I slipped the ring on her finger. She grabbed my hand and pulled me to my feet. We were in the middle of a long embrace and everyone was clapping and cheering again. I felt a slap on my back, then I heard a voice that I had not heard in a very long time.

"It's about time you made an honest woman out of her, brother," Braden said from behind me. Jill pushed me back a little and kissed me again.

"Surprise!" she said through tears and a quivering voice. I turned to face my older brother.

He was thinner and he had a full beard. He looked malnourished and tired, but it was my brother. I looked over his shoulder as Megan and my nieces walked into the room. Allison and Kalin looked like they had aged five years but there they stood. The surprise continued when Alex's' parents and little sister walked in. He bolted from the table and embraced all of them.

THE RANCH

"My God Braden, I was starting to think I would never see you again!" I said as I gave him a bear hug. When the embrace ended and I stepped back, he spoke again.

"Boy have I got a tale to tell you little brother. For now, let's celebrate and for God's sake, let's **eat!**"

THE END

EPILOGUE

Jill and I were married on the 9th of July that year, 2017. While we wanted to keep it a fairly small affair, it just wasn't going to happen. Mayor Calvert was there as were several members of the sheriff's department. The 40 men and women from Teams 1 and 2 were accounted for as well as the 25 members of Class 3. Major Jackson performed the ceremony and his original 20-man team provided security for the event. There were also several dozen members of the Elko community present. My brother was my best man and Jessica was Jill's maid of honor. Jessica, Susan and Megan had worked tirelessly to give Jill a wedding dress that was handmade. I was stuck wearing the one suit that I had brought with me from Reno.

Life at the ranch had settled into a routine again and we were finally able to get on with our lives. The threat of violence had diminished greatly, thanks in great part to Major Jackson, his men, and the men and women of the graduating classes. They had gone to tremendous lengths to bring about the return of civilization. Mayor Calvert had made sure that Elko was the epicenter of the local movement to regain what we had lost the night the EMP hit us. Elko had a working hospital, sheriff's department and in many ways its own working military. While the numbers were staggering, Elko had beaten the odds and on the one-year anniversary, still had a population of a little over 8,000 residents, almost 50 percent of its original population.

The government did eventually pull itself together and as was predicted; Texas led the way. One of the glaring changes they made was to get rid of all the career politicians. They put into place term limits on the House and Senate of no more than two terms in office and those terms were limited to just three years each. The new Supreme Court also underwent some major changes. The Judges were now elected, not appointed. There were seven Judges, one from each region of the country and they were limited to two six-year terms. Every state had one Senator and two Representatives. Each individual was limited to two terms, no matter what office they had served in. The new election process wasn't really anything new. The Electoral College still existed, but he days of the career politician were over. Lawyers and Bankers need not apply.

Our new President was a woman by the name of Jane Dixon. She had been a career cop before the balloon went up. By all accounts, a hard charger and not one to take crap from anyone. Her fledgling administration was on a three-pronged attack. First, deal with the invading gangs from the south. Second, deal with the violence and gangs at home and third, get the infrastructure back up and running. If you answered directly to the President, never ever say the words "I don't know" or "I can't." That was a good way to find yourself unemployed

On May 14th, the day after the arrival of my brother, Jessica and Jake welcomed their daughter into the world. She was perfectly healthy, and they named her Jillian Marie Fields. Of course, Diane Walker and her infant son were allowed to stay at the ranch even after Andy had been killed. She feared we would turn her out, but we put that fear to rest in short order.

Some of our critics, yes, we did have a few of those, said that we should have done more to help the people instead of playing army. Usually it was said over a meal we helped to provide in a safe place we also helped to provide. My answer to them would be to stand a post. Leave the comfort and security of your home, leave the hot meal, and spend some time putting your life on the line for people you will never know. When you have done that, maybe then we can have an honest conversation.

Yes, we moved very quickly to pick up our guns. Yes, we moved quickly to use them in defense of our lives and the lives of innocents. Yes, we would do it all again. Those who moved quickly were the ones who survived. We proved that point. Those that failed to act quickly, perished quickly.

There were two types of survivors after the EMP. There were those like us, the ones who did what they could to help others. Then there were those who did what they could to exploit others, like Marvin and his group. Even with the new government cracking down on the latter groups, they still existed, and they were still growing and getting stronger. Hopefully the good guys would continue to grow and get stronger too.

To those of you who manage to read this, stay prepared. It was said that it doesn't matter what you prepare for, just prepare. You have the advantage now of having survived a catastrophic failure of civilization. Never forget what you have learned, never again rely on technology and never again rely on the Government to come bail you out. You know how to be self-sufficient and you know how to survive. Pass those skills on to the future generations so that they may never have to suffer the tragedy that put us on our knees. And never lose your humanity. Doing so could find you on the business end of a gun.

Little did we know how soon we'd be relying on ourselves again......

THANK YOU FOR READING!

If you enjoyed this book, we would appreciate your customer review on your book seller's website or on Goodreads.

Also, we would like for you to know that you can find more great books like this one at
www.CreativeTexts.com

Made in the USA
Coppell, TX
11 January 2024